my favorite midlife crisis (yet)

# my favorite midlife crisis
## (yet)

Toby Devens

SOURCEBOOKS LANDMARK™
AN IMPRINT OF SOURCEBOOKS, INC.®
NAPERVILLE, ILLINOIS

Published by Sourcebooks Landmark, an imprint of Sourcebooks, Inc.
P.O. Box 4410, Naperville, Illinois 60567-4410
(630) 961-3900
Fax: (630) 961-2168
www.sourcebooks.com

Library of Congress Cataloging-in-Publication Data

Devens, Toby.
  My favorite mid-life crisis (yet) / Toby Devens.
    p. cm.
  ISBN-13: 978-1-4022-0747-1
  ISBN-10: 1-4022-0747-6
  1. Middle-aged women—Maryland—Baltimore—Fiction. 2. Women gynecologists—Maryland—Baltimore—Fiction. 3. Menopause—Fiction. 4. Midlife crisis—Fiction. 5. Best friends—Fiction. 6. Female friendship—Fiction. I. Title: My favorite midlife crisis (yet). II. Title.

PS3604.E885M9 2006
813'.6—dc22

                                        2006006325

Printed and bound in the United States of America.
VP 10 9 8 7 6 5 4 3 2 1

# Acknowledgments

My thanks to so many for their support in the writing of this book.

First, Fouad Abbas, MD, gynecologic oncologist, who took time from his grueling schedule to provide detailed information and relate relevant experiences in the operating room—he was of enormous help, as was Dennis Gleicher, MD, always available to answer medical questions. Vivian Goldman also directed me to good medical information. Thanks to Sidney Ossakow, PhD, for leading me over complex scientific terrain. Fiber artist extraordinaire Carol Bodin walked me through the process, actually had me working at a loom—she gave generously of her time and information. Lenne Lipton, audio-visual and conference specialist, helped me figure out the tricky parts in those areas. If I missed the mark on any of the details provided by these experts, it was my error or my choice to shape fact to the demands of fiction.

Thanks to dear friend Jan Innes whose cushy shoulder and keen editorial eye got me thorough the inevitable rough spots. To Jean Louise Reynolds for decades of advice, insider info, and lots of laughs when I needed them most, and to Candy Cole for her insights into the man/woman dynamic. I am grateful to Linda Hayes who helped reestablish the connection with my talented writer colleagues in Maryland: Ruth Glick, Cronshi Englander, Kathryn Johnson, Binnie Syril Braunstein, Nancy Baggett, Patricia Paris, Linda Williams, Connie Hay, Joyce Braga, and Joanne Settel. They know their stuff and graciously shared it. I'm especially indebted to the remarkable Randi DuFresne who connected me with my agent, Elaine English. Elaine is a skillful and steady champion. And heartfelt thanks to Chassie West whose calm, considered guidance always brought a fresh perspective to my thinking.

Writer Alan Zendell provided suggestions and comradeship and Toba and Andy Barth and Eleanor Feingold were funds of energy and information. My editor Hillel Black deserves my warmest appreciation for seeing potential in the original and applying his brilliant editorial skills, vast experience, and gentle counsel to shaping the ultimate version of this book.

My parents Esta and William Devens stood by me in spirit; I cherish the memory of their goodness and humor. My daughter and friend Amanda Schwartz reached out to help: her medical information was spot-on and her eagle eye caught blips along the plot path. Most important, her unfailing encouragement and love were there for me, as always. Starting her on her remarkable life is my proudest achievement. And, finally, my gratitude to Sam Ponzcak whose infinite patience and caring never fail to astound me—I am so blessed to have my own midlife turned sweet and productive by his strong yet gentle presence.

# Chapter 1

S o, how many times last month did you engage in sexual intercourse?"

Elaine Markowitz, a realtor, fifty-two and tummy tucked, shifted uncomfortably in her chair, disturbing the beige and teak tranquility of my office overlooking Baltimore's Inner Harbor.

"You sure my name isn't going to be published in this article, Dr. Berke?" she asked. "My mother's still living. She has cataracts, but she reads."

"No names. Just numbers, I promise. And it's an important study."

Elaine raised a skeptical eyebrow. "About sex?"

We'd been through this once, but now I clicked off my physician voice and turned on my woman-to-woman voice, warmer and more reassuring. "About female sexual interest once we reach menopause. And about our levels of activity and satisfaction. There are so many myths out there. Like Mother Nature flips the switch when we turn fifty and shuts us down. Which I don't for a moment believe, but I'd like to prove it. With statistics."

Better. Elaine settled back in her chair.

"We need to get the facts out to the general public and to gynecologists, especially," I pressed. "After all, the more we all know about the women we treat, the better we can meet their needs."

"Yeah, right. Okay," Elaine said. "Let's get rid of the myths. Sure. Ask away."

I'd already whipped out my survey sheet.

Policy requires that every woman coming into the OB/GYN practice of Potak, Berke, and Bernstein, MDs for her annual physical and Pap test gets five minutes of chat time after we've invaded her most private territory with a gloved finger and a warm speculum. I make it ten. I *like* my patients. Because I'm a gynecologic oncologist and not an obstetrician/gynecologist, most of the women I see are older. Which provided a handy population for studying the impact of age on sexual activity.

I'd been administering this survey for six months. I worked from a sampling base of a hundred. Excluding the single women in their eighties and nineties who have vaginas like prairie dog tunnels, nearly impenetrable, 30 percent of single women fifty and over in my practice reported dating at least once in the prior month. Twenty percent had been laid in that time frame. About 12 percent noted a significant other with whom they lived or an exclusive relationship with a longtime lover.

Preliminary conclusion: don't count us out. Which was supported by my clinical observation. At least half of the women I treat are divorced or widowed, and I was handing out enough samples of Astroglide and KY Jelly to slide the entire East Coast into the Atlantic. So I knew my single patients were sexually active.

By the time I got to the second page of my checklist, Elaine Markowitz was happily sharing with me the details of her relationship with her forty-one-year-old boyfriend. "He's the stage manager at the Fells Point Dinner Theater. And, I'm not exaggerating here, he looks like a young Brando and screws like a young Bugs Bunny. Five times a week at least. But, honestly, I could go every day. He makes me feel thirty-five."

She did seem to have a dewy freshness about her as if her corpuscles were boogying through her veins and I told her so, though in more clinical terms.

"Part sex, part Dr. Fischman. Look closer." She leaned in. "This is so wonderful. You're a doctor and you can't tell. The man is a miracle worker." I proffered a noncommittal smile. *Bland. Bland was good. Lessens those cartoon parentheses around the mouth.* "I had a full face lift," Elaine chortled. "The whole shebang all at once. Eyelids, brow, chin." She stroked the adolescent tautness of her neck. "I felt like shit for two weeks, but it was worth it. Kevin never would have looked at the old me. Men look through fifty-year-old women, not *at* them, right?"

I gave her a how-would-I-know stare and changed the subject to estrogen patches.

As I droned on, Elaine actually strolled behind me to get a better look at a photo of Whit and Drew taken when the twins were five, bundled in snowsuits and mounted on kiddie skis. One of our family Christmas trips to Squaw Valley. Now Whit was in med school in Chicago with a law student girlfriend and Drew was pulling straight A's at the Art Institute of Boston. Whit looks like me, but takes himself very seriously. Drew is my ex-husband Stan all over. Nicer than Stan, though. A better person than Stan.

Elaine lifted the picture of my boys and interrupted my monologue. "Having kids really ages you. All the worry." She turned to appraise me from under scaffolded eyelids.

"You could get rid of those forehead wrinkles of yours. Botox. Or a peel. Nothing drastic."

That stung. I thought I'd done a nice job of hiding my accordion forehead under wispy bangs. "Thanks for the tip. I'll keep it in mind."

When she left, I headed for the powder room to peer at my reflection, which hadn't been giving me "you're the fairest in the land" lately. Still, what I saw wasn't so bad, even with the forehead pleats. Blonde hair kept glossy by weekly trips to Melik at the Istanbul Salon. Many little highlights to suggest sun streaks. Cream-and-roses skin inherited from my mother, which, alas, tended to fretworks of wrinkles. But I plumped it up with stuff that ran me eighty dollars a jar at Nordstrom's, and I calculated that at fifty-four I could pass for forty. Okay, forty-five. Maybe.

I noticed a bit of eyelid droop on the left side. And a shadow of a wattle under my chin. The sad truth is that women of a certain age must choose between face and body. Enough fat to keep your face youthfully plumped is enough to make your thighs porky. Go for the slender body, and neck up you're drawn and sunken. My personal trainer and I opted for steel biceps and a tight ass, at some cost to my face.

Hank Fischman, one of the top plastic surgeons at Johns Hopkins Hospital, was a former colleague. Maybe I'd give him a call. They used to peel your entire face back from your forehead for a face-lift. Ugh. I can roll an ovary around in my hand and slit into a belly while humming Mozart, but I couldn't do plastic if my life depended on it. Still, there had been recent advances in the full-face procedure. Before I made an appointment with Hank, I'd go online and see what was new in the Ponce de Leon business.

I couldn't believe how shallow I was becoming.

*Chapter 2*

To compensate for all this meditation on my aging exterior, I decided to subject myself to something that would plumb the very depths of my emotional being, something that would Roto-Rooter out any residual gunk of guilt, shame, and self-loathing. I drove up to Annapolis for a meeting of FRESH, a support group for discarded husbands and wives of recently out gays. FRESH is an acronym for Former Rejected Ex-Spouses of Homosexuals. At my first meeting, I'd mentioned to the president of the Maryland chapter that I thought the use of Former and Ex might be a trifle redundant. "Intentional," he'd said, smiling gently. "What is more redundant than the heterosexual spouse of a homosexual?" Point taken.

Unlike AA or Overeaters Anonymous, FRESH provided wine and cheese and permitted smoking on the frequently correct assumption that most of us had tailspinned back into former vices after the revelation. Also, the disclosure of last names was encouraged since it was a FRESH assertion that none of us had anything to hide; we were the innocent victims of circumstance. Also we might want to date each other.

The idea of FRESH members coupling had, at the beginning, smacked of the cast-banging of two broken-armed lovers. But then, Harry Galligan piqued some interest. My favorite uncle had been called Harry and so far the FRESH Harry had been just that, avuncular. That night, he winked at my entrance, patted my back as I walked by, and whispered, "Glad you made it, Gwyn," but that was it.

A half hour in, with the wine flowing, Mark Silva, the chapter president, clapped his hands for attention and shouted, "Let's get seated for Sharing." Sharing was the FRESH term for the open-heart surgery that bares your inner pain.

We gathered in a supportive circle around a man whose wife dumped him the previous week for *his* secretary. "To be honest," he said, "I always had a little sneaky for my secretary. Never acted on it, of course. Then Brenda and Alison met at the company picnic. The next week they had a date for drinks and began the affair. Last Wednesday, they called me into the conference room to break the news. I'm still reeling."

"Of course you are. Very understandable. And so recent. This is the worst time, Fred. Time and friendship heal, believe me." Mark Silva was also the resident clucker and tsker. And he was given to hugs, gender neutral, which freaked out a few of the men. "Correction. Not just me. Believe *us*." Applause.

Our second newcomer, a heavy woman with a mustache and a five o'clock shadow (I diagnosed polycystic ovary syndrome from eight feet away) related that her husband's parting shot had been, "And you need to know that I never really loved you." Essentially invalidating ten years of marriage. So gratuitous. Need to know? The bastard. I really did want to hug her, beard and all. Instead, I got out my Kleenex.

Pam, sitting next to me, reported on her husband's phone call of the evening before. He was going to Thailand for a sex change operation and asked her to be there when he told their children. She was anguished. We were anguished for her, with her. Twelve people in a circle murmured sympathetically. Two of us were sobbing. How ridiculous that I was one of them.

Harry Galligan lightened the moment by giving the treasurer's report. Harry was a pleasing contrast to my wiry, wired ex-husband. A lumbering Irishman with a PhD in physics, Harry worked at the Naval Research Lab in D.C. Not your standard issue scientist, though. He once told me that he spoke six languages and did a mean tango. Not bragging. Maybe flirting. His wife had left him for a famous local politician, a burly Irish woman who looked more than a little like Harry. "Well, she's lost my vote," Harry liked to crack. These days he seemed mildly amused and somewhat philosophical about the wife's defection. But I'd heard from one of the longtime members that he'd shambled into his first meeting with booze on his breath and his tie askew, just about collapsed in the middle of his story sharing, and had to be helped to his seat.

He didn't come off as a personality prone to surprises, but at the end of his report he said casually, almost as an aside, "You know," hitching his neck at me across the circle, his eyes soft with concern, and I felt my heart tumble, "Gwyn has never shared with us. She said she wasn't ready. But she's been coming to meetings for five months now."

*Had* I? Five months? I always decided to make the drive last minute, so I never marked it on my calendar or entered it in my PDA, which meant it didn't count. A non-event.

"Gwyn?" Mark Silva prompted in his kindergarten teacher voice. The bearded lady gazed at me expectantly. The transsexual's wife put her arm around my shoulder and squeezed, so I figured *what the hell, my story isn't worse than any other*, and I shared. Boy, did I share. Even after two years, I shook telling the story of what my friend Fleur called The Treachery.

I told them how at the housewarming for Crosswinds, our new beach house on the Delaware shore, I'd opened the door to a storage room to see, in a nanosecond flash, a picture that would be branded forever into my little gray cells: my husband of twenty-six years entwined in the arms of his lover, his mouth against the mouth of Brad Ventner, Crosswinds' decorator whose taste I never liked anyway. Startled, they broke apart and for a ghastly, surreal moment we all stared at each other. Stan, Brad, Stan's yippy Chihuahua that he always brought everywhere, and me. Then the dog started barking and Stan started babbling something I couldn't hear over the roaring in my ears. I spun away, the dog leaped, I raced for the stairs, the dog charged ahead and partway up darted under my feet, pitching me forward on the $80 a yard Berber carpeted steps, snapping my ankle. I'm a physician; I'd known immediately it was broken. I'd also known that a lot more than my ankle was broken and that it would take a lot more than a cast to fix it.

"And the next day, Stan came back to Crosswinds to collect some clothing and he stood at the foot of my bed gushing this torrent of confession, details I really didn't want to hear. But with my foot propped up and my ankle casted, I was trapped. At one point, he shouted at me: 'Look, I'm fifty-four years old. I don't have another fifty-four years to get it right. I can't, I shouldn't, goddamn it I *refuse* to tamp down my real feelings anymore.'"

"Like it was your fault," Pam said, shaking her head empathically.

"Well, I suppose I should have known. I mean, yes, the night before he proposed, he confessed that he'd had what he called a dalliance with another Columbia journalism student, a guy in his dorm, when he was a sophomore. But he maintained it was an isolated incident of generic horniness that landed on whatever was close at hand. I thought, okay, a one-time thing. Which can happen. Experimenting."

I sniffed, holding back the tears. "Then over the years when he spent all those nights out, well, he's a publisher. He runs two magazines. He took people to dinner. That's what he told me. Entertaining was part of the job."

Preoccupied with my work, with my kids, I was clueless that the smooth fabric of our marriage was being ripped all along the seam by Stan's lust hunts in the streets of Mt. Vernon, Baltimore's largely gay neighborhood.

"When he became obsessed with the beach house, I figured it was just a midlife crisis. But still, all that time with the decorator." I sang the same old heartbreaking tune in a tremulous voice, "I should have known."

"No. That wasn't your responsibility. You're the victim here," Mark Silva shouted from the drinks table. "Just remember that."

"And then Stan apologized. Sort of. He said, 'I really am sorry I lied to you. But I thought if I got married, I wouldn't feel the way I felt about men. I thought the marriage would cure me.' That's what he said. Cure him. Thank God there was the length of the bed between us, because I don't know what I would have done if I'd been able to reach him. Especially when he said, 'I love you. I always will. You're the mother of my children. But this thing with Brad, this is different, this is *in* love.'" My voice failed. I was grinding my Kleenex to dust.

Mark Silva, tisking, came up behind me to refill my wine glass. My hand was trembling so badly I splashed merlot on his fine white shirt.

What I didn't say was that I fell off the deep end after that. Thank God the HIV tests turned out negative, but I felt sick, looked sick, lost thirteen pounds in three weeks, and drove to the Safeway in the middle of the night to buy a pack of Marlboros. Me, a doctor. And I cried myself to sleep for six months straight.

"I'm fine now, though," I said, tears streaming. "I'm doing well. Really." At which point, Harry stood up, nearly knocking over his chair, bisected the circle with his ursine lumber, and handed me his handkerchief. Folded. Clean.

Later, during the socializing part, he brought me a plate of cookies. "You must think I'm a real shit for pushing you into sharing. Not that it wasn't necessary for you, but still…"

"You didn't," I assured him. "I should have shared months ago."

"You were processing," he said.

"Am I processed now? Like cheese?"

Harry laughed. I had the feeling he liked me.

When it was time to go, he walked me to my car, gave me a hearty hug, and kissed my forehead. No one had kissed my forehead in forty years. Maybe he was taking my emotional temperature.

"You had a milestone night tonight. You should be proud of yourself, Gwyn. But don't be surprised if you get some rebound from the release. Anxiety. Sleeplessness. I'll check in with you during the week. Just to see how you're doing."

He watched until I pulled out of the lot. It was midnight when I put my key in the lock. Five past when I called my friend Kat Greenfield who was widowed and a fiber artist, so she was up weaving at odd hours. Not my other friend and neighbor Fleur Talbot who got to Madame Max, the dress shop she owned, at 8 a.m. and went to bed, alone, around ten.

Kat and I talked for eight minutes about Harry Galligan and twelve minutes about her not being able to take over the whole bed. Her late husband Ethan's side was still sacrosanct. She wouldn't even roll there in her sleep. When I hung up the phone, I stroked the back of the receiver. *Nice phone. Give me some good calls this week. Someone with a deep voice who wants nothing more of me than a little attention.*

My prayer was answered. Sort of. God has a demented sense of humor.

The next voice I heard was my father's. He roused me from a deep, dreamless sleep shouting, "You need to telegraph your sister and tell her the birds arrived."

"Dad," I said, "the sun isn't even up. Go back to bed."

"Fine. But you'll call your sister."

I have one brother, no sister.

"And tell her about the birds. Sure, Dad. Does Sylvie know you're up?"

"Sylvie who?"

Oh God.

My father woke me around five nearly every morning. "I just saw your mother in the mirror," he'd say. "She was stark naked and playing around with some old geezer I never saw before. I think she's lost her mind!" Or: "I just wrote a check for $10,000 to the All American Aluminum Siding Company. They're starting tomorrow." Or the telegram about the birds.

Why couldn't I bring myself to put the phone on answering machine mode? He probably wouldn't know the difference. His tangled ganglions didn't register the distinction between reality and electronically reproduced reality.

But I wouldn't do that to him. He was the parent who'd stayed up with me through my chicken pox for four nights running. The parent who'd run interference on the crazy other one. My protector. A sweet little gnome of a man whom I loved with all my heart although I wasn't sure who was currently inhabiting his body.

I needed to speak to his caretaker Sylvie *again* about her going to bed earlier so she could be with him when he woke at 4:30. Weeknights, she stayed up until midnight watching a TV show in which a medium communicated with the spirits of the departed. Then she was so socked in sleep she didn't hear my father prowling the house in Alzheimeric zigzags before dawn. We'd had this conversation before, Sylvie and I. She made promises, but the lure of the dead was stronger than the big bucks I paid her to look after the living.

I would not put him in a nursing home.

# Chapter 3

I'd been hoping, but by Sunday Harry hadn't called.

"Well you can't just sit there moping over an imaginary lover," Kat said, hovering over my paper-strewn desk like a seagull over a landfill.

"Believe me, this look of desperation you see has nothing to do with Harry Galligan," I said as I shuffled through grant application forms.

"Those proposals can wait." Kat tugged them from my hand. "You need to take a break."

"Yeah, well the patients can't wait," I sighed. "When I think of these women falling through the cracks, it's just terrifying. STDs are going untreated. Cancers aren't being diagnosed. Women are going to die needlessly."

On mostly my own time, with grant money and some donations I'd scrounged up, I'd operated the Women's Free Clinic in West Baltimore for seven years. Then the previous spring, the Clinic had come to a grinding halt when its funding dried up. For two months, I'd pumped my personal savings into the project. But it took on water faster than I could bail it out and in June, it sunk. Now hundreds of women from the poor, mostly black Baltimore neighborhood it served were without basic GYN care because they were uninsured or underinsured and couldn't afford to see a doctor. I was determined to find the money to start it up again.

"How many grant applications have you sent out?" Kat asked.

"I'm working on the eleventh. So far, I've heard from seven. Out of those, six declines. One foundation managed to spare $2,000. That won't even buy surgical gloves." I sunk my head in my hands.

Kat peeled my fingers from my forehead one by one. "Enough for today. You're drowning in black and white. You need color, people, something to lift your spirits. Come with me to the exhibit opening. I promise it will be fun. And don't you want to be able to discuss contemporary sculpture when you go out with someone who knows about art?"

"Please, I have no prospects of going out with someone who wears his baseball cap backwards."

"Exactly. No prospects. Time to go prospecting," Kat said.

So I gave in.

But an hour later I really wished I hadn't because as Kat and I made our altogether innocent way across the gallery floor, from behind a sculpture labeled "Sleeping Python" constructed of knives, forks, and ladles, my ex-husband Stan appeared with (they were actually holding hands) Brad, the decorator, who would have been the other woman had he been a woman. Both wore jeans. Stan had lost weight and he'd tucked in his black T-shirt to show off his Scarlet O'Hara waist. His jeans were varnished on, so tight you saw every lump and bump. He'd worn Levi's casual cut when we were married. With a dress belt.

Brad spotted me first and nudged Stan who nodded.

"Move it," I hissed at Kat, who did a little bewildered two-step in the wrong direction.

Too late. "Ladies," Stan said as they oozed over. "Enjoying the show?"

"Interesting," I said. "Seminal. Highly original." I glanced down at my program while Kat presented a frozen half smile. She'd disliked Stan even in his heyday. When we were in college, he used to call her Hippie Dippy Katie and Lucy Liberal, and she once threw a plate of waffles at his head. He'd been doing an imitation of Jane Fonda making a pro-Cong speech, a nasty takeoff in falsetto with a hand on his hip. We should have known.

"Oh, I can't stand it," Brad said, eyeing a metal fish sculpture. "The halibut. He's done it with spoons for scales. It's perfect, Stan. If it's under a thou, I'm buying it for the store." With Stan's financial backing, Brad had opened a gourmet shop in Rehoboth not far from the beach house. Preciously named The Cook's Tour, it carried imported foods and overpriced kitchen tools. "Visualize it in the spot right next to the counter where the light pours in." He marched off.

"I like your new hair, Kat. It's very becoming," Stan said.

I looked at Kat. He was right. It was different. She'd colored out the gray and trimmed it a little so it just dusted her shoulders. Subtle changes I'd missed. I was suddenly overwhelmed and angry all over again at the unfairness of it all. He noticed hairstyles now, Stan the Insensitive, Insentient. Back in the marriage, I could have dyed my hair purple and shaved it into a mohawk and he wouldn't have raised an eyebrow. Drew told me the last time his father visited, he'd brought photo albums and wept reminiscing about the twins' birth. How moving it had been. The highlight of his life. This from a man who when I'd gone into labor asked me if I could hold off a half hour; he had an editorial meeting at four.

For our sons' sake, I try to maintain a civil relationship with my ex-husband, and that afternoon we managed a few minutes of careful chat about the boys. Just as I was ready to jump out of my skin, Stan drifted back to Brad. I heard them laugh, which in my paranoid state, I decided was directed at me. At my fat ass specifically. Which I knew, intellectually, was as small and hard as a stale biscuit. But my reaction was not intellectual. It was two feet south of my brain, tearing at my heart. Then they moved together to stand hip to hip, shoulder to shoulder, their bronze and blonde highlighted heads almost fusing, sharing the program as if it were a prayer book. Brad slipped his free hand into Stan's back pocket. I wanted to die or to kill. Take your pick.

"You okay?" Kat asked.

I wheeled on her. "What the hell did you do to your hair?" Lots of misplaced hostility. She looked at me with sympathetic eyes, which is why she has been my friend since college.

"I decided Fleur is right. It's been nearly two years since Ethan's accident. I can't go poking around in widow's weeds for the rest of my life. Dyeing my hair seemed to be a good statement, to me if to no one else. You know, 'Look at me. I'm not an old lady with gray hair. I'm an old lady with black hair. And I'm back in circulation.' Do you think this sends the message that I'm available?"

This was interesting enough to distract me from Stan and Brad, now yakking it up with the sculptor of this culinary menagerie—the guy whose face was on the front of the program.

"You're not old," I said reflexively. "And yes it sends the message. You're radiating availability. Men are going to drop like flies." Suddenly, a wave of vertigo washed over me, the kind that swamps you when you're losing your bearings. It was disorienting that Kat of all people was paying attention to her appearance, trawling for men. And Stan had exploded out of the closet with Brad. Was I the only one stuck in the muck of my old life? "You look great, I'm just surprised. You haven't messed with your hair for years."

"I dyed my hair because I was so fucking cold," she said. And when she told the story, it made sense. She'd been out Friday night as the fifth wheel with two other couples. They'd gone to Ford's Theater in D.C. and the air conditioning had been on full blast so that even the sweater she'd brought wasn't enough. One of the women had whispered about how cold it was and her husband removed his jacket and draped it over her shoulders. Then the other husband had done the same. "And there was no one to drape me," Kat said wistfully. "If Ethan were alive, I would have had a jacket. But I sat there shivering for two acts. Not just from cold either. I realized how goddamned alone I am. And decided to do something about it. The hair is a first step. What do you think?"

I told her it was a brilliant first step. That I was proud of her. That the restored darkness brought out the violet of her eyes.

"Not violet. Periwinkle." It was the sculptor, Lee Bagdasarian, who'd come up behind us. "Eloquent eyes." He was young. Younger, anyway. Early forties. Interesting slash handsome. Roman gladiator nose and a cowlick of glossy hair I wanted to lovingly smooth.

"Eloquent show," Kat fired back. "I really like your work." He made a modest demi dip and smiled at both of us. "You're Gwyn and you're Kat." And then the eyes veered off me. For good.

"Stan Berke tells me you're a fiber artist," he said to Kat. "That you showed at the Clayton." They talked weaving for ten minutes while I hung around like a potholder to avoid the Stan and Brad Show. Kat told Lee how she especially admired his hippopotamus made of colanders, strainers, and cheese slicers.

"Have you seen the plate-ypus?" he asked her. Just her. "He's got a lot of style, this guy. Come on, I'll show you." She lifted an eyebrow at me. I inched a tiny nod of approval, like a mom sending her daughter off to the prom. He steered her with a hand on her back. Very intimate for a new friend.

And that is how Kat met Lee on the day she sent out her first signal and why I slogged home by myself through the wet streets of Baltimore.

———

I live eight floors up in Waterview, a condominium building in downtown Baltimore. Stan and I moved here after the boys left for college. It was perfect for the two of us. Light-filled and low-maintenance, it has a huge living room window that sweeps over a panorama of the Harbor. I always close the curtains before I leave the apartment just so I can open them to the magnificent view when I return. The dazzling sunsets make my eyes water with pleasure. Even on that rainy August Sunday, just beyond my terrace, gulls lifted into an opalescent sky. So calming. Like a Japanese painting. I watched for a few minutes before turning to the winking red light of my answering machine.

Message 1. Sylvie, my dad's companion. No hello. She barreled right into "Your father thinks he's back in Norway. He thinks he's seven years old and I'm his sister Margrit.

He's been pulling my hair all day. We need to talk, Dr. Berke."

Message 2. Dan Rosetti, my father's geriatrician, telling me Dad's newest symptom, leg cramps, might be a side effect of his Alzheimer's medication. "Let's cut him down from ten milligrams to five and watch him."

Dan was my age, a Yale grad, up on the latest advances, but at heart a physician of the old school, caring and hands-on. Literally. In the office, he'd hold my father's bony hand or wind an arm around his fragile shoulders while talking with him in his gentle, soothing baritone.

"If we get more agitation going down to five mgs, then we'll have to tweak," Dan continued. I sighed. My father was pulling Sylvie's hair, the first sign of dementia-related aggression, and we were reducing his meds. No wonder I felt we were teetering on a tightrope.

"I also want to start him on something new, ArCog. The studies look promising. Just keep an eye out for muscle weakness."

A tightrope without a net.

Message 3. Just what I needed, the nasal drone of Summer Greenfield Ellicott, Kat's married daughter, making a surprise, unwelcome appearance in my kitchen.

"Gwyneth, I'm looking for my mother," Summer drawled in that grating whine she'd found at two and perfected over the next twenty-five years. "Tim has come down with a stomach bug and I need her to stop at the Rite Aid and pick up a prescription." She inhaled an exasperated breath. "If she'd only get a cell phone. Anyway, if you connect with her, have her call me." Click. God forbid a please or thank you.

Poor Kat. I didn't blame her for pleading a technology phobia and refusing to carry a cell phone. She'd be at the beck and call of Summer and her husband, Tim the Dim, 24/7.

Message 4. My son Drew just to catch up.

Message 5. My friend Fleur asking when I saw the plastic surgeon would I please find out if he liposuctioned double chins.

Message 6. My service. Which was unusual since one of our junior associates, Bethany McGowan, was covering that weekend. I returned the call to my patient Freesia Odum, dispensed soothing advice, and squeezed her in for an emergency appointment. Since the Free Clinic's closing, Ms. Odum took two buses to get to my office. She had no health insurance. I saw her gratis to the increasing irritation of my partners in the practice and the outright hostility of the hired help, the younger docs. Especially Bethany, who had a sharp tongue and no respect for her seniors. Especially me.

I wondered if Neil Potak had told her I was the one who tried to blackball her at the new-hire conference.

*I should have stuck to my guns.*

On Thursday, I kept my appointment with Hank Fischman. I hadn't seen Hank since we'd done a pediatrics rotation together at Hopkins. He'd been handsome then and he still looked good. Better maybe, with the Antigua vacation tan and the silver sideburns. His skin was smooth, which could have been an advertisement for his partner's skills or just proof of the natural male aging advantage.

Hank examined my face under the ultraviolet light. He tugged the skin under my chin. Took a digital portrait. Then he escorted me out of the exam room to his office and motioned me to a chair across from him.

"So, how long have you been divorced?"

I raised my eyebrows, then quickly lowered them before my surprise dug three new crevices in my forehead. "Actually divorced? Final papers? Seven months. I didn't know you kept up."

"I don't. Call it educated guesswork. You do it all the time with your patients, I'm sure." He steepled his fingers, a major doctor gesture. "It's my experience that women who have recently been divorced or widowed and who are ready to get back into the social swim come to me for a lift. It's more than surgical, of course. It's emotional. They think they're in competition with thirty-year-olds and they want a fighting chance."

"Can you blame us?" I quickly corrected myself. "Them?"

"No, of course not. What they don't realize is it doesn't work that way. Men who are interested in thirty-year-olds aren't interested in fifty-year-olds looking thirty. They want the real deal. It's more than just physical. It's all wound up with mortality."

"You did Elaine Markowitz. She doesn't look thirty."

"Elaine needed it for her work. The young fry were nibbling at her sales. And she's been divorced seven years. One year is my absolute minimum. You need to get the emotional stuff worked out first so your expectation for the surgery is realistic. I'm not saying that if you want it badly enough, you won't find a surgeon to take your money. But your skin is entirely age appropriate. You have very nice fifty-year-old skin. Would a lift help? Sure. It would refresh your look. Come back to me in a year or two."

"Okay," I agreed with an eagerness that surprised me. Up to that moment, I'd thought I wanted the surgery.

"You could use a little help around the eyes, though. The left one is a drooper. Droopy lids make you look tired. Blepharoplasty is an outpatient procedure these days. You'd be surprised what getting rid of that sag and that pocket of fat can do to improve your appearance. Here's a brochure." He pushed over a pamphlet featuring on its cover a gorgeous female who appeared to be a college freshman. The headline, in twenty-point boldface type, read, "Look Younger, Sexier, and More Competitive."

"I'll think about it." I heard myself sighing.

As I got up to leave, I made departing patient chatter à la Elaine Markowitz. From the gallery of personal photos lined up behind him, one especially caught my eye. Hank with a darling toddler in his lap. "Your granddaughter's adorable," I said. "They're so cute at that age."

He swiveled. "Ah, my pumpkin Carolyn. Yeah, she's cute but a handful. Actually, Carolyn's my daughter. That's her mother. Tiffany." He pointed to the largest frame. Within its gold borders, a stunning brunette smiled a perfect "I have everything" smile. The absolutely straight teeth had not yet begun to shift back into their pre-orthodontic positions. She was, stretching it, thirty-five.

"Lovely," I murmured, wondering if my wince would etch a new line. I couldn't help myself; I said, "I remember Linda. Laura? From back at Hopkins."

"Lisa. She went into dermatology. Damn fine physician. We divorced a few years ago." He smiled sheepishly. "You know. You grow apart."

"And Lisa, did she remarry?"

"Still at liberty."

Of course.

He moved behind me as I bent to pick up my handbag. He tapped my chart against my shoulder. "No charge for the visit," he said. "Professional courtesy."

*I should charge you*, I thought, *for pain and suffering. For making me even more self-conscious about my drooper, for intro-*

*ducing me to the beauteous young Tiffany, every menopausal woman's nightmare.* "Well, you just stop by and I'll be glad to return the favor," I said. He gave me a quizzical look, then the lightbulb zapped on and he laughed.

"Same old Gwyn," he said. "Still the comedian."

Years ago, when we were doing that pediatric rotation together, Hank dressed me down for wearing a hat shaped like a duck to make the kids laugh before I stuck them. Quack, quack, jab. This was the seventies when such behavior was considered unprofessional.

"You're a doctor," he'd scolded. "They need to trust you. If they laugh at you, how can they trust you?"

"Since when are trust and laughter incompatible?" Or pain and laughter.

"All right, Gwyn," he said now, his hand on the door. "Call me if you want to do the eyes. Otherwise, here's the prescription: stay out of the sun, drink lots of water, and eat salmon. There's some very interesting research going on with fish oils and skin elasticity. And don't work too hard at it. Your skin is fine. You're a good-looking woman. Some nice man would be lucky to have you."

"You don't happen to have his name, do you?"

Hank laughed uncomfortably. He never *had* known when I was kidding.

*Chapter 4*

When I opened the door to Waterview's first floor workout room the following Saturday, I saw Fleur Caldwaller Talbot, all 275 luscious pounds of her, on the treadmill. Not sitting on its rubber tread finishing off a pint of Ben & Jerry's Karamel Sutra. Not hanging her hot tub towel on its handlebars. Not stretched along its length, her head pillow-propped, watching HBO on the wall-mounted TV because she was too cheap to subscribe.

Our Lady of Perpetual Languishing was walking a treadmill that was rolling at 1.9 miles per hour as '70s soft rock pumped through the ceiling's speakers.

"Well, now I've seen everything. This must be what they mean when they say when donkeys fly. Donkeys are honest-to-god flying."

"And...assholes...are honest to...*puff*...god...running their mouth."

I could hardly keep a straight face. Fleur was wearing sweatpants and a T-shirt inscribed "Born to Triathlon," a sweatband holding her chestnut hair off her damp, pink forehead, a small towel draped around her neck, and the wild-eyed look of a hamster on an exercise wheel gone haywire.

"Well, I'm very impressed. But sweating to the oldies isn't exactly your thing, Fleurie. You want to tell me what this is about?"

She reached into the basket hooked to the treadmill, withdrew a folded section of newspaper, and tossed it at me. "Make yourself useful. Read," she commanded. "Aloud. So I'll *really* hear it and can close this fucking chapter in my life once and for all."

I sat down on a bench and read. "Bambi and Jack Bloomberg of Baltimore City—oh, Jesus—are proud to announce the birth of their son Mason Saul, August 23, Sinai Hospital, seven pounds four ounces, twenty inches long. Ah, Fleurie." I halted. It was just too painful. Around the same time he started to collect social security, Jack Bloomberg, Fleur's boyfriend of fourteen years, left her for a thirty-four-year-old Hooters waitress. Now, eleven months later, he was a daddy.

"Go on, dammit." Fleur said, and I heard tears behind the voice. Fleur? Tears? Extraordinary for a Baltimore Talbot whose family crest reads *Nunquam Demonstrate Dolorem:* Never Show 'em It Hurts.

"Mason Saul is named in loving memory of his late grandmother Minnie Selma. Paternal grandfather is the late Louis Irving Bloomberg. Maternal grandparents are Lucille and Duane Tuttle of Lusby, West Virginia." I dropped the paper on the bench. "You didn't know she was pregnant, right? You must have almost passed out when you came across this."

"I didn't. Quincy did," Fleur said, swiping her nose as the treadmill slowed to a halt. "He brought it in to me. He *wanted* me to see it. He said, and I quote," Fleur swung into her shop manager's effeminate yet earthy singsong, "'Woman, you need to know that Jack Bloomberg's new life is signed, sealed, and *dee*-livered and you'd better get your shit together and get yourself one of your own because it's getting a little late to be a big-assed, purple-dressed bridesmaid and *never* a bride.'" She scowled on the emphasis. Her never-married status was a sore point with her.

I broke into a laugh. "You really do have him down pat."

"Yeah, well he said to tell you that in regards to getting a life, the same goes for y'all."

I stopped laughing.

———

Fifteen minutes later Fleur was out of the shower, into a robe, and toweling her hair. "The thing is," she resumed, "I decided Quincy had a point about getting a life. Actually, I've got most of what I want, but there's still a piece missing. With luck, it's not too late to find it. At least according to that study of yours, there are women out there getting laid and more at our age." She ran a comb through her hair. "I want the more part." She watched my eyes widen with surprise. "What's the big deal? I just want to get married."

Her reasons, she assured me, didn't have all that much to do with Bambi and Jack. Though marrying well might make a pretty piece of revenge. Down deep, she just wanted what Kat and I had, even if we didn't have it anymore. Someone to put her first, to walk hand-in-hand with her into the sunset.

Fleur reminded me she'd always thought she'd get married. She had a hope chest as a teenager and a boyfriend in college but he went off to drop bombs in the Mekong and when he returned home, he brought a Vietnamese wife with him. Fleur was just about over that when the women's movement made marriage unfashionable, and she got distracted with grad school and building the business.

"By the time I looked up from my desk, my waist was gone and my Aunt Ellen's wedding dress wouldn't have fit me anyway even if the best men hadn't been snapped up in the first round. I felt lucky to find Jack. You know I loved him. I was pretty sure he loved me, at least for the first ten years. But I guess he loved his mother more and then when Minnie died, he was free to do what would have killed the old biddy: marry a thirty-four-year-old gum-chewing hottie whose hillbilly family thought Jews had horns."

"Jack's in the past, baby."

"I'm only using him as an example of someone who got what he wanted. So now it's my turn. But I figure no one's going to hand it to me, right? I've gotta make it happen. So I came up with The Plan."

"A plan?"

"Yes, Gwyneth. To get myself married." I must have looked dubious, because she said, "Why not? I have an MBA from Wharton. How hard can it be?"

Fleur was something of a business genius. Her family was old Baltimore money and she could have spent her time on volunteer boards and the ladies-who-lunch circuit. But she put together Madame Max and made it the most profitable plus-size apparel shop in the Mid-Atlantic. *Charm City* magazine named her one of its "Best and Brightest."

"And it's not a plan," she corrected. "It's *The* Plan." She climbed on the scale, peered at the numbers, groaned, and stepped off. "Which in my case means losing seventy-five pounds to even get me in the running. Beginning with the treadmill. Fifteen minutes a day for a start. And as of Thursday noon, I am officially on a diet. Yesterday I had yogurt for lunch and a Lean Cuisine for dinner. Total: four hundred and eighty calories and nine grams of fat. This morning for breakfast I ate Kashi, which tries to pass for cereal but really is an indigestible paper product and should be stocked in the aisle with the Charmin. The worst is I've given up regular Coke for Diet. Ugh! It tastes like it's processed in Chernobyl and whatever they sweeten it with gives me gas."

"You and I have talked about dieting before. I'm all for your losing weight for the right reasons and in the right way but this crash dieting doesn't work and it's—"

"Speaking of crash, do you know you can be a crashing bore? Let me tell you, it's unwise to lecture a woman who has given up chocolate. She will chew you up and swallow you for lack of something high in cocoa butter."

"Fine. Do it your way," I said. "Not that I think you have to be thin to attract a man. There are millions of women out there who are overweight and married—"

"To men they met when they were twenty and looked like Calista Flockhart."

"—and many women of our age who are pleasantly plump and attractive to men."

"I am not pleasantly plump. I am obese. I am also fifty-five years old, which is handicap enough. I need to have a fighting chance." She grimaced as she pulled up fresh sweatpants.

"You're right. Good for you. And one of these days you're going to land a combination of Wolf Blitzer and Zubin Mehta and live happily ever after in the Waterview penthouse with your own private manicurist."

"Zubin Mehta? You really are a nerd. I was thinking more of Jack Nicholson fused with maybe a sixty-year-old Johnny Depp and we live on his yacht off the coast of Cannes where I'm attended by young Greek cabin boys with perpetual hard-ons."

"Sounds reasonable to me," I said.

"You think I'm kidding but I'm serious. Come on upstairs and I'll show you how serious. And if you're real nice to me, I'll put one together for you. Kat, too. No charge. Don't shake your head, Gwyneth. Are you not single? Oh, sweetheart, you are the singlest. Stan has moved on. He's got Brad. You've got zilch. It's time for you, too."

"Nonono—"

"Come on. You can't tell me you don't want to do it again. The love part, I mean," Fleur said as she gave me a push into the back of the elevator. She pressed four.

"Honestly, I'd be too scared to trust the love part. Look what it got me the first time around." I winced at the memory.

"It got you married for twenty-five years, two kids, and a beautiful life."

"Beautiful on the surface. But dig down and it was all a big lie. Thank you anyway, but my plate is full. God knows, I have enough on it with my father and trying to revive the Clinic. The boys call twice a week. And I have my work. I love my work." There it was. My life. All wrapped up in a pretty package. So what if on lonely Saturday nights I felt that what it contained was a little dull. Dull was better than something sharp enough to carve your heart out.

I sighed. "I'll admit it might be nice to have someone to read the Sunday *Times* with. Catch a movie with. No commitment. Nobody's heart on the line. But really, I'm good the way things are."

"Well, good isn't good enough for me." Fleur spun around at her condo door and twirled the key on its ring before inserting it into the lock. "Follow me and I'll show you my key to the future, I'll show you…" she shrugged her eyebrows à la Groucho, "The Plan."

Fleur had crammed into her study a new four-drawer file cabinet containing hanging files with tabs that read "Internet," "Personals," "Matchmaker," "Clubs and Interest Groups," and "Networking" which she flourished as if she were displaying a diamond necklace.

"My strategies. But that's down the line. Everything begins with this." She withdrew five stapled pages marked "Business Plan." I leafed through, from Feasibility Study to Implementation Milestones, as she explained each component.

"Right now I'm researching Internet dating. You know, like Lovingmatch.com."

Well, I didn't know really. But I was willing to learn.

On a purely theoretical basis, that is. *It's okay for you, Fleur*, I thought. But me? Not on my dead Barnard-educated ass.

Which was absurd. This was a brave new world. We needed to be brave new women.

"All it takes is filling out a profile and a $40 member fee. Are you game?" Fleur stared at me hopefully as I paged through the downloaded application for Lovingmatch.com. My application for medical school had been less complicated, but then I was only trying to qualify for mastering endometrial surgery, not hooking up with some DWM who likes long walks on moonlit beaches and Barry Manilow concerts.

"You want me to go on Lovingmatch.com?"

"Well, pardon me if it's beneath you," Fleur responded, suddenly haughty and looking very much like that Gilbert Stuart portrait of her umpteenth-great-grandmother hanging over her sofa.

"It's not that. Look, if something comes along, I won't turn it down. But I'm not going after it. That's not my style."

Fleur's eyes shot evil darts. "Your call. In any event," she pulled up a folder thick with pages, "I know you're exceedingly busy." There was a tang to her tone that might have been sarcasm. "But in your spare time, on the toilet or whatever, I'd be really grateful if you'd review The Plan and tell me if I've left anything out. Make suggestions."

I was swamped with work. Chart reviews. Grant applications for the Clinic. But I nodded.

"And will you at least come with me to GlamourGal Photo tomorrow?"

Now that sounded like a hoot. "The one in the mall with the women all sexy, pouty, and peach-colored like a *Playboy* centerfold? Of course I'll go with you. I'll even call Kat to see if she wants to come." I was eager to make amends, prove myself, be a friend.

Anything but go on Lovingmatch.com.

———

An hour later, Ethan Greenfield's voice answered Kat's phone. She really needed to change that answering machine message. Ethan had made Kat a widow when he took the full force of ten tons of steel piping rolling off a flatbed truck in front of him on I-95. It was very disconcerting to hear his voice from the grave talk about being unavailable and promise to get back to me.

"Have a peaceful day!" Ethan said genially. *You too, Ethan,* I thought. *Wherever you are. And tell Kat to call me.*

When she did, I invited her to join us the next day for the photo session.

"Sure. But if I'm a few minutes late, start without me." Small pause. "I'm having brunch with Lee at 10:30. Four hours should be enough time to eat an omelette."

"Lee? Lee, the sculptor? The forty-year-old very good-looking sculptor?"

"Well, he prefers to be called a construction artist," Kat said. "And he's forty-three."

I would not be diverted. "Katrina, you are having a certified date. Yay for you. But why brunch? Why didn't he ask you out for tonight? He's not married, is he? Married men don't do Saturday night."

"He's not married and he did ask me out for tonight. I told him I had other plans. I don't really have any but it seemed so date-y, you know, Saturday night. I'm having second thoughts now that I'm actually on the brink. I'm not sure I'm ready for this dating business."

"Kat, Ethan's been dead for a year and a half. If not now, when? Now listen, don't order onion soup with the gooey cheese. And no fettuccini. You don't want to battle fettuccini on a first date. And no sushi, promise me. Because you have to cram a whole piece into your mouth and it makes you look like a blowfish."

"It's brunch, Gwyn. Do I have your approval for a mushroom omelette?"

"Perfect."

# Chapter 5

That evening I attended a dinner party at the home of my accountant Lenny Shapiro and his wife Faith. Lenny and I go back thirty-three years, before his comb-over and my cellulite. Stan retained him when we were young and then, about the time he started sending back wine in restaurants, dumped him for some arrogant kid from a large Episcopalian accounting firm.

After Stan dumped *me*, I rehired Lenny to oversee my assets. Our relationship had never been more than "sign on the dotted line, please," though since my divorce maybe he'd added an extra dollop of gallantry for the poor maiden set adrift in the stormy sea of singlehood, but never anything sexual.

So at the party, when Lenny started rubbing my back as he discussed the deteriorating situation in the Middle East and then when his hands slid below my waist to cop a quick feel of my behind, I mean, really, if all this was intended as a political statement, it whizzed by me.

"Jesus, Lenny." I spun on my heel to dislodge him and nearly crashed into Faith Shapiro who had popped in unexpectedly with a tray of miniature knishes and caught the tail end of the episode. She sent a withering look in her husband's direction, gripped my shoulder with hands of steel, and steered me out of the living room.

"How tall are you?" She stopped midway and backed off, assessing. I am a shiksa for goddsakes with a German mother of Wagnerian proportions.

"Last time I was measured, five nine," I said.

"And I used to be five three. You're five seven. But if you wear three-inch heels you'll be five ten and that'll be perfect. The guy I had in mind—"

"What guy?" Were we in a new soap opera? I was still trying to figure out whether I was going to remove my assets from Lenny's surveillance first thing Monday morning or wait until after tax season.

"His name is Jeff Feldmacher. Not Jewish," in a whisper. "A retired ballplayer with the Orioles, but very smart. Would I fix you up with a dummy?"

"Are you fixing me up?"

"That's the idea." And the light dawned. Get me hitched and I would no longer lure certified public accountants into acts of wild sexual abandon.

"He's very rich, an entrepreneur. I don't know what business, but he does very well. *Verrry* well. Handsome. With hair. Also, he's tall."

"Yeah, I figured. How tall?"

"Six six, I think. So you'll wear high heels and be up to his shoulder, which is nice. I'll give him your number." *For which act of kindness, you are to keep your ass to yourself* was the unspoken addendum. Sold.

My first fix-up in months and the guy had hair. Not bad. For a start.

———

"I can't go through with this," Fleur muttered. It was Sunday afternoon and she had spectacularly fallen off the diet wagon at Giuseppe's Gelato, a tool of the devil conveniently located in the center of the Harbor Mall. Over a triple dip of pistachio, hazelnut, and *stracciatella,* she gazed at me balefully. "I mean, this putting your picture on the Internet—it runs counter to everything I was brought up to believe. Ladies do not compete for men. Ladies do not put themselves on display. Ladies do not divulge their personal history to people they haven't even met. Their innermost needs and desires. Ladies—"

"Ladies went out with Bess Truman and white gloves," I interrupted through my own satanic mouthful of rum raisin. "You cannot observe your grandmother's niceties if you want to be successful with The Plan. We're not talking hand-to-hand combat for the last man on earth. We're talking tastefully admitting a select stratum of highly eligible men into the email version of your parlor."

"They must have gone really heavy on the rum in your gelato." Fleur scraped the bottom of her paper cup with her plastic spoon. "But what the hell, it's worth an afternoon, right?"

Suddenly Kat appeared, shimmering like an angel in diaphanous gray silk and twinkling silver jewelry.

"Well, you're early," I greeted her cheerfully. "How did you know where to find us?"

"Just an educated guess," she said, sinking into a plastic and chrome chair. "It was this or Sharper Image, and this involves calories."

"Get yourself a gelato and we'll talk about your date."

"No gelato, thanks. I'm stuffed to the gills. Why was I so sure this guy was a vegetarian? There you go. Linear thinking. He is an artist, ergo he is a vegetarian. He had bacon and sausage with his cheese omelette."

"My kind of man," Fleur said. "Lee the Sculptor."

"Please stop referring to him as Lee the Sculptor. You make him sound like Ivan the Terrible or Vlad the Impaler or—"

"The date," I prompted, licking my lips with anticipation. I was only dating vicariously these days.

"I told you this was not a date. It was just two people interested in art talking about it. Besides, he's much too young for me."

"An eleven-year difference. When you're ninety-one, he'll be eighty. No big deal." I wasn't going to allow Kat to lose steam over a mere chronological detail.

"Oh please," Kat grabbed my spoon and swiped a mound of rum raisin. "This person wasn't alive when Frida Kahlo died. We are lifetimes apart."

"He's probably dynamite in bed."

"He probably wants kids. He's never had kids."

"Well, it's not a biologic impossibility. There's in vitro. Surrogate mothers. The science is rapidly advancing. Soon Medicare will be covering obstetrics."

"Don't be absurd, I am not having kids at my age. I did it when I was supposed to. I wouldn't even consider a long-term relationship with a man young enough to be my son."

"Only in West Virginia," Fleur said.

"And I will probably not go out with him again if he asks me."

All of us heard the probably, and two of us traded smiles.

"Okay," Fleur said, raising her enormous bulk to standing. She was glorious in full height. Like the *Titanic* before the iceberg hit. "Enough of your problems, Kat. My turn to make an ass of myself. Who wants to watch?"

We all did.

The receptionist at GlamourGal Photo was maybe seventeen years old and what my sons would have called "hot" in a skimpy halter top that should only be worn over young, sprightly boobs, a belly-button ring visible because her jeans were slung to her slim hips, and four-inch platforms upon which she rocked with apparent boredom.

She and Fleur gave each other the once-over. Fleur said, "I have a two fifteen. Talbot. You're going to make me beautiful, are you not?"

The receptionist answered seriously, "Gavin's good. He'll do the best he can."

I watched Fleur's shoulders sink.

Gavin worked with her for more than an hour. He draped her like a Greek goddess in a swathe of champagne-colored satin revealing just a hint of cleavage, he turned up her collar to slenderize her neck, he brought out the red feather boa which Fleur snaked around her shoulders like Mae West ("I'm molting here"). He posed her head-on, three-quarters "to bring out your angles," and from the back with her head twisted around for a come-hither look.

He laid out the digital proofs for us to select from. "You look perfect. A little bit DAR, a little bit rock and roll. We're going for seductive but not someone who looks as if she might eat her young."

Fleur examined the proofs with a scowl. "I look like a water buffalo with this fat hanging under my neck."

"Honey, forget your neck. With that smile, do you really think anyone will look at your neck?"

*Right on, Gavin.* He managed to elicit a tighter version of the dazzling smile Fleur produced for the camera. Fleur chose three poses and handed over her Visa card to the receptionist who said robotically, "I hope you have enjoyed your GlamourGal Photo session. Would you like to apply for our GG Discount card that entitles you to five years of studio sittings at 10 percent off?"

"No, I would not. I plan on becoming a nun in an order that prohibits photographs," Fleur deadpanned.

"A nun," the girl said breathily. "My great-aunt is a nun. That is so cool."

Outside in the brighter lights of the mall, Fleur said, "I must have been crazy to think this was a good idea. There is no way in hell I'm going to put any one of those pictures on the Internet."

"But you have to," Kat said. "People want to see what they're getting into. Would you buy a pig in a poke?"

I slid her a lacerating look. Kat is splendid with visual images, not quite as adroit with words.

"Then I'm not going on. Forget the Internet. Forget The Plan. Fuck The Plan."

I've seen this sudden stalling out in patients before they're wheeled into surgery. Second thoughts before undergoing the experience that might save their lives. "Fine, but if you don't do the project, it will be the only thing being fucked. Think about it."

"Think about this." Fleur shot an elegant, well-bred middle finger at me.

The final word. For now.

# Chapter 6

"Hello, Doc," my father said to me at six o'clock that evening as I let myself into his tiny East Baltimore row house. He waved at me from the hollow of his chair, a behemoth of a brown corduroy La-Z-Boy that nearly swallowed him up.

I leaned over to kiss his forehead, and he reached out a bony hand to stroke my hair. Dark and small, he was the antithesis of your typical Scandinavian stereotype although he came from unadulterated Norwegian stock. He used to brag he never weighed more than 135 pounds in his life. For the last few years, he'd been tipping the scales at 115. He hadn't cared for red meat when red meat was in favor, had no taste for sweets back then, and so, I thought, eyeing him sadly, he will live on forever, his heart ticking merrily, his brain slowly but inexorably disintegrating.

Sylvie was the latest in a succession of round-the-clock caretakers, Caribbean ladies of infinite patience who did the job that should have, by rights, and would have, in another era, fallen to me.

"He's been very good today," she reported, putting down her copy of the *Caribbean Voice*. "Not agitated at all. And he cleaned his plate for lunch. He does like that chicken I do."

She talked about him in front of him as if he weren't there. I wanted to pretend he was, so we had discussed this, Sylvie and I, but to no avail. "It don't matter I tell you," Sylvie had insisted. "He don't know. And if I have to take you in another room to tell you t'ings, you lose your time with him."

"Dad," I said, "it's Gwyn."

"I know who you are."

"Who am I?" I challenged him to repeat it. Numbers were still remembered. Phone numbers. Bank balances. But names disappeared as they were uttered.

"You're Doc," he said.

"And who is this?" I pointed to Sylvie, hoping the new medication Dan found for him might have kicked in, kicked away some of the tangles.

"Ah, that's my hon."

All women, except for me, were "hon." All men were "captain."

He didn't know us, but he did appreciate us. Some days he stood for hours in front of the wall my mother had decorated with family photographs, a documentary of our survival under her demented dictatorship. At least pinned to the wall, we were still and quiet which was all she'd ever asked of us. In spite of her, or because of Dad or who knows what interplay of forces, my brother and I grew up to stay out of jail and pay our taxes. Rolfe, who looked stunned until adolescence and then stoned in his portraits, managed to become a chemical engineer, marry Nadine, and father three kids. He moved to California decades ago and made it east to see Dad twice a year. My father's maintenance fell to me. Fair enough. I'd sopped up most of his attention as a child.

While Rolfe stayed under my mother's radar, I was the thorn in her side, the bee in her bonnet, the fly in her ointment. I looked like her which for some reason galled her, and from the time I was four I talked back to her in polysyllables she didn't understand. She hammered away at me with everything she had.

I was eight when she went into Springfield State Hospital for the first time. Eleven when she made her first suicide attempt, by overdosing on Thorazine. The shrinks diagnosed schizoaffective disorder. There were short pre-hospitalization periods when she heard voices and spun delusions. But most of the time she was just dreadfully depressed and over-the-top angry. Principally with me who, in her muddled mind, was always out to get her. So of course I deserved every slap, every pinch, and in adolescence, the occasional slug.

Dad did what he could to protect me, and when the opportunity presented itself for my escape, he made sure I got out. Rolfe went to the University of Maryland for its low tuition. To pay my way at Barnard, Dad drove a cab at night in addition to his day job working a furnace at Bethlehem Steel. Three hours after I called home to report my acceptance to medical school, my mother took a bus down-town and leapt off the top of the Bromo-Seltzer tower.

Up and out of his chair, remarkably sprightly for an Alzheimeric eighty-two-year-old, my father shuffled over to stand beside me. He clasped my hand. We stared together at these pictures that took up so much space in his minuscule living room, and I realized they were as meaningless to me as they were to him.

"Who is this?" I pointed to my mother. Dan said to keep pushing him to remember. Every cell retrieved is a small victory.

"That," my father said confidently, "is the USS *Arizona*. A grand battleship before they sunk her in Pearl Harbor. Terrible tragedy."

Indeed. What a fabulous place, the human cerebellum.

"You know what?" I stroked his hair. "I'm in the mood for a Big Mac, how about you? A nice fish sandwich?" We did this nearly every Sunday, a treat for him. "McDonald's. What do you say?"

"Oh, my. That's a good one," he laughed. "McDonald's." That name he remembered.

At dinner, he tore off pieces of the fish and cheese sandwich and fed himself while keeping a careful eye on his dessert, a fried apple pie. After my mother's suicide, he'd developed a sweet tooth.

"Eat your fries," he instructed me, briefly lucid. "Enjoy yourself, it's later than you think."

Not so crazy.

When I dropped him off, I reminded Sylvie to hide the phone so he couldn't call me at five o'clock in the morning.

Then, feeling guilty since he asked so little of me, I changed my mind. "Let him call," I told her. "I can always go back to sleep. It's no big deal."

She shrugged at me as if I were just another neurotic American white lady, which I am, and steered my father toward the La-Z-Boy. Two steps in, he shook her off and turned to me.

"Okay, Doc," he tipped an imaginary hat. "Give my regards to Broadway." A song he used to sing to me when I was nine or ten and couldn't fall asleep because of some hissy fit my mother had thrown earlier in the evening. "And remember me to Herald Square."

I had already kissed him good-bye when I handed him over and I was just going to wave from the door, but now I ran back and kissed him again on his soft, paper-dry cheek. For my reward, he returned the kiss, the first kiss from him in a long time. Then he patted my cheek, moved back a step, and surveyed me, his nearly colorless eyes sparking with some emotion. As if he were really seeing me.

Two years before, the American Association of Gynecological Oncologists had awarded me the Turnbull Prize for my work at the Women's Free Clinic. A great honor.

This was better.

I arrived home to find a message on my answering machine. Harry Galligan, finally making good on his promise. He was at a conference in Topeka, but he didn't want me to think he'd forgotten me. He hoped I was doing okay after my FRESH sharing.

Not a word about seeing me or even phoning me when he returned. So much for fantasies of being wrapped in his warm, pipe-tobacco-scented embrace.

The next morning, I was steady-handed and absolutely focused as I prowled through the reproductive organs of my uninsured patient, Freesia Odum. Ms. Odum, age forty-six, had a huge fibroid tumor hunkered down in her uterine wall. This, and three other sizeable tumors, were the cause of her excessive bleeding. I'd tried everything short of surgery to shrink these four big mamas. But now we'd come to the end of the line. Freesia Odum had a six-month-old granddaughter, LaTanya, to raise, and she certainly didn't want any more children of her own. So I went about removing her uterus without my normal reluctance, leaving her healthy matched set of ovaries intact.

I don't like to perform unnecessary surgery, but when conditions call for it, I do love to cut. In those horrendous weeks after Stan made his confession and knocked my world out of orbit, the only place I could find a semblance of peace was in the OR. There is something empowering and, I think, healing to the surgeon as well as the patient in slicing deftly through live tissue, dicing and splicing as Neil Potak calls it, and putting everything to rights. Funny, I have always been a lousy housekeeper, but I'm a skillful surgeon.

Of course, there are times when nothing you do is going to make it well, and those are the days you think you should have been a marketing major. But Freesia Odum's pelvic cavity offered no surprises, and when she came around in recovery I could tell her honestly, "You're going to be fine. You'll probably live to be a hundred and be around for LaTanya's grandbaby."

She was too groggy to speak, but her hand crept out to grab mine and press it to her lips. I thought of my father working that second job to get me through Barnard and blessed his currently addled soul.

Case closed, I thought. But in fact it wasn't. Every week, the staff of Potak, Berke, and Bernstein gathers for our medical review conference. We cover all the challenging cases on the docket, sharing experiences and getting instant consults from our colleagues.

In the middle of reviewing Freesia Odum's procedure— "Six millimeter squamous cell. Highly impacted. One three millimeter—" I was interrupted. Interrupting a colleague mid-review is considered bad form, and I wasn't surprised that this breach of professional protocol was executed in the exquisitely grating voice of Bethany McGowan, MD.

"This Freesia Odum is your uninsured?" she asked. As if she didn't keep a running tab on my billing.

"Freesia Odum has no medical insurance, that is correct." I'd been leaning over the patient chart on the conference table. Now I drew myself up and inquired with lavish politeness, "May I continue?"

"I thought it was settled that we weren't going to absorb any more uncovered cases." Someone had given her leave to say this, I realized, or she wouldn't have dared press on. She darted a glance at Seymour Bernstein (likely culprit), who continued staring at the table, and then at Neil Potak (wouldn't have put it past him, either), who was furiously retracting and reloading his ballpoint pen.

"I'm sorry," I said, my voice thick with sarcasm, "I don't think you qualify as my monitor. You've been associated with this practice for what, a little over a year? I was present at the creation. In your place, I would not presume to chastise a senior partner for her professional choices." Deservedly tough.

The little ferret's face turned bright red but she didn't lower her gaze. I slashed on. "I don't know if they taught medical ethics at Harvard," as a child of blue-collar Baltimore, Johns Hopkins-trained, the Harvard thing had always rankled me, "but we have an obligation here to treat patients. True, we cannot treat every patient without regard for ability to pay, and these days we seem to be guided less by the Hippocratic Oath than by the bottom line. Nonetheless, when we see a patient in severe distress, it is our social and moral responsibility to at least consider whether we can afford to absorb that patient's fees."

"We're not a nonprofit, Gwyn," she had the temerity to back talk me.

"Jesus," I said.

"Besides, that service area has Covenant as a safety net hospital." She made "service area" sound like downtown Baghdad. "Covenant absorbs these cases. I don't know why we—"

"Covenant takes only uninsured emergencies, as you know." I was seething. "They don't do routine care or non-emergency surgeries."

"But," she smirked as if she'd got the goods on me, "Covenant just got bought by UltaMed. That's a major corporation. Who's to say they won't increase community outreach? Which, we need to remember, is not part of our mission."

Cold. Very cold. I wanted to slap her. Neil glanced at my face and said quickly, "Let's move on please. This is sidetracking us."

"Why don't you do a study on this, Bethany?" Seymour interjected. I figured him to be the lead horse in the field of possible coconspirators. Divorced and always on the make, he'd come on strong to Bethany when she joined the practice, but I thought she'd rebuffed him. Now I wasn't so sure. Was this a setup? "See how many pro bonos we've all done. Cost to the practice. Then we'll be able to balance it against good-will in the community, PR, abstract stuff like that."

"Fine," Neil said. "Do the numbers, Bethany, and we'll take a look at them."

I steamed silently.

As we drew to a close, Neil said, "I was supposed to go to London for the IAGSO meeting, but Cheryl is having back surgery. Anyone want to fill in?"

Bethany's hand shot up. She was that dorky kid everyone hated back in junior high for being first with the answer. Call on me, call on me. Ugh.

I cut her off at the pass. "Actually, I'm going, Neil. There's a session on adjuvant therapy for stage 1B1 ovarian they asked me to chair." Lie, lie, lie. He could check the program. "Last-minute fill in."

"Well, that settles that then," Neil said.

Our policy is never to have more than one doc at a time absent from the practice if we can help it. Bethany did not look happy. *Play with the big boys, take your lumps.*

After the meeting, Neil crooked a finger at me and I followed him into his office.

"You okay?"

"Sure," I answered, "why do you ask?" Knowing.

"Well, you seemed somewhat emotional in there with Bethany. Don't you think you came down a little hard on her?"

"Oh, for godssakes. She's a pompous pain in the ass. And out of bounds. Where does she get off telling me who to treat? It's not like I'm standing on North Avenue handing out coupons for free hysterectomies."

"You've done five procedures without charge so far this year, Gwyn. Look, I know the Clinic was close to your heart and you feel we should take up the slack now that it's shut down. But we're not a free clinic, and we do have to keep an eye on the numbers."

"This is a highly lucrative operation. It wouldn't hurt to give a little back."

"The times they are a-changing," Neil said. "We cannot afford liberal largesse. We are not a welfare provider." I'd heard this too many times before. Neil is way to the right politically. "You're how old? Fifty-four? You'll be retired in a decade."

"Not necessarily," I said, shocked. This was the first time either of the partners had brought up the age issue.

"Give or take a year. And Bethany is thirty. She has thirty-five years left to work. Look at her background: Harvard and Hopkins. We don't want to lose her. Let me also remind you it's in your best interest to have the practice continue to be a solid moneymaker since it's going to support you in your retirement. Think about it."

And back off, was the unstated sentiment. Back off, old gal. You're nearly history.

After I left, pulse racing but head held high, I called my travel agent to book my flight to London.

*Chapter 7*

Tuesday didn't get off to a promising start.

While I was still chomping on my breakfast bar, my secretary put a call through. The director of the senior center where my father spent his Tuesdays apologized profusely for bothering me at the office, but Dad was about to flunk out of adult day care. "We're very concerned because Mr. Swanson refuses to interact with our A-Team," her cutesy-poo name for the Alzheimer group. "He wouldn't participate in music therapy, personal expression, or the reminiscence activities designed to stimulate memory." Apparently all he wanted was to sit with three of the fully cognitive senior women and snooze to the clacking of their knitting needles.

Well, that sounded like a good choice to me, like my father was using what was left of his noodle. But if he got expelled, I'd have to scramble for coverage for Tuesday, one of Sylvie's two days off, so I said, absolutely, I understood the benefits of socialization and stimulating his synapses and I'd speak to his doctor and get back to her.

Three patients later, the receptionist ambushed me with the morning mail. On top of the stack was a response to one of my grant applications for the Clinic. *We regret to inform you…* the letter began, as if reporting a death. I was getting down to the last funding sources on my list, but I refused to even consider abandoning hope for the Clinic. I'd think of something. I *had* to.

At least my afternoon lecture to first-year medical students went well. But their youth, their brightness, their eagerness to take on the world with its smorgasbord of options left me mildly depressed. And late. Late was a problem because Fleur and I were going to dinner and she took tardiness as a personal affront.

Therefore I was distracted and hustling when I barreled through the door to her shop and crashed into her former longtime squeeze Jack Bloomberg barreling out. The thing is, I should have recognized him instantly from the smell of his cologne. Then again, it had been a while since I'd been engulfed in Jack's eau de Pine-Sol and I hadn't gotten a look at him when we collided, so I had to hear the "Sorry" he tossed back over his shoulder in his unmistakable gargle before I thought, *Oh, my God, could it be?* I spun around to see him trotting down Pratt Street into the setting sun as fast as his Florsheims could carry him. Even from the back, he looked thinner. And, oh Lord, he was wearing a toupee. But there was no denying that splayfooted gait, the rolled shirtsleeves, and the open vest flapping like wings. My heart sunk. Fleur's ex was back. For—believe me—no good reason.

Inside there was no Fleur in sight, but I spotted her manager, Quincy Dickerson, exiting her office wringing his hands. When he saw me, he broke out one of his fabulous magenta-tinted smiles and strode my way, arms spread wide for an embrace.

"Kiss, kiss," he said and did just that, first on one cheek, then another, European style. He backed me up to arm's length. "Now you're a sight for my gorgeous brown eyes. Love the hair. The blonde is blonder, right?"

"Just a few highlights around the face. It's supposed to add a youthful glow."

"You could pass for thirty-five."

"Liar."

"Well, yes, but didn't it make you feel better for just a teensy second?"

Quincy rocked with delight at his own wit. He was a big man and a bigger woman, but man or woman, he always looked stunning. By day, he wore replica Armani suits a tailor in Cherry Hill whipped up for him. Three nights a week and on weekends, he was Queenella LaBella down at the Rhinoceros Lounge, a gay nightclub on South Charles Street, parading in fabulously glitzy evening gowns he ordered at discount through Madame Max.

"Quincy, tell me I didn't see Jack Bloomberg coming out of here."

His face fell. "Husband of Bambi, father of bambino in the flesh, though I have to admit a lot less flesh than he used to lug around." He pursed his lips. "And how did you like the dead possum on his head? Anyway, there was much activity behind closed doors which I assume didn't end with hugs and kisses from the looks of Madame. And just now, when I tried to give the tiniest bit of advice to the lovelorn, she snapped my head off. Um-um-um," he said as we both turned to watch Fleur emerge from her office. "Look at that face. Not a happy bunny. Make sure she orders two martinis at dinner."

"Sake," I said. "We're going to the Kyoto Inn."

"Oh, God, raw fish. Eating like seals. What is wrong with you people?" As Fleur drew closer, her fake customer-smile fading, Quincy hoisted his bulk from the banquette.

"Good luck, babykins. Take care and beware. And don't make it another hundred years before I see that fabulous face." With an air kiss, he was off.

"About time he got his fat ass back on the floor," Fleur growled after he had skittered away. "I have had more than my share of fat asses for one day, sitting or standing or trying to squeeze themselves into Vikki Vi capri pants three sizes too small. Let's get out of here."

At the Kyoto Inn, she took her mood out on her diet, ordering about thirty dollars worth of sushi and a mountain of tempura. When the diminutive Japanese waitress bowed away, leaving six plates behind, Fleur said, "Don't give me that look. I'm on Atkins. Or South Beach. I can never remember which, but fried is allowed. Okay, not the rice, but I deserve it. It's been a rough day."

"I can only imagine. I ran into Jack on his way out. Or he ran into me. Don't worry, he didn't stop to chat. I don't think he even knew who I was." Fleur swirled her California roll furiously in the soy sauce. "Ah, poor baby. You want to talk?"

"No, I do not. Not to you and not to Quincy Dickerson who'd better keep his nose out of my business or he or she is history. And I'm not a poor baby, Gwyneth, although I know you mean well. I'm a big girl in every sense of the word and I do not need anyone, not a transvestite Dear Abby, not even you to tell me how to run my life."

Feelings hurt, I fiddled with my napkin. "We don't want anything bad to happen to you, that's all."

"Nothing bad has happened. Nothing at all will happen. Look, Jack stopped by to return something of mine. No big deal. Case closed. Let's eat."

That was an order so I snared a shrimp dumpling. She speared a Dragon Roll stuffed with shrimp tempura and crowned with slices of lobster.

"Umm. Why does *trayf* taste so good?"

"*Trayf?*" I'd never heard the word before.

"It means unkosher in Yiddish. Meat from animals that oink and wallow in mud and creatures that scavenge the sea floor. The lowest of the low." She popped another pinwheel of solid cholesterol into her mouth and chewed blissfully.

Fleur, whose family had funded the Talbot Memorial Window at Trinity Episcopal Cathedral in Roland Park, fancied herself an expert in all things Jewish. She'd learned all about Torah and Talmud, kosher and non when she converted five years back thinking it would goose Jack into marriage. His mother was still alive when the romance got serious, and the old lady planned a fatal heart attack if he married out of the faith. So Fleur took instruction from a rabbi thinking if Mother Bloomberg approved, Jack would propose. She even went through the mikvah, the ritual bath, and became an official nonshiksa. Except Jack never gave a rat's ass about religion. He only went to synagogue to please Mama. When she died, all bets were off.

"You still go to temple?"

"On the high holidays. And I can still turn out a mean potato pancake at Hanukkah. But do you remember how Jack loved Christmas? I can still see him on the ladder hanging decorations. He really had a hard-on for that tree. It made him feel like Jimmy Stewart in *It's a Wonderful Lif*e." Jack again. And *she'd* brought him up. "Fine," she continued, "if you must know, he came over to return a bracelet I lost. When they moved out of his townhouse a few months ago, Bambi found this under the bed." She rolled up her sleeve, tugged a gold bangle over her broad wrist, and handed it to me. "Under the bed, isn't that priceless? Oh, I wish I could have been there when she saw the inscription."

"Jack and Fleur, forever and a day," I read aloud.

"Yeah, his watch never ran on time either."

I handed back the bracelet. "And he had to bring it over in person? Why, because he wanted to show you his wig? We have mail service in this country. What's wrong with UPS? Or he could have just dropped it off at the Waterview desk. And if Bambi found it months ago, why did he take so long returning it?"

"All wonderful questions. And the final *Jeopardy* answer is, I don't know. I didn't ask. I don't care. I took back my bracelet and said thanks and good-bye."

"Yes, but did you say good riddance?"

"Oh, for godsakes, I knew I shouldn't discuss this with you. Let's please change the subject. Lighten this up. Talk to me about cancer."

By dessert we'd had enough rice wine to mellow us out. "So what's happening with The Plan?" I asked, wanting to make sure that after Jack's visit, the project was still a go.

"It's coming along," she said. "I was thinking, maybe I'll register with Jewlove.com."

"Jewlove.com. You're kidding!" I laughed, snuffling tea up my nose.

"See what you're missing? There's a matchmaking site for everyone and anyone. Blacks, Jews, black Jews. People with every interest. Every twisted sexual practice. Every body type. I'm going on Fabulousfatties.com and Lusciousnlovely.com. You ought to go on Ivydate.com. It's restricted to people from the top colleges. Connie deCrespi met a droolworthy Princeton lawyer on there."

Constanza deCrespi, who was supposedly descended from Italian aristocracy, was Fleur's attorney and the woman she held up as the epitome of upper-class cool. I'd met Connie and she had everything Fleur credited her with: charm, brains, a laid-back elegance. Just fifty. Divorced with a ball-breaking settlement. Looking around for husband number two. Online, yet.

"When she found out he had a shoe fetish, Connie dropped him. But still."

"I'll think about it," I lied. "Did you finish filling out the Lovingmatch profile?"

"Almost." She extracted the downloaded application from her handbag, snapped open her eyeglass case, and nudged a pair of magnifying half-glasses along the bridge of her nose. They gave her round, soft face a touching gravitas.

"My screen name is brighteyes. I'm cheerful and low maintenance. That's what men want, right? Not to be bothered? I mean, this is the gender that invented the TV remote. Okay. I'm a Whig politically and the only thing left to decide is my body type. I get to choose from petite, athletic, slim, trim, anorexic/bulimic, and sunk way down at the bottom, like big fat rocks in an ocean of skinnies, three categories for the jumbos: buxom, voluptuous, and Rubenesque. Which do you think sounds the least porcine?"

"I like Rubenesque," I said finally. "It conjures a picture of boobs bubbling over a laced-up bodice."

"Rubenesque it is," she wrote with a flourish. "So there I am in a hundred words or less. I'll send it in tonight."

"Good for you. I'm proud of you, kiddo. You started this project; you're going to see it through." I tried to make the question a statement. "I really admire your perseverance."

"Yeah, well I think perseverance is sexy. As in 'the woman can really give good perseverance.'"

Brash and bright, but for all the surface toughness and braggadocio, Fleur has a nougat center, soft and sweet. Jack leaving her for the waitress had almost killed her and now he was back, poking his formerly bald head where it didn't belong. Damn it, I didn't want to see her hurt again.

"Don't get sidetracked, Fleur. Not by anything or anyone, okay? Remember your business plan. Your goal is marriage. You want to be married."

"I do, I do." She lifted a spoonful of green tea ice cream in a toast. "Well, here's to getting what I want and you getting what you want which is...what the hell *do* you want?"

I could feel the rice wine smudging me into sentimentality. I took another sip, thinking. "I guess what I want is for the clock to be turned back to when everything was right with the world. Except it never was, was it? So that won't work." I was surprised by the sting of tears. "But you know what would be nice? To be able to trust someone again. It would even be nice just to trust myself again. Stan knocked that out of me and I guess that's what I want, more than a head on the next pillow." Where did all that come from? I blotted my eyes with the napkin.

Fleur reached over and patted my arm. Then, in typical Fleur fashion, she cracked the emotional moment. "And I thought all you wanted was a subscription to *Twat: The Review of Gynecology*. No more sake for you." She moved the sake decanter, poured the last drops into her cup, and hoisted it. "As I was saying, here's to you and me and getting what we want."

"And Kat, don't forget Kat," I said.

"Oh, honey, she is probably at this very moment getting what she wants. Nevertheless, banzai one and all."

———

The softshell crab roll must have disagreed with me, because I was up and heading toward the Tums when my father called at seventeen minutes past four the following morning.

"I just wanted to tell you that the captain stole my razor."

He spoke in a code I was beginning to understand although it wasn't always consistent. This time I was pretty sure he was trying to tell me Stan had been there. My ex-husband visited my father once or twice a week. Occasionally, he gave him a close shave with a safety razor, unlike the quick swipe with an electric shaver Sylvie gave him. Credit where it's due, Stan may have walked out on me, but he hadn't deserted my father.

Before he could tell me more, Sylvie grabbed the phone.

"Mr. Harald came into my room, stuck his hand under the pillow, and stole the phone from where I was hiding it. You can't keep anything from him. And the other night he got in bed with me. Didn't do nothing, but it was a fright to wake up with him next to me."

"You need to lock your room at night."

"He peed in the rubber plant yesterday."

"You threw it out, I hope."

"I didn't grow up in a shack. Of course, I threw the stinky t'ing out. But tomorrow it will be something else. I'm putting you on fair warning: I don't know how long I can take this."

"Are you quitting, Sylvie?" I heard the desperation in my voice.

"Not yet, not until I get me another job. I need the money too bad." At least she was honest. "But it's gotten out of hand. If you don't mind me saying, you ought to start thinking about a nursing home."

I felt something rise in my throat. It may have been the softshell crab. I thought it was something even less digestible.

"Is he nearby?"

"Standing right next to me. If I turn, I knock him over."

"No more talk of nursing homes, then. Not in front of him."

"Well, you'll have to do something soon. No good you putting your head in the sand. He's going downhill quick."

"Well, please give me a couple of weeks, at least. Can you promise me that?"

"He's pulling on me."

"Put him on, please." When I heard him breathing his raspy former-two-pack-a-day wheeze, I said, "Daddy, go back to bed. It's still nighttime."

"Okay," he said.

"I love you, Daddy."

"You've got it, hon," he said.

Not Doc. Hon. We just slipped down a step on the ladder into the abyss.

# Chapter 8

On Friday towards evening, I opened the door to God's gift to women and Faith Shapiro's gift to me. Jeff Feldmacher, winner of the Cy Young Award, famous for his back-to-back shut-outs in the World Series three decades before, was tall and toothy with a full complement of inert anchorman hair and an appealing fretwork of laugh lines around his eyes. When Faith Shapiro said retired ballplayer, I figured Cracker, but on the pre-date phone call he'd come off charming, a cultivated southern gentleman. In the flesh, well, he had mighty attractive flesh.

Moving with the easy grace of a natural athlete, he paused before my hall mirror to smooth his hair and check his teeth for stray bits of food, then ambled across my living room, his turquoise eyes taking it all in.

"You like art," he said, looking at the best of what Stan and I had assembled over the years. "I collect Neiman. You know Neiman? He does a lot of sports-related art."

We rode the elevator down with Lou Goodkind, 14A. Lou took in Jeff, vacuumed him up and down a few times with his eyes, and finally said, "Aren't you...?"

"Yup," Jeff said.

"Hey. Jeez." Lou extended his hand and said, "Thank you for many hours of pleasure," as if Jeff were his favorite hooker. He nodded at me as Jeff slipped his arm around my shoulder and I could tell I'd picked up megapoints on his scorecard.

Jeff Feldmacher's silver Mercedes had the license plates BALLS 14, his old Orioles number, and six rounds of country western in the CD player.

"You know anything about baseball?" he asked me as we approached Camden Yards.

I used to. My father, the rabid Orioles fan, took me to games from the time I was six until I lost interest at fourteen. We'd sit in the bleachers at the old Memorial Stadium, higher than heaven, hotter than hell, nosebleed territory where he'd keep score in his program while I stuffed my face with hot dogs. He got us both out of the house in summer for night games, where you could see the soupy air, thick with gnats in the light. Shimmering down below was the field, brilliant, faceted with shadows of the players moving, twinkling, more like an emerald than a diamond, an emerald ocean that could sail you away from someone yelling at you all the time and flailing the air with her hitting hand as you ducked by. My mother eschewed all sports that did not draw blood. She watched boxing on TV, screaming at the fighters to go for the kill, and she loved hockey—not the game, the brawls. To irritate her, and because I had a crush on Brooks Robinson, I memorized the Oriole lineup and pinned an orange-and-black felt "Birds" banner to the bulletin board above my bed. But that was more than forty years ago and I hadn't kept up.

I told Jeff I'd gone to plenty of games with my father when I was a kid. He said, "That earns you a B+ in my book." He flicked me an appraising look. "At least you know how the game is played. So I don't have to start from scratch. I usually have to start from scratch. It's a bummer."

I stared at him, wondering what happened to the charm I'd heard on the phone. Who killed Rhett Butler?

At Camden Yards, we sat in a box over third base reserved for Jeff's business clients. He let me know he owned half an office tower in downtown Baltimore and part interest in two restaurants. He didn't talk much to me after that. He concentrated on the field, grunting and whooping at appropriate times and chewing gum so hard his jawbones moved like tectonic plates in a Mesozoic shift.

Fans stopped by for autographs. Most of the people who remembered Jeff Feldmacher were over forty, but at the seventh-inning stretch we were rushed by three women in their mid-twenties wearing short shorts, halter tops, and Dundalk hairdos—homemade peroxide streaks in perms half grown out.

Did I ever have breasts that high? I knew for certain I'd never walked out of the house with my nipples outlined like elevator buttons against clingy fabric. As if this weren't blatant enough, they'd powdered their cleavages with gold dust.

"God, you girls are a sight for sore eyes," Jeff said, as if I weren't sitting next to him nibbling on my barbecue sandwich. He looked down only long enough to sign one exposed hip, one patch of smooth, tight skin below a belly-button ring, and one front triangle of a satin thong. For this last, Terri tugged down her jeans while executing a mini bump and grind. Jeff's voice was wet with suppressed drool. "Nothing more beautiful than a beautiful woman. And I got me a triple here. To Chris, To Denise, To Terri with an i. With love, Jeff Feldmacher." He poked his tongue through the o of his lips as he wrote. He drew a little baseball next to his name.

On the drive home, Jeff said, "Faith Shapiro tells me you're divorced. Twelve years out for me. She's about your age, my ex. Very wrinkled though. Lives in Florida. A sun worshipper and a smoker. You look good for...how old are you? Faith said she thought late forties, maybe fifty."

Faith Shapiro knew damn well how old I was. Her husband did my taxes.

"I'm fifty-four."

"No kidding. I wouldn't have guessed. You're an eyeful. Really well maintained. Money helps, right?"

At my door he said, "I told Faith I usually don't date women over forty or under five foot nine, but she said to broaden my horizons—you were a special lady. And she was right. You've got lots of class, and class makes up for just about anything. What do you think? Should we do this again?"

"Sure," I said. Hating myself. I've addressed a thousand gynecological surgeons about para-aortic and pelvic lymphadenectomies for staging purposes in ovarian cancer, yet I still could not bring myself to say, "Look, we are not a match made in heaven. Have another wonderful twelve years chasing twenty-five-year-old amazons with enough saline in their tits to float the USS *Constitution*. But count me out."

"That would be nice," was what I croaked, wanting to bite my tongue clear through so the tip landed on his $300 Bruno Magli loafers.

"Great. Think about where you want to go next week." He pulled me into an awkward hug.

Five minutes later, while I was reading my email in my underwear, my doorbell rang.

"It's Jeff," the voice through the door said. "Can I use your bathroom?"

"I'm ready for bed," I answered. "There's a restroom on the first floor, next to the workout room."

"I'll never find it. Come on, it's urgent," he wheedled.

*The man could have irritable bowel syndrome,* I thought. *Or horseshoe kidney. Or more likely at his age, prostitis.* How could I deny an ailing man access to the facilities? I'd taken the Hippocratic oath.

I threw on a robe, opened the door, pointed, and watched him dash to the powder room, though not so fast that he didn't take in my robe.

Standing in the hallway, I finally heard the toilet flush, the faucets gush, and then Jeff was in front of me, all six feet six of him, bare from the waist up, shirt slung over his shoulder.

"What do you think you're doing?" I was beyond stunned. "Put your shirt on."

"You sure?" He held out his arms so that he looked like a hairy-chested, well-muscled Jesus. *Come unto me.* "I took a Viagra back there. It will only take a half hour, and we can put the time to good use. It would be a shame to waste it."

"Get your goddamn shirt on. And get out of here. Now."

"You're missing out on some wonderful sex. I bet you don't get a lot these days."

"Out!" I shouted loud enough to wake 8B.

"Okay, okay, your loss, sugar."

I gave him a final push across the threshold.

"I'll phone you," he called back over his hairy shoulder.

———

When my father checked in at nine the next morning—Sylvie having hid the phone in the oven overnight—I said, as thanks for those salvation games he took me to at Memorial Stadium, "I have regards for you, Dad. From someone named Jeff Feldmacher. Do you know who that is?"

And my father, who didn't know his own name, said, "Go Birds!"

———

The following afternoon, I sat next to Fleur at the Istanbul Style and Day Spa while her nails, painted Bitchin' Red, dried and Tracy the manicurist ground an emery board against mine.

"I actually shoved him out the door," I concluded my Jeff Feldmacher story. "Now he'll probably sue me for assault."

"He deserved it. He was a real asshole," Tracy said. Twenty-three, college educated, she took no guff. She had what she proudly called "a potty mouth." All of the female staff at the Istanbul were young and American. They peppered their conversations with foul language. The men were Muslim and looked the other way.

"What bothered me most was his assumption that I'd be so grateful for the attention at my age, I'd keel over with open arms."

"And spread legs," Tracy said. She was a therapist to all her clients. Better than a licensed shrink, too. The psychiatrists I know are badly screwed up. Also, they talk among themselves, which puts your business on the street. Tracy kept it in house.

"Pity fuck," she said. She motioned for my hand to soak in sudsy water. "You never heard of a pity fuck? Where guys feel sorry for you, you know, and like do it as a favor to you. Like if you have acne or cruddy teeth or something gross like that. Men will fuck a milk bottle, so what does it matter to them anyway."

"For godsakes," Fleur waved her wet nails, "this woman is not a pity fuck. Look at her. She's stunning, elegant. She's a veritable Grace Kelly."

"Who has been dead for over twenty years," I said.

"Who's Grace Kelly?" Tracy asked.

Fleur and I shook our heads simultaneously and grimaced with the pain of it.

Tracy said, "So you know that Mrs. Greenfield is upstairs being waxed, right?"

Our Mrs. Greenfield? Kat? Who back in college had grown her underarm hair long enough to be braided? Who'd refused to shave her legs as a protest against the war in Vietnam and as a gesture of solidarity with oppressed peoples everywhere? That Kat?

"Room four," Tracy said. "Bikini wax with Grushinka."

Now, I have had a few bikini waxes in my time. A bikini wax rips stray pubic hair off the margins of the pubis and the upper thigh where bathing suit meets cellulite. It is a procedure Torquemada could be proud of, and personally I would rather go through an unmedicated root canal than submit myself to such medieval torture. But Kat laying her body on the altar of smoothness, a willing sacrifice for a bikini wax, now that was a phenomenon that demanded our attention.

Like teenagers, we abandoned Tracy's table—my right hand was unpolished, Fleur's nails were still tacky—rushed the stairs, and broke into the massage room.

We scared the hell out of Grushinka, preparing the waxing strips. Kat, stretched out on a massage table, just blinked at us and sighed. "I was expecting you."

"Look," she said after we ragged her about the waxing, "I'm trying to open my mind to new experiences. And it's not as if I'm going from hair to bare in one fell swoop. My legs haven't been shaggy for years. I started shaving the day Nixon resigned over Watergate, remember? To celebrate Amerika's emancipation from that lying bastard."

Dear Kat of days gone by, for whom every cosmetic renovation had been a political statement.

"Besides, we're going to the beach tomorrow and I didn't want to frighten the fish. And Lee was talking about doing a piece called 'Katrina All at Sea'."

"Well, he's not working in marble," Fleur said. "I mean, if you're made out of forks, it's okay if you're a little bristly, right?"

"You really like this guy," I said. "Going away with him after knowing him only a few weeks."

"We're staying at his sister's. In separate rooms."

"You can have the house in Rehoboth," I offered. "Drew's using it next weekend, but this weekend it's empty. It's big enough so you could have separate wings."

"Thanks, but I want the sister around. Guaranteed celibacy. No hanky-panky. I won't let myself get too involved so that when he takes off, I'll be cool with it."

"Takes off. That's ridiculous," I said.

"There's an eleven-year difference between us. And his last girlfriend was twenty-nine."

"And that's a fourteen-year difference. Which obviously didn't bother any of the parties involved."

"It's not logical, I know. It's not fair. Double standard. Sexist. Old men play. Old ladies lose. But that's the way it is. So, I'm determined to have my fling, but with no expectations except to enjoy it while it lasts." Kat turned her face towards the wall.

"Kat, for godsakes, you're not in a nursing home." I worked to swallow a lump in my throat. All this talk of age made me queasy. Until lately, I'd never in my life had a problem attracting men. Even after splitting with Stan, I'd managed five or six dates and not one of them mentioned my age. But last night, Jeff Feldmacher had been set to shtupp me figuring I would be grateful for this act of carnal charity and today Kat, who had always exhibited a radical's disdain for the superficiality of physical appearance, was having the hair torn from her thighs to hold on to love. Maybe we were all in more trouble than I'd thought.

The Russian lady bent toward Fleur. "You have little mustache on upper lip. I could take care of in five minutes," she said. "Is not your fault. Is not you are ape. Just shadow above lip. From not much hormones like when you were girl. I can zip off in four minutes."

Fleur stared at her, then dropped back to whisper, "How do you say fuck you in Russian?"

"Kat," I said, touching my friend's cheek so she turned it to me, "if it's Ethan you're worried about, betraying him I mean, one of these days you're going to need to let go."

"Maybe we're just friends, Lee and I. Soul mates. We have similar interests."

"What happened to the fling? A minute ago you were flinging, now only your souls are mating?" Fleur had her hand on the doorknob, eyeing the Russian lady warily.

"Why is everyone pushing me to have sex with this man? If I want to I will, but when I'm ready and I'm not ready. Anyway, I have to lose ten pounds first. My stomach is disgustingly flabby. And I've got to figure out how I'm going to ask him to take an HIV test. These days, you've got to plan for these things."

She was right, but she sounded so prim I thought I was hallucinating. Where was the braless beauty who used to write poetry about the joyous abandoned sex she played out in a sweet haze of marijuana on tie-dyed sheets? What happened to my rapturous flower child of yesterdecade? Turned conventional by time, it seemed.

More than flab, this made me sad.

*Chapter 9*

On Saturday night, with nothing better to do, I went online to check out Fleur as brighteyes on Lovingmatch.com, sweetstuff on Largeandluscious, and Xshiksa at Jewlove. Gavin at GlamourGal had worked his final computer magic on her photo and the result was a knockout Fleur with cut-glass cheekbones and the jawline of a twenty-year-old. To check out the competition, I browsed the ads of other females fifty to sixty. Everyone was peppy, chipper, trim, fit, emotionally strengthened by life's adversities, and eager to start over. The courage of these women exhilarated me. Their numbers depressed me.

As I prowled among the lonely hearts, I was stopped by a banner headline offering a free two-month membership on the website Ivydate.com. My Barnard diploma qualified me. All I had to do was fill out a profile.

Not me.

*Woman in search of man. Between fifty and death.* I slugged in my preferences. Just for the hell of it, because it was this or actually watching Larry King, who droned on in the background.

HighIQutie. That's the name I entered for my *nom d'Internet.* Then I wrote a profile in five minutes flat. Love

Bach and Telemann, Italian art, Thai food. Looking for honest, trustworthy, cultured man who's passionate about work and life. Accent—French, Italian, British, Southern—a bonus. Sense of humor/wit essential.

Then I scrambled through the boxes of photographs I'd promised for a decade to sort, and found one to use with my profile. My neighbor Jean Coogan had taken the picture a few weeks before The Treachery. The boys were gone all that July; Drew in Cape Cod as a counselor at an arts and crafts camp, Whit hiking through Bulgaria with a group of like-minded overindulged college kids. I thought I had it made. Everything stretched infinitely ahead. The beach, the ocean, the day, my appreciated life. I was at its sweet center, a pearl layering gorgeous time. Soon Jean would walk on to her own blanket and book and I would be left to the temporary isolation I loved, facing the sheet of linen afternoon hemmed by prospects of sunset with Stan, sipping pinot grigio, watching the sea, and listening to him talk about his day spent hunting down vintage wicker with Brad, the decorator. He failed to mention that he was getting buggered in the new eighteenth-century Italian provincial bed while I was focused on the waves. That detail would emerge in the divorce interrogatories.

The woman in the photo looked blissfully unaware. On the beach under a floppy straw hat, oversized Jackie Kennedy sunglasses hiding my eyes, nose pinked by the sun, I smiled with genuine pleasure at the expanse before me. I was displayed in high menopause with a body ten pounds heavier than before or after. And for all the patients I counseled who were in the same state, the intractable thickening of my waist had infuriated me. The bathing suit, navy with vertical white stripes, was my effort to slim at least what the world saw. I lost those defiant last ten pounds that fall in the melting off that for me always accompanies crisis.

Now I smiled at the photograph, admiring from a distance the feminine curves that frustrated me then. No one but my closest friends and family would recognize me in this photo. Perfect for a lark. I scanned it in. Pressed *submit,* reassured myself that nothing would ever come of this folly, and promptly—the way I misplaced the names of the new, unfunny crowd on *Saturday Night Live* now making background mayhem—forgot about it.

My father liked to sit on a bench in Patterson Park and watch...what? I wondered if what he saw was just a jumble of fragments, shards of shifting images without meaning but with some beauty. There must have been something out there striking some chord in there, because he sighed frequently and deeply on those outings, I hoped with pleasure. This Sunday, the sun was warm, the grass smelled of scallions, kids kicked up dust with their bicycle wheels and yipped on the bumps. Maybe something broke through.

He ate his ice cream cone like a child below the level of self-consciousness, with a wide flat tongue that I didn't remember from his good days. Perhaps the small muscles were beginning to slacken. A slight tremor in his left hand plunged his thumb through the cone so the mint chocolate chip ice cream flooded through the hole and dripped down his shirt. I wiped his face with a napkin, dabbing at the green cream on his cheek. He grabbed my hand to stop my fussing, then turned it over, jerked it up, and planted on my palm an unexpected, sticky kiss.

"I need some money," he said, as I delivered him back to Sylvie.

He said that nearly every week. He was obsessed with money, which is typical for Alzheimer's patients. There is nothing in the literature about this, but much anecdotal material.

Sylvie had scolded me before. "You keep giving him all this money and then he hides it who knows where and it's lost forever. Give him play money."

So I'd stopped at Toys "R" Us and picked up a pack of kiddie cash for the inevitable demand and when he asked this time, I peeled off a fifty, three tens, and two fives, while Sylvie nodded approvingly at my side.

He looked down and scowled. "What are you trying to do to me here? This is fake money. It's a joke, right?" Very coherent. A flight into lucidity. Then, crash. "I know what you're up to, Helen. You've switched money on me. You've got my real money hidden somewhere, right? Piling up so you can run off on me." Spittle gathered at the corners of his mouth. Thirty years too late, he was telling my mother off. He shouted in my face, "You were born a bitch, you'll die a bitch. May your soul be condemned to eternal damnation." Without warning, he reared back and shoved me so hard I careened sideways into the beveled edge of a china cabinet, which carved a short, deep slice below my eyebrow. Blood gushed. I snatched the crocheted doily off his chair back and pressed hard, but my father saw and recognized the red. His face collapsed. He bawled like an infant, gulping air to fuel his sobs.

"It's all right, Daddy, it's all right," I kept repeating, trying to stanch the blood with one hand and reach out with the other. "Come on, Daddy, I'm fine. See?" I cupped his chin and tilted his head so he could see my forced smile. "It was an accident. I know you love me. You'd never hurt me on purpose." But the only thing that comforted him was the sucking candy with a honey center Sylvie slipped into his mouth.

When he'd quieted down, she lowered him into the old chair and switched on the television. She talked in front of him, but he didn't seem to hear. His attention was locked on the Game Show channel.

"I don't know about this," she said. "This is a new t'ing. The pushing and shoving. He never did do that before. Oh, I don't like that. We're in a new phase here. I tell you, I'm not one to put up with physical abuse. I didn't let a husband do it; I'm not about to let an old man do it. I don't like this phase. No indeed, don't like it at all."

I was going to London for the conference I'd hijacked from Bethany McGowan. I couldn't leave my father without coverage and there was no time to find a suitable fill-in.

"I'm sure you can handle him, Sylvie. I'm sure this is an isolated incident. But just to let you know how much I appreciate the way you care for him. Wait..." I dug through the junk in my handbag, found my wallet, and placed a fifty-dollar bill in Sylvie's palm, an obvious bribe. I was buying time. Sylvie eyed it suspiciously, then held up to the light. To make sure it wasn't play money, I presumed.

On my way out, I checked my eye in the mirror. It would need a steri-strip to minimize the scar, but compared to the gouges my mother left me, it was a nick. When it healed, it would be hardly noticeable.

———

I must have sounded desperate when I called for an appointment because by Monday I was at Covenant Hospital's Gerontology Department sitting across the desk from Dan Rosetti while my father tried to recite the alphabet for the psychologist in the next room.

"His shoving isn't unusual," Dan said. "Some of my gentlest patients lash out from time to time. We don't know exactly why. It could be that this acting out marks a further decline. Which is a damn shame. Harald is a sweet guy."

Dan Rosetti was also a sweet guy. His eyebrows knit with empathy when he gave me the news that wasn't really news, and when he talked to my father, it was man to man, not doctor to patient, or worse, doctor to disease. My father adored him and always struggled to climb out of his illness when they conversed. He may have flunked the cognitive tests, but Dad could still manage formulaic small talk with Dan. The superficial patter is the last to go. Dan always seemed touched by the show and he would either ruffle what was left of my father's hair or rub genial circles on his back as he listened. Geriatricians know that most of their patients don't get enough physical contact, but Dan was more hands-on than is recommended for physicians in our currently litigious society. Fleur said that was the warm Mediterranean in him.

It was Fleur who'd suggested we see Dan when my father began showing signs of befuddlement. She liked the way he managed her mother's osteoporosis. In a trick of fate, Fleur had inherited the big frame and the padding that upholstered it from her Grandmother Broussard. Mother Talbot, on the other hand, was a trim little number who'd never weighed more than a hundred pounds and, now that she had the bends, measured all of five feet. But if her bones were porous, her brain was dense with fully functional cells. "Daniel Rosetti may be Italian," she'd told Fleur recently, "but he's not like one of those crude gangsters on HBO saying that awful F-word all the time."

"The old girl thinks he's God and he'll keep her alive forever," Fleur said.

Now Dan scrawled the name of a new drug on his prescription pad and slid it over to me. "This might calm him down, but I can't guarantee it won't make him lethargic."

"No, let's just let it go. Next time I'll remember to duck."

"You all right, Gwyn?" he asked. "I know this can't be easy. There are support groups you might find helpful. If you're interested, I can give you a few phone numbers."

*No, no, not another FRESH,* I thought. All I said is, "I think we're okay for now."

"If it's any comfort, they're onto some really promising leads in the research. One of these days there's going to be a major breakthrough. Probably too late for Harald, but..." he shrugged and I filled in the blank, *maybe in time for you. Otherwise, you too may wind up fingerpainting with your mashed potatoes and thinking Eisenhower is president.*

Alzheimer's. Worse than the F-word.

# Chapter 10

A few days later, on a mockingly vibrant autumn afternoon, I said good-bye to one of my patients. Twenty-nine, mother of a toddler, lovely, accomplished, she'd come into the office with Stage 3 ovarian cancer and pleaded with me to buy her time.

Together we fought the crab for twenty months, a tug-of-war I thought I weighted for victory with chemotherapists and radiologists and experimental protocols. Wrong again.

With everything we know, with all our science and our technology, our data and our skills, clinical medicine can still be a crapshoot. The slip-on-the-banana-peel school of medicine teaches you not to take the credit for a save and not to hold yourself entirely responsible for a patient's loss. Which doesn't make it any easier to lose one.

I sat at her bedside and let my dying patient console me. "You did everything you could, Dr. Berke. I couldn't have asked for a better doctor."

She whispered this final benediction even as I was powerless to do anything more than increase her painkillers, wrap her glacially cold hands in my warm ones, and not turn away when my eyes filled.

Which is why I decided to fix myself a martini on a weeknight.

I came home early, changed into sweats, turned on the news, and headed for the vodka. I bent over the wet bar to pour myself two fat fingers of Smirnoff. Therefore, my back was turned when Bethany McGowan plunged the knife deep between my shoulder blades.

I heard the nasal voice first. It whirled me around, showering martini on my blouse. Oh, it was her, all right. In living color, the weaselly face magnified by the TV set. I must admit someone had done a creditable job with her makeup. And her shiny dark hair, which she usually wore sleek against her skull, had been fashionably tousled. From beneath the white lab coat peeked a pale blue spread-collar silk shirt. Expensive looking. If I were a woman concerned about pre-cancerous uterine dysplasia, I'd think Bethany was a reliable resource. Except that every September for the past decade, *I'd* been the one facing the camera during National Pap Test Week. *I'd* been the gynecological talking head on WJZ-TV urging Baltimore's women to get their cervixes swabbed.

But this year, the commemorative week had slipped my mind, and the health reporter hadn't called me. Whom did she call? Not Bethany certainly. Potak? Bernstein? One of the seniors who passed the call to Bethany? The bastards. I fumed as Bethany explained the difference between regular and thin prep Pap smears and described cell changes in cervical cancer. You'd have thought oncology was her specialty when 90 percent of what she did was obstetrics. She knew from first trimester vomiting and last trimester hemorrhoids. She was a mommy-sitter and a baby-tugger, for godssakes.

By the time Bethany's sermon gave way to coverage of a five-car pileup on I-70, I was punching numbers into my phone. Neither Potak nor Bernstein, alerted by caller ID, would pick up. Fine. I'd ambush them tomorrow before I'd had my caffeine. While I was still a madwoman.

At eight the next morning, Seymour Bernstein leaned back in his leather chair looking desperate to press a button that would project him beyond my fury. "The truth is, they asked for Bethany. Well, not exactly for Bethany. But they wanted a younger face. Not my words, Gwyn." An artificial smile exposed twenty thousand dollars' worth of oversized dental implants. Since divorcing his comfortable high school sweetheart wife, he'd been dyeing his grayish hair a one-dimensional beaver color and worn a perpetual ersatz tan. Some members of our junior staff had spotted him dancing spastically at nightclubs around Fells Point, frantically hunting the younger gazelles.

"That's ageism, grounds for a lawsuit," I said, steaming.

"Against who? The station? Bullshit. It's just demographics. They're trying to capture the eighteen-to-thirty-four market, where the money is. The big spenders."

"Mature doctors give off an aura of authority and confidence," I persisted.

"I couldn't agree with you more. But I don't schedule for WJZ. They wanted young, but experienced. It was going to be Ken Dempsey, and he stutters, or Bethany. I thought she did pretty well. Photographs nicely and she has a calm, understated presence."

That was a shot. As was his next volley. "And I thought it was a nice consolation prize after you pulled London out from under her. I got a mailing from IAGSO. I didn't see your name on the faculty. Typo, I assume."

The s.o.b. He'd probably called Don Iverson, who was in charge of the program for the Academy. And I'd neglected to cover my tracks.

"Well, you could have had the courtesy at least to tell me about Bethany's appearance," I countered, sounding as lame as I felt.

"And you'd have reamed me a new one and we'd have had to call a meeting and take a vote and God knows what while the reporter would be on the phone to Frank Lustig over at Union Memorial and we'd have lost the coverage. Sometimes it's best to just get the job done and deal with the consequences later."

He sighed and reached for his Palm Pilot, then turned mournful eyes on me. "Look, I'm sorry you're fifty-four. Hell, I'm sorry I'm fifty-nine. But it's the reality. We've got plenty of good work left in us, Gwyn. That's not the issue. But they're nipping at our heels, the young turks. So cede them a little space graciously. Do a little mentoring. Teach them the craft, not just the skills. You're a good doctor; pass it on."

"And then go gentle into that good night," I said, turning to the door.

Behind me, he expelled a groan of exasperation which slid into a higher key as he sang out, "Ahh, Bethany, come in, come in."

The newly celebrated Dr. McGowan poked her head around the doorjamb. How long she'd been standing within eavesdropping distance was anybody's guess. The hazel eyes lit on me for the briefest moment, all blank innocence, then bounced over to Seymour Bernstein where they acquired a smoky light.

"Hope I'm not intruding, Sy," she said. Her voice was nauseatingly melodic. I backed up to catch the panorama of the exchange.

"Always time for you, Beth," he began, then added for my benefit, "...any."

And I got it. Or thought I got it. His delight in seeing her could have been the relief of a drowning man spotting a lifeboat. After all, she'd interrupted a conversation that reduced him to tearing his dyed hair. Then again, she was leaning forward in a peach silk duplicate of the shirt she wore for her TV appearance, lab coat unbuttoned, bezel-set diamond pendant swinging in the shadow of her cleavage, one shapely leg—ending in a very unprofessional three-inch tapered pump—extended. Her lids lowered. His lips moistened. Seymour and Bethany, a couple? Beth and Sy, on the sly? She was thirty. He was fifty-nine. Mentoring? Teaching her the craft? Was I paranoid? Or was I, once again, the last to know?

The following morning at nearly the same time in nearly in the same place, I almost crashed into Kat emerging furtively from Neil Potak's office.

She could have been in for a routine check, so why, when she saw me, did she look as if the pulse in her forehead was about to strum "Nearer My God to Thee"? Her eyes met mine and she jumped back like a crane readying for flight, arms flapping, string handbag swinging.

"Hi," I said. "Everything okay?"

"Yeah. Fine."

I paused. It's a physician's trick. Wait a beat and even the shyest patient will feel compelled to fill the silence, sometimes with helpful information.

"I just needed to get something checked out."

"Good. And everything's okay," I made it a statement. We were walking in rhythm now and she followed me into my office.

"It's just a urinary tract infection. I kept getting up all night to pee. I had a little blood in my urine this morning. So I figured why play around. I called and Marie said Dr.

Potak had an opening and could fit me in. He gave me an antibiotic and something that will turn my pee orange. No big deal. Could be from anything, from the air."

Honeymoon cystitis. Too much intercourse in too short a time irritates the urethra. Common among newlyweds. Evidently, Kat and Lee had quite a weekend, in spite of the sister in the next room.

"All right," she conceded, as if we were arguing. "I slept with him. God."

"Well, that's nice. It's been a long time for you. I hope it was a good experience."

My placid tone disarmed her. "Not a great move, huh? Too soon? It just happened so naturally. I think it would have been *un*natural to deny ourselves." Kat recited the litany of the free-for-all seventies.

"Well, you always had good instincts. Obviously, you feel you know Lee. And trust him. And he's not made any noises like the sex has scared him away, right?"

"Just the opposite. He's been calling three times a day." Kat smiled a wicked smile, leaned forward, and morphed before my eyes into my college roommate, the wild-haired, pot-smoking, placard-waving, bead-shaking Kool Kat I loved. "My God, Gwyn, it was like I was in my twenties. I was popping orgasms like bubble wrap. The most I ever had at one time. Oh, and we watched porn."

"In his sister's house?"

"No, I was afraid we were too loud, so we went to a hotel the second night. Porn! Me! Maybe I was wrong about porn. About it being another capitalistic tool for the oppression of women. Even though the women were wearing seven-inch heels and going down on two guys at once, they were getting as much as they gave and it was stimulating. Except..."

I held my breath.

"Ethan. I feel I betrayed Ethan. I know it's illogical and ridiculous. He's dead and I'm alive and he would have wanted this for me. To be happy..."

*Well, yes,* I thought, *but maybe he wouldn't have cheered for the multiple orgasms.*

"...and our sex life in the last few years before he died was beginning to slow down. He smoked all that weed when he was younger and he thought maybe that had something to do with it. But you get used to the slowing down and I thought, well, I'm into menopause so I wasn't exactly burning with desire. At least before the estrogen. And now with Lee, I feel reborn. But Summer thinks I've lost my mind. She's absolutely livid."

Summer was a stiff-necked little prickette who supported the most outrageously right-wing political causes with the money she and her equally tight-assed husband had reaped from the sale of their dot-com. The only explanation for her being Kat and Ethan's kid was a switch in the hospital nursery.

"Summer knows you slept with Lee?"

"Oh, God, no. Not even went away with. I told her I was spending a few days with you at the beach house. I didn't think you'd mind the little white lie. She's crazy enough thinking I'm even dating again. She says her father's body is still warm and I'm dancing on his grave."

"Hardly. Ethan's been dead for a year and a half."

"You're right," she said firmly. "Why do we let our kids lay this emotional blackmail on us? Summer is married. She has a life of her own. Why can't I have mine?"

"You can and you should, sweetie," I said.

"You think so? Really, Gwynnie?" Even back in college when she was setting fire to her bra, Kat had looked to me to hold the extinguisher.

"Sure. The experts say when you're ready to move on you'll know. Looks like it's time."

Kat nodded. "Lee's a really good person. I'm not saying it's love. Too soon, right? But we've got feelings for each other. I just wish he were ten years older."

"He will be in ten years. Hang in there."

She sent me a wry smile. "Move on. Okay. One of these days maybe you could help me tackle Ethan's closet. I've been putting off cleaning it out but I think I can do it now with some moral support and a few extra hands. As long as Summer doesn't get wind of it."

"Sure. I've had some practice. Before Stan came back for his clothes, I got into his closet. There's a homeless guy panhandling on Biddle Street wearing a $600 Italian suede jacket."

"Oh, that's terrible." Kat allowed a fluty laugh, her high moral character nonetheless offended. "All right, we'll do it. Soon. When you call Fleur, see what she has open. And call her today, please. She didn't want to bother you at the office. Something about Bethany McGowan on TV last night and keeping her distance until you cool off. But she wanted you to know she even found a man online for you. Some shrink in Bethesda who collects English porcelain and nineteenth-century commodes."

"That would be Stan," I said, smarting. "I'll give him Stan's number, maybe they can hook up."

She looked at me with soft eyes. "It's going to happen for you, too."

I knew she was trying to be kind, but I felt myself icing over. "I've probably got a mob of furious patients in the waiting room and Marie has been giving me the evil eye every time she passes the door. So..."

"I'm glad you have your work," Kat said, as if it were all I had.

Which may have been true but I really did not want to hear it.

## Chapter 11

Over the next week, Fleur received more responses to her Lovingmatch.com profile and set up dates with Pokey's Pal for Friday night and Mitch247 for Saturday.

"Who's Pokey?" I asked Fleur as she sorted her files on the sofa in my home office.

"Pokey is his pet. A hedgehog. He actually asked me if I would like to pet his Pokey."

"He didn't! Please tell me you're planning to meet this person in a public place."

"Of course. And I have a whistle and pepper spray on my key chain, just in case. Accessories for the well-dressed twenty-first-century woman. Dear Lord, is this what we've come to?" She shook her head in dismay. "Of course, a hundred years ago I'd be the crazy spinster locked up in an attic room. And modern technology has got me *two* dates in *one* weekend. So," she lifted the glass of iced tea I'd provided, "here's to the twenty-first century." She gulped tea, and said on the swallow, "Any plans for the weekend?" Then looked contrite as soon as the words spilled.

"Sure, Paul Newman phoned to say he and Joanne were finally splitting up and would I be his date for the Golden Globes."

"You could be dating, you know, if you weren't such a snob about the Internet. If it's good enough for Connie deCrespi whose grandfather was a count, it should be good enough for you. And I don't know if you've noticed, but there aren't hordes of men knocking down your door these days, so unless you want to sit home every weekend, you might think about getting off your ass and doing something about it."

"I signed on to Ivydate.com," I said, stung by Fleur's words into confessing.

"You didn't." She banged her glass down on the coaster. "Well, shut my well-bred mouth. I take back everything I just said. When?"

"About two weeks ago."

"And?"

"And I don't know. I never checked back."

"Oh...my...God. Let's get to that computer, girl." Before I could stop her, she took over my keyboard "Username?"

"HighIQutie."

She fired off a give-me-a-break look.

"Password," she barked. When I hesitated, she growled, "Tell me your fucking password. You can always change it."

"Twinmom."

"Here we go." Her lower lip dropped. "Yikes! Your mailbox is crammed. This cannot be because you're a HighIQutie. What photograph did you put on there, something from the *Sports Illustrated* swimsuit issue? Twenty-three messages. Beginning with LuvinLaw. Oh, Gwyneth Margrit, I think we hit the jackpot here. You can't leave now," she moaned as I headed for the door.

"I'll be back." I needed a vodka and tonic.

I stood in my kitchen holding my glass under the ice dispenser. The glass was a Waterford highball from a set Stan's staff at *Berke's Business* had presented him on the magazine's tenth anniversary. The crystal radiated prisms like a flawless diamond and hefted like it weighed three pounds, empty. The fridge was a subzero behemoth designed for a large family or for a couple who gave lavish parties, not for a single woman who lived on Lean Cuisines. The stove, brushed steel, had been purchased at a restaurant supply house. Its size was laughable now. Wherever I looked in my three-thousand-square-foot condo, I saw only the best, the biggest, the most expensive.

I thought of all the women who'd been abandoned with nothing or worse, debts to pay, damaged children to raise, bruises to nurse, and I despised myself for having so much and appreciating it so little.

But truth to tell, I was not entirely ungrateful. I'd slept on a rollaway cot in the living room until I left for college because the second bedroom went to my brother. I had one drawer in my parents' dresser for my stuff, which my mother prowled through. As a teenager, I showered at a girlfriend's house every day because someone was always in our postage-stamp-sized bathroom, and no matter what bug spray my father used, we couldn't get rid of the silverfish that scaled the slopes of our bathtub. So I did know how good it was to have money and space, comfort, cleanliness and, most of all, the options it brought. Still...I would have given it all up for what happened not to have happened, for Stan to have been as straight as I'd thought he was and devoted as he played at being throughout our marriage. Given it all up, lock, stock, and Waterford for that. But I didn't have that choice.

So I splashed too much vodka on my perfectly sculpted ice cubes, filled the glass with tonic, sniffed back the gratuitous self-pity, and shuffled off in my bedroom slippers to see what the real world and Fleur had in store for me.

She was fanning herself with a sheaf of papers. "I've gone through the messages, pulled up the profiles, and triaged them for you." She cracked a piece of ice between her teeth. "I've whittled the field down to five good ones."

I riffled through the printouts. "Gumbo? I don't care if he is a periodontist, I will not go out with a man who calls himself Gumbo. This one's too short. He'd come up to my belly button. And this one looks like an aging Elvis. Didn't anyone tell him long sideburns went out around 1986?"

"He's a world-renowned mathematician. He'll probably win the Nobel Prize one day, but if you're so shallow as to be put off by something as superficial as appearance, fine. How about TonyTiger? Princeton. Columbia Law. He wants to snuggle down in front of the fire with the right woman." I scanned the message which began, "Hi, beautiful lady!" crumpled it, and slam-dunked it into the wastebasket.

Fleur withdrew her hand from behind her back. "I knew it would come to this so I've saved the best for last." She flourished a paper. I snapped it out of her hand and peered at the image, slightly fuzzed by my printer. The picture was of a nice-looking guy, squinting into snow-reflected sunlight. He was posed on skis, all geared up. His hair was going, but he had fine, even features and a good smile. Maybe he'd been to Gumbo. "He's too thin."

"How can you tell in that ski suit? He could have a beer belly hidden under his jacket. Would that make you happy?"

"I like men with a little flesh on their bones."

"You are not making soup here, Gwyn. You are auditioning a potential date. What's with you and thin?"

"Oedipus complex, I guess. You met my dad. He's a flyweight."

Fleur snatched the paper from me. "You need more help than Tracy can give you. Listen. 'Creative, well-read, public-interest exec. PhD. Fifty-eight. Devoted to personal growth and change. Passionate about the outdoors. Seeking educated, affectionate woman for long-term relationship. Love of Mozart and *Jeopardy* a plus.' Now that ain't chopped liver." Fleur smiled smugly. "And read his email."

It was coherent and clever. He said my profile intrigued him. He thought I was attractive. He liked my smile under the Jackie-O sunglasses.

"Okay, he sounds interesting," I grudgingly acknowledged. "What do I do next?"

"You write him. His user name is Enviroman. Don't look at me that way. Sit. I'm getting myself more tea. Type."

Six emails and two phone conversations later, I made my way across the sunset-splashed concrete lip of the Inner Harbor towards my Sunday lunch date. As soon as I saw him, I knew I was in trouble. Without the kapok and the quilting of the ski jacket, stripped down to a pair of faded green slacks and a green T-shirt reading "Save the Bay," Zack Butler, aka Enviroman, looked as self-righteously skinny as a celery stalk. Not my type at all.

We wandered among the street performers in silence. Zack had waxed poetic in his electronic messages and turned up my pilot light with his Back Bay Boston accent on the phone. In person, he was about as talkative as Calvin Coolidge. The mime passing the hat had more to say.

At brunch, under the influence of his cranberry juice on the rocks, he droned on nonstop. About himself. Zack was a radical vegetarian and environmentalist. He shared with me his passion for the native Maryland Blue crab. Not to eat of course. He whined endlessly about his ex-wife, with whom he was in a major love-hate relationship. And about his irritable bowel syndrome. This last while I was eating my salad.

Which was topped with strips of sirloin. Now that really freaked him out. When the check arrived, Zack extracted from his change purse (no wallet; a brown plastic change purse with a prissy metal catch, just like the one my mother used to carry) a coupon for a 10 percent discount on our lunch. "Please, let me know my share," I said. "I really would like to pay."

"Fine with me," he said. Total time expended on this entirely superfluous event: one hour twelve minutes.

Back in the Waterview lobby, I heard a clunk-clunk behind me and turned to see Fleur barrel by, her face the color of meringue with a strawberry spot on each cheek. "You all right?" I called to her. No answer.

I caught up with her at the elevator. She stayed tight-lipped until the doors closed.

"Mitch247?"

"He took one look at me and said, 'Jeez, you don't look anything like your picture. Nothing personal, but I don't date fat women.' Nothing personal! Could it get more personal? The bastard."

"And I take it Pokey's Pal was a washout last night."

"The Johnstown Flood."

I followed her into her apartment. She headed toward the kitchen.

"Ben and Jerry," she said. "Now those are men worthy of a woman's trust. The rest aren't worth a bucket of warm spit."

She pulled out a quart of ice cream and dug each of us two baseball-sized dips. "I'm beginning to think Chubby Hubby is the only hubby I'll ever have." She licked the scoop. "Well, I've spent fifty-five years without a husband. I can manage another twenty or thirty." She tucked a couple of Oreos into the dishes.

"Fleur, don't let one lousy date derail you. There are all kinds of losers out there. You don't own the patent." I described my encounter with Enviroman. The wife, the bowels, the discount coupon. "How suave, as we used to say in college."

We were both laughing by the time I finished.

But not for long. "You-know-who called last night," she said suddenly.

Which could have been any of Fleur's cyber suitors. "Funguy4U?"

"Jack. My Jack. Well, not my Jack anymore. Bambi's Jack. Well, not Bambi's Jack either, at least not for long. Or so he implied."

I groaned. "I thought you sent him packing when he showed up at the shop."

"I did."

"Yeah, well obviously he didn't get the message. And can you see how he's manipulating you? Calling to tell you he's leaving Bambi."

"He never said that. Not in those words. But he implied...oh, I don't know what he implied. It was late and he sounded like he'd had more to drink than he's used to. Jack was never a drinking man. Gambling. That he liked. And his cigars. But she doesn't let him smoke anymore. Because of the baby. And she has him on a low-fat diet. Lots of fish. Jack hates fish."

"He's leaving his wife because she makes him eat salmon?"

"Not just that. He sounded overwhelmed. The baby's been sick. They haven't even had the bris yet. They were worried it was something really serious, but turned out to be gastric reflux. Mason's on medicine now, but he still keeps Jack up all night."

"Well, I'm sorry for Mason, but I can't say Jack has my sympathy. So he loses a little sleep. It serves him right for procreating at sixty-five. A man collecting Social Security should not be changing diapers unless they're his grand-children's."

"And Bambi gained forty pounds with the pregnancy."

I looked at her questioningly. Fleur's weight never bothered Jack. They happily ate the top of the food pyramid together. "He thinks she's having hormone problems. He says she has a short temper. That she yells a lot. He says he misses me. How comfortable it was. You never know what you have until you lose it."

"He didn't lose it. He threw it away."

Dead silence.

"Fleur," my tone was a warning.

"Don't worry, I'm steering clear of him. He wanted to go out. Just for coffee. Just to talk. And I said no."

"Of course you did. If you said yes, I would have peti-tioned the court to declare you mentally incompetent."

She twirled her spoon in her ice cream. Fudge soup. If my mother had been there, she would have slapped Fleur for playing with her food.

"I loved him," she said. "Please note the past tense. Still, when he walked into my office the other day, I nearly passed out. And last night when I heard his voice, I actually felt my heart turn over in my chest."

"Of course you did. It was trying to send signals to your brain. Alert, alert! Common sense and self-preservation, man the barricades!"

"He sounded so sad, Gwyn. I kept feeling 'poor Jack.'"

"Poor Jack? Are you forgetting what kind of shape you were in when he left you? On the verge of a clinical depression. That's what your poor Jack did to you."

"Point taken. But it was easier to hate him last night when I still had Mitch247 on the horizon."

I peeled the package of Oreos from her fingers and shoved it in the pantry. "There will be other men. Not Mitches. Good men who want a good woman, which is you. There are thousands of them on those websites. You'll find someone and if you don't, being without is better than Jack Bloomberg. Ugh, I can't believe the gall of the man. Running back to you at the first sign of trouble in his marriage. Who are you, the Salvation Army? I guarantee you, when the baby's Zantac kicks in and Bambi loses five pounds, he'll forget you ever existed. Promise me you won't get involved with him. Even for coffee."

Her eyes widened and filled, and she exhaled a sigh so deep, it ruffled the napkin in front of her. "Promise," she said.

But since her hands were in her lap, I had no way of seeing if she was crossing her fingers.

## Chapter 12

Kat lived in Columbia, a planned city west of Baltimore that began as a haven for reconstructed hippies and old-guard liberals back in the sixties. Her rancher was sheltered by trees that gave way to woods behind. To the left were the herb and vegetable gardens for which Ethan had turned the first earth and which Kat still tended, although her heart was in the flower garden, riotous with mums and impatiens on this warm Indian summer afternoon. As I crossed the brick patio, I noted that the family room was open to whatever breeze wafted in the vicinity since, in spite of my warnings, Kat left her sliders and screens open to mosquitoes and rapists and wouldn't even consider wiring the place for alarms. Only the tinkle of wind chimes announced my entrance.

"Hello," I called out and three cats dashed out of nowhere to nuzzle at my ankles. Denny and John scattered in my path, but Mama Cass stuck around, mewing, as I checked rooms for Kat. I finally found her in the huge walk-in bedroom closet, paralyzed in front of Ethan's third of the closet space. She seemed a little quavery. Not teary, but on the brink. She was wearing Ethan's NYU sweatshirt over decades-old jeans and held a brown crewneck in one hand.

"Goodwill?" She poised it over a heap of clothes. "Or Tim?" Summer's husband.

"It has a hole in the sleeve. You can't give it to Goodwill in that condition. Give it to Tim. His kind likes clothing with holes. It says they're too rich to care."

"That's old money," Kat said. "Tim is very careful about looking just right."

"Well, throw it out then." I regretted saying that when I saw her stricken face. "Oh, Kat. I'm sorry. But you know if Ethan were alive, you'd steal it from the laundry basket to put it out with the trash."

"You're right. But he's not alive and these are the last of his things." Kat's mouth twisted with pain and I reached out to squeeze her free hand.

"I know, sweetie. This has to be rough on you."

"It happened so quickly. He's here, then swoosh he's gone and there's this need to hold on to anything you have left."

Some of my patients take years to die, giving up molecules of themselves each day so their family gets used to their absence little by little. Ethan had been there at breakfast and vanished before dinner. Kat never knew what hit her. Hopefully, Ethan never knew what hit *him*.

She reluctantly dropped the sweater to start a third pile. She pulled out Ethan's robe and held it against her cheek. "It barely smells of him anymore. I slept in this robe every night until the smell faded away." Then she straightened up and said abruptly, "I feel guilty about Lee. Maybe Summer is right. Maybe it's too soon."

Summer. Of course. "Only *you* know that, sweetie," I hammered the point. "But remember, if Summer gets cold in the theater, *she* has someone to give her his jacket. And you're not shopping for engagement rings so I don't understand why she's got her knickers in a twist over a few innocent dates."

"Not so innocent."

"But she doesn't know that, does she?"

"Summer has very strong intuitive powers. Even as a child she could pick up on things you didn't want her to know."

"Like a witch," I mumbled, my head turned into a row of trousers.

Kat expelled a small groan as she swung out a clutch of hangers with Ethan's shirts. "Let's just do this," she said firmly. "Let's just get this over with before I change my mind."

———

By six, we had three bags of Ethan's clothes standing at the front door and Fleur, Kat, and I were seated around the table set on the patio, rewarding ourselves with Chablis and a tray of grapes and cheese. Fleur had been incommunicado for a week. I'd left a few messages, then emailed and got a *Don't worry—I'm just busy* reply. So I let it go. Now she'd emerged from her silence with smudges under her eyes and an aura of depression casting a blue shadow on her normally rosy complexion.

As a result of Mitch247 and probably Jack, she'd been neglecting The Plan, and Kat, assuming my role as its defender, tore into her. "This isn't like you, Fleur. I can't believe you have nine emails from three websites sitting on your computer and you haven't opened them. Doesn't it drive you crazy to ignore them? It's like Christmas. All these wrapped presents and who knows, one of them might contain just what you always wanted."

"Yeah, or a salad spinner or one of those fish plaques that sings, 'You Are My Sunshine.' I'm better off not know-ing, believe me." Fleur's voice had a defeated ring.

"You were so gung-ho until that idiot commented on your weight. One lousy slight—"

"From a guy with very few front teeth."

"My point exactly," Kat said. "Now what kind of judge of beauty could this man be? Why should a toothless clod have the power to sidetrack your life-enhancing project?"

Fleur popped a grape between her own perfectly aligned front teeth. "Because he's a man and men have power. Even the cruddiest of them. They're born with it. It's part of the package. With the penis and the testicles."

"This isn't about Jack, is it? You haven't heard from him again, have you? After that b.s. about leaving Bambi." Kat sounded so innocent with that wispy voice, but she could be sly.

"As a matter of fact, I have," Fleur said, too casually. "He called last night. The baby's finally well enough to have his bris and Jack called to invite me."

"You're not going, of course," I said.

"Well, actually..."

"Oh, Fleur!" I was outraged.

"Before you jump down my throat, Jack made it a personal request. His sister Bea isn't driving anymore. Cataracts. So he asked me to pick her up. Bea has always been very nice to me."

"You're treading on thin ice here," I cautioned.

"I think Fleur is safe," Kat said. "I can't imagine a man coming on to you at a bris. I'd walk around clutching my crotch and keeping my distance from any life form that can hold a knife. As far as Jack goes, it's my personal opinion that—"

Before she could finish, a deep voice emerged, like a tossed hat, from the side of the house. "Uh-oh, Kat's going to get personal. I am *really* intruding." Then Lee

Bagdasarian, Kat's new beau, materialized holding a bottle of wine and wearing a sheepish, endearing grin. "I know, I know, I should have called first."

We turned to stare at Kat who jumped up, eyes wide with surprise, warm with pleasure.

"Don't be silly," she said. "You're just in time for dinner. No really, we'd love you to stay." And we all buzzed agreement. "I have enough food for an army. Grilled veggies. Couscous. Salad."

Fleur said, "And we'd be interested in a man's point of view in this conversation we're having. About circumcision. You know, snip-snip where it hurts."

We all heard Kat's intake of breath and Fleur quickly added, "Or not."

We lingered over dessert. Lee was telling us about his trip to Ethiopia and how he learned leather sculpture from Amhara tribesmen when Summer Greenfield Ellicott burst through the open slider onto the patio.

She blinked in the oranging sunset, looked around, took us all in. She'd never met Lee, who was sitting next to me and across from her mother, and you could see her trying to figure out the connections. Was he with me? Fleur? Or was this the man who was after her father's old job?

Kat was obviously flustered by this unexpected appearance. "Well, another surprise visitor." ("Like a Marx Brothers movie," Fleur whispered to me.) She introduced Lee, and Summer nodded, but her eyes seethed.

"Have some fruit," Kat said. She grabbed the serving spoon and waved it over the bowl like a wand that could transform it into something her daughter might want, something that would bring a smile to her scowling face. Summer shook her head no, glanced towards the platter of cookies, and backed off. She had the tired, puffy look of someone working too hard from the inside, like the patients I see who have chronic pelvic pain.

It always amazed me how she didn't resemble her dark, thin, and quietly earnest father, or her dark, pear-shaped, softly molded mother. And as soon as she'd understood what was really important to them, Summer disdained her parents' political and social views. This broke Kat's heart. But she kept on trying. She remembered her own easy relationship with her Ethical Culturist mother and she hung in there trying to win over this mismatched daughter who wore Baltimore Country Club getups of plaid or toile with matching headbands and lived in a huge colonial decorated in chintz and portraits of someone else's illustrious Calvert-related ancestors.

"The pineapple is really sweet," Kat pressed.

"Nothing for me, thank you," Summer said. "May I please see you *inside*, Mud-ther?" It was a command.

Until Lee thought to close the sliders, we could hear enough to know that Summer came over to borrow Kat's Cuisinart and found the bags of Ethan's clothes at the door. We heard "how could you"s and "betrayal" and lots of "Daddy"s. There was an uneasy silence around the table for a few minutes and then Kat and Summer appeared in the kitchen window, which hung over the flower garden. The window was open, and the voices were audible from the patio. Kat stacked dishes while Summer ranted on, and we couldn't help but hear Summer's screeching "My God, he looks my age! You've lost your mind, Mud-ther!"

At which point, Lee stood up and announced, "I think I'll walk off Kat's delicious dinner. I'll be back," and vanished into the woods.

Fleur and I deliberately made a clatter clearing the table and only really exhaled when we heard the front door bang so loud the cats yowled. When Summer was a teenager, Ethan removed the door to her room as punishment for her slamming it to make her points. She had a vile temper.

Kat was at the sink, scrubbing away at the couscous pot as if she could Brillo off the cruddy part of her life. Her face looked collapsed and pale. "Should we go in to her?" Fleur asked, and I was considering our options when we saw Lee slip behind her and wind his arms around her waist. He nuzzled her neck and whispered into her ear, and it wasn't long before her face took on structure and a healthy color.

"She'll be okay," I said. "For now, anyway. Long term, I wouldn't make book on it."

*Chapter 13*

I let myself into my father's house a little before noon. The first thing I noticed was no TV blare. A bad sign. If depriving him of his television was Sylvie's idea of punishing an old man, she'd have to deal with me.

Then I heard the music, a gentle reggae beat, set low, and I remembered it was Monday, Sylvie's day off, Blossom's day on.

A sloe-eyed, dimpled beauty of nineteen, Sylvie's cousin Blossom might have been my dad's favorite hon. All day long, she played her Jamaican CDs. Sometimes she danced while doing her chores. Sometimes she pulled my father to his feet and tugged him around with her, which made him chuckle.

Today, the scene in the living room was peaceful. My father, freshly shaved and combed, snored in the La-Z-Boy, an empty Friendly's ice cream cup his lap. As I smoothed out his Orioles afghan, he twitched something resembling a smile. Chocolate mint dreams? Dreams are nonsensical to start with. What happens when waking sense dies?

Blossom stopped waggling her head to the tropical beat long enough to acknowledge me with a wave. She licked chocolate from her lips and continued spooning up her hot fudge sundae.

As I tried to decode the tableau, Stan emerged from the kitchen with a cup of tea, which he placed in front of Blossom who awarded him a gold-toothed smile. "Everything's under control," he whispered and reached behind Blossom to plump her pillow. He was sporting a row of six silver bracelets on his forearm to match the huge Mexican silver and turquoise belt that held up his low-rise jeans and as he plumped, he tinkled.

"You can talk in normal voices," she said, hitching her head at my father. "When he's out, he's out."

"You're not working today?" I was unaccountably irritated with my ex. It wasn't even noon and I had already been usurped.

"I just stopped by to check up on him. Brought some ice cream."

Why did this scene grate me so? Stan caring for my dad. Maybe because ultimately he hadn't cared for me. Which was probably not entirely true; my pain was talking.

"He is also Mr. Fix-It, Mr. Stan is. See what he did with the kitchen door?" Blossom said.

"It's no big deal. While I'm here, if there's something that needs fixing, I fix it. This wasn't a major problem. Not like the stuffed toilet last time." I hadn't known about last time.

Stan walked me over to the swinging kitchen door that would swing no longer. He'd installed a hook and eye on the outside, high enough for the tall Jamaican women to lock, but beyond my father's reach. Simple, but I hadn't thought of it.

"He can't get in when I'm not watching or if Sylvie turns her head. He can't set fire to the house." Blossom seemed satisfied.

"I had the tools," Stan shrugged. "It took me three minutes, tops."

"It should do the trick, thanks," I managed to say, but the words were stones in my mouth. I thought, *If you're Mr. Fix-It, how come you were so talented at taking my life apart?*

"My pleasure."

Stan had become unfailingly gracious to me as soon as he knew he was out of the marriage. Of course, with Brad in the wings, he wanted the fastest settlement money could buy and we'd come to a quick agreement about the condo and the rest of the stuff of twenty-odd years. The beach house was the only booty we'd squabbled over and I don't think he would have fought for it by himself. That war flew Brad's flag. He'd egged Stan on, he and the lawyers who had to earn their fee. And that's why I'd battled for it. In the end, I think as much as Stan loved the Rehoboth house, he gave it up with saintly relief, to expiate his guilt.

But that was just a down payment. He knew he still owed me.

My father woke up drooling. He rubbed his sleeve over his mouth and said, "Hiya, Doc." I was Doc again, thank God. It was almost too good to be true, so Doc examined him.

I squatted down to his level and motioned to Stan. "Do you know who this is?"

My father squinted. Then his colorless eyes filled. "That's the Captain. That's my Stan the Man, the best damn son-in-law on God's green earth."

Stan teared up. Me too.

"Well, this is a gift from God. Let's pray that it lasts," Blossom murmured, breaking the spell.

"Be grateful for the moment," Stan said, and I wondered at this recently revealed tenderness. It had not been a hallmark of his personality during our marriage. Maybe it came out of the closet when he did.

I didn't love him anymore, but his presence always reminded me that I once did. So when he said, "If you haven't had lunch yet, I'll treat. There's a place in Canton with great burgers," I backed off.

"I thought you only do chicken and fish."

"I can slip in a burger. Brad's out of town. At a spatula show or something." He smiled sheepishly. Brad ate no meat. Please, did I really want to go there?

"I'm overbooked at the office. Sorry." I was aiming for pleasant.

"Some other time." He reached out, then thought better of it. He didn't dare touch me. "Enjoy London," he said. "Sylvie told me you'll be gone nearly a week."

And didn't Sylvie have a big mouth. I must have winced because he added, "No really, have a good time. I told her if they need anything I'm a phone call away."

"Mr. Stan's number is on the refrigerator," Blossom said.

"Well, thanks," I surrendered. I could be gracious too.

That night, arriving home late from the office, I found a message on my answering machine: "Gwyn, this is Harry Galligan. From FRESH. What happened to you yesterday? You missed the FRESH picnic." Hadn't known there was one. "And we missed you. Hope you're doing okay and we'll see you again soon. Take care."

Before I could plan the repartee or lose my courage, I pressed redial. It was only nine thirty but Harry must have gone to bed early because his voice sounded just roused. He seemed pleased to hear from me and we caught up on the picnic. He told me he'd been traveling a lot, though not to glamorous places. I told him I was leaving for London in the morning for a week. And he said, "Ah, well that's a shame. For me, not you," he immediately corrected himself. "Because I was thinking you might want to do dinner this Saturday night."

My rotten luck.

"I would have liked that." And decided, why not? "How about *next* Saturday?"

Harry's voice inched up a happy notch. "That works for me. I'll phone you the day before. I'm looking forward to seeing you. Outside of FRESH, I mean."

After I hung up, I crashed. That call to Harry topped twelve hellish hours at the office. I'd gulped down Dannon's on the run between examining rooms and my father. Now I discovered in addition to being exhausted, I was starved. The hell with it, I called Domino's. If indigestion kept me up all night, I could sleep on the plane.

When my house phone beeped, I switched on the closed circuit Waterview TV channel. It was a condo rule to visually confirm the identity of visitors before buzzing them in. "Yo, Domino's," the delivery man shouted into the wall mike. He had a thermal pizza box balanced on one hand. Legit. And behind him hovered an apparition that looked sickeningly familiar. Fuzzy in black and white, but unmistakable. The new patent-leather hair, the three-piece suit with the remnants of a gut hanging over the belt, the jacket slung over one arm, and the vest unbuttoned—no one else on the planet made that particular fashion statement. Jack Bloomberg. Visiting Fleur, of course.

He slipped in behind the Domino's guy, so it was too late to call her. And what would I have said, anyway? And who'd crowned me queen of advice for the lovelorn? It wasn't as if my romantic life was going to win the Dr. Phil Award for Fully Functional.

Still, for the first time in a long time, it had promise.

Funny though, tonight I'd gotten no thrill from Harry's voice. No kick. What I did get was a nice gentle feeling from a nice gentle man. Why did that disappoint me? Wasn't that just what I needed? Nice?

# Chapter 14

The first time I flew to Europe, I was twenty-four years old. I had a few weeks off between medical school graduation and the July kickoff of my Hopkins internship and Stan charged my tickets to his parents' credit card so I could join him in London. They never squawked about that. He was an indulged only son and there was no denying him anything, including a trip around the world when he finished grad school, and me, of whom his family didn't entirely approve given my shady background.

I flew a Pan Am red-eye, leaving at six from Baltimore and arriving in London around nine the next morning. People used to dress for flying before air transportation became so proletarian that today it's like hopping a winged Trailways.

For this exalted occasion, I wore linen pants with a Villager madras shirt and Bass Weejuns, the preppy traveling costume Debutante Barbie would have worn for a transatlantic flight. While the rest of America's twenty-four-year-olds dressed in torn jeans and scruffy sandals in honor of the Third World, I was doing a hand-over-hand up the ladder and yearned with all my being to pass as top rung.

At sunrise, the captain roused us to announce we were approaching the coast of Ireland. I craned to see that it really was emerald green in the first light and wept at the thought of how far I'd run from Streeper Street and at the miraculous turn my life had taken. Back then, I believed in miracles more than I believed in myself. Hammering my way through a miserable childhood, holding on through a worse adolescence, and all the while getting the grades so I could get out, I didn't catch on to the cause and effect. All I knew was that somehow I had Stan, I was going to be a doctor, and all my options were open and all of them were good.

As we made our initial approach, I looked down and realized my linen slacks were a wrinkled mess. There was no way I was going to let Stan Berke see me less than perfect. I managed to haul down my carry-on from the overhead rack and quickly change in the tiny bathroom. When I presented myself to an open-armed Stan at Heathrow, it was in a fresh wraparound chino skirt. So many years ago. So many attitudes ago.

———

This trip I traveled business class on British Air, the ticket paid for by the practice, and slept through the flight. Heathrow Airport was a madhouse, as usual. The lines at passport control for British citizens were worse than those for non-Brits. A group returning from Disneyland was noisily cranky and a crowd of pensioners back from holiday in Ibiza made for mass confusion.

So when my line moved faster than expected, I was caught off guard and had to rummage for my passport which turned my handbag into a volcano spewing pens, Tums, business cards, Lifesavers, a comb, and my passport case onto the floor.

"You've done it now," the voice behind me murmured. "Made a dreadful mess, haven't you? Allow me."

What I felt next is what the French call a *coup de foudre.* A lightning strike to the heart. An immediate cardiac shock that doesn't involve the brain at all. In fact, standing there in the few seconds it took for the yet unseen person behind me to scoop up my scattered stuff, I felt lightheaded, as if my brain had drained from my cranium. We're not necessarily talking love here. Nothing that arduous. In my case, it was more like walking smack into a force field. Or maybe mainlining high-grade heroin.

It's not a rare syndrome, this *coup de foudre.* Dear Abby gets letters about it all the time. "It was World War II, I was a soldier on leave at a USO dance, and this beautiful girl was standing at the edge of the floor..." Songwriters put it to music: "I took one look at you, that's all I meant to do, and then my heart stood still."

Mind you, this reaction was produced by hearing the gentleman say all of twelve words in what I would have wagered a week's salary was a London—probably Mayfair or at least Knightsbridge—accent. I know my accents and this one was top of the line.

Had I ever been hit with anything like this before? Not with Stan, the only man I ever thought I loved. The fact is I hadn't even liked Stan when I first met him. I went out with him to fill in on a double date. Not my type at all. Too pleasant. Too accommodating. It was only after I finally saw him through my mother's eyes and knew she would have despised him and all he stood for—the background, the promise, especially his desire for me—that I could love him.

Now I turned to smile my thank you and faced a perfect match to the voice. The man was elegantly handsome with steel-gray hair and a Cary Grant chin cleft deep enough to sink a putt into. He had very even, very white teeth and a smile so jolly it deserved a laugh behind it. Straight nose. Intelligent eyes the gray of Beluga caviar. Tall and solid looking. Neatly packaged in a blue and white striped shirt and khaki trousers. At his feet lay his suitcase. Over one shoulder was slung a black leather laptop case. Over the other, a carryall imprinted with the letters IAGSO followed by Vienna and the dates of the previous year's meeting. UK and U.S. passports tucked into its outer pocket proclaimed his dual citizenship. When he saw my glance rest on them, he said, "Today, Uncle Sam's line was shorter. Wasn't that a stroke of luck? Well, now I think we have all your treasures."

Both his hands were full of my retrieved things. These he presented to me one by one like a cashier counting change, laying on a dazzling smile throughout the transaction. "And finally your passport. You need to keep a better eye on that. They won't let you in without it, you know. And it would be a shame to miss England in September. It's a very pretty time of year. We only get rain every *other* day in September."

"Very kind of you," I said, clutching my passport.

He said, "Not at all."

I glanced at his left hand and noted no wedding band, looked up, and caught him staring at my left hand. We both laughed.

I was juggling two bags so I couldn't manage a handshake, but I worked the dimples inherited from my mother, not that she'd ever used them. "Gwyneth Berke," I said, pausing to let the name sink in. "You're attending the IAGSO meeting?"

He seemed surprised. "Yes," he said and waited a beat too long to introduce himself, because the passport control officer raised his voice impatiently, "Next. Next, please.

Shall we keep the queue moving, please?" The woman behind my anonymous Englishman glared. I shrugged hopelessly and scurried.

*But all is not lost,* I thought, *because he has to be behind me and if I walk slowly enough, after his passport is duly stamped there is only one hall out and he will catch up to me and finish the introduction.*

"Madame, do not tarry please. This is a security area. We ask that you step briskly." A uniformed airport officer waved me along.

And then, suddenly, my Englishman was next to me and past me, whizzing by without even a glance in my direction, but headfirst, like a bull, charging three men who were waiting just beyond the security gate, one waving, the other two nodding genially. The waving man I recognized. Harris Jance, MD, PhD, inventor of the famous Jance scissors that slice through tissue like butter, and president emeritus of IAGSO. A Scotsman of grand years and grander repute. The two men with him were middle-aged, Asian, both bow-tied and blazered, the standard successful-doc uniform that crosses all borders.

"Simon, good to see you," Jance said as I traversed the cement floor parallel to them, moving as if the air were liquid and I was *verrrry* slowly swimming through it. "You know bleh-bleh"—couldn't make it out—"Tashiki, of course."

"Yes, yes," Simon said, bowing over the handshake. "So kind of you to come."

"But I don't think you know bleh-bleh Phan. Bleh-bleh Phan, Simon York."

"A pleasure, sir," Phan said. "I read your paper on bleh-bleh-bleh..."

Simon York.

Ahh. Simon York.

So that was my cavalier. The famous, infamous Simon York of New York's Kerns-Brubaker Medical Institute which, along with Sloan-Kettering, was one of New York's crown jewel cancer centers. I'd seen Simon York before, but only from a distance. On the podium. Across the vast plains of a meeting room. A first-rate surgeon, he was also a biochemist who'd studied under Nobel laureate Georgi Popovich years before Popovich copped the Nobel Prize for medicine. Contender for the Lasker Award for achievement in medical research a decade ago, edged out by a colleague of mine at Hopkins, the ophthalmologist Al Sommer, York was supposed to be brilliant, but ferocious to work with. Charming but difficult in the clinches. He was so out of my league, it took my breath away.

Ah well, it had been a lovely moment. It was nice to know my hormones still had the power to frazzle me. I tucked away the *coup* experience like a lace handkerchief, reassured to know it was around but something I didn't have much use for anymore.

———

As it turned out, I attended the two sessions in which Simon York was participating. I'd checked them off the preliminary program back in Baltimore. He was doing some amazing science that I thought might eventually benefit my patients.

I had a question, but after the first session, before I could approach him, the panel disbursed and he vanished.

I did run into an old friend, Davis Standish, who'd practiced in Baltimore before moving to Southern California. Davis is what Fleur would call a player. He had his hands (and, some of my colleagues implied, another skillful appendage) up some very famous snatches. With his wife languishing at home with MS, he was the perfect extra man to escort his movie star patients to premieres and charity events. I'd kept up with him in the magazines as he grew older, richer, and more recognizable with his silver hair pulled back into a ponytail and his gymed-up muscles straining the sleeves of his tuxedo. I'd always liked Davis. I gave him credit for bucking the old guard and living his life with gusto, but the pompous academicians who made up the golden inner circle in IAGSO shunned him.

Still, he was a very good surgeon and he came to all the meetings to keep current. We greeted each other warmly once a year. Today, I got a Euro-Hollywood kiss on both cheeks. The mild flirtation we'd cultured but did not act upon went back to serving on the same Med Chi committee in Maryland in the eighties. We used to lunch occasionally to discuss committee business, nothing more.

"You look wonderful, Gwyn." He backed up. "And it's not plastic either. It has to be good genes."

*You should only know*—I thought of my mother, the nutcase, and my father with Alzheimer's. But he was right, the skin genes were pretty good.

We chatted about old times and at the end I said in farewell, "I think I'd better get going. I'm heading for Simon York's paper two floors up."

"Ah, Simon. A few years ago I sent him a patient with a nasty papillary serous carcinoma that, frankly, I had no experience dealing with. I thought she was a goner, but he pulled her through and as a thank you gift she planted two million in his lab. There's no doubt the guy's brilliant and obviously he can turn on the charm."

*Oh yes*, I thought, remembering our encounter at Heathrow.

I sat in the third row for Simon's presentation and

allowed myself to be thoroughly impressed. Good work, well presented, and you could hear the buzz from the audience when he finished.

By the time I got to the front of the room, the crowd around him was large and I paced its fringes. Simon spotted me while talking to Marv Feller from Liverpool. Our eyes caught. His narrowed, then sparkled with recognition. He kept talking but he never lowered his stare and suddenly he smiled right at me. When Marv backed off, a German woman I remembered from other meetings pushed forward. Big, blonde, and insistent, she must have seen that Simon was distracted, lifted one hammy arm, and placed her hand on his shoulder to get his attention. This made him smile wider, and he actually shrugged at me as if to say he was helpless to escape. I shrugged back and moved away from the crowd.

So much for our brief encounter of the third kind. So much for Simon York.

———

"I can't believe you're taking estrogen. You must have a death wish." Alicia Griffith, MD, FRCP, gestured menacingly with her fork. "You've read the recent findings. Might as well take cyanide."

I sipped the last of my coffee as I defended myself. "I tried going off last year and by the end of the third week I was lighting up like Times Square. And I'm lethargic without it. Even on the lowest dose, I'm getting hot flashes, but at least they're manageable. Please don't dish up the Boston study about adverse effects. We all know the literature flip-flops every three days."

Fedora Croscetti, the youngest of our group at forty-seven, shook her tousle of dark curls and clicked her tongue at me.

For the past two decades, five of us colleagues and friends have held an annual reunion at the IAGSO meeting. We communicate the rest of the year by email, trading professional opinions and personal chitchat. That night, we were up to dessert at Wordsworth, a tony nouveau Brit restaurant designed to counter all the stereotypical trashing of English cooking. Isabelle Rousseau leaned over to trade me some treacle tart for a dollop of my toffee pudding. "Don't be so hard on poor Gwyneth," she said in her charming French accent. "I couldn't live without my little estrogen pill. I take it unopposed, without the progesterone which gives me a mustache and acne. I know, I know, I'm risking uterine cancer. This is why I get cleaned out every summer with a D and C. It's worth it. Without estrogen *le vagin* is so dry." She flicked a glance at me.

Alicia jumped in. "Did you say *le* vagin? Don't tell me vagina is a masculine noun. The French are so perverse. Ugh. As for taking unopposed estrogen, that's daft," she said, sniffing like the highborn English lady she was. Sometimes her superior Oxbridge tone irritated me. "I assume you're not recommending such a regimen for your patients."

"I tell my patients it is roulette, the entire hormone replacement issue," Isabelle responded.

"Funny," I said, "I tell mine it's a crapshoot."

Preethika Patel delicately sipped tea, her face screwed up with concentration. A slender, serious-looking woman of sixty with a thriving Delhi practice, she'd worn the white widow's sari the year before. Tonight, her sari was blue and silver, a flattering complement to her dark hair streaked with gray.

Now she said, "In India, the upper classes, those who can afford it, take hormones. The others treat with herbs, like saffron and Shatavari and aloe gel to rub on the genitals. In the villages, they are probably safer than we are. If you believe the latest breast cancer findings."

"So you don't take estrogen?" Alicia, the boldest of us, pressed. Preethika was reserved. Not shy. Just a soul comfortable inside herself and not banging at her own doors.

"Well, I don't get hot flashes. I sleep no better or worse than any widow. I do worry about osteoporosis. And the verdict isn't in for Alzheimer's. So your answer, Alicia, is no, I don't take estrogen, but you're damned if you do, damned if you don't."

A pondering silence washed over us. I thought, *We are all in the same boat, some of us riding the waves, some of us bucking them.*

We paid our check and were making our way out of the dining room when Alicia slowed down and arched back to hiss, "Power table." She cocked her head toward the far corner. "The big guns are breaking bread. Bedell and the entire governing board. And isn't that your friend David Standish?"

"Davis," I said distractedly. "Davis, not David." I was looking elsewhere at the same table. At the back of someone in a Harris tweed jacket. Not sure. Maybe. Probably not.

"How did Standish get to sit among the anointed? He's a certified pariah. Much too Hollywood for those old farts."

"You didn't hear?" Fedora's lip curled. "He put up half a million dollars to underwrite the Arlis R. Bedell Prize for gynecological research." Diverted for a moment from the tweed jacket, I was speechless.

Alicia was never at a loss for a crack. "Add money, a pinch of arse kissing, and stir. Voilà, instant respectability."

By the time we reached the cloakroom, we were a jumble of voices. But one stood out. Isabelle saying, "And who was that sitting next to Simon York? The redhead."

So I was right. My heart gave a little leap on "Simon," then on "redhead" sunk not quite like a stone, more like a pebble.

"She was very close. She had her cheek almost against his cheek. And her hand was on his shoulder, did you see that?"

I had. "His wife?" I ventured, despite the absence of a wedding ring.

"That was not the gesture of a wife," Fedora said dryly.

"The redhead is Beata Karnikova from Prague. You know her, Isabelle. You served on the policy committee with her." This from Preethika.

"Ahh, Bitti, the Iron Maiden. She is very intelligent and *verrrrry* ambitious."

"Young?" That was me again.

"The far side of forty," Alicia said. "But not very far. And well preserved."

"Are they an item?" It was a casual question.

"Bitti and Simon York? Well, I never thought so until now. Anything is possible, I suppose."

"Personally I think he's *un bourreau des cours, trés* sexy," Isabelle said. "I like a man with a strong jaw."

"Oo la la. Very practical of you," Alicia said, which set us giggling like schoolgirls as we walked through the lamp-lit London streets.

London was balanced on the cool cusp of autumn. The air was thin, clear, and ginger-smelling. A moon, one day short of full, hung high and to the right of Big Ben. I thought again how lucky I was to be here. How much fun dinner had been. How grateful I was to have friends like Alicia, Preethika, Fedora, and Isabelle, even if I didn't see them more than once a year.

I loved that these very accomplished physicians could gossip and giggle with the best of them. I cherished the silly stuff. And if it was childish, well, the hell with that. I'd missed a real childhood, so I took it when I got it.

Back in my room, I called my father and pried Sylvie away from *Judge Judy*. He was doing fine, she assured me. Mrs. Parente, his friend from the senior center, had dropped off a box of cannoli. He'd wolfed down two. He hadn't asked for me, but he'd talked to my message machine at 5 a.m. and seemed content with just the sound of my voice. Sylvie put him on and I listened to him babble about someone he saw in the bathroom mirror. The best I could make out was that he thought he saw his sister, Margrit, in the reflection of his own face. My Aunt Margie died in 1993.

After we clicked off, I sat on the edge of the bed with the phone in hand, thinking about calling Harry Galligan. Now that was the man for me. With all the other pressures—my dad, trying to revive the Clinic, the Bethany McGowan–Seymour Bernstein axis of evil—what I definitely did not need was someone demanding, someone as complex as, say, a Simon York.

In the end, though, I decided against phoning Harry.

# Chapter 15

Not that I looked, especially, but for the next two days I saw neither hide nor silver hair of Simon York. Leaving the scene of a meeting in progress isn't uncommon. Your practice pays for your trip to Paris or Maui. You drop in on a few sessions and then take off for more glamorous nearby locales. Such games are played with skill and frequency among my peers.

Simon could have been fly-fishing in Scotland for a few days or he could have been a guest at a country estate in Shropshire. On his arm and in his bed, Bitti Karnikova. Because Bitti was also nowhere to be seen.

Well, good for them. The tingle had faded. My circuits were wired for work. The meeting absorbed all my attention.

I'd planned a self-indulgent evening of room service and relaxation, but when I returned to my hotel room after the second day's program, I found an envelope slipped under my door. Inside were an invitation and a note on hotel stationery from Davis Standish.

*Gwyneth. I didn't have a say in the guest list or you would have received this weeks ago. Hoping it's not too late. I'd really like you to join us. Davis.*

Which is how I wound up with the cream of the gynecological crop at the Tate Gallery reception in honor of Davis Standish, benefactor of the Arlis R. Bedell Prize. This wasn't a group I'd normally feel comfortable with. The board was comprised mostly of men, outstanding in their specialties, who tended to network professionally and socialize with each other at these meetings. The two women were magnificent specimens of female overachievers who'd given up too much get to the top of their profession. Arlis Bedell's prodigy Rachel Cohen-Goldberger was fifty, with a biblical face, the figure of a sylph, and the saddest eyes I'd ever seen. Her husband and infant son had died in a boating accident twenty-five years before and she took all that pain and fury and channeled it into her work.

Angela Barola dressed like a drudge and wore a perpetual scowl. Never-married Angela rose through the macho Italian ranks to distinguish herself as one of the most skillful surgeons on the planet. She was legendary for grit under fire and for her work with the Italian feminist movement. Also a research scientist, she was reputed to get by on two hours of sleep a night. She looked it, but she and Rachel were legends, heroes among the community of female physicians. We showed them off to our daughters as proof that if you surrendered your life to your work, you too could stand among the crowned heads of your profession even if you didn't swing testicles.

It was a good-sized crowd that wandered through the galleries of the Tate. Rachel stopped to say hello. She carried a glass of water that could have been gin. After she drifted away in her miasma of sadness, I followed the party meandering through the five huge galleries. In the third, while examining a Constable, I heard a voice close behind me. "Gwyneth Berke?"

I turned to someone who looked vaguely familiar, sounded more familiar, and whom I couldn't place for the life of me.

"Hi," I said vacantly, "I'm sorry, I don't..."

"It's okay," he answered, in a soft—central European? No. Moroccan? No. Ah, Israeli—accent. Which didn't help at all. "I don't expect you to remember me. It was long ago and far away. Ari Ben-Jacob. Hopkins. I was a lowly resident. You were chief."

I stepped back. "Ari! It can't be. What happened to the mustache? And you were so skinny."

"Yes," he smiled. "With the big Adam's apple. And the tic. You can't possibly have forgotten the tic."

I didn't answer because it really had been a major tic, very distracting. He'd get out two words and his eyes would squint once, then twice. Like Morse code.

But the tic was gone. The Adam's apple had receded into his tree trunk of a neck. The impossibly curly red hair had darkened and relaxed into gentle waves. Ari was a nice-looking, broad-shouldered man with an engaging grin.

"What a change. Look at you! What happened to you?"

"What happened to me is what happens to everyone. Life happened to me." He shrugged charmingly and changed the subject. For fifteen minutes we chatted about the fate of former colleagues. As we wound down, he said, "So, I read your paper in the June *Archives*. It was very interesting to me. I have a relevant case I'd like to discuss with you. If you have the time." He took a deep breath. "Look, I'll bet you haven't eaten anything and you know it's not good to drink on an empty stomach. Not that I blame you, the hors d'oeuvres are lousy. Will you be my guest for dinner tonight? It would be my pleasure."

*What could be the harm of it,* I thought. The old boys and

the two old girls were networking among themselves. Davis Standish was velcroed to the woman he arrived with, a dazzling redhead of maybe thirty-five. And Ari was right, the hors d'oeuvres really were dreadful.

"I think I'd enjoy that," I said.

By ten o'clock, I'd expounded on treating his case, we'd caught up on both our lives, and two bottles of wine had caught up with us.

"Well, Gwyn," Ari vamped, his eyes glistening with cabernet and perhaps something else.

"Well," I smiled. "I really need to be getting back to my hotel. I want to get to the early morning sessions."

"And I am leaving at 6 a.m. for Tel Aviv. It's my daughter's eleventh birthday day after tomorrow, and my ex-wife is making a family party. I've seen what I came here to see. And I can't miss Ronit's birthday."

"It's an early day for both of us."

"Yet I don't want the night to end," he said, covering my hand with his. "I had a crush on you, did you know that? A schlemiel like me. But I'm not a schlemiel anymore and we're both free now. Living in Israel, I can't promise you much more than an evening of pleasure…"

It wasn't my heart that caught this time. It was certainly not my brain, given that this man was fifteen years younger than I, he was once a kid under my supervision, and I wouldn't see him again for a year at least. It was the same thing men are slave to all the time—the siren call of the crotch-stirring moment. And for once in my life, I took the call.

Who would have thunk it? Ari Ben-Jacob was as sleek and muscled as a dolphin, and he moved in the tangle of sheets as if they were his natural element. He did not murmur love. But he had a very well-developed vocabulary of lust. Oh, he was good at this. He did all the right things without thinking, the way a born dancer moves instinctively and gracefully to the rhythm. And he took pleasure in giving pleasure.

"Look at you," he said, presenting naked me to myself in the mirror. "You're beautiful."

I averted my head from the full-length image as I'd been doing for the last decade, and he said, "No, no, look. You have wonderful shoulders."

"Shoulders?" I laughed, thinking, *Boy, he had to reach for that.*

But he protested, "Shoulders can be very sexy." He traced around my clavicle with his finger, then kissed inside both hollows. "So sexy, all of you."

"Me?" I said, yearning to hear.

"You don't know this? The tall, beautiful blonde, so intelligent, so cool on the outside, but one senses the heat beneath the surface. What could be more enticing?"

He tipped my chin up with one finger, forcing me to see my reflection. "Look at your neck. Like a queen. You should be feeding peacocks in a Jerusalem garden. Your body is so exciting." He inventoried me head to toe.

I didn't let on that what he saw was a conjurer's trick worked by desire and low lighting. An illusion.

And then it didn't matter. Because we were involved in lust for lust's sake. Which is what I was there for. No more. The adventure tossed me back to my Barnard days when the mantra was "If it feels good, do it." I'd done it, though not as much as some. *So, thank you, Ari Ben-Jacob*, I thought as we lay together in post-coital bliss, *for a lovely misplaced moment in time that made me feel nineteen again.*

———

The next day, Fedora and I were having a pre-dinner drink in the hotel bar when Bitti, walking through the lobby, spotted Fedora and lifted a limp wave.

"Poor Bitti." Fedora hunched over her wine glass. "She looks so washed out. Redheads lose color so quickly. But of course, vomiting and diarrhea for twenty-four hours will drain you of color whatever your complexion."

"Bitti was sick?"

"Horribly. She thinks it was from something she ate at Wordsworth the other night. I saw her this morning at breakfast. All she had was tea and toast and to me she looked still a little wobbly on her feet, which is normal after two days in bed."

Two days in bed. Not with Simon York in Shropshire or wherever. Not that it mattered, but it warned me I needed to stop jumping to conclusions about men. Stan had done that to me. Eroded my trust, made me a touch cynical. Time to let that go and give all God's children the benefit of the doubt.

———

The XXVI IAGSO Annual Congress was gavel-pounded into history and by eight the next morning the hotel lobby swarmed with attendees awaiting airport transportation. My flight was scheduled to depart at eleven. Preethika's flight to Delhi left at around the same time. We shared a taxi to Heathrow.

The bellman was loading our baggage on his trolley when a group of four men emerged from the lobby door to stand next to us under the hotel canopy. Then Jai Prasad, one of the IAGSO board members, removed himself to chat with Preethika. That opened a direct line of vision between Simon York and me.

Simon nodded, looked puzzled, then it seemed the light dawned. "Back in a moment," I heard him say to Arlis Bedell.

Before I could catch my breath, he was at my side. "We never got to complete our introduction at the airport. But the program did that for us, didn't it? I did see you after my session and I wanted to talk to you, but Inger Schroeder pinned me down. Formidable woman. One doesn't cross Inger. And then by the time I extricated myself, you'd vanished. Did you have a question?"

"I did, but I can't for the life of me dredge it up right now." I was having either an inconvenient hot flash or I was blushing, something I hadn't done since second grade. In any event, the sudden burst of heat temporarily wiped out my memory. I sucked my lower lip trying to remember.

He tugged his gaze from my mouth to my eyes where it locked, very intense. In sunlight, my Nordic blue eyes go sapphire. I flashed him the bling.

"Not to worry," he said, taking my hand. I wasn't imagining it—his thumb was massaging the soft flesh between my thumb and forefinger. Then he did that thing with his mouth attractive men do, that twist of a smile that turns a woman's center to soufflé. "If you think of it, jot me a note. I'm in New York, at Kerns-Brubaker."

"Simon, Jai, the car is here," the man standing next to Arlis Bedell called out. A black Rolls limousine had pulled up to the porte cochere.

"Coming!" he didn't turn away. "Oh, yes, I want you to know, I read your bit in *Issues* last winter. Impressive stuff. You're working on a follow-up, I presume?"

"Simon!"

"Sorry. I'm being summoned, Dr. Berke. " He remembered my name. "By the way, I like your perfume." He leaned in. "Tuberose. Very sensual. But subtle. It suits you." Backed off. "Got to go."

"Bon voyage," I said on a gasp. With a wave he was off.

The last I heard of him, he was instructing the bellman, "Take special care with that one," pointing to a black leather laptop case. Then he scrambled into the limo, the driver closed the door behind him, and that was that.

Except if there was one thing I'd learned in my fifty-four years on this unruly and unpredictable planet, it was that *that* is hardly ever that.

*Chapter 16*

The office, my first day back, was a happy shambles. Marie Lansing, our chief appointments secretary and office manager, announced she was getting remarried and moving to Boston. Everybody was thrilled for her. Including me. Though I felt as if my right arm had been lopped off at the elbow.

"We're going to miss you, Marie." I couldn't contain a sigh.

"You're all going to be fine. I trained Barbara to take over as soon as I had an inkling I was leaving. And there are three gals coming in for interviews this week to fill the empty place."

Seymour was going to handle the interviews. Based on his hiring of Marie ten years before, he fancied himself an expert on human resources.

"Do you have a moment?" Her rapidly blinking eyelids telegraphed nervousness. Which wasn't like Marie.

"Of course."

She closed the door to my office and slipped into the chair across from me. "You know, Dr. Berke, I don't tattle doctor to doctor." Which was true. She not only protected us from our patients, she protected us from each other.

"This isn't easy for me to say, but have you noticed any-thing, ah, unusual going on between Dr. Bernstein and Dr. McGowan?"

I hummed a noncommittal note.

"God, I hate this," Marie said, smiling weakly. "I've been losing sleep over whether I should tell you, but it's for the good of the practice and now that I'm leaving..."

Oh, shit. I really didn't want to hear this. Then again, such knowledge might come in handy.

"And I figured I ought to mind my own business. But it's gotten too obvious to ignore. And it's during office hours. I mean, they can't keep their hands to themselves. When they think no one's looking, he'll...you know...grab for her...you know, breast. And I caught her patting his...uhmm...backside. That kind of inappropriate behavior. Some of the staff are picking up on it. Gossiping. Which isn't good for the practice. So I thought I ought to tell you. I mean, I'm more comfortable telling you than Dr. Potak, him being a man."

*Take this with a grain of salt*, I reminded myself. Marie disliked Bethany. All of the support personnel did. Not entirely unwarranted. Even after repeated warnings, Bethany treated them like indentured servants, snapping orders and expecting immediate heel-clicking attention.

"I'm not sure what you can do about Dr. Bernstein, his being a partner and all." She left unsaid what I knew the staff thought, that Seymour was the village idiot, always chasing after very short skirts barely covering very young legs. He was incorrigible, but untouchable. Bethany, on the other hand, did not have tenure.

"This is a wonderful practice," Marie said. "Please don't let that woman destroy it."

"You did the right thing by telling me. I'll deal with it.

You can leave us with a clear conscience." I gave her a reassuring shoulder pat. Then I went out to spy on the enemy.

You didn't have to be James Bond, believe me. When they passed in the corridor, they slithered against each other like lizards on a hot rock. Reviewing papers in Seymour's office, they leaned hip to hip. They traded lascivious glances in the coffee room, and there was an excessive use of tongue on Bethany's part as she licked Coffeemate from the rim of her mug.

Now that Marie had alerted me, the hanky-panky was obvious. You could smell the musk and feel the electricity when you were in the same room with them. Ugh.

Still, despite all the sexual current I caught passing between them, I had no solid evidence, no reason to call Bethany on the carpet and take her down a peg, no excuse to defang the young pup nipping at my heels. In surgery, I was absolutely focused, but around the office I watched every move the suspects made and in the exam rooms my more observant patients noticed something was off.

One of my favorites, Sondra Delgado, told me I looked under the weather.

"Jet lag. But you look fine," I switched subjects. "You've lost three pounds. Your osteoporosis test came back with great numbers."

"Yeah, I work my ass off for them." Sondra had a zesty way with words. She taught poetry writing classes at the local community college. She also led aerobics workouts at the Unitarian church. She was a knockout at sixty-four, which gave me hope.

I'd scraped the cells I needed for her Pap test, but she was still in the stirrups when she said, "Look at my pubic hair."

I lifted the drape.

"It's white," she said.

"So is the hair on your head." I'd been seeing Sondra Delgado for twenty-five years and she'd been a silver-haired beauty in her thirties. One of those premature grayers with golden skin that lit up against the silver.

"But my pubic hair has always been black. I had a big black bush. Now look at me. It's almost all white, what's left of it."

"Well, pubic hair does thin out and will eventually gray with aging."

"I want to dye it. That's my question. Can I dye it? You're smiling. If you laugh, I swear to God I change doctors."

"It's not you," I assured her. I was caught in the memory of seeing Kat in the nude for the first time. We shared a room in college and she was changing into her pajamas and there it was, a dark shock of kinky pubic hair, a black  bramble that didn't resemble anything I knew. I'm a naturally fair Scandinavian and I'd hunted down Annie Johansson in the showers for confirmation that a scant drift of pale hair is a perfectly acceptable variation on the theme.

Now here was Sondra Delgado smiling back at me, but with tears in her eyes. "You've got to think I'm so shallow to worry about this when you have patients with cancer."

"Not at all," I said. "If it's important to you, it's important to me. But I don't think dyeing it is a good idea. The pubis is a delicate area and you could have an allergic reaction."

"Damn. As you might have guessed, there's a man involved. I haven't slept with him yet, but I know it's going to happen and I'd be so mortified for him to see me like this. Like an old lady."

"Well, his pubic hair is probably gray also."

"It's different for a man."

I thought but didn't say, *you're* telling *me*? "Why don't you shave it? That's what the *Playboy* centerfolds do. It's supposed to be very sexy. I have to warn you, it may itch at first. But if you keep it shaved, you should be fine."

Sondra sat up. "You...are...brilliant. No, I mean it. That's an absolutely brilliant solution. That's why I see a woman doctor. And not one of those thirty-year-old know-it-alls who hasn't the foggiest idea of which end is up for someone my age. I knew I could bank on you, Dr. Berke."

Yes, it was only pubic hair, but it gave me a burst of confidence to know that age counted for something in a practice with its own thirty-year-old know-it-all.

Wednesday, at our monthly financial update, Seymour and Bethany prudently seated themselves across from each other at the conference table. Fifteen minutes in, with Neil deep into a discussion of profit/loss variables, I noticed Seymour get this goofy, dreamy look on his face that I'd seen enough times to know had nothing to do with bookkeeping. Eyes front, I slid a manila folder from my lap to the floor, then ducked to retrieve it, and...eureka! Proof positive: Bethany had extended a single shapely leg and her unshod foot was gently massaging Seymour's crotch into a giveaway bulge. I bobbed back up to send her a "we will have a talk, young lady" glare and watched her face turn the color of a mushroom.

## Chapter 17

**Y**ou've got to be kidding. She was giving him a toe job in the conference room?" Fleur laughed with such gusto, I feared she might pitch herself into the pyracantha bushes lining the path to Kat's studio.

We'd pulled into Kat's driveway simultaneously on Saturday morning, answering her summons to help her decide which of her weavings to select for an upcoming gallery show. Now Fleur and I trudged together up the hill to the glass-enclosed addition Ethan had built as a fiftieth-birthday gift to his wife.

"It's not funny, Fleur. It's a breach of professional behavior. It's unconscionable."

Fleur blotted her eyes with a tissue. "Yeah, well, maybe you need to lighten up. So they're hot for each other. So they engage in a little foreplay sub rosa. It's not as if they're shtupping patients. They're shtupping each other. And you told me Bethany's a bitch and he's a jerk. So it's a perfect match."

"That's not the point. It was in the office."

"Under the table."

"Not always. Why are you defending them?"

"I'm not defending them. But do you really think it dishonors the entire medical profession for one of you to get caught with your foot on your boss's dick in the conference room?" She broke herself up again.

Why did I even bother? Fleur, close as we are, could never understand why I was so outraged at this desecration. That's what it seemed to me, anyway. Because I wasn't Bethany McGowan whose family was one of those Eastern shore estate clans with money to send their daughter to private schools and on to Harvard, or Seymour Bernstein who'd followed his obstetrician father into the family business. Medicine had rescued me from my lousy beginnings. A crazy, abusive mother. An overwhelmed father who, until he got the job at Beth Steel when I was twelve, barely supported us on his janitor's wages. I could count the books in the house on one hand. So medicine gave me a life and work that I love. I didn't practice my father's Lutheranism or my mother's Catholicism, but I did practice medicine. And if occasionally I got the giggles in the Church of the Holy Speculum, I never defiled the premises.

Fleur was panting, but she managed to say, "All right, seriously, have you talked to them about it?"

"Not yet. I haven't had the chance. Right after the meeting, Seymour left for Chicago for some course he's taking. And Bethany very conveniently came down with the flu and hasn't shown up for the last two days."

"Well, they can't duck you forever."

"I can't decide who's more culpable. Bethany, who's sleeping her way into a partnership, or Bernstein, who's taking advantage of her ambition."

"Bernstein. He's the senior. He should know better."

True, but it was the junior breathing down my neck, poised to kick my ass into the sunset with a foot that had been places I didn't really want to think about. What I did enjoy contemplating, what I anticipated with wicked satisfaction, was the look on her face when I asked her to step into my office for a private talk about a very private matter.

My smirk gave way to a sigh when I contemplated the long list of things I should have been doing that Saturday morning instead of sorting through Kat's tapestries. Laundry to catch up on after nearly a week away, a paper to finish for the October deadline of *Annals of Gynecology*, notes to organize for a talk I was giving in Philadelphia the following weekend, a haircut before my date with Harry that night, and I'd wanted to take my father to see Dan Rosetti, one of the last of a dying breed of docs who kept Saturday morning hours.

It wasn't as if Kat really needed us. The two men who owned the Charles Street Gallery had selected the pieces— tapestries, rugs, shawls, and other wearables—for the exhibit, but she thought they picked the most saleable ones, which might not be her best work. Lee had made his choices. But since he was a sculptor with an eye biased for form, she wasn't sure she entirely trusted his judgment either.

She must have been desperate to turn to Fleur and me for our opinion on, of all things, art. Fleur's taste in art ran to thoroughbreds grazing in meadows, hunting scenes, and portraits of dead ancestors. I'd grown up in a house with fiber art—the Last Supper painted on velvet hanging over the couch. One of the perks of dating Stan had been borrowing his taste in everything, the way I bummed his cigarettes.

I'd told Kat that Fleur and I were the Laurel and Hardy of art connoisseurs, but she'd insisted she needed us. She was nervous about the exhibit. It was in a major Baltimore gallery. The *Washington Post* art critic had promised he'd be up for the opening.

When women call women for help, we drop everything and rush to the rescue. I'd flown to Kat's side when her sister Melanie died of breast cancer a decade before, and left a full waiting room to hold her hand through her mother's last hours. Fleur let Quincy run the store for three days during the punch-drunk week after Stan KO'd me with The Treachery. It's the law of the coven. Sister down! Sisters rally!

As we approached Kat's studio I thought again that Ethan Greenfield must have loved his wife extravagantly to have built her such a workplace. After his parents died, he sunk most of his moderate inheritance into his organic vegetable business, which was really a compost heap, turning dollars into fertilizer with amazing efficiency. But he'd set apart a chunk to pay for building this studio addition for Kat which, architecturally, was as crisply angled and clean lined as a Swedish church.

Inside was all earthbound practicality. The single room was huge, with picture windows and a skylight so the studio was flooded with natural light. Just beyond the door, a long trestle table held pots of dyes, foam brushes, and a table loom. Dead center, three floor looms sat, one dressed for Kat's latest project. In preparation for the show, the candidate tapestries were displayed on the far wall.

Kat stood to one side of them, shoulders slumped. Her eyes were focused not on her work but on her daughter whose face was closed, emotionless, as if she'd pulled down every shutter and slammed every door. Kat's face was readable: sadness and pain. It was obvious we'd walked in on a major moment.

"Hi, Kat," Fleur said, but neither of us moved beyond the door where we'd stalled out when we saw Summer. Fleur didn't like her any more than I did. "Hello, Summer.

What a surprise! We didn't know you'd be here, did we, Gwyn?"

"Summer is pregnant," Kat announced. Flat out, no preamble, just "Summer is pregnant," without joy.

"Well, isn't that nice," Fleur said as she flashed me a look. I knew she was thinking *Rosemary's Baby*.

I recalled being surprised midweek to see Summer emerge from an exam room and, spotting me, smile and lift her hand in greeting. Unusual, the smile and the wave. She must have just gotten the news.

"Yes, it's very nice for Summer and Tim. But not so wonderful for me." Kat dragged herself out of Summer's direct beam. I saw the sadness drain from her eyes and something igneous replace it. She began to pace. "Summer has just given me an ultimatum. Haven't you, Summer? It seems I have a choice to make. And if I make what Summer has decided is the wrong choice, I may never see my grandchild. Because I'm not going to be permitted—that was your word wasn't it, Sum—or maybe it was allowed, I'm not going to be allowed to have any contact with my grandchild if I don't meet Summer's condition. And Summer's condition is that I have to stop seeing Lee to see the baby. Isn't that right, Summer? That's it in a nutshell, isn't it?"

"What?" Fleur exclaimed. But Summer said "Mud-ther!" at exactly the same time and that took precedence. "Mud-ther, I can't believe you!" Summer's nostrils flared. She was finally open for business. "This is a private matter, a family matter. I can't believe you would spread it around to the immediate world."

"Gwyneth and Fleur *are* my family since your father died." Kat gestured us to come closer.

"Oh, please. This is between us. You have no right to bring them in on this."

"Why? Are you ashamed? Because you ought to be." Circling her daughter, Kat picked up speed. Gutsy Kat was making a comeback. "Forcing me to choose between someone I care about and my grandchild. You ought to hang your head in shame."

"No, *you* ought to hang your head in shame. My father isn't dead two years and you're running around with that Armenian—"

"Summer!" Kat put up with a lot from her daughter, but she would not tolerate prejudice from anyone. "His name is Bagdasarian. Lee Bagdasarian."

"Whatever. For godssakes, the man is ten years younger than you. You're like one of those old ladies you read about who get swindled by these con men, the young gigolos, on cruise ships and like that. I mean, think this through. Do you really believe he's going to marry you? Well, he's not. You'll see. You'll come out of this Bag-whatever thing with a broken heart. I suppose in the end, that's your choice. My choice is I'm not going to let my child see his grandmother sleeping around like some kind of, I don't know...slut or something."

A moment of silence followed. We were paralyzed into a shocked tableau, even Summer who suddenly looked as if she were about to cry.

I broke the silence. "You know, Summer, this room is very toxic. There are all kinds of fumes in here. Dyes and turpentine to clean brushes..."

"I use only natural dyes. No chemicals," Kat corrected.

I ignored her. "You're in the very early stages of your pregnancy. Your fetus and you have a lot of growing to do." I'd used the same soothing voice when I was an intern doing my psych rotation. "And you really don't want to expose either of you to the toxicity in this room. It's my professional opinion that you really ought to leave now. Just to be on the safe side."

"Yeah, if you want to be safe, you'd better get out now," Fleur said. She was seething.

"Is that what you want, Mud-ther, for me to leave with nothing settled?"

Kat nodded. I didn't think she could speak.

"Then I'll call you tomorrow. When we can talk in private." Summer gathered her handbag, swung the cardigan half of her heather-colored sweater set over her shoulders, and with that flouncy walk she'd had since childhood—"The Princess Snotty Walk," Ethan used to call it with pride and fondness—sashayed past us, shaking her head disgustedly all the way.

Of course, she slammed the door behind her. So hard a shower of yarn cones flew down from their pegs on the wall and bounced in her wake.

We never did get to choose the show pieces that afternoon. Kat required comfort and counsel.

"Even with grown kids, when a parent dies, they know they can't exhume him, but they can tend the shrine," I told her.

"So I become what, a nun? I'll always love her father. I explained that to her. Nothing will change that. But she wants me to stop my life." She rubbed her eyes as if that could clear her vision. "I don't even know where this is going with Lee, but I'd like to find out."

"Then do," Fleur said. "Don't let yourself be blackmailed."

"I'm going to have a grandchild, Fleur." Kat uttered this slowly as if she had to spell it out for Fleur, who'd never had a child. "Can you imagine if I can't see it?"

Fleur looked hurt, but she said, "Summer will change her mind."

"She might," I agreed. "She'll really need you through the pregnancy and when the baby is born. I've seen it happen even when there's been a longtime estrangement. The new mamas need their own mamas and that wins out in the end."

"You may be right. I hope you're right. But what if you're not? You know Summer," Kat's voice cracked. "Can I take the chance?"

Oh, yes, I knew Summer. She'd hold her mother's heart to the fire. I had a feeling that Kat would, in the end, have to make a choice.

———

"I just hope she doesn't buckle under the pressure," Fleur said, as we walked together to our cars. "That brat of hers really knows how to apply the thumbscrews. Kat's a smart woman. But she gets all caught up in the emotional crap."

I'd been waiting for the right moment to bring up Jack Bloomberg. Experience taught me if you confronted Fleur at the wrong time, she pulled up the moat.

"Too much feeling, too little thinking. I guess it's her artist's mentality," she concluded.

There was my opening. "So you logical business types don't get sucked in by the emotional crap."

Fleur was sharp enough to pick up the innuendo. She ground to a halt, her thumb on the car remote.

"What the hell does that mean?"

"Ah, Fleur," I sighed. "I saw Jack on the condo channel the night before I left for London. I was letting the pizza guy in and right behind him there was Jack waiting for you to buzz him up."

"Jesus! A person's life is an open book at Waterview, isn't it? In my case, a very dull open book."

"Look, I'm not trying to pry. It's just that I'm worried you—"

She cut me off. "Oh, for godssakes. You want a play-by-play?" She sunk down onto a garden bench Ethan had placed under an oak tree shading the cars. "Fine. Maybe it will do me good to get it off my chest. Sit." She inhaled a deep breath. "Okay. That was when? Monday? Nothing happened that night. It was all tea and sympathy. Or if you want to get picky, black coffee and sympathy. He just wanted to talk. Bambi is having problems nursing the baby. Maybe the kid doesn't like the taste of silicone. So, that was the first night."

"There was a second night?"

Fleur stared at her nails. "The second night we talked about Bambi's postpartum depression. She gained forty pounds with the pregnancy and she's still eating for two. And the baby's reflux is better, but now he's got some kind of scalp rash. Jack wanted my advice. I reminded him I had no experience with pregnancies or babies, thanks to him."

"Let me get this straight: Jack's having problems with his wife and he comes running back to his former girlfriend. My God," I said, "that man has a lot of challah."

"Chutzpah. Chutzpah means nerve. Challah is a kind of bread. I agree. Now. For some reason, while it was happening I was flattered. I also thought..."

"What, that he might leave her? Fleur, you wouldn't have taken him back!"

"Nah. Not after I had some time to think about it." There was a moment of silence in memory of Fleur's finally buried dreams.

"You didn't ask me if I slept with him."

"I didn't think it was any of my business."

"Like that's ever stopped you. As it turns out, I didn't. Not that I didn't try. Don't say it, Gwyn. Whatever you can say about my character, I've already thought about myself. All I know is at that moment I was figuring here's my chance to get back at Bambi for taking Jack from me. Tit for tat, you could say. And it seemed so natural with Jack pouring out his heart, resting his head on my shoulder, then against my bazooms. It seemed the most natural thing in the world. Don't forget we'd been together fourteen years."

"Oh, Fleurie."

"There's always going to be feeling there."

Ari Ben-Jacob had whispered that when we said our good-byes. Once you love, does the germ of it remain dormant forever in your blood? Years later, it's not the same virus, but a mutation. Harmless, unless your resistance is low.

"Maybe I still love him. Maybe it's just affection we have for each other. Whatever. But when the actual moment of truth arrived, he couldn't. Or wouldn't. Who knows? I guess it hit me then that he really loves her. That's what the power failure was all about. So I personally buttoned that ridiculous vest of his and sent him home to Bambi and the kid."

"Good for you."

"Yeah, well don't hand out any prizes. If he could have, I would have gone through with it. What does that make me?"

"Human," I said.

Fleur had come clean. It was only fair that I make my own confession. Oddly, I felt more reticent about my *coup de foudre* with Simon York than I did about hurtling into the sack with Ari for my first genuine one-night stand. So I skipped Simon. But Fleur got a kick out of the Ari story.

"Perfect. No strings. No regrets," she commented when I was through telling it. "That's what you want, isn't it?"

"Sure," I said, as if I were.

"I *am* impressed. You've got a young stud in London and good old Harry waiting in the wings this side of the pond. Everyone should have such an abundance of riches. However, all is not bleak on my horizon. I, too, have some prospects."

"Good for you. Does this mean you've revived The Plan?"

"Yup, I figured why should Jack have all the fun trapped in a miserable marriage? I want my turn. And I made three contacts on Lovingmatch this week. One guy seems okay. We talked on the phone last night. He knows the difference between Larry King and B. B. King." She twisted her mouth into a hopeful smile. "We'll see."

*Chapter 18*

Five great things about Harry Galligan:

1. He arrived for our date carrying a bouquet of flowers, multicolored with lots of tinted carnations, in a cone made of transparent film that told me he'd picked it up either at the Safeway or from a roadside vendor. I found this very sweet.

2. He looked polished. Not slick, but as if someone had taken a chamois to him and buffed him to a glow. His shoes gleamed. His cheeks were burnished with rosy Celtic color. Even the back of his neck, where his hair appeared freshly cut (unlike mine) and the curly auburn was faded, had been barber-shaved to a pewter finish.

3. He ordered a porterhouse the size of a football field and a baked potato the size of a football at Ruth's Chris Steak House and finished everything on his plate as well as the creamed spinach and sautéed mushrooms on the side. All this he washed down with bourbon. Good all-American boy.

4. He didn't drone on about his ex-wife at the dinner table, which was commendable first-date behavior, even though the idea of a woman running away

midlife with another woman was fascinating. (Not a man with a man though. Of course.) For part of the dinner, I thought about whom I would choose to boff if I suddenly turned lesbian. Fleur and Kat were immediately excused. None of my friends qualified; they would all talk a blue streak in bed, which was an advantage of having sex with men.

5. When we ran into Fleur and her date in the lobby at the end of the evening, Harry gave her the once-over, the way a man would once-over a twenty-eight-year-old bombshell. In the elevator, he said to me, "Now that's a good-looking woman." The man had taste.

Five not-so-great things about Harry Galligan:

1. He shot his cuffs through the sleeves of his jacket and hiked his trousers when he sat down. Stan once told me that cuff-shooting and trouser-hitching were dead giveaways of a lower-class background and, guttersnipe snob that I am, I've never forgotten it.

2. He smelled of Old Spice or Canoe. *(Do they still make Canoe?)* Whatever, it was a scent that transported me back to my horrendous high school days and that depressed me right though my second glass of wine.

3. His shirt was made of something unnatural and when his jacket flapped back you could see through its nylon translucence the outline of his undershirt, one of those scooped neck numbers only Andy Capp and my father still wore.

4. He rambled on about a "Science Friday" program on NPR that somehow segued into a moment-to-moment recapitulation of his recent visit to Ireland. When the waitress recited the daily specials, I made her

list the ingredients in the Louisiana Seafood Gumbo just to get a break from the grand tour of Dublin. His table talk made me want to lay my head between my bread plate and my water glass and take a nap.

5. He surprised me with a good-night kiss that could have been the Mr. Nice Guy equivalent of the pity fuck.

<u>Three nasty things about me:</u>

1. I couldn't quite manage to hide my disappointment that Harry wasn't the person I'd signed on for. And how fair was that since the gap between fantasy and reality was one I'd dug myself?

   I'd been so excited when we set up this date, certain he was the man of my dreams. Why do women invest prospective lovers with attributes that would make Harrison Ford duck his head and say "Shucks, ma'am"? Now that the date was here, he was just Harry. Pleasant. Attentive. But no tingle a la Simon York or Ari Ben-Jacob. And life, I'd recently decided, was too short to waste on no tingle.

2. I was incredibly boring. Incredibly.

3. When we ran into Fleur and her date in the Waterview lobby, I dissolved in giggles as the date kissed my hand. Who was this guy and why hadn't we discussed him at length? All I knew was Fleur looked like she was ready to strangle me. As I cracked myself up over the continental guy with an honest-to-God pompadour, a major pinky ring, and very wet lips, she sent me her haughty to-the-manor-born look. No one did haughty better than Fleur. I was abashed but couldn't stop giggling even when Harry flashed me a warning signal. *My mother was right, my baptism didn't take. I am a sinful person.*

Two things I liked about me, in spite of my mother:

1. I apologized to Harry for my rudeness.

When he said fairly casually during the good-night ritual at my door, "Let's do this again," I got all ruffled and told him I was going to be out of town the following weekend giving a speech to an audience of menopausal women. That stopped him in his tracks.

"That's okay," he said finally, "I didn't have a specific date in mind."

*Take that, you self-important MD-type.* Then maybe he regretted backhanding me, for that's when he planted the surprise kiss.

After we disconnected, I said, "It was fun, Harry. I'm sorry if I was such a pain tonight. It's been a tough week and a lousy day. Earlier I mean." Thinking about Kat and Summer.

"I'll call you," he said.

"Drive carefully."

My feet were killing me. For the hundredth time, I swore I was going to give up anything higher than one-inch heels. Once I could sail along on three-inchers, but lately even namby-pamby two-inchers were hell on my feet and lower back. I needed to unhook my bra. I wanted to peel my panty hose down from their control top to their sandal toes and toss them over the balcony and far, far away into the water, which shimmered the reflection of a full moon. *Lunacy. Dating at this age is sheer lunacy.* But I vowed to do it again sometime. Dumb persistence. That was the second thing I liked about me.

## Chapter 19

On Monday morning, before I could execute my planned ambush on Seymour Bernstein, Bethany materialized at my side, clutching a balled-up tissue in one hand. She looked awful. She was either suffering from the cold I thought was fake or she'd been crying.

"You shouldn't be working sick. It's not fair to your patients. Or to the staff." I resumed scanning a radiology report on my next patient.

"If you have a moment, I'd like to talk to you," she sniffed. "Please."

"In my office."

Sitting across from me, she said, "I want to apologize." She pulled her skirt down over primly crossed knees. The skirt was longer than those she'd been wearing during the last month and the feet that tapped to a nervous internal beat were clad in what looked to be Red Cross shoes. Sturdy and not at all sexy. I imagined she'd given some thought over the weekend to redeeming her image and dug her pre-affair wardrobe out of the closet.

Her voiced cracked when she said, "I feel horrible about what happened the other day."

"You should."

"I don't know where my head was."

"You need to keep better track of all your body parts, Bethany."

"Agreed. I know what you're thinking."

"Do you?"

"But believe me, I am sincerely sorry."

*Sorry for her behavior or sorry for getting caught,* I wondered. "Look, if you want to..." I searched for a word to use with prissy bluestocking Bethany, then remembered I was addressing someone who foot-groped a colleague in the boardroom, "...screw around with Seymour, that's your choice."

Her eyebrows took off. Surely she wasn't shocked by my use of "screw." Maybe back on the estate in Easton, they didn't talk about it; they just did it wherever and with whomever they wished. As members of the congenitally elite, they were entitled. Maybe that's what I detested about Bethany. That inherent sense of entitlement I'd never felt and could never feel, the one, along with Gerber's strained peas, your wellborn mama fed you with a silver spoon.

"You're both single and above the age of consent. Seymour is so far above the age of consent he probably signed his ID with a quill pen. But that's your business. It's only mine when you make it mine. And the staff's. You and Seymour are the hot topic in the coffee room. They're not blind, you know. This is indefensible, unprofessional conduct."

"You're right."

"You're damn right, I'm right. And why do you have to bring it into the office, anyway? You both have apartments. With bedrooms."

She wrung her tissue and mumbled, "Seymour gets turned on by—"

"Enough." I held up a halting hand. I really didn't want to hear any more. "Just know this, I'm not going to allow you to climb the ladder on your back. Not in this practice."

"What!"

"Oh, please. Spare me the outrage. Let me tell you something, my generation worked too damned hard to bury that load for you to come along and dredge it up again."

"You've got to be kidding," Bethany said, leaning forward to dig her nails into my desk. "You can't possibly think that I'm sleeping my way into a partnership."

"That's exactly what I think."

"My God. My God." She sunk back in her chair, shaking her head incredulously. "I don't expect you to believe this, but I love Sy. I do. I know he's thirty years older than I am and sometimes he's a little rough around the edges, but that doesn't matter to me. I'm in love with him. And he's in love with me."

We both observed a moment of silence while Bethany recovered from and I tried to process this revelation. Sy and Beth in love. You might figure them for some recreational slap-and-tickle, but love? That was like a romance between Godzilla and Mothra. I said finally, "Well, I'm thrilled for you. But it's no excuse."

"You're right. We got carried away and we've been stupid and thoughtless." Lids were lowered. "I assume I should start sending out my CV? I mean, you've got your ammunition now so you can do what you've been wanting to do for a long time. Fire away."

"No one's firing anyone," I said. "You're a good doctor, an asset to the practice. I consider the matter closed. For the time being anyway. We have discussed this…ummm…situation and," I decided to give her a break, "it remains between us, and of course, your boyfriend. Who, by the way, has been avoiding me. Eventually, I'll tag him in the hall and we'll talk this through."

"I'd rather speak to him myself first, if you don't mind," she said.

*I bet.* Then again, I didn't relish a duel between partners. Bad for the practice. "Fine. But make sure he knows how ticked off I am. And that one day we'll have our own little chat, Sy and I."

She nodded. "Are you going to tell Neil?" Who would have been appalled. Neil was a stickler for observing the code of ethics.

"I'd rather we resolve this among the three of us."

"Thank you." No tears. No sniffles. Her cold was apparently miraculously cured.

"You're welcome," I said, turning to my computer. Dismissing her. But I watched her from the corner of my eye. And she knew I'd be watching her very closely from now on. One misstep, one shot across the bow and she was done for. She and Seymour Bernstein both. One word to Neil and heads would roll. Hers anyway. Seymour would keep his, but lose major face. So there would be no more talk about my age, my retirement, my mentoring young up-and-comings, my taking a backseat to the young'uns because the exit sign was lit. I had a garlic necklace to protect me from the vampires. I was safe now.

For the moment, anyway.

———

Two days later, *I* was on the receiving end of a scolding. "You really are becoming a one-dimensional person. Working nonstop. And don't tell me you don't have time for anything else. There's always time for romance. Like there's always room for chocolate," Fleur grumbled as she scowled at my reflection in the long mirror of the Istanbul Salon and Day Spa on Wednesday evening.

While Attila cut her hair and Melik highlighted mine, we sat in adjoining chairs, nibbling sandwiches from carry-out containers in our laps.

"You don't understand. I've done fifteen surgeries so far this week. As far as I'm concerned there's only one gender on this planet." I wiped mayo from my lip. "Your point is moot anyway. It's not like the men are lining up for me."

"You have Harry Galligan," Fleur reminded me. "Who, from everything you've told me, is a national treasure."

"Harry's wonderful," I agreed. "But I'm not sure I'm going to see him again. No tingle."

"Now you want tingle? I didn't know tingle was on your wish list. Fine, you've revised," she surrendered. "Which means you're still shopping."

"I don't want to shop. I don't have time to shop," I said.

"How long does it take to log on to your computer? When was the last time you opened your email from Ivydate.com?" My reluctance to be Internet matched continued to be a sore point with her. "Okay, so maybe he won't be a doctor with great pecs and genuine Israeli circumcision, but there are some good men out there. Isn't that what you're always telling me? 'If you dig around a little, Fleur, there are lots of good men, or good enough anyway.' But only for me, right? Not for you, you hypocrite." She grunted with exasperation. "And you're fucking spoiled to boot."

Melik must have registered the "fucking" because his eyebrows shot up. He plucked a square of aluminum foil from my outstretched hand, brushed it with bleach, and wrapped it around a hank of my hair. Very focused. "Too much gray," he'd announced when I walked in. Just what I needed to hear. "Gray coming in fast. Color today. More blonde."

Fleur and I talked freely with only the stylists around. They didn't speak much English. Melik knew "shorter," "longer," "blonder," "darker," and when he finished with you, "absolutely gorgeous, honey." And probably "fucking." I was beginning to think, with maybe the addition of "harder," "softer," "higher," and "lower," that should be the limit of every man's vocabulary.

"What about this Ben-Gurion or whatever his name is? Has he emailed you?"

"No." Which was fine. Ari was a fling. Flings are like firecrackers. Once flung, you really can't get a second bang out of them.

There wasn't much to mention about Simon York. Still, his memory tickled. "There was another man," I said, finally.

Melik pointedly examined my scalp. It was a sham, his thick accent, his limited vocabulary. My Turkish hair stylist was probably an Oxford scholar.

With many polysyllabic words, I described my encounter with Simon at the airport. "Fleur," I asked, "did you ever have a thunderbolt hit you? The first time you met Jack, did you feel like you couldn't catch your breath?"

"Actually, yes. I met Jack when I walked in on him taking a piss in the men's room at Chiapparelli's. I thought it was the ladies' room, that's how bombed out on Strega I was. But no thunderbolts. For what it's worth, my theory about thunderbolts is at the first sign of one, run, do not walk, to the sunny side of the street. Thunderbolts end with someone getting burned."

"You're probably right. But for this kind of feeling, I might be willing to take the risk. It's all moot, anyway. I only spoke to him twice. I've been thinking of maybe writing a follow-up note. I had a question for him that I never got to ask. Purely professional. And he said to drop him a note."

Fleur's head jerked so violently, she knocked the scissors out of Attila's hand. "No shit. In case you are completely out of touch, that's what is called a come-on. But of course, your being Miss Manners who just happened to be born in an East Baltimore row house, you decided it might not be proper to go after this guy. Look at that face," she rebuked me, "you're making yourself a permanent scowl."

I leaned toward the mirror to check. Melik yanked me back. "Maybe I should get Botoxed. And I've been thinking about having the eyelid lift done."

"You don't need plastic. You just need to cut down on that cockamamie schedule of yours. The pace is going to kill you. I hope you write this York person and he writes you back. And then I hope he screws you until you beg for mercy. God knows you need a little diversion."

"Dryer, honey." Melik sent me off to get the blonde streaks baked into my hair.

Fleur shook off Attila and trotted after me, "Look, why don't you come with me tonight? I'm going to the Gee! Spot. I need to find something special for an up-and-coming date with the guy from Saturday night, Eldon. Well, up and coming if I play my cards right. And if you're worried we'll be seen, don't. It's all private. Very discreet."

The Gee! Spot, an upscale, by-appointment-only sex accessory shop, was owned by Antonia Guest, one of Fleur's ritzy chums from prep school. How's that for taking revenge against your country club childhood? Could you shove your middle finger any higher than that?

"Some other time," I begged off. "I'm really beat and I

have to prepare my speech for the Menopause Forum on Saturday, plus I've got surgery first thing tomorrow."

"You really need to lighten up, Gwynnie. Smell the roses before they fucking wilt. Come on, it'll be fun. I'll buy some crotchless panties and a new pair of handcuffs," I fervently hoped she was putting me on, "and you can pick up a vibrator. Antonia has an amazing selection."

"I don't need a vibrator."

"Yeah, you do. And I bet you don't even have one."

"I do. Somewhere."

I'd bought my first vibrator back in college. Before Stan. It was the size, shape, and approximate heft of a rutabaga, and it had the bad habit of faltering at the most inopportune moments. When sex with Stan petered out in the last few years of my marriage, I dug it out of a back closet. It gave up the ghost finally a few months after he left me. I was too depressed to replace it.

"Well, you might think do-it-yourself action is beneath you," she persisted, "but a good vibrator is better than nothing at all which, since you're tossing out Harry, is what you've got."

I was mildly insulted. "Maybe, but I prefer something a little less mechanical."

She eyed me sadly. "Sweetheart, at the rate you're going, all work and no play, no man and no prospects, you're not only going to use it for sex, you're going to dress it up and take it to dinner."

Wrong.

———

The following morning, at six, my phone rang.

"Gwyneth Berke?"

"Uh-huh." My father had roused me ten minutes before from an exhausted, dreamless sleep. I was still groggy.

"I've wakened you, haven't I? Not a good start. This is Simon York calling." Pause. "Of Kerns-Brubaker. We met at the IAGSO meeting." Long pause. "You there?"

"Sorry. It's just that you caught me getting out of the shower." Lie. He'd caught me sitting on my bed, legs swung over the side.

"It's rather presumptuous of me to call. You do remember me?"

"Yes, of course, Simon."

Long pause. Throat cleared. "Ah, good." A breath that sounded like relief. "The truth is, Gwyneth, I've been wanting to get in touch with you since London. We kept missing each other at the meeting. And you had a question I never got to answer. Which I'd like to do. So I thought, well, I'd give you a call and see if we might…uhm…get together."

"I see," I said, as I bolted to my feet where I was hoping my brain might kick into gear.

"But I've been out of town. Saudi Arabia, actually. So this is the first chance I've had to call. And then I'm a bit awkward when it's not…ah…entirely professional." Deep breath on both our parts while that last bit hung in the air. "Anyway, I screwed up my courage and here I am."

"Very brave of you," I countered, which wasn't half bad for early morning repartee.

"Don't you think?" he said with a laugh. "Look, I know this is terribly gauche to say, but I just touched down and I haven't been in my office for more than two weeks so I'm in something of rush. What I called about is to find a time when we can get together. I'd like that to be soon, and then we'll talk about that question you had for me, and anything else your heart desires."

For a research scientist—a notoriously slow, methodical,

and cautious species—he was galloping along at breakneck speed.

"Are you free this Sunday by any outlandish chance?" he asked.

Shit and double shit.

"Actually, I'm in Philadelphia this weekend. Speaking to five hundred women on Saturday about the risks of HRT." I credentialed here.

Credentials ignored. "Ah, Philadelphia. I've consulted at the Abramson Center there. The city is quite nice. How about I train in?"

"Into Philly? Just for the day?"

"New York is hardly more than an hour by rail. Why not?" I heard clicking in the background. He was typing into his computer.

"Well, Sunday afternoon, I promised to do breakout sessions with some of the women from the day before..."

"Breakfast, then? Right, here we go. I could be in by nine thirty, at your hotel by ten, and on my way back by noon. Just enough time to see what we shall see."

"Well, sure," I said. Brilliant.

"And the name of the hotel is?"

"The Marriott. Downtown."

"McMarriott. Remind me to tell you of a much nicer alternative for next time. Gwyneth?"

"Yes?" I just wanted to get off the phone.

"I'm glad I called."

"Yes, well I guess I am too."

That sent him into peals of laughter.

When he clicked off, I stabbed #6 on my speed dial. "Fleur," I said. "Simon York just phoned."

"The English thunderbolt?"

"One and the same. We have a date for breakfast on Sunday."

"Fast worker. Ah well, I suppose this means I'll have to return the vibrator I picked up for you last night. He'd better be good, your Brit. The Magic Bullet has five speeds."

# Chapter 20

At thirteen, I won the public speaking contest at Ferdinand C. Latrobe Junior High School reciting from memory "Renaissance" by Edna St. Vincent Millay, all one hundred and fourteen lines of it. The phrase "How can I bear it, buried here" invariably made me cry. I tried not to, but I wept saying it on stage. And who knows what the judges saw? They hung a medal around my neck.

My parents and brother waited for me at the back of the auditorium looking like no other family in the room, the school, the universe. Standing with them was the principal, Mr. Cohen, who said as I approached, "Here she comes, our champion orator. We're very proud of Gwyneth. A straight-A student, and I don't have to tell you she's quite talented as a public speaker."

My mother, her eyes hot coals, nodded. My father said thank you. And Rolfe leaned behind the both of them to whisper at me, "You're going to get it."

That night I padded down to the basement, inched out the loose brick ten bricks in from the side of the furnace, a hiding place I'd fashioned when I was ten.

"Fuck you. Fuck you. Fuck you. Fuck you." I said the phrase out loud for the first time in my life, although I'd thought it for a couple of years. I shoved the medal to the back of the hollow among other treasures that would have been confiscated had my mother known about them.

The next morning after my father left for work, she asked me to show her my medal. I told her I left it at school.

"Well, I want it," she said. "You only won it because all the other kids were shit. Don't let what that old kike Cohen said go to your head, Miss Too-Big-for-Her-Britches, Miss Quite Talented. Miss Poetry. Don't think you're better than everyone else, because you're not."

"I don't," I said.

"Yeah, you do, you just say you don't because you know I won't put up with that fancy-pants attitude. I know what you're thinking. But it ain't going to work. I'm too smart for you. I'm going to wallop that show-off out of you."

Which she proceeded to do, with a vengeance.

Years later, when she was shrinking and I was growing and she didn't dare touch me, I dug out all the stuff I'd hidden in that hole. The medal, the silver cross my Aunt Margie gave me for my sweet sixteen, some coins from baby-sitting money my mother hadn't got her hands on, a photograph of my father's mother I'd rescued from the trash. On our second wedding anniversary, Stan spirited the medal from my jewelry box and hung it on a gold necklace, which I wear every time I face an audience.

You would think after my mother tried to beat it out of me I would have lost my taste for poetry but I never did, and I'm still good speaking in public, in love with the sound of my own voice magnified and the way the audience gives back to you when you hit the mark.

Onstage in Philadelphia, I filled the next to the last seat on a panel of five. At one end, Peggy McGrory, PhD, anthropologist and author of *Hot Flashes and Hottentots: A*

*Survey of Menopause Among the Girquas of South Africa*, read through her notes. Next to her sat Charlotte Springer, a proponent of menopause done naturally with herbs and acupuncture. Then Sidney Luskin, a cardiologist from the Penn's Women's Health Program, then me. The chair on my other side remained empty, its absent occupant's name-plate flipped facedown.

"Before we turn the afternoon over to our distinguished panel, we have a surprise for you." Andrea Chung-Parker, MD, the Forum's president, leaned over the podium.

A surprise indeed. I hadn't been informed and from the scowl on Sid Luskin's face, I wagered he was in the dark, too.

"Last night, I was at a dinner party given by the governor of Pennsylvania, and one of the other guests was a woman who has just about single-handedly turned menopause from almost shameful to almost fashionable. When I told her what we were up to today, she asked if she could be on our panel."

A rustle of speculative whispers rushed through the crowd.

"As always, she's coming through for women's issues. For twenty years, this extraordinary human being has shaped the minds and opened the hearts of America. Though she lives in New York City now, she is truly Philadelphia's own..." which gave it away and a collective "Ohhh" swelled from the seats to the stage. They knew. Even I—who watched television only for the news and Brit wit—now knew the identity of our mystery panelist whose loyalty to her hometown was legend. The women rose to their feet before Andrea could announce her name, and then it got lost in an outburst of applause and cheers so you could barely hear her shout, "Fortune Simms!"

Iconic to half the planet, in life looking like a Masai warrior at six feet four inches, wrapped in a garment of purple and yellow tribal print, Fortune Simms strode on her endless legs to center stage, lifted her arms into a grand V, and shouted her signature question, "Who's In Charge of Your Life?"

The audience, comprised of five hundred MDs, PhDs, MSWs and MBAs, sent back the response in one voice, "No One But Me."

I heard Sidney Luskin mutter, "Shit, this will be a circus."

But it wasn't. We presented our ten-minute talks to a rapt audience. The energy generated by Fortune's appearance swept up everything in its path. She really was a multimedia phenomenon, galvanizing her public to whatever was her current pet project. And since Fortune was about to hit her fiftieth birthday, her daily talk show had been obsessively concerned with osteoporosis, arthritis, and, ta-da! Menopause.

I popped out my standard speech, warning about mistaking cancer symptoms for the normal signs of menopause. But I felt supercharged and the familiar phrases snapped as if they were fresh. Afterwards, I called for questions from the floor. One had to do with vaginal dryness and there was a general swish as half the audience took a swig of water. "Change of life should change the sexual part of your life only for the better. Let's put the men back in menopause," I said, which elicited a mix of laughter and applause and a whoop from Fortune.

From a center table, a woman shot up, hand waving. "Arletta Washington, Black Women's Support Alliance. My question has to do with racial differences in the menopause experience. Specifically, do black women undergo a different kind of menopause than Caucasians? Because from what I hear when we all get together, it sure doesn't sound the same to me."

"In what way?" I prodded.

"For one, we seem to suffer more and whine less."

When the laughter died down, I said, "What you're observing has also been noted in some studies. Whereas Caucasian women may see menopause as a signal of aging and slowing down, African American women tend to view it as a liberation from the responsibilities of childbearing and even welcome it as a time to pursue their own interests."

"Amen," Fortune stage-whispered.

"I saw this firsthand when I ran a free clinic in downtown Baltimore with a mostly African American patient population." In the margin of my vision I registered Fortune's gaze sharpening, and after I took a few more questions she lead a generous outburst of applause.

At the cocktail reception following, she made her way to my side. A large man wearing a headset and a blazer with an FS emblem on its pocket stationed himself a few steps away, his eyes always on her.

"So, Doctor Gwyn," she'd nicknamed me already. "Looks like you knocked them dead out there."

"Not exactly a sterling recommendation for a doctor," I said with a laugh.

"Now that's what I mean. That's exactly what I'm looking for."

"I'm sorry?"

"The quick wit. The sassy mouth. You relate as a human being, not only as a doctor. I watched how you connected with those women when you took their questions. You didn't pull any of that high-and-mighty doctor crap—you know, the scientific jargon, the superior attitude. You respected them. You *honored* them."

This was Fortunespeak. Not my style, but, God knows, it worked for her.

"You're a natural for television and you'll be great on my show. No, wait, let me finish." She cut off any possible protest. "Around the holiday season, we're planning a series on making and keeping life-changing resolutions. And of course, at the top of the list is health. You'd cover the gynecological angle. I'm not sure of the format yet. My producers can work it out with you. You'll be doing the women of America a great service."

I envisioned Bethany McGowan wracked with envy, Seymour Bernstein incredulous and awed in that order.

I said, "Since you put it that way, how can I decline?"

"Wonderful." She laid on the glorious Fortune smile. "We pay scale. But I'll personally make a donation to that Baltimore clinic you manage."

"That's very kind of you. But we had to close the Clinic for lack of funding."

"Really? Well, that's a *damn* shame. How much would it take to reopen?"

"At least a half a million." I hadn't just tumbled off the turnip truck. Fortune Simms's pockets were unfathomably deep.

Before I could get on with my pitch, my fellow panel member Peggy McGrory wiggled her way into our duet. She carried a copy of *Good Times, Good Fortune,* Fortune's guidebook through the perils of middle age. The books were stacked near the bar, gifts to the Forum officers and the panel.

Peggy offered up her copy as if it were an animal sacrifice. I peered over as Fortune signed it, *Dear Peggy*

*McGrory: You are in charge of your life. Fortune Simms.* You'd have thought that Peggy, a full professor at Yale, winner of a National Book Award, and a former member of the U.S. Olympic Women's Luge Team, might have drawn that conclusion for herself. But no, she read the inscription with the same reverence she would have accorded the Dead Sea Scrolls and simpered her thank-yous as she backed away, nearly bowing.

I handed over my book. It was intended as a gift for Sylvie so there wasn't going to be a "Take Charge of Your Life" inscription, which might prematurely launch her out of my father's cockeyed universe in East Baltimore.

We did a little negotiating and ended up with *To Sylvie, a caring woman. Thank you for being there,* which Sylvie could read as being in front of the old RCA every day watching Fortune or being there for me and my dad, keeping him out of a nursing home.

"Then we'll see you in December." Fortune handed my business card off to the man in the headset.

"Wouldn't miss it for the world," I answered.

———

That evening, still wound up, still full of myself, I called to check on my father. After going nowhere with our standard opening mishmash, I said, "Today I met someone you see on TV every day, Daddy. Fortune Simms. You know Fortune Simms. The tall African American lady on channel 11. 'Take charge of your life.'" Who knew which memory was sharp enough to break through the Alzheimer's membrane?

"Who is this?" he said, his agitation mounting.

Sylvie commandeered the phone. "He's okay?" I asked.

"Mr. Harald needs to drink more water. But he shoves the glass away."

"Give him tea and orange juice. Sylvie, I met Fortune Simms today. I had her autograph her book just for you."

"Is that right?" Unenthusiastic.

I barreled on. "She wants me to be on her show next year."

"We don't watch it anymore. Too much talk of health problems. We've got enough of health problems around here. Why do I need to hear about how my bones are going to crumble when I'm old and gray? We watch *Maury Povich*. Now that's an interesting show. Today was about girls who fell in love with their stepbrothers."

Which helped put everything back in perspective.

## Chapter 21

Sunday morning, as I got ready for breakfast with Simon, my hands, always steady in surgery, jiggled applying makeup, skidding my eyeliner on a landscape of fine wrinkles.

I still hadn't decided whether to let Hank Fischman smooth out my eyelids and lift my brows. A couple of hours in his surgi-center and I'd have twenty-year-old eyelids in a fifty-four-year-old face. Ah, the hell with it. I smudged the kohl and told myself smudged was the latest style and that Simon, a cerebral man, wouldn't care anyway. He'd be focused on what I said and not on how I looked. He'd be interested in my endothelium, the lower cells where the real work takes place, not my epithelium, the topcoat that is vanity, all vanity.

I pacified myself with this thought while smoothing on a shimmer of lip gloss. The label claimed to "add the plumpness of youth to thinning lips and prevent the lipstick feathering that arrives with age." Arrives with age. As if there were a party. As if anyone would invite it.

At a quarter of ten, the hotel phone rang. Simon said, "Am I too early? I caught an earlier train," sounding a bit nervous. Which I found sweetly disarming.

Emerging from the elevator, I spotted him rocking on his heels, biting his lip.

"Simon?"

He laid eyes on me and broke out a smile. I'd been wrong about the cerebral. He measured me like any man, took my hand, and backed me off to get the whole picture. "You're worth the trip. You really are worth traveling to bloody Philadelphia. I'm starved. Are you hungry? Let's get some breakfast."

He wore a V-neck sweater that appeared to be cashmere and carried a camel-hair jacket and tweed cap, its Harrods label visible. His shirt glowed a genteel blue above pleated chinos. His feet were shod in obviously Italian loafers fashioned from the hide of unborn piglet. Disgustingly beautiful. The shoes. *He* was just knock-out handsome.

We talked about safe things at first. My survey. His research. I'd steered the seating so he was positioned on my left, my better profile, and between bites of scrambled egg I remembered to keep my head high, which hoisted up the neck slack. The Marriott had considerately bathed the room in warm, peach light.

"I really do think you're on the right track with your study. With proper care, you should turn out a respectable piece of work." I reeled from the backhanded compliment, but he was smiling impishly. "Now, let's talk about what really matters. I think people are more important than ideas, don't you?"

We presented our lives. I censored my history, transforming my mother into an eccentric who died of unstated causes when I was twenty-one. Nor did my divorce suffer from a burden of detail. Something about a divergence of paths. We were all very civilized. If not for us, then for the sake of our twin sons, the brilliant Whit, the artistic Drew. Simon seemed satisfied with this vague bio, as washed in flattering light as the dining room. I spouted these white lies with only the most fleeting discomfort. He didn't ask a single question.

And then he floored me with his honesty.

His marriage had been complicated. It had produced a son, a teenager now, with "issues." The divorce hadn't been pleasant. Then again, few are. Cynara, the ex, was a decent woman, but, according to Simon, "had never really grown up. She's forty-six going on sixteen."

My first thought was: forty-six. Eight years younger than I. Argh. Bad start. Second was forty-six going on sixteen sounded like a nifty trick to me.

I sipped my coffee, trying to look sympathetic.

"The truth is I was less than the perfect husband and father. Far too involved with my work. And so in the last few years Cynara found someone who would give her the attention she craved."

"'Cynara. I have been faithful to thee, Cynara, in my fashion,'" I quoted the poem I'd learned in high school, not unaware of the irony of the line, and saw his eyes light. He chimed in so we chanted together, "'And I am desolate and sick of an old passion, Yea hungry for the lips of my desire.'"

The hovering busboy stopped fiddling with our water glasses and looked at us, first at Simon, then at me. Had he heard the walloping beat of someone's heart?

Simon covered my hand with his. "My word, you are a find," he murmured. Then his eyes clouded. "You need to know something, Gwyneth. And this may all seem very premature to you, but best lay it all out in the open at the outset is what I believe, so you'll know what you're dealing with."

"I see," I said. Of course I didn't. I couldn't imagine what dark secret Simon York was about to confess. Was he practicing gynecology without a license? Fudging research data? Sniffing reagent chemicals under the fume hood? Cross-dressing in a mere PhD's lab coat?

I waited, breath trapped in my lungs.

"Well, the truth is, I'm not all that successful at my personal relationships," he said, and my breath came whooshing out. That was it? He was confessing that he was as fucked up as 90 percent of the dating world? I couldn't help it, I laughed. And then I protested.

"Really, Simon," I said. "I can't believe—"

He laid his finger against my lips to shush me. "No, I want you to hear the unvarnished truth straight away. The fact of the matter is I'm just not very skilled at the human give-and-take. For which I take full responsibility, but it's also true that I didn't have many positive role models. My father died when I was six, in another woman's arms, my mother made sure to tell me. She wasn't much of a mother either. Packed me off to boarding school right after Papa's funeral. So I never had any training in that area." He shoveled a forkful of scrambled eggs, never taking his eyes off me, as if he had more to say. So I took a bite of toast.

"My record on that score is not something I'm proud of." As he wiped his mouth with the cloth napkin, he looked genuinely pained. Then he brightened. "Still, I'm not a bad chap, really. And I'm working on it. Learning how to develop caring relationships. I've been reading all the latest self-help books you Americans are so good at writing. I'm taken by the quickness of the process, the efficiency. And I really do want to do better. I *know* I can do better if I just find the right person to do it for. With."

That dumped us into an uneasy silence for a minute filled by piano music as a tuxedoed man played Cole Porter circa 1935 behind us.

Fortunately, before too long the waiter arrived with Simon's tea. A pot of it. With a plate of lemon slices. Which broke the mood.

"Lemon, oh, no, no. Milk, please," he sent him off briskly. To me, back in his cheery mode: "I never understood this American penchant for lemon with tea. Don't you find it barbaric?"

"I drink iced tea with lemon," I said. It was a patriotic statement.

"Iced tea is an abomination. But let's not squabble." His eyes twinkled. "We have so little time. In fact," he glanced at his watch, "it looks like I'm going to have to be on my way if you're to get to your session. But we'll do this again very soon, won't we? See each other. Do you want that, Gwyneth?" He creased his forehead as if the answer were in doubt.

"Yes," I said. Well, croaked more than said.

In the lobby, he swung his jacket over his left shoulder and with a single, well-executed yank surrounded me with his arms, his scent. He kissed me. A strong yet tender kiss. I was too astonished to put any muscle behind my return. "I'll be in touch," he murmured.

"Good," I said, with just the right touch of confidence. And the warmth I felt climbing from chest to cheeks as he sent me a chipper last wave from the backseat of his cab, I decided wasn't a hot flash. Not this time. It was a happy, youthful glow.

———

He called the next morning at six, Haydn in the background, the rustle of papers in the foreground. "And how is Gwyneth this morning?"

"Too early to tell," I ventured, which elicited a chuckle, but registered.

"Apologies. But this is really the best time for me to call. I do all my clinical work in the morning, just stack up the surgeries. That way I can be in the lab by noon. So I need to get an early start. And once I swing into action, I get so busy, it's difficult to extricate myself."

"I didn't mean..." thinking, *Great, you've torpedoed him before he's even set sail.* But no.

"I've got a miserable day ahead so I figured I'd give myself a shot of sunshine before tackling it," he said as we both heard the distant beep that signals *callus interruptus.* "Whoops," Simon said. "That's mine I think. Probably my nurse. Got to go."

"Yes, of course. Me too."

———

Simon liked to keep in touch. He called mostly in the morning before he went off to the hospital. But sometimes at bedtime, just to say he was exhausted and couldn't talk much but wanted to hear my voice. I looked forward to those calls. We laughed, shared bits about ourselves. Occasionally, he made suggestions. A book I might like to read, a CD I should own. He was into geopolitics and chamber music. "What's that playing in the background?" he asked one night during the first week.

"Dinah Washington."

"Is she one of those rock and rollers?"

I saved that one for Whit, my jazz aficionado. He got a kick out of it.

We made a date, Simon and I, not for the coming weekend, but for the following. He laid out the plans. He'd fly to Baltimore and stay at the Harbor Place Hotel within walking distance of Waterview. "I'll try to get away for two full days. We'll have fun," he assured me. "I wish it could be sooner. We're busy people, you and I. But now that we've found each other, we need to find *time* for each other. Don't you agree, Gwyneth?"

Before I could answer, he got beeped for another call.

———

The entire week turned out...well, interesting, as I'd taught my sons to say when faced with Grandmother Berke's cooking. Life is a stew—sometimes it's palatable, sometimes it triggers the gag reflex.

Midweek, my father had a flight into health and we managed a two-minute rational conversation about my brother Rolfe rarely coming to see him. Nothing new. Although I was the main target for my mother's temper, from the time he was around three, my kid brother developed skills to duck the family drama. He'd burrow in a closet or dive under a bed, preferring even darkness and dust bunnies to the white hot fury of Mama on a rampage.

These days Rolfe visited for Easter and once in the summer, which was all his wife would allow. Nadine and Rolfe had known each other since fifth grade, so she'd been exposed to the Swanson family soap opera in prime time. I didn't blame Nadine for wanting Rolfe to keep his distance from his crazy clan.

"So it all falls on you," my father said. "It's not fair that you carry all the burden."

"You're no burden." I kissed his paper dry cheek.

"I know what I am. Sometimes I don't know *who* I am, but I know what I am." Which made both of us laugh, but my father brushed away tears and I swallowed mine.

On the Stan front, boyfriend Brad asked to borrow a cut crystal punch bowl he had Stan cede to me in the settlement. I wasn't only gracious during the conversation with a man I detested, I arranged to leave the bowl for him at the lobby desk with a recipe for Stan's favorite champagne punch.

I returned Seymour Bernstein's curt hello with a cheery one and complimented Bethany on her picking up an early stage ovarian cancer from some vague symptomatology. I asked after my patients' families and made sure the speculum was warm. I tiptoed through each universe trying to be a better person, more loving, forgiving, understanding, in hopes that God or nature or whatever wielded the power over my fate would continue to smile down on me. A lot of this was Simon-inspired, of course. And I hadn't even slept with him.

"You're putting me on," Fleur accused, after I caught her up. "All that hearts and flowers phone porno but no real sex?"

"Good God, when? Between the eggs and the scones? We only had breakfast."

"You were in a hotel. Okay, the restaurant. But you had a room. Was the elevator broken?"

"It was a first date, Fleur. And not even a real date," I protested.

"Oh, please. Should I sing a few choruses of 'Havah Nagilah' to remind you of a recent toss in the hay?"

"This is different."

"This has the potential to be serious, right?"

"Could be."

"Which means Harry Galligan is definitely out of the picture?"

She surprised me by remembering his last name.

"I'm not sure. Maybe. No."

Which might not have been fair to Harry given my initial attraction to Simon, but it was early in the game and

I wasn't quite ready to count the Irishman out. My brain told me he was a better match for me than the Englishman and I was pushing for my brain to take over from my heart or my gizzard or whatever was driving this initial rush of feeling for Simon York.

# Chapter 22

Thursday afternoon, Neil Potak popped into my office. Which alarmed me even before he opened his mouth because this particular partner, unlike the gregarious Seymour Bernstein, wasn't big on socializing. Neil's last pop-in had been the year before to tell me something had exploded in the autoclave in Examining Room Four.

"Any news on funding for the Clinic?" he asked now, gazing through my window where thunderclouds crowded the sky over the Inner Harbor.

I'd heard from the last prospect on my list. I said, "The Pearlmutter Family Foundation isn't funding startup projects. I'm still digging, but there's not much out there I haven't approached. Still," I tried to catch his eye, "I'm telling myself the pressure's off a little with UltaMed buying Covenant. Maybe they'll pitch in and get those patients on board."

Neil examined his very clean fingernails. "Listen," he said. "This is just a rumor so far, but I just got a call from a friend of mine at Covenant. The buzz over there is UltaMed is closing down the hospital. Giving it six months. They've called a staff meeting for," he checked his watch, "about now."

I'd been playing with a gel pen. Its extra-fine point glided perilously close to my wrist.

"That's got to be a mistake," I said. "There's no other hospital in a ten mile radius. They can't shut Covenant down."

"Everything turns on the bottom line these days." He shrugged. "Covenant's been hemorrhaging dollars for years. So maybe UltaMed is amputating. Seems like a logical move to me. You have a gangrenous foot—you cut it off."

I sent him a shocked look. "These are human beings we're talking about, Neil, not mixed metaphors. If Covenant shuts down, where are these people going to go?"

"Not here," Neil said much too quickly, his sharp amber eyes finally settling on me. "Bethany's dragging her feet on getting out the final report, but I've seen her preliminary draft on our pro bono numbers. We can't afford to absorb these uninsured patients. Not anymore. Not even a few. And you should know Seymour backs me up on this."

"Sonofabitch," I muttered after he closed the door. Then I phoned Dan Rosetti's office. My father's doctor was chief of gerontology at Covenant. If anyone could separate truth from scuttlebutt, Dan could. His receptionist said he'd been called to a 3 p.m. meeting of department heads. It was 3:15. Those hatchet meetings never lasted more than a half hour. If I hustled, I might be able to tag him on the way out.

I drove through West Baltimore under a steady drumbeat of rain. The famous white marble stoops fronting the formstone row houses were stained gray by the gloom, and a soggy mulch of early October leaves clogged the gutters. Everything looked as raw as I felt.

This neighborhood was a west side version of the one I'd grown up in across town. Working class. A tavern on every corner. A laundromat and a check cashing service flanked the storefront that used to house my women's clinic. It was now the Beulahland Tabernacle of Joyous Prayer. Covenant loomed like Old Mother Hubbard over the neighborhood, its red brick skirts spread across two city blocks, its bonnet, a smaller silver replica of Johns Hopkins Hospital's gold dome, washed dull in the dreary light. Just as my mother had hauled Rolfe and me to Hopkins for earaches and poison ivy, the folks around here used Covenant as their doctor's office.

No more.

When I hit Dan Rosetti's reception area in Covenant's physicians tower, his appointments secretary said, "He's still in the meeting, Dr. Berke. You've heard the latest?" She slashed two fingers across her throat.

I nodded. "Is it official?"

"Just came across on WBAL news." She glanced at her desk radio. "I've been working here twenty-one years. As my kids would say, this really sucks. Not for me so much. I just keep thinking, what's going to happen to our patients? All these poor seniors don't take change easily. Especially the Alzheimer ones."

I hadn't thought about that. My dad took the same green chair on every visit. Picked up but didn't read, couldn't read anymore, one of the large-print magazines stacked on the side table. He'd be lost in a new place.

"Gwyneth?" Dan Rosetti's voice rose behind me. I felt his hand light on my shoulder and turned to see a grim smile.

"Oh, Dan," I said, emotion flooding, surprising me. "What the hell is going on?"

"My office." He hitched his neck in that direction. "I'll tell you everything I know."

What he knew was my worst nightmare realized. UltaMed had filed the legal papers to sell Covenant. More official in this day of media power, they'd already released the news to the press.

"Covenant's a lost cause," Dan said. He'd been with the hospital since his residency there, which added up to three decades.

"And what happens to you?" I asked.

"Oh, I'll be fine. Union Memorial has been after me for years. They've got a first-rate gerontology department. The problem is Covenant has been eating the charges for a few patients of mine. Don't ask me what's in store for those folks now. Unless." He pressed fingers to his forehead. "I was thinking about you in there. About your clinic."

"My clinic," I sighed. "There *is* no clinic and it doesn't look like there ever will be. I've hit every foundation that sounded even remotely promising. I'm at a dead end, Dan."

"Maybe not," he said.

The phone rang. Dan peered at the caller ID. "One of my patients. Probably saw the bad news on TV. This shouldn't take long."

I took the moment to glance around his office. Awards from the Knights of Columbus, Polish Home Club, and Sons of Italy thanking him for his volunteer service shared the wall with his diplomas from Yale and Penn Medical School.

Sitting on his bookshelf was a mug painted with "#1 Dad" that had all the pixie charm of a kid's summer camp crafts project. And beside the mug, the inevitable clutch of family photos. In one, a younger Dan with pure black hair stood straight and proud as a Roman soldier beaming down on his captured Saxon bride. The wife was fair and pretty. In her lap perched a child of six or so, hair as flaxen as the mother's but bearing her father's generous smile. A more recent portrait of Mrs. Rosetti revealed how well she'd aged into what I guessed were her early forties.

By the time Dan hung up the phone, I'd already shifted my stare from the photos. There was not going to be a repeat of the debacle with Hank Fischman, the plastic surgeon, and the photos of his trophy family. Knowing too much about my colleague's private lives, their younger wives, was a passport to depression.

"So, you're having problems getting funding," Dan said, eyebrows knit pensively. "But I think with Covenant closing, you may have a better chance. Especially if you expand your vision somewhat. Now don't jump on me until you've heard me out. It's a women's clinic. No question. But now the need is even greater."

I chewed a knuckle, listening.

"One day a week, you add a pediatric component. Many of the women who come to see you have children. So this is a natural. We bring in some volunteer docs." He mentioned two of Baltimore's best pediatricians. "I guarantee you, if these guys don't sign on, I can find people who will. Or maybe we just do an open clinic one day a week. See whomever. Male. Female. All ages. Hell, I'm trained in internal medicine. I'll give up a morning. Maybe a day."

I shook my head, astounded at his offer. When the Clinic was operating, it was tough for me to squeeze one afternoon out of the practice. I'd added two nights a week on my own time and for the rest hired a couple of young physicians eager to moonlight. "This is very generous of you," I said. "You really think you can give up a day?"

"Why not? I'm fifty-seven years old. I'll be negotiating a new contract and I figure I can write my own ticket. I like to think I got into medicine to treat people, not their wallets. The Clinic will give me the opportunity to prove that."

What an amazing man! For a moment, in the gloom that was both outside and inside, hope flickered.

Still, every silver lining has its cloud. I found mine. "What makes you think we can bring this off?" I asked. "A full-service clinic even for one or two days a week is going to take serious money for staff, equipment, insurance. If I couldn't get backing for my little storefront…"

"Aha. But with a broader patient base, we might have a better shot at landing some grants," he countered. "If you like, I'll help you write the proposal. Anyway, think about it."

I promised I would.

And I did. I even sketched out a revised mission statement. But then something came up and for the next few weeks I found myself preoccupied with a situation that was even more urgent and much, much closer to home. Kat was in trouble.

*Chapter 23*

No call from her in nearly a week and then when she surfaced, I wished she hadn't. Not that way.

I was checking on my patient after a four-hour procedure Friday morning. My arches hurt, but I was still on my surgical high in the recovery room when my pager went off.

I located an empty cubicle and returned Kat's call. I thought maybe she wanted to talk about her gallery show, which was scheduled to open in a few weeks. Or that she needed to vent about Summer or Lee. I forgot she never called during the workday except in an emergency. She'd phoned when her sister was diagnosed with cancer and when the police called about Ethan. Now, I heard her voice and it was hollow as bamboo.

"Gwyn, I've found a lump in my breast."

Friday midday isn't a good time to discover a lump. Many of our docs start their weekend early. When Kat called, Neil Potak, her gynecologist, was on the far nine at the Woodholme Country Club. At the hospital, the Breast Imaging Center wound down by midafternoon and the odds of getting someone to take a look or a feel were dicey.

Unless you had connections. I had connections.

I told Kat to sit tight and give me five minutes. I called Radiology four floors down and snagged the chief tech Renee Carson on her way out and turned her around. She tagged Leah Abramovitz, my favorite radiologist, and within a half hour we pulled a team together for an unscheduled mammogram.

I caught Ibrahim Sukkar having a late lunch at his desk. He was the doctor I saw for my own breast check and he had the discerning fingers of a blind man. "Abe, I would consider it a personal favor if you'd take a look at my friend." I explained the situation.

"Of course," he said. Twenty minutes later, Kat reeled into the radiology waiting room looking as if she hadn't slept in days. Ashy complexioned and tangle haired, she'd thrown on one of Ethan's salvaged windbreakers over jeans and a T-shirt. Watching her remove it with jerky preoccupied movements, seeing those frantic eyes, I was glad I'd rallied the troops.

I hugged her, then held her hand while she rattled on nervously, "I'm so glad you're here. I can't believe you rounded up someone to see me. God, I can't even talk my mouth is so dry. I want a cigarette. I haven't smoked for fifteen years and I would kill for a Salem. That's how crazy I feel. Logically, I know it's probably nothing; 80 percent of lumps are benign, right? It's not like this torture is something brand-new." Kat had moderate fibrocystic disease. "I've been carrying around these two bags of jelly beans since I was thirteen and I've felt lumps before, but this is different. This feels like a piece of peanut brittle, but with one peanut in the center and no sharp edges."

I didn't like the sound of it, but I was saved from having to dissemble by Renee Carson flashing us her broadest smile.

"Hi, Dr. Berke. You're looking good. You can come in now, Mrs. Greenfield." Renee read her face and added tenderly, "It's okay, baby. We've kept the machine warm for you."

"Oh, God, I hate this."

We all hate it. For whom the bell tolls and each year you figure you've run out of time and it's about to toll for you. During my own mammograms, I'm bathed in agita, just another terrified woman. The precious MD, all the education, counts for nothing when it's your breasts in the vise. And I say the same prayer every year: "Forgive me for everything and protect me against wildly multiplying cells in the name of the Father, the Son, and the Holy Ghost, amen." I can't remember the last time I attended church except as a wedding guest, but I always promise that if I get through this mammogram with a passing grade, I'll start again. I never keep the promise.

I sent Kat off with another promise, one a friend could make but a physician couldn't. "Whatever it is, we'll take care of it. You'll be fine."

Fifteen minutes later, she shambled back to the cubby, teeth chattering, ties undone. "Oh, sweet Jesus, I'm glad that's over. She's a nice lady, that Renee. She says you operated on her years ago. She thinks you hung the moon. She says it shouldn't take long. Dr. Abramovitz doesn't have anyone ahead of me."

Renee drew back the curtain. "I hate to do this to you, but we need to reshoot. Now I don't want you to jump to any conclusions, sweetheart. This makes us all crazy, so I know what you're thinking, but I just want to position you a little differently. Here, let me help you with your gown."

As Kat slid by her, Renee widened her eyes at me.

The film of Kat's breast looked dicey and Abe Sukkar persuaded her to let him do a core needle biopsy that same afternoon. At four thirty, he delivered Kat back to me gulping breaths, but by the time we reached the hospital garage, her brain had already made its initial adjustment to the shock of dreadful possibility. Such a pliable organ, the brain. You'd think it would explode with some of the thoughts it has to process. But no, it just reconfigures its cells and moves on. Unless it goes nuts.

"We won't know until the lab work comes back. For now, it's inconclusive. Dr. Sukkar's words. Which means it could be..." She couldn't go on.

"It means what Abe said. Until the pathologist examines the cells under a microscope, it's just a questionable mass."

"Mass. That reminds me. I want to go to Mass on Sunday. Time to up the bidding in my bargaining with God." Kat twisted an ironic smile. "The agnostic in the foxhole. I'm such a cliché." She inhaled tremulously. "Four days of not knowing. It's like some medieval torture. By Tuesday, I'll be a total wreck."

"It's going to be a long weekend. Can Summer stay with you?"

"Summer's in New York with Tim, visiting his parents. I'm not going to screw up her outing."

"Lee?"

"No, not Lee. That's over. I haven't seen him in a week. We...all right *I* decided this was better for everyone concerned. Before it got too serious. Don't look at me like that."

"He's a great guy, Kat."

"There are other great guys. Let's just hope I'm around to enjoy them."

"Oh, Kat, you will be."

When we got to her car, she insisted on driving herself home. I didn't argue because medically she was in shape to drive and emotionally it wasn't a bad idea. Steering through rush hour traffic was an acceptable metaphor for what she was going to be doing over the next few days. Let her have the illusion, at least, of control.

"It will do me good. I'll put on QSR, blast out the Golden Oldies, and pretend I'm sixteen again. When life was simple and you didn't have crap like this to worry about." Her history. Not mine.

"Well, take it easy. I'm going to stop at home for a few things and then I hope you have fresh sheets on the guest room bed because I'm staying with you this weekend," I said.

"No. Really. It's okay, you don't need to. I'll be sleeping most of the time anyway."

"Maybe. But when you wake up and need a shoulder to cry on or you have any questions, I want to be there."

Surprisingly, she didn't protest further. "I really got lucky when I drew you in the dorm lottery, lo those many years ago. Don't think I don't know it." She squeezed my hand.

"Yeah, I could have been Brenda Cofee with the b.o. or Susie Lemberg who dried her diaphragm on the radiator, remember?"

That teased a smile. "I mean it. You and Fleur, I don't know what I'd do without you."

"That reminds me, I should call Fleur. If it's okay with you."

"Yes, it's okay, I guess. Sure. She'll be royally pissed if she's out of the loop."

"Knowing Fleur, she'll probably want to stay over, too."

"Hey, we're keeping a vigil here, not having a pajama party." But she looked pleased. Then in a quick turn into her subconscious, she said, "I don't care about the breast, you know. They can take it. They can take both of them. I've never fixated on my breasts anyway. Italians are ass people. A nice round ass, now there's a real symbol of womanhood. I'd fight like hell against an assectomy, but they can have my boobs. I just don't want to die. Not that way. I watched my sister die of breast cancer and I don't want to go down that road." She shivered.

"That was fifteen years ago. There are all kinds of new roads to go down that don't end in the place your sister did."

She slid behind the wheel of the trusty old Volvo she'd owned for a decade. I crouched by the open door. "You sure you're okay?"

"Yeah, I'm just scared shitless. I feel like such a coward. I'm trying not to catastrophize. That's what Ethan used to say I did. Always expect the worst. Well, maybe he can serve as my intermediary with God. Head death off at the pass."

"Ahh, Kat."

"You're right, you're right. For once, I'm going to visualize a happy ending. The biopsy comes back negative, no bad cells. It could come back negative, right, Gwyn? It could be nothing, couldn't it?"

I gave her the only right answer. "It certainly could be nothing." The "could" was the truth. But it was the "nothing" that became the weekend's mantra.

*Chapter 24*

Nature sent Kat a mockingly beautiful weekend to anguish through. The October sun shone, the temperature soared, and the warmth turned up the souvenir scent of summer flowers and the misplaced loamy aroma of spring. Stretched out in a patio chair, she spent the daylight hours overlooking her garden as the wind chimes tinkled and endless cups of chamomile tea cooled on the tray table next to her. Fleur and I observed a respectful silence and checked on her every few hours.

On Saturday, Harry Galligan tracked me down on my cell phone. He knew it was last minute but did I have any interest in catching a movie that night?

"Ah, Harry, what a nice idea," I said, "but I'm staying over with a friend for the weekend. She had a medical scare and now she's waiting for some test results. It's tough marking time by yourself. I'm here to lend moral support."

"You're doing the right thing." Pause. "The person with the medical problem, it's not that lady we met in your lobby, is it?"

I had to jog my memory. "Oh, Fleur. No, no. As a matter of fact, Fleur's staying over too. No, it's a different friend. Her name is Katherine, Kat."

"Well, tell Kat I'll be thinking good thoughts."

"I'll do that."

"Better yet, how about I come over later and bring you gals some Chinese food? You have to eat. And I'm sure no one's in the mood to cook."

"Wants to bring dinner," I mouthed to Fleur who nodded an enthusiastic yes.

"That's very kind of you, Harry, but I think this is a no-man's land for a couple of days."

"Ah, female problems. I understand. Maybe we can reschedule."

"Right."

After I hung up, Fleur said, "Wasn't that nice of him to think of bringing food? He's such a sweet man. And you're trading him in for a limey you've meet twice who lives two hundred miles away." She tapped her forehead. "Sharp, very sharp."

"Who's trading? Am I trading? It's much too early to trade," I said.

"Look how excited she got," Kat said, winking at Fleur. "The woman is most definitely trading."

———

That night, Kat downed three-quarters of a bottle of wine all by herself. By ten we were all quite squiffed and very giggly.

Fleur entertained us by reviewing her latest e-men.

"I've been online a lot with the Whiz, who's an aerospace engineer, and with Rocketman, who's not. Rocketman has a problem with premature ejaculation, hence the name. Stop that cackling, the two of you! There are worse afflictions and at least he's honest about it upfront."

The hysterical eruption that burst from Kat probably had more to do with her own situation than Fleur's inadvertent pun. All her emotions were very close to the skin. Fleur was providing a fine diversion. For a while, anyway, the patient's mind was teased from thoughts of doom.

"Seriously," Kat choked back her laughter, "I admire you for putting yourself out there with all these men. In your place, I couldn't do it."

"Aren't you lucky you're not in my place, then," Fleur answered. She didn't know Kat had broken up with Lee. But now Kat gave us the details. She'd told him their relationship was getting too serious too fast and they ought to take a hiatus to cool things down. To his credit, Lee hadn't given up without a fight. He argued against a separation. They could slow down for a while. See each other every other week. No, she insisted, she needed time and space.

"He said he cared about me and he thought I felt the same way. He felt we had a future. He was so surprised. And hurt." Kat's eyes clouded with the memory.

"Sure. He's crazy about you. And you're just crazy. I can't believe you gave up your wonderful Lee. And for what? To satisfy your daughter's outrageous demands. When did you have your backbone surgically removed?" Fleur asked, then looked shocked because the word "surgical" bounced us back into the frightening present. The loss of Lee, painful as it was, paled in comparison to losing a breast or your life.

Kat got there even before we did. "I'm comfortable with that decision. Especially now. Lee is young. He has his life ahead of him. Let him spend it with a healthy woman."

Fleur sprung to her feet. "That's ridiculous. Jesus! You're going to be fine. Right, Gwyn? She's going to be fine." She folded a slightly resistant Kat into her arms. "I am such an idiot. I didn't mean to upset you. You have enough to deal with. Shit. You're a surgeon, Gwyn. Why don't you sew up my mouth?"

———

Tuesday morning passed with no lab results for Kat. That afternoon, I attended a baby shower for one of our nurses in the boardroom at which Mindy, Seymour's new hire, made her debut. Brunette, fluffy, cusp of thirty, legs like a thoroughbred colt. She licked frosting from her fingers with scientific concentration. Another one with a prehensile tongue. Speaking of which, Bethany bobbed in for a minute to grab cake and shot a troubled glance at Seymour. He declined to register her entrance with as much as a blink, continuing his conversation with Neil and Ken Dempsey in a testosterone pocket near the window. But as he left, he touched my shoulder and rasped, gangster-like, out of the side of his mouth, "A word?"

We ducked into the empty snack room. He spoke quickly, as if we were about to be arrested by the thought police.

"Bethany came to me the other day with some cockamamie story that you think that she and I are...*grmph*...having some kind of inappropriate relationship."

I let him sweat. It was a pleasure to see his forehead glaze over like a petit four.

"Let me assure you, there is nothing untoward happening between us."

I snorted, but daintily. "Well, you might want to tell that to Bethany. She seems to think there is. Actually, she's under the impression that you two are in love."

Which elicited a cartoon smile. Wiggly at the edges. Like when Woody Woodpecker is about to go *splat!*

"Love?" he repeated. "She can't be serious. Now that proves we're talking about an unstable person. I'm no psychiatrist, but this is clearly a case of wishful thinking combined with vivid imagination. You need to consider the source."

I dearly wanted to smack him. "Sources, Seymour. Me among them. I suppose I hallucinated her foot creeping into your crotch under the boardroom table. Look, what you do on your own turf is your own business. When you bring it into the office, it becomes mine." *And Neil's* was the unspoken threat.

"Gwynnie," he said, as if we were pals, "I don't know what you saw or think you saw, or what the rumor mill is churning out or what crazy supposed confession you heard from Bethany McGowan, but she and I are not involved. Never have been, never will be. That's the truth, take it or leave it."

Before I could say, "Leave it," Barbara poked her head in. "Dr. Berke, a Kat Greenfield on line two."

"Send it into my office."

All this carping suddenly seemed petty and frivolous with Kat's life on the line.

"Dr. Sukkar just called. He got the lab results." Kat sounded calm, almost lighthearted. Relief washed over me. Then she said, "It's cancer."

Rocked back, I managed to stammer, "I'm so sorry, Kat. Are you okay?"

"Yeah, fine actually." I heard a quivering intake of breath. "All right, maybe not fine, but okay. Now that we know."

"Uhmm." My patients had taught me how to listen.

"The third shoe has fallen. You know I've been waiting twenty years. With my mom and Melanie getting hit, I figured it was just a matter of time for me. So now it's happened, and Dr. Sukkar can cut it out and if I'm lucky, I can get on with my life."

"Absolutely," I agreed. "Did he say anything else? What kind of tumor? What he has in mind for treatment?"

"Yeah, he talked about the tumor stuff. I wrote it down." She shuffled through papers. "I don't know where I put it now. You can call him. Actually, I have two little tumors."

An alarm buzzed. Multifocal tumors are disease multiplied. I said, "Little is good."

"He says they're really close together so he can take them both out in one scoop. I'd lose a lot of tissue but keep the breast. Then I'd have to have radiation. The other option is a mastectomy." She slurred the word as if to soften its serrated edge. We inhaled at the same time. Then Kat said, "The more tissue he takes, the better the chances of getting it all, right?"

"Actually, a study just crossed my desk…" I groped for papers, feeling around for my comfort zone. But Kat didn't want to hear any more and interrupted me.

"That's okay. I have time to think this through. Dr. Sukkar says it's not life threatening if we hold off a week. I need to get a second opinion for the insurance company anyway. You'll give me a name. And I have to call Joel and Dirk. The gallery guys. To postpone my show. What do you think?"

Life is so seductive, we rush back to it as soon as we can. Kat was worried about reprinting invitations even as the bad cells nibbled up the good cells.

"Let me talk to Abe and see what we're dealing with."

"We," Kat said, her voice softening. "You're in this with me, right, Gwyn?"

"Shoulder to shoulder. To the barricades."

"How seventies." She forced a laugh. "To the barricades, sure. But to the end? I mean, to the bitter end? If worse comes to worse, I don't want to suffer like my mother and Melanie."

I was pretty sure what she was asking of me. In that event, I would help her, but not the way she wanted.

"Which won't happen," I said. "Have you called Summer?"

"I'm at Summer's. She's having terrible morning sickness. Ugh, what lousy timing for this cancer crap. Summer hasn't needed me since she was ten or eleven and now she does and I can't even be there for her."

"Of course you can. And you will. You'll dance at your grandchild's wedding."

"Only if it's the waltz, the fox-trot, or the funky chicken. Those are the only dances I know. Do you remember how it used to irritate Ethan that I couldn't lindy? He was such a good dancer. He...oh God. Poor Ethan, he must be so worried about me."

"Cry it out," I urged as she gave in to sobs. "Cry it out, baby. It's good to cry."

I could have used a good cry myself, but Mindy was waiting to set up shop in my office for her first shot at sorting through my files and when I fled to the staff ladies room, I found Bethany camped out on the lounge crying hard enough for the both of us.

Actually, from a clinical standpoint the news about Kat wasn't all bad. Ibrahim Sukkar told me she had an infiltrating ductal carcinoma in her right breast. Very close by sat a ductal carcinoma *in situ*, a tiny noninvasive DCIS that also needed to come out. He could remove the breast, but he saw no need, nor did I. He'd do a lumpectomy, targeting both sites and removing plenty of surrounding tissue to make sure she was free and clear, after which she'd require radiation to kill off of any stray cells.

Not two minutes after I hung up with Abe, Simon called, unusual for midday.

"I miss you," he said, out of the blue, his voice all warm and toasty.

"I miss you too," I said with a sigh.

"You needn't sound so sad. It's good we miss each other. It bodes well for the relationship."

"It's not that. Kat, the friend I told you about? Her surgeon just phoned with the lab report. Malignant."

"I'm so sorry, Gwyneth," he said. Then his voice went from sympathetic to colleague-to-colleague as we discussed her prognosis.

Winding down, I said, "Thanks, it was good to be able to talk it out. It's nice that we speak the same language. I'm really looking forward to this weekend with you." An understatement. The prospect of two days with Simon was the bright light at the end of this dark tunnel of a week.

"Ah, about this weekend. The reason I called. I was wondering if we might postpone my visit. Just for a bit. I've got an article coming due for *Cervix*." One of the more fetchingly named of our academic journals. "And I need time to smooth out the bumps by my Monday deadline."

"Damn." I bit my lip against the disappointment, then stiffened it. "Well, business before pleasure, I suppose."

"Oh, dear. It sounds monumentally depressing when you put it that way."

"Unless..." I pulled a fast switcheroo. I invited him to the beach house. I hadn't been to Rehoboth since August, but Drew had stayed over recently and he was the tidy twin so it would be in fine shape to show off. Simon could work on his paper in Stan's study, which overlooked the sea. "Very inspiring," I assured him. "I know what it's like to be under the gun so I'll stay out of your way. But if you want to take a break, the beach is really lovely this time of year."

"How can I resist such an offer?"

"You can't," I answered, pleased with myself.

"Sold," he conceded with a laugh.

# Chapter 25

With Kat's diagnosis, I crashed head-on into my own mortality. My patients didn't sound the same grim alarm in me, but there was nothing like a little cancer in your own circle of friends to make you feel you had fifteen seconds to live. The warning prompted me to book an extra hour with my personal trainer. Twice in three days, I called my sons on some hokey pretext, really to tell them how much I loved them, and I made an appointment with my attorney to update my will.

Fleur approached danger from a different angle. She pushed harder to get hitched while she could still make it down the aisle without a walker.

The Plan hadn't stalled out, but it wasn't exactly zooming down the road to the wedding chapel either. Many men, nothing in platinum with baguettes to show for it. Nonetheless, Fleur was convinced that all she could do was play the odds. The more potentials she met, the more likely she'd find husband material.

Within hours of Kat's mammogram, in a death-defying frenzy, she signed up for a dating service called Cocktails for Two and its spin-off, Supper at Seven. If a slippery old codger escaped those two nets, she could catch him at

Linen and Silver, a dinner plan for the over-fifty crowd. All this eating and drinking would be hell on her diet, but she was determined to lasso a date for New Year's Eve. And she held me to some promise she said I made to go with her to Hannah Pechter's, a matchmaker from Pikesville, a Jewish area in the suburbs.

"Don't tell me you don't remember saying you'd go with me Thursday night."

Sometimes I thought Fleur made these things up. She dug around in her wallet and handed over a business card.

"Shidduchs and Sheitels," I read. "What's a *shidduch*?"

"A *shidduch* is an arranged match. A *sheitel* is a wig the orthodox women wear. Some sex-crazed rabbi invented the myth that a woman's hair holds the power to distract men from holy things. And this was way before conditioners. So only a husband can look upon his wife's natural tresses. For the rest of the world, the religious babes tuck their own hair under a wig as soon as they say 'I do.' They're really very good quality, these *sheitels*. All natural hair. Hannah sells them on the side."

At the last moment, she persuaded Kat to join us. "Come on," Fleur urged, "you need a good laugh. This should get an 8.6 on the Rickles scale."

Before Kat could change her mind, Fleur and I zipped by to fetch her. The evening was mild for mid-October but Kat was dressed for the chill December in her soul. Her skirt was one of those Mexican striped things she favored, longer than Hannah Pechter's modest midi, and she'd wrapped a fringed shawl tightly around her. Over that, a jacket.

"Welcome to Shidduchs and Sheitels, where the elite meet and greet." Hannah shooed us in, then backed up to take Fleur in with a measuring gaze. "I wish I had a hundred like you. They're going to batter down my door."

"From your mouth to God's ears," Fleur said, and the matchmaker stared at her as if she were something edible smeared with cream cheese.

Then she said, "For you, Fleur dear, I've got ten hand-selected prospects on video. You'll look at those tonight. If nothing appeals to you, next week you'll look at ten more, and if you don't like any of those, I'll send you to my brother-in-law the optometrist to check those beautiful blue eyes of yours. Come, let's get started."

Following her tiny figure down the hall, we passed a room lined with shelves of wigs on disembodied, featureless foam heads. "That's my other business. Mostly it's for religious women, but we also have some for cancer patients. For when they undergo chemo."

I heard Kat's tread hesitate behind me and reached back for her hand.

Hannah's viewing room was dominated by a big-screen TV. On the coffee table, she'd arranged a carafe of coffee, four mugs, a large plate of strudel, and a manila folder. Fleur automatically reached for a piece of strudel and Hannah automatically moved the plate towards Kat and me.

"This is my middle son, Yossi," Hannah announced, as a thin, prepubescent boy entered the room. "One day, he'll take over the business and then it will be third generation." She spat twice in her hand, saying, "Poi poi," which Fleur explained was a shield against the evil eye that could steal your good fortune. "Why am I so successful? Because I provide a personal service, not like on the Internet where you could be talking to a convict for all you know. Here everyone fills out detailed questionnaires. Fleur described herself to a T. Then you make a video. Yossi will video Fleur tonight and, just as I show you videos of them, they see a video of you."

"You're going to make a video, Fleur? You never told us," Kat said, obviously tickled. I was glad she'd come with us. Shidduchs and Sheitels was just the right medicine for her troubled heart.

"Do we have to do this?" Fleur groaned.

"Please, you're going to be wonderful. The quality will shine through. Now let's take a look at the cream of my over-fifty crop, selected personally by me for you. Yossi will pop the videos in and out." Hannah handed Fleur the folder which contained a profile and photo of each candidate. "I recommend you make notes or you'll never remember the nuances. And please, don't write someone off just because he has a mole or a lisp. We're all made in the image of *Hashem,* but that doesn't mean exact. No soul on Earth is perfect. Kat, there's a rheostat above you to dim the lights. Yossi, shove in Milton Rosenthal, please."

Milton, sixty, bald and baby-faced, led the video parade. He'd lost his wife the year before. Most of Hannah's men were widowers. "At least you know these are not fly-by-nights or love 'em and leave 'ems. These men were happily married and they want to be again."

Fleur nodded somberly. She'd had her fill of fly-by-nights.

Ira sold real estate. Very successful but he had psoriasis. Ken and David whizzed by.

Fleur jotted furiously.

Next came Elliot, who spoke with a slight British accent. I perked up. Fleur shook her head no. Elliot had a sweet smile and a winning personality but kept kosher.

Barry, Mark, Howard, Lester, and Sandy followed in a blur. And last, but certainly not least: Victor. "A raincoat salesman. But high-end. Very attractive. The women flock to him like birds to birdseed. Unfortunately, the kind he attracts, he doesn't want. Listen."

"What I'm looking for is someone kind and generous, with a zest for life. A person who will share my interests such as Chinese cooking and going to flea markets. I'm also a sailor of sorts. I keep my twenty-two-foot Sunseeker docked in Annapolis, so I'm looking for a first mate."

Kat and I snorted and Fleur rolled her eyes, but she placed a check mark next to his name

At the end Fleur decided on Howard, Victor, Barry, Ken, and Milton. Five more than she'd come in with.

"Excellent choices," Hannah *kvelled*, beaming like a lighthouse.

I asked Fleur, "Are you going to mention that you're a convert?"

Hannah vetoed the idea. "Don't go into it. They take one look at you, they know you weren't born Jewish. They also know you're Jewish now or I wouldn't take you as a client. You don't have to delve deeply for the introduction. Howard, the periodontist, didn't mention he had prostate cancer. He's cured."

Fleur had been a thin child until she turned eight, she once told me. After her father—the spouse with the money—divorced her mother—who had the better pedigree—Fleur and her brother Kenyon began to smother their sorrow in Cheetos and chips. Kenyon was pushing 350 pounds when he died of a heart attack at forty-eight.

I didn't define Fleur by her weight, but too often she did.

While the camera rolled, Fleur also rolled merrily along with her narrative. She talked about her work, her interest in early American silver, and her love of English mystery novels. Then she said, "And I like all kinds of cuisine, as you might have noticed."

"Yossi, stop the filming," Hannah called out. To Fleur she said gently, "I don't think you should bring it up about your weight. It's self-evident. Why make it an issue? They'll see zaftig. Many men appreciate zaftig, but there's no need to emphasize."

"Right." Fleur resumed to explain why she never married. "When most of my friends were meeting and dating their husbands-to-be, I was in business school. Soon I started my own successful business, and I was spending all my time doing that and marriage didn't seem a priority." Hannah nodded happily through this. "Then I met that special someone and fell in love. We were together for fourteen years, but he never seemed to get around to proposing."

"Cut!"

"The way it works," Hannah said at the door, "is I'll show your video to the five men you selected and they take it from there. And Fleur, if you don't get a call by mid-week, phone me. Sometimes they need a little nudge."

I had the feeling she had a set of very sharp elbows.

She handed us our jackets. "It was nice meeting you, Gwyneth. What kind of name is Gwyneth, if I may ask?"

"I'm half German, half Norwegian. But I think it's an English name. My mother took it from a book with a heroine named Gwyneth." Doubtless one of those trashy novels she'd devoured. As if her fantasy life weren't sufficiently vivid.

No score on any count. Fleur tried to give me a boost. "Gwyneth is a doctor."

Hannah looked puzzled, as if she couldn't quite fit the idea of doctor with this shiksa in a sweatshirt and jeans. It clicked finally. "Really? And your specialty is...?"

"Gynecology. I'm a gynecologic oncologist, which means..."

"I know what oncology means," Hannah said. "You're unusually attractive for a doctor. A classical face. It's a shame you're not Jewish. And you, Kat. So sweet and quiet. You're not currently married either, I see."

Kat wasn't wearing her wedding band. I hadn't noticed before, but it must have vanished between cleaning out Ethan's closet and the farewell to Lee.

"I know I could find someone for you. If you sign up tonight, I'll give both you and Fleur a 10 percent discount."

"I'm not Jewish either," Kat said.

"Greenfield?"

"My late husband was Jewish, but I never converted. I'm Italian. Catholic. Kind of lapsed Catholic. And you wouldn't want me anyway. I'm damaged goods." Kat's laugh was brittle.

"What did you say?" I couldn't have heard correctly.

She ignored me. "I was just diagnosed with breast cancer. I'm being operated on next week. I may wind up with one breast. I don't think they're coming out of the woodwork for single-breasted women."

"You're right," Hannah said. "I won't disagree with you."

Fleur's face blanched, except for two pink alarm spots on her cheeks. And I said, "My God, that's ridiculous!"

"Please," Hannah held up a halting hand. "Let me finish. Kat could be right that there are some men out there who would reject a woman with one breast. Who knows what evil or pettiness lurks in a person's heart? But what I'd say to you about those men is why would you want them?"

"I don't want them. I'm just saying no man would want me."

"You think so? Because of a missing breast? I can tell you for a fact there are men who couldn't care less about a breast. They look deeper, to what beats under it."

"Thank you, Hannah, that's very kind of you." Kat shrugged on her jacket as she shrugged off Hannah's comforting words.

But the indomitable Hannah would not be brushed aside. "I just wish you were Jewish so I could prove it to you. So I could line them up for you."

"Really," Kat said, showing her discomfort, her need to get out of there. She'd been distracted for the moment by Fleur's adventure, but now the entertainment was over and it was dark outside.

On the car ride home, I fumed, "Where did that come from, that bullshit about damaged goods? That's not you talking, Kat."

"Maybe not the old me. Maybe that's the new one-breasted me."

I let it go by. But Fleur couldn't. "First of all, I didn't know you decided on a mastectomy. Second, whatever you decide, you have a man who would love you for yourself. Do you think Lee would leave you because you have one breast?"

"Lee is irrelevant. Don't bring up Lee."

A few minutes later she mumbled, "Summer thinks Dr. Sukkar is medieval for even considering a mastectomy."

Aha and of course. "Summer thinks?" I seethed. "Did Summer earn a medical degree when we weren't looking?"

"And even if he just scoops out a big hunk of my breast, she's afraid I'll look distorted. She really thinks he should do two small lumpectomies. She says breast-conserving surgery is what everyone is getting these days."

I shouldn't have, but I lost it. I spun around in my seat and fixed on the shadow of her. "Just listen to you. This is not highlighting your hair or Botoxing your forehead. This has nothing to do with what everybody is getting, as if there's a fashion to breast surgery. And it's not like Abe is pushing a mastectomy. He offered you the option of a lumpectomy. He thinks you'll do fine with that. Yes, he has to remove more tissue than if there were only one tumor. But if you're not happy with your appearance, you can always have reconstructive surgery."

"I want to be able to look at myself in the mirror without cringing."

"That has nothing to do with your breast, Kat. If you don't want to cringe when you look at yourself, stop giving in to Summer whenever she puts the screws to you."

Of course, I was sorry as soon as I said it. Kat made a *umpf* sound like she'd been punched and I curled into a cocoon of guilt and regret in the front passenger seat. Snapping at Kat when she was so fragile was unforgivable. And who was I to dictate the terms of her relationship with her only child?

Then, just as we pulled up to her door, Kat's new cell phone beeped. It was Summer, from the emergency room. She'd been throwing up all day and Tim was concerned she was dehydrating and insisted on driving her to the hospital. She was already hooked up to an IV to replenish her fluids and they were going to keep her overnight. Tim was with her but she wanted her mama. I couldn't blame her for that. But she'd forgotten her overnight case. Could Kat pack it for her? She just couldn't bear those icky hospital gowns. And don't forget her hairbrush.

Which steamed me all over again, but for once I kept my mouth shut.

By the time we rerouted to Summer's and dropped Kat off at the hospital, it was after midnight. Fleur was bleary as we walked through the Waterview lobby, but she revived enough in the elevator to say with some passion, "I can't believe Kat's allowing Summer to run her life. Taking orders from that prissy little twerp. Ditching Lee. It really burns me."

"Bottom line, it's none of our business."

"Of course it is, we're her friends."

"Her nonjudgmental friends until she gets the cancer taken care of."

"Yeah, whatever," Fleur muttered, grudgingly. "But I swear, if everything turns out all right on that front, I'm going to take Summer on. Face-to-face, femmo a femmo. Either that or call Lee and make him come to the rescue."

"You wouldn't. You'd better not."

"Just watch me!" Fleur said.

# Chapter 26

Simon's beach weekend with me began on a shaky note. In spite of his Church of England face, he was pulled out of line at Kennedy, wanded, and frisked, a jolt for someone whose standard airport greeters, like Dr. Tashiki back in London, tended to fawn and bow. Then he got stacked up over Baltimore-Washington International for twenty minutes and I turned up late because an airport cop chased me into circling for a half hour. So I expected a grouchy traveler. But no, when I picked him up at the arrivals curb, he radiated good spirits.

He slid into the passenger seat and pecked my cheek. "I think the entire country is having a nervous breakdown—except for you and me, of course," he smiled. "As for you, when I didn't see the car I concluded you'd probably given up on me. But all's well that ends well."

While a horn blared behind us, we sat just looking at each other. With the silver hair, the chin cleft, the clever gray eyes, he really was a stunner.

Then *he* said to *me*, "I'd forgotten how damned attractive you are, Gwyneth."

"Well, thanks. But we'll see if you feel the same way Sunday after two days together."

He threw his head back and gave a hearty laugh. "Ever the optimist, are you? We're going to have a wonderful time."

By the time we arrived at Crosswinds, he was beat. I was wiped from the drive. We collapsed. In separate bedrooms, of course.

Saturday morning I woke to an anemic disc of a sun cranking itself barely above the waterline. From my window, the sea looked insipid, the sand chilly and uninviting, and I wondered whether this beach weekend with Simon was one of my better ideas.

Surprise. He was up, dressed, fully charged, and tossing through the kitchen drawers when I walked in on him.

"About time, you slugabed." He gave me a soft citrus-scented kiss on my neck.

"I like your aftershave," I whispered, tingling down to my flip-flops.

He nuzzled the hollow of my shoulder. *Oh, God.*

Gently, I managed to tug myself away to toast bagels and brew the coffee he opted for instead of tea-bag tea. Over breakfast, he regaled me with stories about his recent trip to Saudi Arabia, where he'd treated the women of the Royal Family. Afterwards I set him up in Stan's study, a room the size of New Jersey, with a seven-foot-long Eames elbow desk that I'd bought to replace Stan's antique partner's desk.

"Anything else you need?" I asked from a chary distance.

He surveyed the desk, the sumptuous oak and leather ergonomically correct swivel chair, the light falling on his laptop screen from the wide-angled view of the beach through the window wall, and finally me.

"I need a real kiss," he beckoned. "Can't work without one." He corralled me into his arms. Oh, the man could kiss. This one was hot and sweet and tasted of hazelnut coffee.

I caught my breath and plunged into a second kiss. And then, dear God, something delicious stirred below the equator. Before I had time to relish that sensation, he released me.

"There, that should hold us for a while. Why don't you do whatever it is you do Saturday mornings? Pop in about eleven thirty and we'll see how far I've got with this damnable paper." He applied a hand to my back and gently but firmly shoved me toward the door.

Simon liked women. You can tell when a man really appreciates the opposite gender. Stan, for example, thought we were an inferior species and got itchy and bitchy in our company. This was something I observed throughout our marriage but understood only in hindsight. Simon, on the other hand, brightened with pleasure in the company of women. So I wasn't surprised that women seemed to like him back.

My neighbor and Crosswinds' architect Sue Duffy, for example. Handsome at fifty, Sue was built like a mythical creature: beautiful woman waist up, all ass below. As an architect and a big-butted woman, she prided herself on seeing beyond structure. Her practiced eye drove through the struts and bones into the core strength of a house, she'd once told me. I suspected it worked with people too, because as she and Simon conversed, her eyes sharpened, calculating. Poised for good-bye on the threshold, she said out of his hearing, "Now that's a fine example of the best of imported goods. When was the last time I had a conversation about Christopher Wren and English baroque architecture? Sweetheart, this one's a find."

That afternoon, Simon discussed Persian art of the Qajar period with Yasaman Shariyeh, owner of the Afsoon Art Gallery, all of thirty-five and exotically beautiful with velvet brown eyes and luminous golden skin.

As we were about to leave with his purchase of a small print, he handed her his business card. "If you find the match to that print, call me."

"Yes, of course." She glanced down. "I'll do that, ah, Dr. York." Very proper, although she brushed her fingers against his in the transaction. He looked at me and frowned as if she'd misinterpreted his interest.

Back outside, he bent down and rubbed his cheek against mine, like an eraser, erasing all doubts that I was his one and only. Then he wound his arm around my waist and we meandered like that to Rehoboth Avenue.

He halted in front of the window of The Cook's Tour. "You need loose tea and a tea strainer instead of those tea bags you use."

"Not here," I said quickly, trying to steer him away from Brad's shop. "Their prices are sky-high. There's a shop down the street..." But he barreled in and I followed, praying.

Brad was not in evidence. *Thank you, God.* No Stan either. *Amen.*

Betsy Whitkin, who'd once cleaned Crosswinds as part of a Merry Maids crew, was languishing behind the counter reading *Cosmo* when we interrupted her. She nodded at me and talked to Simon about English cheeses until I led him into the aisles of Brad's overpriced inventory. We collected a tea strainer, sacks of Darjeeling and Assam teas, a box of Duchy Gingered Biscuits, and a jar of Fortnum & Mason gooseberry preserves. All of which, it turned out, got him hot, because back at the house after a proper English tea, I'd barely wiped the crumbs from my lips when he took me in his arms and said in a hoarse voice, "I want to make love to you, Gwyneth."

Well, yes of course, I'd known when I invited him it would happen. A beach house. Waves crashing. Gulls cawing softly in the distance. As the day chilled down, I'd turned on the gas fireplace in the living room which made authentic flickering shadows on the wall. Thanks to Stan's state-of-the-art stereo system, flamenco music throbbed throughout the house. Everything encouraged us. Nothing stopped us. God knows, I wanted it. Whatever had stirred up the original *coup de foudre* was still working. My mouth was so dry with longing, I could barely get the words out.

"Do you have protection?" I murmured. STDs were an age-defying menace.

"I'm a physician, my darling. Of course."

"HIV test?"

"Last time a month ago. Negative." So romantic, the language of twenty-first-century love.

What did I expect going in? Well, supereducated men tend not to be fabulous in bed. They work too much in their eggheads. Overthink the process. Make love as if they'd learned it from one of those Arthur Murray charts with the footprints. One, two, three, bump; four, five, six, grind. Lousy rhythm, no music. So I suppose I expected nerd-a-go-go.

I got Baryshnikov.

Joined at the lips and the hips, we inched our way into the bedroom. Two feet from the bed, groggy with lust, I fumbled with the buttons on my blouse.

"No, let me," he said. With his surgeon's nimble fingers, he unbuttoned me, peeled down my jeans, and tossed them. As I fought to breathe, he teased me, slowly unwrapping me from the last layer of overpriced Victoria's Secret froth, brushing velvet kisses on my shivering flesh.

"Oh, God, Simon," I heard myself slur, felt myself slip into that gorgeous drunken state where inhibitions crumble and every gesture is played out in slow motion.

And then the cool air against my flesh stirred a frisson of worry. Just in case, I'd draped a silk robe the color of crème brulée on a side chair. Just in case, I'd set the lights low. And from the bedroom fireplace, gaslight flickered camouflaging shadows. But still, my nude wasn't a sprightly twenty-year-old's nude. Not even a ripe forty-year-old's nude. And Simon, I expected, had his choice of vintages.

He said, "Don't," as I reached the robe. "Let me see you. Please, darling, I need to see you." I let the robe drop, heard his quick intake of breath. "You're beautiful," he whispered. And that "beautiful" released me so I could stop fretting about myself and concentrate on him as he slowly, tantalizingly removed his trousers and shirt and stepped over them.

Simon York à la carte, all muscle, curly chest hair, and burning eyes looked—if this were possible—better than Simon York in his usual state of Savile Row perfection. Think Heathcliff with that quintessential English face, the sensual hint of overbite, the square jaw burnished with five o'clock shadow. Think great English lion. The one the sun never sets on. Think normally sleek silver hair, a tousled mane. Noble features softened by desire.

And then he laughed, a deep rumble. "Look at what you've done to me." He smiled down on the huge hard-on in full salute. "That's from you. And *for* you. Do you want that? I want to give you that."

Oh, I know Fleur likes to say, "It ain't the size of the clapper that makes for the toll of the bell." And she's right in principle, but I gasped at the sight of Simon so huge, so ready for me. I went to him. Ran my fingers down his muscled back. Gripped his shoulders and pressed myself to him. Rocked against that urgent hardness and heard his low growl before I slipped my tongue between his teeth.

He returned my kisses. So deep. So wet. Against his warm flesh, I inhaled Eau de Simon, a wild perfume of citrus aftershave, sweat, and musk. I licked that sweet saltiness, then traced my tongue down his neck and heard his breath go rough. He glided a path along my cleavage, drew wet circles to the left, to the right, put his mouth to one nipple then the other. I moaned my arousal. And as his tongue slid its descent, I swayed and staggered back against the wall, beyond hot, beyond fevered, approaching throwing off sparks.

And yet I said, "Don't," to the top of his head as he sunk to his knees. "Not yet." Meaning not that I wasn't moist with eagerness but that what he had in mind was so intimate we needed more time to…

He looked up at me, his eyes intense. "Please. I want to. You do want me to."

I nodded and lost him. Lost myself in him as he worked that devilish tongue. Faint with pleasure, I braced myself against the wall and just…let…it…happen.

When he came up for air, he murmured, "You taste like honey." Answering every woman's question, every woman's secret fear. "Delicious. God, I want to fuck you." So said my brilliant British scientist whose usual vocabulary was pristine, and I was putty. Literally, I felt my flesh melt into something yielding, malleable, able to be shaped to any desire. We hit the bed, tumbled onto my six-hundred-count Porthault sheets, and really messed them up.

Simon, the gynecologist, knew where all the hot spots were buried and precisely what to do when he uncovered them. While the guitar played a frenzied *bulería* in the background, we strummed each other until we were both taut, ready to snap. So that when finally he entered me, it took only seconds before I crescendoed, soared, spasmed, went off in all directions. Then he drove to his finish, gaze locked on mine, letting me watch those pure gray eyes cloud, then flame as he shuddered.

Not once in my life, in all the years I'd made love, had I ever seen a man climax eyes wide open. That windows to the soul cliché? Absolutely true. I felt magically connected to him.

Afterwards, as I lay in his arms, he said, "God, that was lovely, Gwyneth. Everything I'd hoped for. More than. You were wonderful."

"You were," I said, barely breathing.

He took my hand and kissed its palm. "*We* were," he said.

At sunset, we took our martinis to the deck. While Simon swiped a red pen over his article for *Cervix*, I stretched out at the other end of the wicker sofa, my feet in his lap, finishing off the previous Sunday's *New York Times* crossword. Occasionally, I tapped into his brain for a lost word. From time to time, I stole a glance at him. The sheaf of silver hair falling over his forehead, the twitch of his jaw as he concentrated, the squared shoulders under a gray merino crewneck like the ones the rich kids wore back in college—all this tingled me down to my toes, which he massaged with his free hand.

In the background Isaac Stern fiddled through the Brandenburg Concertos. "Do you play bridge?" Simon asked, not looking up from his editing.

"I do. How about chess?" I asked. "Do you play chess?"

"I do," he said.

It was a match made in dork heaven.

Except that heaven lasts forever, and our weekend was running out. Still, there were many weekends ahead. Why shouldn't there be? I closed my eyes and stretched the moment the way women do, prematurely. Why couldn't we go the distance? Why couldn't we end up as The Drs. York? Writing papers together. Making fantastic love into eternity.

If not, if Simon and I ended badly, well then, I would have had a wonderful love affair with a brilliant, charming man. More than a fling. Something to remember fondly while rocking on the nursing home porch.

That's what I told myself as the flaming sun dipped into the turquoise sea, just like a sappy painting on velvet.

---

"Remember fondly? Oh honeybunch, are you kidding yourself," Fleur said, chuckling, when I confided that on Sunday night. "Let me tell you, if you and Simon get something going and he breaks up with you, if Simon does you dirty, you're just another Jerry Springer biker chick wanting to tear his eyeballs out. We're all primitive creatures when we're pulling the knife from our guts. Okay, so you had sex. Which you're not going to talk about because well-brought-up women don't. Except you weren't well brought up, so it's an affectation."

"The sex was dynamite," I said, failing to suppress a smirk.

Fleur blinked at me as if I were some new specimen of Gwyneth she hadn't come across before.

"Listen to you. Dynamite, huh? That's a surprise. The Brits are not known for sexual proficiency. Brussels sprouts, yes. Sex, no."

"Well, he was incredible," I said. "It's been years since I had such a big…well, you know…"

"You had A Big You Know? Then he must be good. Because honestly since menopause, my You Know hasn't been that big. I think it's all hormone related. Blood rises to your face for a hot flash instead of settling in the nether regions where it's needed."

"The vast majority of women over fifty report an increase in the intensity of orgasm," I said.

"This is your *farkuckteh* survey again, right? That survey has gotten us all in trouble. I'll tell you it was a hell of a lot easier back in Jane Austen's day when fifty-five-year-old ladies put on their lace caps and retired to play whist. Sometimes I wonder if civilization has really made any progress."

"Your date last night was lousy, right?"

"Yeah," she said, "the pits."

# Chapter 27

I brought back souvenirs from my beach weekend with Simon. Occasionally, the memory of his chiseled profile on the next pillow would surface. Or I'd get ambushed by a flash of him buttering his toast or laughing at something I'd said. These blips of pleasure didn't interfere with my work, mind you. I saw patients, performed surgeries, watched CNN, ate my yogurt, but occasionally a thought of him jingled the serotonin receptors in my prefrontal cortex and passing a mirror, I'd catch a glimpse of my goofy smile.

Early in the week, Kat got a second opinion on the best way to treat her tumor that agreed with Abe's first and now that she knew what had to be done, she just wanted to get it over with.

Kat's lumpectomy was really a partial mastectomy and Abe and I had gone toe-to-toe with her insurance company to buy her an extra day in the hospital, after which she'd require some looking after. She intended to stay with Summer and Tim for a few days. The plan was for me to stop in over the weekend to do the post-op care that made Summer blanch when I described it.

"Well, isn't she the delicate flower. It doesn't sound so

bad. Hell, I'll do it if you show me how. You can even go to New York if you want to," Fleur said.

Simon had invited me up for the weekend, but under the circumstances, Kat came first.

"Atta girl," Fleur cheered. "Friends before lovers. It's nice to know you've still got your priorities straight. And you know, Gwynnie, when the lovers are long gone, the friends are still there for you."

"That's so comforting." I said it as a joke but, deep down, I meant it.

Simon was disappointed when I postponed my visit, but he understood. "Of course, you must be there for your chum. You have a good heart to go with the not-so-shoddy brain. In fact, I think you're quite wonderful. You do know I like you very much, Gwyneth."

I swallowed a major lump. "And I like you very much." We both paused reverently at our display of feeling, and then I added, "God help us both," which really broke him up.

———

I couldn't change my two surgeries scheduled for Thursday afternoon and wouldn't rush them. And although I intended to get to Kat before they wheeled her into the operating room, the pelvis of my second patient, Mrs. Violet Sandler, aged eighty-two, had other ideas. Working around adhesions from her previous procedures was like picking through scotch tape. By the time I reassured the family and stripped off my scrubs, Kat had been in Abe's hands for more than an hour.

I made it into the waiting room just as he emerged to tell Summer, "It went the way I like surgeries to go—short and sweet. We won't get the final pathology results for a few days, but let's take it one step at a time. Your mom did fine in there."

Me, he motioned aside for a more detailed assessment. The bottom line was he had to take more tissue than he'd anticipated, a major chunk, and Kat might want to seriously consider reconstructive surgery. But the prognosis was good: if her luck held, she'd get five weeks of radiation to prevent local recurrence of the cancer, but she shouldn't need chemo.

After Fleur went off in search of another Diet Coke and Summer found an alcove to call Tim from her cell phone, I slipped into the recovery room to see the patient. I hadn't expected her to be awake, but she was—awake and looking beautiful with her crinkly hair spread on the pillow and her face pale but relieved.

"You did great, kid." I patted her hand.

"Yeah, Dr. Sukkar said. So far. Radiation next. Thank God no chemo." Her eyes shimmered and I knew she was thinking of her mother and sister who'd endured grueling rounds of chemotherapy, Melanie dragging herself to be dripped long after the doctors had given up. "Thank you, God. Thank you, Ethan," Kat whispered to her intervening angel. After a sip of water, "Summer okay?"

"Fine. She and Fleur are outside."

"Together?" Kat grimaced, as if I'd left Dracula to baby-sit Frankenstein's monster. "Listen." She motioned me down to her. "Favor. When you go to feed the cats. In my bed-room, on my dresser"—her voice was hoarse from intubation and she slurred, still thick-tongued—"on top, envelopes. Last-minute notes to my lawyer, others, you...you know, in case, something happened in there." The OR. "Bury them. In a drawer. Don't want Summer to see them. Doesn't need to know her mama's a wimp."

Some wimp. When I stopped by later that afternoon to check on her, Kat was sitting up, legs over the side of the bed, eyes lasering Summer, who leaned against the windowsill, arms folded defensively across her chest. The patient, five hours post-surgery, was chewing her daughter out one decibel level below a shout.

"No, what you don't seem to grasp," Kat curtly nodded an acknowledgement as I entered, "is that at fifty-four I don't have to justify my actions to anyone. I'm a grown woman, your mother, not the other way around, and you have no right to tell me how to live the rest of my life, however long—or short—that might be."

"Mama, please," Summer said. "Don't talk like that. Dr. Sukkar told me…"

"Dr. Sukkar can't make promises. Life isn't infinite, Summer. Your father hadn't so much as a cold in fifteen years. Then he drives to pick up mulch and gets killed in a freak accident. So you have to use whatever life you have because it can end in an instant." She winced as she snapped her fingers. I moved forward, about to suggest she might want to take it easy, but she waved me away. "If I get a second chance here, I'm not going to waste it. I'm going to do what *I* want to do. And you, my darling daughter, need to back off. Understood?"

"But that man is so much younger than—"

"Lee is not the issue here."

"Fine." Summer rolled her eyes. "Whatever."

"Summer Germaine!" Kat's voice rose menacingly.

"Fine. Yes. Right. Understood, Mama."

When I caught up with Fleur later, her response was, "No shit? She really laid the brat out, huh? Here you have a prime example of what does not kill us makes us strong. But does this mean she's back with Lee?"

"I asked the same question after Summer took off. Short answer: no. Lee is too young to be saddled by the likes of her. Kat's words. He's entitled to kids. Not that she knows if he wants any. And a girlfriend with no cancer history and a perfect set of boobs. Not that she ever discussed her surgery with him. Or even told him she was *having* surgery."

"Don't you think he'd want to know? I have half a mind to call him," Fleur continued.

"Half a mind is right. Do *not* call Lee. If Kat wanted to, she would have. Stay out of it, Fleur. Just as she told Summer, you can't live her life for her."

"Sure I can. And I'd live it better. With Lee."

"Well, obviously she has other plans. If Kat wants it over, it's over."

But maybe not.

That night, with Mama Cass and Denny purring and scouring my legs, I kept my promise to Kat and hiked up to her bedroom. On the dresser, she'd built a shrine, probably inadvertently, but she was an artist so who knows? I picked up her silver-framed wedding picture and looked at it closely for the first time in thirty years. She and Ethan had been married in Prospect Park in Brooklyn, which they'd tried to turn into Katmandu with incense sticks planted in the spring earth and lanterns strung in the trees, unlit because they couldn't get a permit from the NYFD. The bride, in a gauzy caftan, appeared light as a dragonfly. The bearded groom looked like the rabbi's twin. Right after Kat's sister snapped that picture, a panhandler made his stoned way through the wedding guests, a good omen Kat had said, lifting all-embracing arms. "Faith," she'd cocked her head toward the rabbi-guru. "Hope," she'd nodded toward her new husband. "And charity." We broke into applause and showered the stoned guy with coins. A happy day so long ago.

Next to the picture, Kat had arranged a vase of flowers—apricot mums from her garden—a small jade Buddha, and the fan of envelopes. One for the lawyer, one for me, one each for Fleur, Summer, and Tim, and one marked in Kat's Picasso scrawl, "Lee." I did what she instructed me to do. Buried them deep in a drawer under the bras she'd get to wear again.

When I arrived home, I found three voice messages.

Sylvie: "Mr. Harald acted up in the barbershop today. Should I call Mr. Stan and ask him if he can cut Mr. Harald's hair next time he comes?"

That one I returned. "No, do not ask Mr. Stan to do anything. I will take Mr. Harald to the barber myself on Friday. Don't worry, I'll be able to handle him, Sylvie." I didn't have to see her to know, without doubt, she was screwing up her mouth in disbelief.

The second message was my son Drew informing me he was coming home next month for Thanksgiving, which was a surprise. Drew, who'd always been closer than his twin to my dad, these days avoided occasions where he'd have to confront what was left of his beloved grandpa. Just couldn't deal with it. So this seemed like a breakthrough. His cooler medical student brother, Whit, planned to have dinner with his girlfriend's family in Virginia. *And why not*, I thought, *let somebody have a joyous celebration*. We would be a pitiful three at the Waterview table: Drew, the sensitive son, his insensible grandfather, and his not-so-sensible mother.

The third message featured the amiable growl of Harry Galligan asking how I was doing since it had been a while and, by the way, how was that woman who was having medical problems when we last spoke? Typical Harry. The man deserved better than he'd been getting from me and even in my Simonized state I felt guilty about it. Calculating that I could work my schedule of tending to Kat to free me for a few hours Saturday night, we made a date. It turned out to be a nice evening. No pyrotechnics, but lots of warmth, which I appreciated as the autumn weather turned chill.

*Chapter 28*

The next month zipped by. Now that Ibrahim Sukkar had plucked the family heirloom out of her right breast, Kat's natural optimism resurfaced. She started her radiation therapy, floating through the sessions on a waft of serenity, visualizing her cancer cells as lotus petals being crushed by Buddhist monks and scattered to the winds. Which was so Kat. I say do whatever works for you, even the alternative stuff as long as it doesn't lure you from top grade western medicine, even if the vote's not in on imagining your way to good health.

Fleur, in her own spurt of energy, ran through four of Hannah Pechter's video studs: one schmuck, two schlemiels, and a schlimazel. But there was a mensch on the horizon. She penciled in Victor, the Chinese-cooking high-end raincoat salesman, for the following week.

At the office, it was obvious Bethany McGowan had taken Seymour's discarding of her very hard. Back to her pre-affair bluestocking fashion style—flat shoes and Puritan blouses buttoned so tight and high up her neck that I feared for her carotid artery—she sulked and skulked around, growing thinner and more dispirited daily, while Seymour—like a vampire sucking every ounce of joy from her soul—grew fatter and more beamish. I kept my eye on Mindy, the new hire, for signs she was being illicitly boinked, but Seymour seemed to have learned at least one of two important lessons: don't play around in the office or if you do, don't get caught.

Apropos of boinking, Simon visited three times. Quick visits, in and out. Literally, figuratively, sexually. But sheet-scorchingly good. And then *finally,* I found a weekend free to make my long postponed visit to him on his home turf.

He owned a two-bedroom co-op in a pre-war building on the Upper East Side which must have cost him a bundle. But unless you knew how inflated Manhattan apartment prices are and the cachet cost of the best neighborhoods, you would think he lived much below his salary. Which had to be way, way up there.

The Westwood was virtually indistinguishable from two other Woody Allenesque drab-chic apartment buildings on a block that also housed a newsstand, a jewelry shop, and a Vietnamese greengrocer. Across the street a row of brown-stones gave way to a deli, a florist shop, a tapas bar, and an antique store specializing in czarist treasures, which was probably a front for the Russian mafia. Maybe that's why the neighborhood was so quiet on a Friday afternoon. And why The Westwood didn't need a doorman.

I nodded maternally at a young man flashing his electronic resident's pass and he flourished me into the handsomely refurbished art deco lobby. The elevator took its sweet time getting to the sixth floor.

"Yes, yes," Simon called through the door in that impatient British manner that made me hot when Jeremy Irons laid it on. A few seconds passed during which I assumed he was checking me out through the peephole and then he opened the door with the security chain latched in case some six-foot-five 280-pound miscreant was posing as "Gwyneth, it's me, Gwyneth."

He unhooked the chain, popped me a kiss, and said, "Hello, my beautiful houseguest." After he hung up my coat, he took me into his arms. "I've missed you terribly. I'm so delighted you're here. Moment," he said, as the phone rang. He checked the caller ID. "London. I'm doing a phone consult. They were supposed to call this morning. Sorry. This is a must take."

He said into the phone, "Martin. Where have you been? Ah. Well, I'll need to make this short. Hold on." Turning to me, he said. "Ten minutes. No more. Promise. Meanwhile settle in. Place is a bit cluttered, I'm afraid. But there's plenty to read and tea's on the boil."

So I made myself a cup and looked around. As for clutter, he wasn't one of the Collyer Brothers, the two old coots who, back in the 1940s, had piled up newspapers and magazines and a hundred tons of junk around them in their Fifth Avenue apartment until the cops found their moldering bodies under heaps of garbage. Not that bad.

Someone had made the beds, cleaned the bathrooms, and swabbed down the kitchen. On its counter sat a spice carousel, a sign or memory of a woman's touch. The contemporary teak dining table shone clutter free, but skyscrapers of magazines rose from the carpet beneath it— *Science, Popular Science, Theoretical Science, Esoteric Science, Incomprehensible Science.* Simon's study must have been designed as a maid's room. Now it was crammed with a computer, file cabinets, academic publications, papers in wild disarray, even half a blueberry muffin that looked like it had been baked around the time McArthur invaded Korea. There were reading glasses scattered in every room.

Sticky reminder squares attached to every flat surface. Simon, it seemed, was your classic absentminded scientist, but sexy.

A half hour after he left me, he found me reading the *New York Times.* "A very productive ten minutes," he said. "Now with that behind us, I can think of a wonderful way to spend the next, say, forty-five." He was nuzzling my neck. "Unless you'd rather an early dinner?"

"Hungry for something else," I said, wondering at the deep vein of sensuality this man had unearthed in me. My quickie with Ari Ben-Jacob had given me a shot of confidence, a reminder that I was still attractive to men in spite of my ex-husband's preference. But I hadn't been inclined to hop a plane to Tel Aviv for more. Simon was different. Just the thought of him stirred desire. And no shame at that. Amazing. Fifty-four and hot at last!

"Not here. Bedroom," I murmured. He had to relocate books and papers from the comforter to the floor to make a place for us on his bed. But we had more than enough room and finally enough time as he undressed me, talking to me all the while, telling me what he was doing as he was doing it, that Mayfair accent making every lusty syllable sound like Shakespeare. Very steamy Falstaff. Then no more talking as he worked his wicked tongue brilliantly in other ways. And I was pretty brilliant, too, much better than I'd been at nineteen when all I had in my repertoire was a single repetitive tongue-flick. Susie Lemberg back in college had us practice on popsicles. No wonder I'd left my dates cold.

When Simon groaned he couldn't take it anymore, I climbed atop so I could look down on that gorgeous face, look into those gorgeous eyes as they turned to molten steel which, once again, tripped me over the edge.

Sated, I collapsed against his chest. He caressed my hair. "Simon," was all I could whisper. I wanted to be nowhere else, wanted the moment to last forever.

As if reading my mind, he pressed my hand over his heart and said, "This is ridiculous. We've seen each other only six or seven times so it's much too early to feel let alone say, but I think I'm falling in love with you."

Still bleary with pleasure, what I heard was the "think." He only *thinks* he's falling in love with me. Then the sentiment hit full force.

Fleur, when I recounted this next part, was ready to have me consigned to a psychiatric institution, eager to sign the admission papers herself. Because instead of letting him stew, wait, bite his nails, yearn, ache, climb mountains, and ford rivers to win me, I replied breathlessly, "I've been thinking along the same lines."

"Have you, my darling?" he said, sliding me up so he could look at me. "Tell me."

I said, grinning at the craziness of it, "I don't know where this is coming from. I'm a rational person. More intellectual than emotional, I've always thought. Not impulsive. God knows, I'm not a teenager. And yet…"

"Yes," he said, "And yet for me too."

After a long, gentle kiss that seemed to seal the sentiment, he leapt to his feet, energized. "Now I really am starved. You too? Would Thai takeaway do the trick?"

On our way to the Bangkok Delight Carry Out, we met up with someone from another part of his life. From the slight drape of skin around the jawline, I estimated her at mid-forties. A little too much eye makeup for workout clothes, but attractive.

She was Dr. Claire Something who was doing some amazing science in his lab and I was Dr. Unintelligible, colleague and friend, from Baltimore. After the introduction, we stood awkwardly sizing each other up. The rest of the conversation, about the impending first snow of the season, raced towards its end.

After Claire had vanished around the corner, I said, "So I'm your colleague and friend, am I?" miffed at the way I got shoved into a sexless corner.

He got a kick out of my annoyance. "What would you have me say?" he laughed. "Girlfriend? Lover?" Then, sobering, "Seriously, Gwyneth, I'm very careful about my public persona. Reputation is a fragile thing. I try to keep my private and professional lives entirely separate." Simon tucked my hand into his pocket as we walked. "I assume you do as well. Claire works in my lab. I want her to concentrate on her science, not be speculating about what I do in my off hours."

"Did you ever date her?" I said. Call it instinct.

Call it a guess. Simon appeared genuinely appalled. "Good grief. Now that would be asking for trouble. Never a wise idea to mix business with pleasure. Except in our case, of course, and we don't really work together." He gave my hand a squeeze.

On the walk back, with the bags of food cooling, Simon made a detour to the local music store where he purchased CDs of classical composers I'd never even heard of and I bought Itzhak Perlman playing Paginini and Ella singing Gershwin. We emerged into the night and just as we arrived on his street it began to snow starry twinkles that lit up the dark. Then something strange happened. Simon halted in front of Friedman's Deli. He cased the block to make sure, I guess, that none of his colleagues from Brubaker out for a nosh would catch his show. Because what he did next had to be out of character for the eminent, the proper Simon York of the impeccable public persona. In the snow-freckled light from the deli, with the aroma of sauerkraut and garlic wafting around us and "Lara's Theme" seeping out of a nearby apartment—or maybe I spun the tune in my brain as I orchestrated the moment—in a scene that was drop-dead *Dr. Zhivago* romantic, he leaned down and kissed me. Hard. With passion pumping behind it. Right out there in full view.

When he released me, I saw his eyes sparkling with maybe astonishment at himself and love for me. That's what love does, propels you into a grand jeté over your own boundaries. With the risk of landing in a bruised and battered heap where your feet used to be instead of in the wonderful wild blue yonder. But worth it, I thought. From the look on his face, Simon did too.

After dinner, I slipped Ella into the CD player and tugged him to his feet.

"No, no, no, no, no. I don't dance," he protested.

But he allowed himself to be dragged into a fox-trot and, wonder of wonders, after the initial crashing awkwardness and after he lost some of his self-consciousness and concentrated on the music, he wasn't half bad. I told him so.

"You're just being kind. I'm a congenital oaf. I know my strengths and weaknesses."

"No, really." I meant it.

"Then I have you to thank." He appeared genuinely delighted at this new trick and with me.

"The way you wear your hat. The way you sip your tea," Ella crooned, the scent of lemongrass filled the air and the moment hung velvet. Simon, moving with newfound grace, whispered huskily, "I guess this makes us a couple. Do you want that, Gwyneth?"

Declarations of love in the afternoon, a couple by evening. I could hear Fleur warning, "So fast?" Still, it wasn't as if I were seventeen with the luxury of unlimited time. My heart, which had bucked into arrhythmia at his question, told me "The hell with it, why not?" I was smitten with this man. He with me. Why not attempt a little boundary leaping of my own?

I nodded, which I hoped he could see in the half-light.

"Then that settles it. We're a couple," he laughed softly.

*And whatever happens,* I sang to myself, *they can't take that away from me.*

But they tried, whoever *they* were, because right in the middle of this perfection, my cell phone went off in my handbag across the room. Sylvie. My father had taken a spill. He'd been unsteady on his feet lately, spending more and more time in the brown recliner, and I'd told Sylvie to keep a close watch on him because I'd picked up a foot drop on the left side a few days before and I didn't trust his balance.

Panic shifted Sylvie's Jamaican accent into high gear. "The t'ing is, I never took my eyes off him. I had my eyes on him all the time. But there was no warning is the t'ing. He just tripped over his feet and went to the floor. He hurt his shoulder. He's holding his shoulder."

I heard my father mewling in the background. "Put him on, please."

"Daddy, are you all right?" I didn't expect an answer. I just wanted him to hear my voice. "Can you move your shoulder? Lift your arm."

Sylvie took back the phone. "He can't lift his arm."

"Sylvie, listen, his shoulder probably isn't broken," that's a rare event, "but he might have dislocated it. Call Dr. Rosetti. See if he wants Mr. Harald to go to the emergency room. And please call me back after you've spoken to him. Don't forget to call me, Sylvie."

"What was that all about?" Simon asked. After I gave him a brief, bowdlerized summary, he said, "Hmm, sounds like you might want to consider a higher level of care for your papa."

*No, I might not want to consider a higher level of care, which is another way of saying nursing home. Not tonight.* "I don't think he's ready. And not to be rude, but can we change the subject? Please."

As if anyone paid attention to me. I heard almost the same words two hours later when Dan Rosetti, not Sylvie, called from the hospital. That dear man met Sylvie at the ER and reviewed the x-rays that showed my father fell smack on his shoulder, causing a separation.

"We've got it covered. The orthopedic guy is slinging him now," Dan reported.

"Is he very scared? Should I come back?"

"No, you enjoy your weekend. We gave him some Percocet and he's enjoying the nurses fussing over him," Dan continued. "Honestly, I don't see a need for you to come back early. Sylvie can handle this. We'll give her instructions about pain meds and ice. And if it will put your mind at ease, I'll stop by tomorrow to see how he's doing."

"A house call? Dan, I really appreciate this. I can't tell you how much."

"No sweat. Harald's a favorite of mine. So just have a good time in the big city. You drive up?"

"Train."

He hesitated, then said gently, "Well, I don't want put a damper on your time up there, but maybe on the way back you can give some thought to next steps. We're about at the end of the line in terms of Sylvie providing adequate care. She'll do for now, but soon…" He left the unmentionable unsaid.

In spite of phoning Sylvie nine times to check on my father, it was a  memorable weekend. We roamed the snow-dusted streets of the Village, caught a Bulgarian film festival in SoHo, visited a Klee exhibit at the Guggenheim, made passionate love twice again. Simon managed to squeeze in a few hours at the hospital between dusk and dark on Saturday,  which soothed him, and then we cooked together—chicken with saffron and olives from a Moroccan cookbook he'd picked up in Rabat. Over the sauté pan, he said, "It's jolly to play house with you. We do very well together, don't we?"

Yet, when I said, after Sunday brunch, "I think I'll head back early. I'm worried about my father," he said, "Yes, we'll get you on your way. And I've got to get moving, too. Time to pack," heading for the bedroom.

I followed. "Pack for what? Where are you going?"

"Uh, didn't I tell you? I'm leaving for Budapest first thing tomorrow. For the SACO meeting. Giving a paper. Be back in a week." He pulled a suitcase from the closet.

I bit my lip, calculating. A week in Hungary and after that he was off to Florida for Thanksgiving. It would be three weeks before I'd see him again.

"Why the long face?" He gave my cheek a quick stroke, then snatched a handful of ties from his closet and tossed them into his carry-on.

When I didn't answer, he dropped the last tie and looked up. "Come here." He folded me into his arms, murmuring, "This is my life, Gwyneth. My schedule is packed. Surely you of all people understand what that's like. But what we have, you and I, is so important to me that I want to grab at whatever time we have together. Even if it isn't enough, it's something, no?" He kissed the back of my neck above my collar.

Wooed and won, I leaned back into his embrace. "It's more than something."

*But not everything,* I had to remind myself when he failed to phone for the next five days.

*Chapter 29*

Who gives a rodent's rear about your Moroccan chicken? And snow drifting down between the skyscrapers while that syrupy 'Lara's Theme' plays in the background? Life is not a gaggy romance novel. Now sex is another story. Are you people still setting fire to the sheets?" Fleur asked when she and Kat finally pinned me down for a debriefing Friday night.

Kat said wearily, "Is nothing sacred?" and waved away the mashed potatoes. During the last few days, the effects of the radiation had caught up with her. Too exhausted to crunch a carrot, for once she hadn't turned up her nose at her nemesis, fast food. Fleur and I had loaded up at KFC before heading out to Columbia to set up supper in her kitchen.

"Sex is not the focus of every relationship, Fleur." I gnawed on a chicken wing.

"Dream on." Fleur shoveled coleslaw. "So when is the next big date?"

"He's spending the holiday in Key West with old friends. Making it into a long weekend. It's been on his calendar for nearly a year. Which works out because Drew's here for Thanksgiving. So no Simon until early December. I've bought concert tickets for that Saturday night. Unless he's changed his mind about coming. I haven't heard from all week. That's not like him."

"Ah, the dance-away lover. Two steps forward, one step back. Trust me, he scared himself with that couple business and now he's into the seventy-two-hour cooling off period. Soon he'll invoke the kick-out clause. I knew it. Don't say I didn't warn—"

"Oh, for godssakes," Kat interjected. "Pay no attention to her, Gwyn. Simon sounds wonderful. I Googled him the other day, just as a lark. There was a photo. He's stunning. No wonder you fell for him on the spot. His CV was a mile long. And he's on some kind of honor's list made up by the queen back in England." News to me.

"Well, la-di-da," Fleur said.

Kat ignored her. "Five days without a call is nothing. Even if he usually calls a lot, because didn't you say he was giving a paper? He's probably swamped. And the man told you he loves you and you're a couple. *You* call *him*. It's way past time to dump those bourgeois conventions society shoved down our throats forty years ago. We're in the twenty-first century here. Could anything be more irrelevant?"

She pushed her plate away impatiently. She'd lost some weight over the last weeks and looked less earthbound, more like a pale, luminous flower on a slimmer stem. Her cheekbones had emerged and her beautiful violet eyes seemed more prominent.

"And you have a perfect excuse. The call from Fortune Simms's office. You can tell him all about that."

Fortune's producer had phoned the day before to prep me for my first appearance on the show. "I don't remember seeing a TV set in his house," I said. " I'll bet he doesn't even know who Fortune Simms is."

"Please." Kat rolled her eyes. "More people recognize Fortune than the pope. I'll bet he'd be thrilled to hear from you. Call him."

"Don't you dare!" Fleur brandished her fork menacingly. "The fastest way to lose a man is to chase him. Didn't your mother ever tell you that?"

"My mother told me Hermann Goering was sending her messages through her molars. But don't worry, Fleur, I'm not going to call Simon. I don't wear white shoes after Labor Day, I don't touch up my makeup in public, I don't send printed Hallmark sympathy cards, and I don't call men. Besides, the last thing I want Simon to think is that he's on a short leash." I turned to Kat. "As for bourgeois—hell, I've spent my entire life striving for bourgeois. Now that I've got it, they'll have to pry it from my cold dead fingers."

———

Simon phoned finally on Saturday afternoon from Budapest. "Hectic conference," he said. "Very busy." I heard background tinkle of crystal and clatter of silver.

He was all wound up over some buzz he'd come across about a rival lab working on a project similar to something cooking in his own. Now it was going to be a race to the finish line. "I'll really have to put nose to grindstone when I get back," he warned me. "Sorry I didn't have a moment to call. And I didn't want to subject you to my black mood." Which didn't sound black now.

"That's what friends are for." For better for worse, I almost said but caught myself.

"You're right of course. See, you're already teaching me about relationships. I'm a slow learner, but don't give up on me, please."

When I didn't answer, he said. "Uh-oh. Do I sense regrets? Still love me?"

"Most of the time," I said, only half-joking.

"Oh, you can do better than that," he said, laughing. "You'll see, all will be well as soon as we're together."

I grumbled, "Which isn't until December fifth, more than two weeks away." And then it would be only for Saturday night because he had a Kerns-Brubaker fundraiser in D.C. on Sunday.

"I know, darling. Too long. But I'll make it up to you."

A woman's voice trilled in the background, "*Siiiiimon.*" Violin music swelled behind him with gypsy passion.

"Magda Zilahy, wonderful old warhorse, chair of our host committee," he whispered. "Looks like our table's ready. I love you, Gwyneth. Take care. I'll phone again soon."

Which he did from then on. Nearly every day. So we were back on track.

———

Thanksgiving was less awful than I'd expected. Much less awful than the year before when Drew had gobbled his dinner bent over his plate, eyes averted from my dribbling father, then declined dessert to exile himself to the far end of the living room with a book. And the old man had known. What was left of his consciousness had registered the abandonment. "Come here, *barnebarn,*" he'd called to his grandson, "sit by me." But Drew had just waved to him from across the room.

Hurt for my dad, anxious for my son, I'd tried, but Drew had refused to talk about it; not to me, not, so far as I'd known, to Dan Rosetti who early on had explained the Alzheimer's prognosis to my sons and invited them to phone anytime with questions or just to talk.

This year I watched, half sad, half proud, as Drew mopped cider from his granddad's chin and buttered his roll. He cut his turkey into small pieces and, when my dad's hand shook too hard to make the journey from plate to mouth, fed him. Major transformation.

In the kitchen as I got out the pie, Drew came in carrying plates, which I took as an opportunity to say, "Thanks for taking care of him. I know you don't think he's aware, but I can tell you've broken through." My father, who'd looked so lost the previous year, had given Drew shining smiles throughout dinner.

"No problem," Drew said, stacking the plates in the sink.

"I know this is hard for you, seeing him this way."

"Yeah, well, it's hard for everyone."

"True. But you've been so gentle with him, I just…"

"Mom, for godssakes, it's not a big deal, really." He didn't look up from scraping plates.

"It is to me. It is to him," I said.

"Yeah, well, the truth is I really didn't want to come today." He turned to me then, holding a scraped plate in front of him like a shield. "I didn't think I could deal with it. But it's Thanksgiving and all, and my not showing up would leave just the two of you. So I called Dr. Rosetti and we had a talk. He explained some shit to me. So now, well, I'm not all right with Grandpa's brain cells checking out, but I can deal with it at least." He put down the plate and wiped his hands on a dish towel. "By the way, don't blame Dr. Rosetti for not telling you. I didn't want you to know. I wasn't sure I could bring this off."

"But you did."

"I guess. So if this turns out to be like his last memory of me, it will be okay, right?"

"Oh yes," I said and kissed him on the cheek.

*Thank you Dan for giving that to my son and my father. Thanks for so much*, I thought, on Thanksgiving Day.

Dinner over, my father insisted on watching a football game, so while I loaded the dishwasher, Drew sat with him on the sofa, arm wound around the old man's scrawny shoulders, explaining the plays. But within a few minutes, Drew told me later, Dad got antsy and began wandering around the living room picking up and putting down the decorative tchotchkes on my tables.

It was only at a commercial break that Drew realized his grandfather was out of his sight. That's when I heard him calling, "Granddad, where the hell are you?"

And then, "Mom, Jesus, Mom. Get in here."

I found Drew standing at the door to the master bath staring at my father dressed in my peach silk robe with the ruffled cuffs. He'd draped a Gucci scarf around his neck and propped on his nearly bald head a hat I hadn't worn in twenty years.

"Nice touch, the feather on the hat. Joan Rivers would love this getup," Drew said. We leaned against each other, stifling giggles, swallowing back tears.

"You've got to face facts, Mom," Drew told me after we'd delivered my father into Sylvie's care, "he's really losing it. If you wait until he becomes incontinent or can't walk, your options are slashed. I know how hard it is for you, but you can at least start scouting out places. You want to have all your ducks in a row when he has to go in."

Which made sense. And eased my heart a little, since I could tell myself this was a contingency, not an inevitability, plan.

"Smart boy, your Drew. You've done a good job with both your kids," Dan Rosetti said the next day in his office after I'd thanked him for intervening. "I'm going to hook you up with Michelle Isaacs, a geriatric social worker who's really terrific. She'll find the right slot for your dad. In the

meantime, I wouldn't worry too much about Harald turning into a drag queen, but let's fiddle with his medication a
bit." As he scribbled on his prescription pad, he asked, "Any
news on the Clinic grants?"

I'd gone over his emailed suggestions for revising my
proposals. He'd come up with some salient points I'd missed.
"Cross your fingers," I told him. "I have two applications
out. Haven't heard yet on either. I'm going to try to send a
few more this afternoon. I've got the day off. Our office is
closed for Thanksgiving Friday."

"Ours too," he said, concentrating on scribbling a new
page.

"You came in for me?"

His head snapped up then and he stared at me with a
look I hadn't seen before from Dan. Tentative. "For your
dad, for you," he said. "The least I can do." He put down his
pen, gave me a cryptic smile, then raked his fingers through
his hair. The last seemed like a nervous gesture, which was
out of character for Dan. He said, finally, "So now I know
your son and your dad like football. How about you?"

I nodded, puzzled.

"Good. Because I've got two tickets for the Ravens
game Sunday. I was thinking that maybe you'd like to join
me."

Was he asking me out? Impossible. First of all, he had
a wife. I darted a glance at Mrs. Rosetti's photo. And Dan,
tracking that, took an audible breath as my astonishment
became apparent. "Ah. You didn't know. Melinda passed
away two years ago. Of an aneurysm. Very sudden."

"I'm sorry, Dan, I *didn't* know." He was full of surprises
today.

"She was a great gal," he said and swiveled around to
adjust the frame. "We expected happily ever after but I don't

have to tell you, the best-laid plans." He shrugged. "Anyway," he swiveled back and gave me the full force of his baby browns, "I'm legally and morally free to ask a lovely woman out on a date. That is, if you're interested."

Under different circumstances, I would have jumped at the chance. Well, not jumped, because according to Fleur, who had the rules of this game down pat, jumping implies overeagerness, which borders on desperation. So no jumping. But I would have happily strolled into a date with Dan Rosetti. Which was currently out of the question because I had Simon. And Simon had me. Big time. We were in love and we were a couple. Officially, even though Simon was, at the moment, in Key West for Thanksgiving and I was facing a man drumming a pen on top of his desk as he waited for my answer.

Which came spewing out. "Honestly, Dan, I'm flattered. But the thing is, I'm seeing someone."

He elevated his eyebrows. "Figures." He flipped the pen into a spin and caught it, as if to say, "Got it. Fine with it. Already flipped it off." What he actually said was, "Well, timing is everything. That's great, Gwyn. Congratulations to the lucky guy."

A lesser man would have gone frosty on me, but not Dan, the ubermensch. The change was subtle. He returned to scratching away at his pad. "Okay, I'm giving you Michelle's number at the office and her cell. I've already briefed her about Harald." Looking up, he showed me a smile that was only semi-detached. When he handed me the page, he was careful his fingers didn't touch mine. Or maybe I was reading more into it than the quick hand-off implied.

He didn't help me with my coat as he'd been doing lately, but gave me a single pat on the back as I exited, the kind of pat he laid on my father and probably on all his ancient patients.

"To repeat, timing is everything," he said, as he ushered me out. "In your dad's case, I wouldn't wait too long. Call Michelle. And enjoy your weekend."

# Chapter 30

I was grabbing a leftover turkey sandwich when Fleur stopped down on her way to Saturday brunch. Not your run-of-the-mill cold waffle and curdled scrambled egg buffet, either, she assured me. This was a special promotion that Linen and Silver, her fifty-plus dinner-dating service, offered their premium members. "A lot of the men are retired and I guess they don't have much to do besides play golf or play with themselves. So they come to these brunches for the all-you-can-eat, which is better than the frozen dinners they microwave at home. They have a few drinks, charm the ladies, and then go home to nap."

She'd dated a few men she'd meet at the L&S dinner fix-ups. "Nothing you want to bring home to Mama, even if Mama would probably accept the bag boy at Safeway at this stage of the game. Look, I know you're not currently in the market, but if all you do is drink mimosas, you'll get your fifteen bucks worth. And Connie deCrespi will be there. You two hit it off, remember?"

Fleur had been hanging out a lot with Connie lately, personally and professionally. Contemplating adding a second Madame Max store in Bethesda, she'd called on the attorney to handle some tricky legal maneuvers for the expansion. They talked about it a lot over drinks.

"Sounds irresistible, but regrettably I'll have to pass. I've got these grant proposals to get out and then Harry and I are meeting for an early dinner."

"Really?" Fleur said. Her voice was icy. "I hope you're not using this guy. To fill in the blanks with Simon, I mean. Because from everything I've heard, Harry has a heart. So you might not want to break it."

My sentiments exactly. When Harry had called wondering if I was as tired of turkey as he was and if I wanted to join him for steamed crabs on Saturday night, I said absolutely. I couldn't continue to string this decent man along. It was morally reprehensible to continue to treat him like a spare part. First I'd mellow him out over a couple of beers, then I'd bid him adieu.

I told that to Fleur, who said, "Good girl. *Crazy* girl, dumping Harry for Simon York—for *anyone*—but good."

If she thought I was crazy for ending it with Harry, she'd have shipped me off to a padded room for turning down Dan Rosetti. But that bit of data would remain forever out of her reach, if I could help it. Just imagining what Fleur could do with that tasty bit of information made my head ache.

———

"Come to papa, baby," Harry Galligan spoke lovingly to a beautiful specimen of Maryland Blue crab steamed red, one of two remaining from the dozen we ordered at Bo Brooks Crab House on Baltimore's Boston Street. He brought the wooden mallet down hard, shattering the crab's shell, gushing spicy juices that soaked the newspaper-covered tabletop.

With an evil grin, he broke off the crab's claws, laid a sharp knife blade against its carapace, dug the sweet lump meat from its eviscerated body, and popped a morsel into his mouth.

Maybe it wasn't the smartest idea to make my farewell address to someone wielding a sharp instrument, but I'd fortified myself with two and a half beers and the time had come.

"You're a good man, Harry," I began.

"Yup." He concentrated on sucking a sliver of crabmeat from his thumb. "And you're a fine figure of a woman." He looked up. "What's wrong?"

Here was someone who could read my thoughts. A rare find. Every woman's dream.

"Wrong?" I quickly swallowed a spoonful of crab soup hoping the pepper might sharpen my senses.

"Well, we haven't gotten very far with this relationship, but something tells me you're about to give me the old heave-ho."

I wondered when he'd mastered that mind-reading trick. After his divorce, I figured, because he told me once that he'd been oblivious to his wife's diddling her politician girlfriend for the last six months of their marriage.

He whomped a crab. "Ah, well, *de gustibus non est disputandum.*" He registered my blank look. "No accounting for taste."

On the money. In Latin, yet. So much for my thinking of him as an overgrown leprechaun. In my dither over Simon, I hadn't given Harry the credit he deserved. This was a person who'd traveled the world. A crack scientist, probably as well respected in his field as Simon was in his. And on the personal level, Harry was empathic.

I put down my spoon. How do you explain a *coup de foudre*? And not explain to Harry that with *him* there was no zap of lightning, not even the sound of distant thunder.

"You're a fantastic person," I began again.

"Wow. First I was good. Now I'm up to fantastic. When you get to spectacular, sell, right?"

When I didn't answer, he said, "Do you want to talk about him?"

It was like trying to break up with Houdini.

"Come on. If I'm so fantastic and you're still not buying, there has to be someone else. No, honestly, I'm okay with it. And I can tell you need to vent."

That was all it took to launch me into a ten-minute monologue about my feelings for Simon, feelings that were, somehow, easier to lay out for Harry than for Kat or Fleur.

So I told him how I'd surprised myself by falling, no *plunging* in love with the guy. Then I kvetched about how tough it was to maintain a long-distance romance. That we had to work at finding time to see each other. "I'm busy. He's busier."

"You say he's tops in his field. How do you think he got there?" he asked.

"But he warned me he's not very good at relationships."

"Credit his honesty."

"He's in Florida for Thanksgiving. And I haven't heard from him since Wednesday."

"So call him, if you're worried. But come on. He's our age, right? We're not like these kids on their cell phones every minute. He's busy down there. He'll catch you up when he gets back. Women obsess over the craziest things."

"You're right." Leave it to Harry to uncomplicate what I'd complicated into a restless night. "And the thing is, I've got so much respect for him. And admiration. He's brilliant, and charming. And cultured."

Harry raised an eyebrow, which could have meant he was impressed or maybe he was just registering the chef's heavy hand with the Old Bay seasoning. "Culture means a lot to you, huh? You a Dundalk girl?" He named the blue-collar area where my father used to work for Bethlehem Steel.

"East Baltimore, Patterson Park," I replied, feeling a non-menopausal flush rising.

"Ahhh." Harry had my number. "Still, I'm a little surprised. You're a physician. And I'd think being married to Stan, you would have hobnobbed with the rich and famous."

"Not really. The business magazine only took off in the last ten years. Before that it was strictly a Baltimore enterprise. *Berke's Law* still is. By the time *Business* made it big, we had our own circle of friends. Most of them are successful. A lot of them have money, but Baltimore isn't D.C. or New York. The major players don't live here." I whacked the last crab. "I've been to a few Washington parties. But I'm not that impressed with the business crowd. My peers are another story. In my field, Simon is one of the golden boys. National Academy of Sciences. President's Commission on Cancer."

"Which means he's a good doctor, but doesn't mean squat about him as a person." He concentrated on buttering his roll. "Ah, pay no attention to me. If you think he's Superman…"

"I'm not saying he's perfect. He's got a hefty ego. All the powerhouses in science do. But there's something vulnerable about him, too, that touches my heart. And I love the cleft in his chin."

"Your heart. His cleft."

The waitress dumped another dozen crabs on the table.

I giggled and Harry emptied the rest of my beer into his own glass.

"Hey, to each her own," he said. "The man with the cleft is obviously what you think you need. So go for it. As long as you're sure you're finished processing Stan. Because your feelings for this Simon could just be a diversion if you're trying to escape old pain."

"I'm past it," I said. "All ready for new pain."

"I'll drink to that." He took a swig of his Sam Adams. "If it makes you feel any better, I knew what you and I had was just a friendship. Now I'm not saying that at the beginning I wasn't hoping it would catch. You know, turn into something more. But I didn't have to be a genius to notice you weren't burning with desire for me. And, not to hurt your feelings, but I didn't fall out of my shoes when we kissed either. Look, if you really like Simon, he must be a good man."

Over cheesecake he took on an earnest look. "This may sound like a cliché, but I hope we can continue being friends. We have a lot in common, and you're easy to talk to. I know you've got your girlfriends, but you might want a man's take on the new guy. And there might be a time when I need a woman's perspective on another woman."

"Is there something you're not telling me?" No wonder my romantic revelation hadn't sent him into paroxysms of grief. He had other irons in the fire.

"In time, my girl, in time. Right now, all I have is wishful thinking. When I have more, you'll be the first to know, believe me."

He laid his hand—big and hairy as a paw—on mine. "I wish you luck, you know that. I'm cheering for you. And for this Simon fellow, even if he is a bloody limey."

"I know you are, Harry," I said, gazing into my mug, trying to read my future in the swirls of Coffeemate, and wondering if I'd just made a major mistake.

## Chapter 31

*M*onday

Back to work. The week after Thanksgiving is traditionally chaos—patients trying to jam in appointments before the holidays. One more "to do" entry checked off their pre-Christmas list. We were swamped.

Our docs handled the punishing schedule in their own special styles. Seymour, his head buried in a chart, barged into anybody in the vicinity. Neil, a darter, snapped at the staff. Ken ran around with an open can of Diet Dr. Pepper sloshing in the pocket of his lab coat. Bethany...now that was an interesting study in how the aspiring mighty can fall. Vanished was the uppity preppy-peppy bounce, the in-your-face nuisance of a presence. In its place, a wisp of gray wool, an apparition, disappeared around corners or slunk hunchbacked, eyes on the floor like Inspector Clouseau sniffing for clues. Very mysterious.

Maybe she was trying to get the goods on Seymour and Mindy, who had the look of thickly applied innocence, like Raphael cherubim, even as he nibbled kisses (Hershey's out of a Precious Moments cup) at her desk. As I walked by, he boomed words like "organization" and "Xerox" which he probably jammed into the middle of sentences about how he liked to lick her ear.

All right, my antennae may have been oversensitive due to Seymour's escapade with Bethany, and his business with Mindy could have been all business. Still, in spite of our being rushed, on the first day back I spotted him parked at her desk three separate times, which is excessive. And if I saw him, Bethany saw him. You had to wonder what she thought. Felt. How nuts this made her. Even if it was all in her head.

Apropos of nuts, Seymour had complained a few weeks before that the cleaning staff was moving papers on his desk. Then he found his beloved Jaguar XJ with a long, deep scratch along the driver's side door. He was positive the scratch hadn't been there when he parked in the garage that morning. Random or creepy? Accident or Bethany or one of his patients exacting retribution for a Seymour Bernstein ham-handed pelvic exam? Seymour is notorious for jamming his jumbo-sized fingers into narrow spaces with the finesse of King Kong romancing Fay Wray.

Who knows what mayhem any of us is capable of when manhandled? The Harvard-educated, silver-spoon-fed Bethany. Me. Do my Turnbull Prize, my guest column in *GynoToday,* my painful absorption of the art of the fish fork and the Renaissance poets override the wild-assed genes of Helen Kohl Swanson? As I watched the Bethany-Seymour breakup drama unfold, I found myself wondering what atavistic gene might surface, what monstrous deeds I might stoop to if scorned.

In the afternoon, a reporter from the *Baltimore Sun,* interviewing me about my upcoming appearance with Fortune, posed questions I could answer.

*Tuesday*

As it turned out, the *Sun* article was well written and the photographer really did know how to light cheekbones. I came off a Tahari-suited, Mikimoto-pearled monument to trust. My colleagues congratulated me and someone even tacked the clipping to the coffee room bulletin board where I was rereading it for the ninth time when my pager sounded an urgent signal.

Seymour's big hands had gotten him into a major jam this time. Generally, delivering babies doesn't take much finesse. You learn the technique in medical school, but you could learn it as easily at the World Wrestling Federation. Just grab around the neck, fingers supporting the head, and pull. It's not a particularly delicate business.

C-sections take more skill, but after hundreds you get the hang of it. Once in a while, though, it can get tricky. You have to maneuver. And sometimes, it's a tug of war between life and death.

The call was from Seymour's circulating nurse who said, "Mrs. Garland is trying to bleed to death in OR 1. We need some help stat," and I took the stairs two at a time.

Mrs. Garland had to be Sherry Garland, whom I met when I removed her mother's cancerous uterus a few years back and who'd stopped, mid-waddle, to chat with me in the hall after her checkup with Seymour the day before. She had a husband and two other kids at home. Lots of people needed her.

In my field, you get an occasional bleeder. I've never lost one, but I've had a few close calls. The worst was a decade before. Removing a pelvic mass from a patient with lymphoma, I found myself wading up to my wrists in blood. With some fancy finger work and thirty units of AB positive, we pulled her through. After that, the word spread that I was adept at snatching bleeders out of the maws of death and I started getting calls from surgeons lacking that peculiar talent.

This time, I hit the OR trotting. Seymour, who never looked anything but overconfident, looked under. Above the mask, his eyes—showing too much white—widened even more for me. Beads of sweat popped on his forehead. This was a C-section. He'd lifted the baby safely out, but the mama refused to stop bleeding. The cause was placenta accreta in which the placenta grows into the uterine muscle. The procedure to separate took more delicacy than Seymour's huge hands were capable of and now we had a fountain. He bobbed a bow as he backed out of the way and I plunged in. You don't even think at this stage, it's all reflex and heart, and you have it or you don't.

This is what I love. The combat. It doesn't have to be mortal, just perilous. When the dragon breathes fire, you slay the dragon. The closer he gets, the steadier your nerve, the better the sword play.

I knew the topography by heart, but Mrs. Garland's internal landscape had been rendered murky and slippery by hemorrhage and for a split second, when the anesthesiologist calmly stated a tumbling blood pressure, I felt my heart lurch with the possibility of failure. I blocked it and focused on envisioning the internal iliac artery, the one that feeds the pelvis. I imagined precisely where it was and exactly how it felt and pushed myself to move swiftly but cautiously.

Found. Then my trusty instruments and I manipulated and clamped and, twenty units of blood later, stemmed the great tide.

After mama got shipped off to recovery, Seymour and I convened outside the OR to strip our scrubs. "That was a bastard of a bleeder. Thank you, Gwyneth." He said respectfully, "You're good." Not *still* good, which would have earned him a curled lip. Just straight, unqualified good.

We talked shop for a few minutes, which pumped color back to his face, and right before I sprinted to my own patient, he said, "That article in the *Sun* this morning? Great coverage. This Fortune thing could be a real publicity boon for us. Try to mention the name of the practice on the show. And see if they'll flash our 800 number on the screen. I told Barbara to prepare the girls out front for an onslaught of phone calls. Between the TV show and the newspaper article, we're going to be inundated. You know, in retrospect you were right about that Pap Test Week appearance on WJZ. You're the pro. I never should have allowed Bethany to do it. She has no media presence."

No doubt she'd lost it when she lost her position under Seymour.

"Actually, I thought she did a decent job," I responded.

Look, with my picture up on Fortune's website and the *Sun* article, I could afford to be magnanimous. Also, I wasn't inclined to let Seymour get away with gratuitous Bethany-bashing. You want to evict the woman's toe from your crotch, fine. But there's no need to kick her to the curb.

"She seemed to have done her homework. She was articulate. Maybe she could have been more comfortable with the camera, but that takes time, practice."

"You're right, you're right," Seymour agreed. "She needs experience. Give her a few years."

All in all, a very satisfying morning.

*Wednesday*

In the midst of feeding my acid reflux with a tuna sandwich eaten at top speed, I took an interesting phone call. From my old chum, Hollywood's gynecologist to the stars, Davis Standish of the silver ponytail and deep pockets. I hadn't seen Davis since the London IAGSO meeting when we'd spent a total of two minutes at the Tate Gallery reception bullshitting. Now, after the small talk, he sprung a surprise on me.

"We put an ad in *Annals* to hire an OB and got bombarded. Everyone wants to live in L.A., right?"

I didn't say wrong, although I would have to be declared brain dead before I would consent to as much as my beating heart being shipped to Los Angeles.

"Anyway, I'm reviewing CVs and I get stopped in my tracks by your office letterhead. I'm not allowed to ask and you're not allowed to tell according to that ridiculous HHS rule, but screw 'em. What do you think of this ummm...Bethany McGowan?"

"Bethany? Really?" I blurted. I shouldn't have been surprised, given the gray outfits accessorized with the matching cloud hanging over her head. But I'd thought she'd tough it out to see if the alleged Seymour/Mindy dalliance might explode so she could pick up Seymour's pieces. You had to give the woman credit; she had too much self-respect to hang around.

Listen to me, over the brim with sympathy when a few months ago the prospect of Bethany's moving on would have filled me with glee. But what was to gloat about? It wasn't as if she were contemplating leaving because I'd racked up a solid win for sweaty maturity over dewy youth. In the grand tradition of women of every age, she'd been trounced by love.

Davis was saying, "Well, I get the feeling from the cover letter that this is very preliminary. My take is she's scouting around, getting a sense of what's out there. But I don't want to miss an opportunity if she's really good."

"She's really good. Her patients love her. She's a work-horse. And she has a first-class brain."

"Yeah, I figured. Harvard and Hopkins. Sweet CV. But what about her psychological makeup? Is she self-actualized?" Ah, the land of the fruits and the nuts and the people who treat them. "Is she a team player? I run a happy shop here. She's not going to screw up my dynamic, right?"

"Your dynamic is safe." *You, on the other hand, might not be. Bethany's taste runs to older, libidinous men of influence.* This I thought but did not say.

"And she's thinking of leaving because?"

I chewed slowly, trying to come up with something plausible. "I can only guess that she's fed up with Baltimore winters. That she wants a practice with a little more glamour. We're kind of East Coast stodgy. And the two other partners are OBs. So there's not much chance to shine here."

"Sounds reasonable." Even better than plausible. "She's smart, she's young. The PC police will cuff me for this, but she's attractive, right? I mean, she doesn't have to have movie star looks, but Californians are really tuned into healthy. So she can't be four hundred pounds or—"

I cut him off because I was about to gag on my tuna salad. "She's very presentable, Davis."

"Super. Listen, you might not want to share this call with her. The ad promised confidentiality."

"My lips are sealed."

"I really appreciate this, Gwyneth. Very generous of you. If she joins the practice, I'll let her know how gracious you were."

"No need."

"Next time I get into Baltimore…"

"Yeah, lunch," I said. And after we hung up, I dropped the remains of mine into the wastebasket.

Driving home that night, my cell phone rang. It was Fleur. "Are you sitting down?"

"I'm driving. So, yes, I'm sitting down. Are you all right? Kat's not having problems is she?" I asked, alarmed.

"Everyone's fine. Okay, slow down or I'm not responsible."

I was caught in traffic. There's always construction around the Harbor to snag you at rush hour. "Consider me slowed. Now what's this headline news?"

"Oh, baby," Fleur said. "Stop the presses. You remember we were talking about Dan's wife's picture on his desk?"

"Yup." Months ago. A sudden, ominous feeling made my stomach lurch.

"He's not married." She paused, I guess to listen for the sound of metal crashing.

I pulled myself together and called on all my acting skills. "Wow! Dan's not married, huh? That *is* a surprise. I'm stunned."

"Me, too. Imagine, no wife. Well, there was a wife, of course. Melinda Pringle Rosetti, one of the Roland Park-Captiva Island-rolling-in-it Pringles. She died three years ago. Back before he started treating my mother. It was very quick. Some kind of stroke." Here Fleur's voice struck a somber note.

"That's terrible," I said.

"Terrible. And my mother knew. The Pringles are in her crowd. She went to the funeral. Can you believe that osteoporotic little vixen never said a word all this time? I think she was worried if I found out Dan was single, I'd go after him myself and screw up her fantasy of waltzing off with him to Sicily or wherever."

"Hmmm," I said. "How did you find out?"

"Not from my mother. Her friend Bettina, the retired nurse, usually schleps Mother to her doctor's appointments, but Bettina's down with the flu so I had the pleasure. Well, after Mother's exam I got some one-on-one time in Dan's office to discuss her condition. I just happened to comment on the photo, ask after his pretty wife, and boom, the bomb goes off. Widowed."

I felt myself withering under a sudden onslaught of hormonal heat. Literally in a flash, the implications of Fleur's prying became sickeningly clear. Dan was going to think I told her about our encounter in his office the week before, about my turning him down for a date. He'd be mortified. No more than I was already. Good Lord, how was I going to face him?

"I'm giving him Connie's number," Fleur said.

"What? No. I don't think that's such a good idea," I heard myself babbling. I unbuttoned as many buttons as I could get to on my coat. I was dripping.

"It's a brilliant idea. Look, I'd go for him myself, if I didn't think my mother would commit daughtercide for screwing with her dream lover. Kat's dealing with cancer, she doesn't need any more excitement. Plus I haven't given up on her and Lee yet. And you, my pretty, have the terminal hots for Simon York, and are therefore out of the running. But I refuse to let a man of Dan Rosetti's caliber go to waste or get scooped up by some floozy like Jack's Bambi."

I leaned on the horn. The colorblind idiot in front of me was sitting at a green light as if he'd rented the space, and I had a SUV growling behind me.

"So we have Connie who's Italian and fabulous and Dan who's Italian and incredible. It's *beshert*. Fated to be. I've already left a message on his machine," Fleur said.

Dan wasn't the fix-up type, I told myself, struggling to

shed my jacket while seatbelted. Fleur's plans for him wouldn't get off the ground, I decided, all the while wondering why I wasn't rejoicing at the possibility of another happy couple. Because no one was good enough for the wonderful Dr. Rosetti, last of a dying breed. That's why. Not even Constanza deCrespi, Fleur's kick-ass aristocratic attorney.

"Hold on," she said, "I've got another call."

I peered into the Honda ahead. The driver was wearing a headset and gesticulating wildly. No sign he was about to move. Fucking cell phones. Making people crazy. I began to inch my way around him.

Fleur was back. "Listen, that's Dan on the other line. I've got to talk to him about Connie. Back to you later."

"Fleur," I said. "Fleur! Damn!" But she'd clicked off as the SUV behind me cut around my right fender in a shrieking arc. I flipped the driver the bird, but she'd already taken off, oblivious. Too late. Too damn late.

# Chapter 32

Just when I thought I'd never get rid of that last Ziploc of leftover turkey, November bowed out, December blew in, a certain Englishman's Saab got parked in my space in the Waterview garage, and I was in his arms. At last. Three weeks without Simon had left me hungry for him. And not only for his artful lovemaking. I would have been happy just to sleep in his arms after the rare luxury of enough time together.

He'd promised me three-quarters of a day and a long night before he had to head down to Washington on Sunday for the tea dance honoring his funding foundation. "Let's just do whatever's fun in your home town," he'd said, leaving the scheduling up to me. Fun for Simon was catching the traveling exhibit of Neo-Impressionists at the Walters Art Museum and I'd bought concert tickets for the Baltimore Symphony's evening performance. After that, we'd have supper in a restaurant where the crab imperial was to die for. Then he'd whisk me home to bed and bliss. That was the plan.

At the museum, we strolled hand in hand, just another couple out for a Saturday afternoon with the clock not ticking. In the East Gallery, I backed off as Simon drew closer to peer at the perfectly arranged points of a Seurat. Suddenly, the way the painting before me cohered from a distance, I saw our big picture: this extraordinary man had come into my life and brightened it, added vivid color and a splash of excitement. And if not a lot of the relationship made sense close up—our demanding schedules, inconvenient geography, and the huge gap in our backgrounds— from the grander perspective, it worked. He made me grandly happy. Swamped by a wave of tenderness, I moved in, reached out, and stroked the boyish back of his neck.

He whirled around and smiled. "Come closer, Gwyneth, you need to see this. The precision of the light fractioning is absolutely scientific. Amazing, yes?" On the upswing of my nod, he pressed his lips against my forehead. "I love being here with you," he said and drew me to him, which is how I felt his cell phone vibrate against my hip.

"Not now," he moaned. He gave me a look of desperation and retreated a few steps. "Yes," he barked into the phone before he even checked the ID window. "It is, indeed." His voice changed as if someone had buttered it. Straining to listen, I heard, "Actually Baltimore. Ahh, understood. About an hour's travel. Yes, happy to. No, no, no problem. Don't trouble yourself over it. Plans were made to be changed, as my dear old dad used to say. Not at all. See you then."

"Gwyneth," I saw his Adam's apple bob as he clicked off. "We seem to have hit a snag." He flattened his lips to a thin stripe of disappointment.

"Jesus," I said. "Don't tell me. The honeymoon is over."

His hand was already on my shoulder and he steered me to the stairs as he talked a steady stream. "My granting foundation. They're all in D.C. for the Brubaker event tomorrow and they pulled an ad hoc committee together to meet this afternoon. They want to grill me about my projects. Have no choice, of course. Vital for me to defend them. My work depends upon their funding."

I almost said, "How about I go with you? I'll find something to do in D.C. and at least we'll have the night together." I'd strung the words in my head, but didn't say them. I'd accepted scraps from Stan for twenty-six years. Never again.

A man who had honed multitasking to a fine art, Simon didn't break stride while taking the pink granite stairs at a clip, buttoning his coat, and telling me, as I panted to keep up, "I'll call you, but I can't say when. Knowing this crowd, we'll be working into the night. I'll be lucky if I can grab a few hours' sleep. May not touch base until tomorrow."

I thought of the Seurat we'd just seen. A female bare-back rider poised on one foot atop a white horse as it raced around a circus ring. The gutsy woman was smiling, no less. Or maybe she was gritting her teeth.

At the bottom of the stairs, Simon turned and saw my face. It couldn't have been pretty. He stopped dead in his tracks. "Gwyneth," he said. "You're endlessly patient, tolerant beyond the call of duty. I wouldn't do this if it weren't essential to my lab. I can't risk offending my major funding source."

His funding source. Unarguable.

"Imagine if it were your Women's Clinic on the line."

I nodded which was his cue to give me one of his winning smiles, this one tinged with sympathy. "Listen, darling, why don't you stay? No need for both of us to have our day ruined."

He had to be kidding.

"Seriously," he said. "See the rest of the exhibit. I'll catch a cab to your place to pick up my car."

"That's ridiculous."

"Our lives are ridiculous, which is what makes them interesting."

"I'd take less interesting about now," I said, ruefully.

"I understand," he said. "You're right, of course. I'll make it up to you, I promise. We'll do better." His knuckles brushed placating strokes along my cheek. I leaned against his chest.

Underneath the cashmere V-neck, I could feel his muscles tensing, gearing up for a dash to the exit. Sighing, I backed off.

He gave me a quick kiss, an eye on his watch. "I'm so sorry, but I *must* go."

Finally, knowing I was being unreasonable, because it wasn't as if he wanted to cut our weekend short, wanted to work instead of play, I said grudgingly, "Good luck."

He was already on the run. "You're an angel," he called behind him.

That evening, Simon's angel, wings clipped, decided what the hell, she'd done Seurat solo, she might as well not waste both concert tickets. It was an all-Russian program, as romantic as borscht, perfect for a solitary woman trying to keep her mind off her vanished weekend, her absconded lover.

I never made it. As I stepped from the Waterview elevator into the lobby, my cell phone went off. At the other end, Sylvie, the implacable island woman, the one who carried my father's craziness with a gently swaying balance, was hyperventilating. In the two minutes it had taken her to pee, she panted, my addlebrained father managed to figure out the complicated lock I had installed on the front door. He'd vanished into East Baltimore. In December. With night falling.

Dear God.

I swallowed my panic and told Luann, the concierge, I had to go find my father. I said aloud, mostly to calm myself, "What I think is that he walked to the McDonald's. My father loves McDonald's. It's only two blocks down from the house. Or maybe he's in the 7-11. We buy Slurpees for him at the 7-11. I'll roll by on my way."

"He can't have gone far," she assured me. "He probably wandered over to a neighbor's and he's sitting on somebody's porch and they don't even know it."

"Right," I said, grabbing any shred of hope along with my car keys. But as I sprinted to the garage, I called the police.

———

Dan Rosetti's theory is that wandering Alzheimer's patients take off in search of something. The goal oriented ones hunt for their mothers or their dead spouses or, if they're in a care facility, for their homes. But Dan says he's sure that the aimless ones are also searching. For the person they once were. Now isn't that enough to break your heart?

Mine was thumping like a drum when I turned the doorknob on the Streeper Street house. On the way over, I'd managed to convince myself that my father was already back home sitting safely in his recliner. But no, he was still on the loose and there was only Sylvie on the sofa, nervously wringing a tissue and, next to her, a police officer jotting down a list of places where he may have lighted.

"You know he has Alzheimer's?" I asked the officer as I tossed my jacket.

Blanchett was her name, a softly cushioned brown-skinned woman. She said, "Yes, Ms. Needam here told me. With folks like your dad, we don't wait. We have uniforms out there already combing the neighborhood. And if it's any reassurance, these are the people we generally find real fast. They never get too far. He has some identification on him, right?"

I nodded. I'd taken away his car when he wasn't looking, but he'd held onto his license. He also wore a medical bracelet.

We spent some time going over possible leads. I dug out his most recent photograph, which was actually of the two of us taken, as if I needed more immediate pain, on the night of The Treachery, in the kitchen at Crosswinds.

"Why, he's a sweetie, isn't he?" Officer Blanchett peered at the photo. "What a nice open smile."

The damn house was like a freezer. Why in God's name was the thermostat set at fifty-eight when my father's old bones needed heat? The tattered Orioles throw he wrapped himself in, winter and summer, was no match for this hollow BenGay-scented cold.

It wasn't Sylvie's fault, I reminded myself. He was *my* father. I needed to be here more often checking up on things, not in bed with Simon or getting my nails done at the Istanbul. Holding Kat's hand and excising carcinomas from patients in peril were acceptably noble activities, but the rest were no excuse. And because of my neglect, my selfish preoccupations, my father was wandering around without a coat in the cold of winter somewhere, who knows where. I bounded up, going for my jacket.

"The Marines have landed!" A familiar voice turned me around to see Fleur leading a rag-tag battalion from the kitchen, a motley and beautiful crew that quickly filled up the small Streeper Street living room. My old flame/new friend Harry Galligan and Mark Silva, president of the local chapter of FRESH. Tracy, my manicurist, who rushed to hug me. Quincy Dickerson, Fleur's shop manager, was doing his Queenella LaBella act at an AIDS fund raiser, but his main squeeze—a butch fireman named Brendan—showed up carrying a huge flashlight and a bag of Starbucks coffee.

And there was Dr. Dan Rosetti, his hand on the shoulder of a stunning young woman who vaguely resembled the ponytailed little girl perched on her mother's lap in the photo on Dan's desk. "My daughter Chrissy. She's been through Outward Bound. Chrissy's great to have in a search party."

When I got her alone, I gave Fleur a hug. "I don't believe this. How did you find out about my dad?"

"Well, of course you didn't call me, not that you have the vaguest idea of what friendship is all about. Luann got a hold of me. I made a few phone calls. With everyone out looking, we'll make short work of this and maybe you'll be able to salvage some of your big weekend with Simon." She cocked her head to get a view of the hall behind me. "So where is he?" Then she read my eyes. "Oh my God, he's not here. Please." She held up a halting hand, impossible to ignore.

Fleur's palms are as big as a man's and she wears a size 10 ring. "Don't give me the crap about his being British and how the governess raised him and the shitty way he was treated at Eton or whatever. Prince Charles would be out there with a flashlight tonight. For your information, Dan Rosetti was supposed to be on his first date with Connie, which he postponed to be here for you." She clucked exasperation. "Of course, your wonderful Simon…"

"…doesn't even know about my father going missing," I finished her sentence. "We were at the Walters when he got called to a meeting in D.C. With his primary funding source."

When she curled her lip, I said, "Do you know how hard it is to pull in money these days? Ask me who I'd go off with if I had a choice between a wild night with Simon or a couple of hours pleading the Clinic's case before the president of the Franzblau Foundation."

She drew a sigh so deep it threatened to pop her bra. "All right, forget Simon. You've got a pack of people out there ready to tear this neighborhood apart. Let's go find the only man in your life you can count on."

"Who doesn't have two coherent brain cells to rub together. Figures. My poor lost father."

It was only when she reached up to wipe the tears from my cheek that I realized I was crying and maybe not just for him, maybe for his poor lost daughter who, in spite of herself and everything her mama said with the belt in hand or the hanger raised, had loyal friends who came through for her like her daddy did.

Now that I knew I was crying, I let myself sink into sobs. "What if he got hit by a car? What if he got mugged? There are junkies out there who will kill for a dollar or two."

"Not for Monopoly money," Fleur answered.

My thready voice spiraled out of control. "Like they look. They shoot first, then they take your wallet."

"Come on, pull it together. You'll have time for crapping out when everyone is home safe and sound." Fleur would make a great prison matron. She spun me around and pushed me along, roughing me up a little when I hesitated. "You'll feel better when you're doing something. Get going."

———

Chrissy mapped out our routes and organized us into bands. Dan, Mark, and Tracy. Fleur, Harry, and Brendan. Chrissy and me. Sylvie stayed back to take calls or just be there in case my father ambled home. The cops had already searched door to door on the block and combed two more in each direction, but we fanned out hitting the high spots along the main drag, Eastern Avenue, and the side streets. Chrissy and I stopped off at a tavern my father used to frequent when too much beer and not the ravaged connections between his brain and his legs made him stagger. We checked out the all-night laundromat, the Greek restaurant where my mother once waved a knife at the waitress for not enough lamb in the moussaka, and the animal hospital where my father, Rolfe, and I carried Snookie, the family mutt, in a bedsheet after she got hit by a car. That happened forty-three years ago, but Dad talked to my dead Aunt Margie so I hoped maybe he'd gone back to pick up Snookie.

At around eleven we shambled in with nothing to show for four hours. A new arrival, the WJZ-TV camera crew, had taken over the living room.

My father's disappearance was the lead story on a slow news night. Eyes smudged with worry, I begged on local television, "Please, please if you see an old man in a brown sweater who seems to belong to no one"—I almost lost it there—"please call the police hotline."

They flashed a number on the screen over my dad's photo. Then the anchorwoman said, "That was Dr. Gwyneth Berke, a local gynecologist, whose mentally impaired father is missing in East Baltimore."

Publicity, but not what Seymour Bernstein had in mind when he encouraged the partners to keep a high media profile.

"You did good," Fleur said after the TV crew had departed and she'd steered me into the tiny, overheated kitchen for a cup of coffee. "You need to get the word out. Which reminds me, did you phone the kids?"

"Whit's in the middle of exam week. Drew's in LA doing that short-term internship at the Hirschorn. I don't want to make them crazy unless there's good reason. Or in this case, awful reason. I'll call them tomorrow if he's still missing."

"Yeah, well, speaking of missing," Fleur peered at me over her cup with lidded tortoise-wise eyes, "have you called Simon?"

He hadn't phoned me, which meant he was still out there pressing the funding flesh or had collapsed exhausted in his hotel bed. I didn't want to disturb him.

"Decided against it. Look," I rushed to preempt her, "I know he's put in a long, hard day. Even if I caught him, he'd have to drive back to Baltimore, then find his way here. And I wouldn't want him roaming around." I waved my hand towards Patterson Park. "This is a tricky neighborhood. He'd get lost out there."

"Because we'd send him out entirely on his own? Because Baltimore is a jungle, unlike New York, which is...?"

"You're right, you're right. But do we really need one more person out walking the streets? And I'm not sure what else he could do. Hold my hand, I guess. But I've got you for that."

I dug my toe into a spot in the linoleum that had started to peel. How many times had I asked my dad to let me fix up the house since he wouldn't hear of moving? But no, he liked the depressing mustard color my mother had chosen for the walls thirty years before and the bizarre collection of clown art she'd hung on them. He'd even refused to let me remove the see-through plastic covers from the living room furniture.

I ran my hand over the Formica kitchen table, sweeping grains of sugar.

"Not ritzy enough for Simon, huh?" Fleur could always see right through me.

"That's not fair." I didn't look up. "He isn't a snob."

"Who's talking about *him?*"

I felt myself simmer with embarrassment as we both confronted my shameful truth: I was uncomfortable with the prospect of Simon visiting Streeper Street and catching a glimpse of my shabby blue-collar beginnings.

God bless Fleur. She'd skewer me later for being a small-minded, self-hating arriviste. And get no fight from me. But for now, she just threw me a pitying look and gave me a pass, along with a refill on my coffee.

*Chapter 33*

I spent all night hunting for my father. With Mark. With Dan. With no luck.

At 2 a.m., outside an all-night pharmacy, Mark and I ran into Quincy Dickerson, who'd raced over from his show to join the search. Though he'd ditched the Tina Turner wig and traded the four-inch heels for hip-hop Reeboks, he hadn't taken the time to cream off the theatrical makeup and I heard Mark emit a disbelieving squeak and watched his irises bloom in the light of the RX sign as he gazed on the remnants of Queenella LaBella.

Quincy winked at him and unfolded a map of Baltimore. "Now here's what I've covered so far. But remember, I've only been on the streets a little more than an hour." He traced a twenty block radius with a magenta-polished fingernail. "I know you're discouraged, but trust me, it's just a matter of time before he turns up. Half of Baltimore's finest is out cruising for him. Right in front of the Polish Home Club, I got stopped by a Charm City cop car fitted out with two very cute uniforms. Just a routine hassle. They thought I was out hustling. Dirty minds."

Mark giggled uneasily.

"Anyway, when I told them I was searching for Harald they gave me these flyers. And tape. I've been taping them to windows and lampposts and you name it. He's the pin-up boy of East Baltimore, your daddy is." I gave him a wry smile and his false eyelashes batted furiously, telegraphing compassion. "Ah, babykins. Someone's going to spot him. Cross my heart. Just wait till morning when the folks hit the streets."

I nodded, yearning with all my heart to believe him. But I knew the effects of below-freezing temperatures on a fragile body and I didn't think we had that much time.

——

At sunup, with my father still at large, Fleur and I sat in the Streeper Street living room trying to come up with fresh leads for the new cop on duty. Male, approaching retirement, basset-jowled, and nursing a bad cold, Sgt. Jamison wasn't nearly as comforting as the nice woman officer from the day before.

He blew his nose, coughed noisily, and flipped the used tissue into the trash basket, peppering the air with his virus. Then he turned a bleary eye on me. "Look, you're a doctor, I can play it straight with you. Every hour that passes is a strike against him. And he's been gone twelve. I read some report that said about half of Alzheimer's patients die if they're not located within twenty-four hours. Plus it's wicked cold out there. So the clock is ticking." For that, God gave him a coughing fit. When he could talk, he said, "On the other hand, we've got squad cars out there looking for him. Someone could have led him to a shelter. He could be sleeping on a heating grate. Miracles do happen."

Fleur threw him a fist disguised as a look and hauled me off to the kitchen where we refueled on Brendan's high-test coffee. Wrapped in a chenille bedspread lifted from

Rolfe's old room, she looked like a soothsayer and, after all our years of friendship, she probably could read my mind. "He's not dead, Gwynnie. His brain may have gone to cottage cheese, but physically he's strong as a horse. They'll find him. Didn't Sergeant Shmucko say they've got lots of cops out there trying to track him down? Let them do their job. Why don't you try to get some sleep? If you think you'll be out of the loop in the bedroom, catch a half hour on the sofa. I'll man the phone so you won't miss anything. Deal?"

"Deal."

But I couldn't sleep. As if I weren't sufficiently haunted by the picture of my father curled up in frozen eternal rest against some dumpster, there was an ice storm predicted for late afternoon. So I went out and knocked on doors and posted fliers under a menacing sky. On my way home, I stopped to light a candle at St. Stanislaus, my mother's church. She'd gone to mass there every Sunday and I assumed that's where she'd made her weekly mind-boggling confessions. And she'd been buried there. If any goodness lurked in that tormented soul of hers, it hovered over the statues of the saints or drifted among the incense at St. Stan's. A long shot, but we were pretty much out of options.

I was brought up Lutheran like my dad—Rolfe, because she disliked him less, got to be Catholic—but I'd never been much for prayer. As a kid, I'd tried, but it hadn't worked for me. Now, brought to my knees by my father, I prayed to my mother, of all people, to intercede. "If you ever loved him, find him for us. Please, Mama." That's how desperate I was.

By the time I left the church, its steps were littered with the first gritty pebbles of ice and ten minutes later sleet was battering so hard, I heard only consonants when Quincy called out behind me, "Gotcha covered." He pulled alongside, swung his umbrella so we could share, and fell in step with me.

"You can take off the babushka now. Not a good look. Unless you're trying to blend in with the simple folk of the Polish countryside. How you doing? Not so hot, huh?"

I could only manage a nod.

"Yeah, me either. How long have you been out?"

I held up four gloved fingers.

"Listen, don't take this like I'm giving up, because that couldn't be farther from the truth. But I think we've done all we can on foot. What say we go back to your dad's house, find us some dry clothes, grab a cup of coffee, and then, if you want, we can take a car out. Just drive around and see if we can spot him. Does that sound like a plan? And we could stop off at the senior center. Has anyone called over there? Yes? Well, how about the lady who brought over that killer rum cake. Let's give her a call. She might have an idea."

Mrs. Parente, the knitter from the senior center. My dad's pal. She hadn't even crossed my mind.

I gave Quincy my first smile of the day, a grateful one. The world's first transvestite detective. And a damned sight better sleuth than Sgt. Jamison who, Fleur told me when I checked in by cell phone, was snoring on my father's sofa, spewing germs like Old Faithful.

"We're heading home," I shouted into the phone over the pelting sleet. "But in the meantime, see if Sylvie can find a Mrs. Parente's phone number. Tell her she's the lady who bought over the cake yesterday."

"Someone brought over cake? There's cake?" Fleur crackled back just before I lost the connection.

We were four blocks from Streeper Street, picking our way gingerly over the slick sidewalk when suddenly the sky split, discharging a blast of icy shrapnel, and I lost my footing. Quincy caught me on my way down and hauled me to my feet. Then he steered me into the closest refuge, my father's favorite McDonald's.

"Let's wait out the worst of it here," he said, as we basked in the warmth and the light. Then he got a good look at me and pursed his lips. "Oh darlin'," he said, backing off, "you really do look like the abominable snow-woman. Ronald McDonald meet Madame Yeti." He grabbed a fistful of napkins and mopped the frost off my face, then wiped his own. "Much better. We don't want to frighten the horses, do we? And now, if you'll excuse me for just a sec, my teeth are swimming. Got to tinkle. Order me a large coffee, black, please. And one of those fried apple pies. That should thaw out my intestinal tract."

He was off. And then, within what seemed like seconds, he was back. I was concentrating on laying out spoons and napkins so I saw the bulky shadow of him on the table before I heard him say, "Would you like fries with this, ma'am?"

I looked up to see a grinning Quincy and, standing next to him, my father.

"Daddy," I rushed toward him. I hugged him. I kissed his stubbly cheek, his forehead, the palm of one hand. I wrapped my arms around his bony shoulders and rocked him. He was my father, but he was also my baby.

When I finally backed off, he said, "So where have you been?" Which made me laugh hysterically. Then Quincy began to cackle and finally my father caught the giggles and the three of us stood there in the warm, greasy, delicious McDonald's air laughing until we cried. After a minute, the men stopped but I was way beyond tears of relief and I couldn't stifle my sobs. I only sucked them up when Quincy said, "You're scaring him." He was right. My father, his face twisted with sympathy, reached into his pants pocket and pulled out a wrinkled gray handkerchief. He pressed it to my eyes. How many times had he done that over the course of my childhood, that gesture that was an apology and an admission of helplessness? Then he pressed it against my nose.

"Blow," he said, very clearly.

I blew and leaned against him, savoring that one sweet moment with the balance shifted.

———

We entered the Streeper Street house triumphantly, Quincy trilling, "Yoo-hoo, anybody home? Look what the cats dragged in."

Fleur emerged from the kitchen and, at the sight of our bedraggled trio, flung the fork she'd been licking into the sink and threw herself at my bemused father. Sylvie, after an initial gasp, slumped against the breakfront, eyes closed, praising the Lord and thanking Jesus again and again. I called the police to report we'd found my dad.

Over a fresh pot of coffee, and soup and bread for my father, Quincy explained how he'd been alerted by the snoring from the next stall and bent over to see legs ending in slippers under the partition. "I said, 'Who's in there, who's in there?' I shouted it a few times which woke him and he called back 'hello, hello' and, of course, I recognized the voice. 'Harald, unlock the door,' I told him. 'It's Quincy, you remember me, Quincy, Gwyneth's friend. I work for Fleur, the lady with the dress shop. Open the door.' Nothing. He wouldn't. Or couldn't. So I had to crawl under. And let me tell you, that was a contortionist's trick. Thank God I'm a dancer and stay in shape. It's a big shape, but it's *in* shape." He bobbled his massive head, appreciating his own joke.

"So I slither under, trying not to think of the germ colonies I'm wiping out on my back. But it was worth it, because there he was, weren't you sweetheart, sitting on the throne. All dressed up with no place to go. Cozy as a cat. His slippers were dry so he'd probably been there since it started icing up."

"And no one saw him in there?" Fleur asked. "For more than an hour?"

"Brendan checked earlier and didn't spot him. Maybe he wasn't there then. And with the storm, the place was nearly empty, right Gwyn? Even if one of the staff walked in, they're kids. They wouldn't question a locked stall with a pair of feet hanging down."

"But you have no idea of where he was before McDonald's?" she pressed.

"Well, he had the scent of French fries on his breath, Nancy Drew. And I wiped some ketchup from his chin when I cleaned him up. The kids at the counter said they didn't feed him. So he'd probably dug himself up a dumpster dinner. All we know is his survival skills kicked in. The wheres and hows of his long day's journey into whatever will probably remain a mystery. He's not telling, are you, Harald? And, really, who cares? He's healthy, he's happy, and he's back. That's all that counts."

After he demolished the last of Mrs. Parente's cake, my father let me take him into his room to check him over. He seemed to be in good shape for a man who'd braved the frigid streets of Baltimore for twenty hours. The only residual evidence of his trial was mild dehydration, even after all the water and orange juice we pumped into him at McDonald's, plus more water, tea, and soup at home. There was no sign of hypothermia, probably because he'd been wearing his ratty old sweater and a blue flannel shirt beneath. Or maybe because intermittently he'd found refuge in warm halls or by steam vents. Or maybe his surprisingly healthy state was the work of my mother. You'd think I would have given up on her, even on her spirit, after what she put us through. But somehow it was a comfort to think she'd zombied up from warmer climes to answer my prayer.

Dr. Dan, who stopped by later to give him a more thorough examination, said Harald was a tough customer who'd live to amble off again. Which is why we needed to talk.

"Later," I pleaded.

Once Sylvie and I settled my father in bed, I hunted down a bottle of aquavit and poured a round for the rest of us.

"To my father," I said, hoisting the toast in the direction of his bedroom. "To safe returns and happy endings. And to Quincy. How can I ever thank you?"

Quincy pressed a multi-ringed hand against his broad chest, honestly touched. "Oh, baby, there's no need. Now I *will* say you're lucky I decided to use the men's room and not the ladies' as I've been known to do in my time. And I'm just glad he was willing to go along with me. I mean, would you trot off merrily with some six-foot black queen in a Judy Garland at The Palace sweatshirt and false eyelashes? The man may be lacking something upstairs, but he still has marvelous taste. So skoal to Harald. Skoal to us all."

Before he left, Dan cornered me in the kitchen. "You don't want to hear this and I don't want to say this, but it's time, Gwyneth. He needs a safer place." I saw the collapse of my face mirrored in his own. We looked distraught. "Michelle says you haven't phoned." It had only been a week since he'd scrawled the social worker's name and number on the paper that was still folded in my wallet. "She'll ease you into it. It may take months to get him settled, so you need to get started now."

And before I left, Sylvie pulled me aside. "I can't go through such a fright again, Dr. Berke. I have blood pressure. So I'm telling you now that I'll work through New Year's, but that's it. And if you're thinking of using Blossom, her new class schedule starts January third so you can't count on her. I'm sorry, but at least I'm giving you a month to come up with someone to watch Mr. Harald." Her eyes were moist.

I put my arm around her. "That's very fair, Sylvie."

Which was true, but I didn't know if I could find a place for him to live in such a short time. And even if I could, I didn't know how I was going to live with myself.

*Chapter 34*

I was still emotionally wrung out when Simon finally checked in Sunday night. He'd been swamped of course and was just coming up for air. He missed me. How was I doing?

I told him about the search for my father. How the old man had wandered for hours in an ice storm without a coat. How I'd been out all night tracking him. I made a point that my friends had rallied. I sniffled as I recounted the McDonald's reunion.

"My poor Gwyneth. It sounds like you went through hell. I'm glad your friends were there for you. But why didn't you phone me? You should have called."

"And you would have done what? Interrupted your meeting? Put your funding source on hold?" I asked wearily. "What would have been the point? Be honest, Simon. Faced with the choice between your work and me, would you have chosen me?"

Dead silence at the other end. Broken finally by his clearing his throat. And then he said, "Maybe you're right about the old Simon. But the new and improved Simon would have been there for you. I would have got though my meeting and then excused myself. Then I would have driven to Baltimore to do whatever I could to help you find your papa. But you never gave me the chance, did you?"

"I thought—"

"I know what you thought. And a few years ago, no doubt you would have been right. But not any longer. Not with you." He let that sink in before he said, "Obviously, we have a way to go in terms of trust, of knowing the other person's heart. Which is one of the hallmarks of a success-ful intimate relationship, yes?" It sounded like he was hitting the self-help books again. Maybe *I* needed to go on Amazon.

"I'm sorry," I said, feeling I'd done him an injustice. Tracy, my manicurist, told me I had major trust issues. Stemming from my mother, aggravated by Stan. Now they were spilling over to my relationship with Simon. "I have a tendency to rush to judgment. I'll work on that," I promised him.

"No apologies necessary. We've both got work to do. Let's not make too much of it. Just think of it as a little bump in what I hope will be a long and happy road."

———

Less of a bump, more like a pothole that swallows you whole.

The following day, mid-morning, I was in my office catching up on paperwork when Mindy put a call through from Simon. Forgoing his normal introductory small talk, he cut to the chase. "You haven't read your *Washington Post* yet today," he said, as if he had a crystal ball.

No time in the morning for such luxuries. I brought the paper to work in my briefcase. If I was lucky enough to get a break for lunch, I read it then. If not, I repacked it and tackled it when I could in the evening.

"Why?" I asked. "Did you make the front page?" That was half joke, half serious. You couldn't put it past him to cop some lofty scientific prize. "It's right here, though." I extracted it from my briefcase.

"Well, I'd like you to read it now, please. Style Section; page C3, above the fold. Right-hand column. I'll wait."

"Won't take long," I said, "I'm a fast reader. Hot Flashes?"

I could almost feel his shudder through the phone. "Yes."

**Hot Flashes**, the headline, was in bold face. Beneath it, a copy block.

> **Ducky and Doc: Romance Sails the Pond?** That was wealthy Washington benefactor Delores "Ducky" Franzblau in the arms of veddy British, veddy famous cancer doc Simon York at the Kerns-Brubaker Tea Dance fund-raiser yesterday at the Ritz-Carlton. It had to have been more than Ducky's contribution of two mil to the prestigious New York institution that brought stars to the eyes of York, who never left her side. The couple was pasted together for every waltz and fox-trot. When questioned about a romance, Ducky gushed, "Just old friends. But very close friends," and the urbane York gallantly commented, "A lovely woman with a generous heart. Can you think of anything more irresistible?"

"Finished," I announced, in a voice that implied "terminated." I was swaying in my chair.

He took a deep breath that sounded like it filled all the alveoli of his lungs. "So you see why I wanted to alert you before you found it on your own and perhaps jumped to erroneous conclusions."

"Hold on," I said. "I'm looking at the photograph."

In it, Simon, more alive than I currently hoped, was staring into the camera, his normally serene features drawn into the human equivalent of The Happy Face, irises jumbo dots, grin carved nearly ear to ear. And he was indeed superglued at the hip to Ducky Franzblau, around whose liposuctioned twenty-three-inch waist his arm was entwined. Ducky was fortyish and attractivish with the best nose money could buy and the too-familiar quotient of adoration in the gaze she beamed up at him.

"Very nice," I said. "Worth a thousand words."

"All of them false," Simon said. When the silence at my end grew thunderous, he broke it with, "Gwyneth, are you there?"

"Here," I said. "Ducky Franzblau. What kind of person is named Ducky?" I rescanned the paragraph, getting zapped by small shocks each time I hit a key phrase. "You were pasted to her," I read. "You had stars in your eyes. You were an item. Jesus, Simon."

"We weren't. It's all rubbish. A gossip column. Made up whole cloth. No better than those supermarket tabloids. This woman is the head of my foundation."

No comment. I used my doctor strategy. Just listened.

"The photographer posed us, inching us together. I suppose I should have been more aware of the consequences but I didn't think anyone would misinterpret what was a congenial gesture. And you can't exactly tell your benefactor you don't want to stand next to her." He paused, then threw what he must have thought was his best punch. "What happened to the trust issues you were going to work on?"

Not smart to get aggressive in the middle of a weak defense. Someday, if there *was* a someday, I'd trounce him in chess. "You want to talk trust? While I was out combing the streets for my father in twenty-degree weather, you were warming up to Ducky Franzblau. This was the meeting you left me for. So much for trust."

"Not true. There *was* a meeting on Saturday. The tea dance was Sunday. You're not making sense here. This isn't like you, Gwyneth. So over the top." He sighed. "Look, this is no good over the phone. We have to see each other. Talk this through. You need to be in my arms where those doubts of yours will vanish, I promise." I heard a frantic rustle of paper in the background. "This Friday you're in Manhattan for that television program, right?"

Right. The first of my two appearances with Fortune Simms.

"I know I told you I have to be in California this weekend for an editorial board meeting." Simon was listed on the masthead of one of our specialty's most prestigious journals. "But I don't leave for San Francisco until midday Friday—ah, here we go—December eleventh. So why not come in early and stay over Thursday. We can put your fears to rest."

"Thursday?" I took a long pause. "I'll think about it."

"Please," he said.

"Fine," I said, with a proper reluctant edge.

"Wonderful." He was instantly cheerier. "Sweetheart, we've something special here. Let's give it every chance."

With that, I didn't slam, but did hang up the phone.

Then I wiped my sweaty palms on my lab coat and read the paragraph a third time. Slowly. For nuances. Chewing a nail. And considered all possibilities, like the scientist I was. My conclusion: if you microscopically examined the context, Simon's comment could have just as easily been interpreted as the response of a grateful beneficiary to a donor's largesse.

Which made me feel a lot better. The problem was, if you're bullshitting yourself, how do you know?

At eight that evening a floral delivery arrived. Fleur spotted Luann, our concierge, signing for it and called up for me to come claim it.

"Flowers. So exciting!" Luann crowed, beaming behind the lobby desk.

"Ducky and Doc Sailing the Pond?" Fleur said. She'd read the *Post* item and for once hadn't given me her uncensored opinion. So far. But she eyed the flowers suspiciously.

I opened the card. "We'll work this out. Together. With love." I handed the card to Fleur. "You can't tell me that's not sweet."

She blew a Bronx cheer. We all stripped down the green and white paper.

"Holy Casanova," Fleur muttered as we stared at three dozen long-stemmed red roses. She gave a wolf whistle. "This must have cost him a pretty penny. I'm impressed. He pulled out all the stops for you. You've got to wonder, though. Is it love? Or is it guilt? Real or Memorex?"

"Well," Luann said, "I think your flowers are gorgeous. And your Englishman—the doctor?—is very distinguished. But I have to tell you, in my humble opinion, the one with the beard, that Mr. Galligan who used to come by? Now he's a real charmer."

"My sentiments exactly. Harry Galligan. He da man," Fleur managed to get out before I turned on my heel and headed for the elevator lugging my roses.

# Chapter 35

Subj: Good Fortune
Date: Sunday 12/6 4 p.m. Eastern Standard Time
From: Fortune@FortuneSimms.net
To: gsberke@md.com

Dear Gwyneth,

Time to energize for your Friday, December 11, appearance on *Good Fortune!* Our other guest will be Dr. Prasad Rao talking about taking stock of your relationships as an end-of-year exercise. A copy of his new book, *Men Are Coconuts, Women Are Pomegranates,* will be in your mailbox by Monday. I suggest you read it before your appearance. It will give you the courage and confidence to own your feelings and speak your mind.

Tips to maximize your power this week:

Be healthy: Avoid alcohol, eat well. Try a juice fast for 24 hours before the show to rid your body of toxins.

Be brainy: Practice yoga, which increases blood to the brain and keeps your thinking cells shipshape.

Be zippy: Rejuvenate your momentum with good sex.

Be centered: Meditate to enrich your spirit. Bless each day
     with a promise to take charge of your life.

Monday: Reap the rewards of being your highest self.
Tuesday: Take pleasure from work and special talents.
Wednesday: Give freely without expectation of return.
Thursday: Love is negotiable. Bargain from the heart.
Friday: Trust the lightbulb moment—the Great Aha!—
     when it all comes together in a flash.

See you Friday in the Green Room for a final briefing.

With love and joy,
Fortune

"A juice fast? Have sex? That woman is six feet four of
high-quality chutzpa. What a control freak. Do you think she
lets that husband of hers pee standing up?" Fleur read over
my shoulder, shedding pork rind crumbs onto my computer.

Kat appeared in the doorway holding a tray with
steaming mugs of ginseng tea and a plate of fruit and
cheese. "You can make fun of Fortune Simms, Fleur, but
she's supposedly studied Eastern philosophy at an ashram
in Tibet. Personally, I think she has some interesting things
to say. About not blaming yourself for life choices, but
taking responsibility for them. And Gwyneth, it might be
helpful to practice that attitude as you're working out your
problems with Simon this week."

Fleur swiped all of the Gouda, sniffed the tea, and
waved it away. "Good luck." She gave me a skeptical look.
"I just don't know about this guy. Maybe Simon York is

brilliant with bacteria or cancer cells but the man *tells* you he stinks with more advanced life forms and you fall in love with him. I mean really, why don't women believe men when they confess their faults? Why do we think we're the one who will finally change him? Even after parades of women have gone down like ten-pins thinking the same thing."

"People *can* change," Kat countered, eyes firing. "It sounds like he's already done some work and is open to more. As for this Ducky person, let's not jump to conclusions. I mean, can we really trust the media to get the facts straight? Everything is so sensationalized these days. And say he did go a little overboard in buttering up his benefactor. It's not helpful to blame him exclusively. Gwyn has to take some responsibility for not setting down ground rules for the relationship early on. Responsibility, not blame. Fortune says blame is a brick wall. Responsibility is an open window."

"And I am a door that will slam shut behind me if you don't stop spouting this feel-good drivel. Honestly, Kat, you are so gullible. Fortune Simms is no philosopher. She's a marketing machine. She's zeroed in on every woman's doubts and fears and she makes millions plastering them with these verbal Band-Aids that—"

"Hush, Fleur," Kat, ever polite, cut her off. "I'm not saying you have to swallow this woman's philosophy whole cloth. But she didn't get where she is without touching some universal chord. Why not just extract what you need from what she offers?"

Why not indeed.

———

"Love is negotiable." Fortune's Thursday quote had been lifted, I discovered, from *Men Are Coconuts,* etc., the 244-page jumble of pop psychology, Eastern mysticism, and off-the-wall horticulture I thumbed through on the train to New York.

I figured if I was going to share Fortune's guest couch with its author, Dr. Rao, the next day, I'd better bone up on his fruity theory. It might also give me some tips for my upcoming powwow with Simon.

The gist of it was that men are coconuts—a simple organism, tough skinned, hairy on the outside, blandly pleasant within. Women are pomegranates—complicated, compartmentalized, in part unpalatable, and difficult to get to the heart of. But when you do, ah the rewards—the seeds of Nirvana, sweet, tart, and juicy. Coconut-men want relationships to be simple and uniformly sweet. When there are problems, hack them open, lay them out. Pomegranate-women pick, pick, pick, suck and spit, suck and spit, which drives the coconuts crazy. Dr. Rao's book counseled women to achieve their relationship goals by coconut-negotiating: slicing to the heart of the problem and presenting the meat of their concerns quickly and directly.

Elephant manure or brilliant strategy? We'd see when I had my talk with Simon. I was prepared to slice.

He welcomed me with everything short of a brass band. The apartment was spick-and-span, as if the cleaning lady had left only minutes before. Playing softly in the background was a romantic rhapsody and Simon had actually lit a vanilla candle in the living room. Overkill, I thought. But still, a part of me was touched he'd gone to all the trouble.

I accepted his kiss, though I didn't give much back.

"We have to talk," I said, as soon as I took off my coat.

"Of course, but there's no need to rush. You've had a long train ride. Change into your nightclothes. I have tea and biscuits waiting. How about I bring a tray to the bedroom? I'll give you a back rub, and you can unburden yourself."

"No back rub, no biscuits."

He looked so stricken I said, "Yes, to bedroom and tea."

There was lavender soap in the bathroom next to my towel and on my side of the bed a vase of roses, mixed red and white. "The florist told me red is for passion," Simon announced, "and white for harmony," this last uttered softly as if he were making a fervent wish.

Denied. When I emerged from the bathroom, I found him leaning back on the pillows, eyes closed. He patted the blanket next to him.

I knew if I got in, if I felt the warmth of that deliciously hairy coconut body against my skin, heard the English accent murmuring sweet everythings, I'd cave. So I stood my ground at the foot of the bed and talked. And he opened his eyes.

I told him how disappointed I was that we had so little time together. That yes, we had tight schedules and yes, we lived in two different cities, but if this relationship were to continue, we'd have to do better. "If we're going to make this work we need to invest more into it. Because relationships are built on time spent together and we spend hardly any."

"That's not entirely true," he protested. "Actually, we've seen each other a good deal since we met in September. This weekend was a disaster, admittedly. But let's review. We missed two weeks because of your friend's lumpectomy. Surely I can't be held responsible for that. Then there was Budapest. Unavoidable. And the weekend I spent in Key West. On my calendar before you and I had even met."

He'd closed his eyes to count, I suppose, because he

said, "We've seen each other a total of eight times over three months. Which is laudable, considering."

"Two or three were only hours long. Just for sex, it seemed."

His eyes snapped open. "That's beneath you, Gwyneth. Nonetheless, you've won the larger point. So let's make it better. Right now. Chop-chop." He leapt out of bed, wrapped himself in a silk robe, and cleared a spot from the clutter on the round table parked next to his dresser. He pulled two chairs close.

We took out our calendars. Mine was a state-of-the-art PDA handheld, which he viewed with distrust. Electronic gadgets weren't Simon's strong suit. His calendar was primitive, a little brown leather notebook, probably crammed with his physician-typical chicken scratchings.

We penned, not penciled, in four meetings over the following six weeks. Two were only half days in Baltimore for Simon, one en route to Slovakia to treat the newly elected woman prime minister, the other a detour on his return from a Miami consult. But we had two full weekends on the docket, New Year's Eve for me in Manhattan and in Baltimore at the end of the upcoming week after his presentation at the GRIA conference in D.C.

I could live with that. For the time being. Long term, I wasn't sure how long distance would hold up. But now wasn't the time to fret about it. Dr. Rao's book had a chapter on living in the moment; "the present is a gift," he called it.

"There," Simon said, closing his calendar, "well done. Lots to look forward to. Now," he gave me a twinkling smile, "any other complaints? This is the time, luv. Let's get them all on the table and deal with them. No unfinished business to ruin our night."

"Well, there's the matter of exclusivity."

"What?" His smile faded.

In spite of the opening throb of a tension headache, I pressed on. "Exclusivity. It might be we came too far too fast. All I'm asking is that if you want to see other women, you let me know so I can play by the same rules."

He gave a mirthless laugh. "Rules? Other women? What are you talking about, Gwyneth?"

I plunged on before I could censor myself. "Ducky, I mean Delores Franzblau. Come on, Simon, it was all there in black-and-white. Look, I don't want to tie you down. If you're having second thoughts, I'd understand." Well, not really. But he didn't need to know that.

Simon enunciated very slowly, as if I had a learning disability. Or spoke only Azerbaijani. "This is all in your head, Gwyneth. As I told you, Ms. Franzblau is chair of a foundation that supports my work. She is an amiable woman with very deep pockets. That's it. You have nothing to be jealous of. No one." He swallowed hard. "Mind you, if you want to date other men, I'd never trap you against your will. But it's not what I want. Is it what you want, Gwyneth?"

"Actually, no," I admitted.

The weight in the room seemed to lift. He leaned forward and took my hand. "Then all this can be about is you're afraid you're not loved." Which may have been partially true, but also let him off the hook. "Is that what it is? Because I can promise you, you are. Very much so. Come with me." He rose, tugged me to my feet, and led me to the bed. He got in, then lifted the sheet so I could slide under and into his embrace. Which was warm, strong, and reassuring. His hands skimmed my skin to shivers. His fingers teased me with pleasure. "Let me prove it to you. There you go. Reassured? How's that? And this?"

I thought "this" was going to be an extension of "that", which had to do with his lips on my... Surprise! He swung an arm over me, pulled out the drawer of the night table on his side, and extracted a small box.

"For you," he said. "From me."

I stared at a lovely gold and jade ring nestling in velvet.

"A token of my affection. Here. Try it on. I guessed your size but, see, it fits perfectly. It was meant for you to look at whenever you need to feel close to me. I need to feel you close right now."

As I lay entwined in his arms, he murmured, "I've been thinking. A few years ago, I had an offer from Johns Hopkins to run a lab there. I turned it down. No reason at the time to make the move to Baltimore." He caressed a breast. Nuzzled an ear. "But now I have a reason. Perhaps I'll give them a call. See what's currently open. Explore my options. How does that sound?" He cupped my chin in his hands. Gazed at me with expectant eyes.

"I love you, Simon," I said breathlessly.

"I do you, darling."

Talk about foreplay!

So just when everything seemed to be falling apart, everything came together. Including me, of course. Sandwiched between Simon's murmuring, "You didn't mean what you said about seeing other men," and his assuming the dead pope position for a full eight hours of post-coital sleep, I achieved the Ultimate You Know *times two*. A first for me.

Give the juicy pomegranate a great big hand.

———

Next morning, he roused me with a kiss to start our two-hour honeymoon. He was in a jolly mood. I was probably certifiably insane: an undiagnosable mixture of euphoria, relief, excitement, and stage fright. With Simon's perfectly chosen words, the calendar entries, the jade ring, and some incredible lovemaking, he'd vanquished all my worries.

He cooked breakfast for me. Okay, only Kashi and soy milk, but he poured. He also handed over the editorial page of the *New York Times,* which doesn't sound like a big deal but you have to think of it like a cat leaving a dead mouse at your feet. Not much of a gift at first glance but considered from the cat's perspective, an offering of great value, enormous sacrifice, and what passes in the species for love.

By ten, fully charged, he laid out my instructions before heading for the lab. He made me promise I'd be out of the apartment by noon, because the cleaning woman was coming in. He showed me fresh towels and demonstrated how to work his new showerhead. He reminded me twice to check that the door was locked behind me when I left. No key necessary, all I had to do was slam. He asked me so many times if I was sure I'd kept the roundtrip part of my train ticket that I was forced to pull it out of my wallet and let him read it just to get him off my back.

Overnight case slung on shoulder, Burberry muffler tucked into coat, he left me with a peck on the cheek and a reminder that he was staying with me in Baltimore the upcoming Friday night after the GRIA conference in Washington. As if I'd forgotten. I wished him a safe flight to California and a productive editorial meeting and waved him off at the door.

After I showered and dressed, but skipped the makeup because Fortune's stylists would do my face and hair, I had an hour to waste. With what Fleur called the *shpilkes* and my father used to call ants-in-the-pants. I wandered around the house, looked through Simon's CDs, attempted the

*Times* crossword, switched on CNN, peered at the photo wall in his study. I went through the books stacked behind his computer printer to see what he was reading these days. Pushkin. Nice and light. Ugh. Something called *How Women Think.* A Japanese poet I'd never heard of. A glossy picture book titled *The Great Resorts of Europe.* And, because God has a sense of humor, *Men Are Coconuts, Women Are Pomegranates.*

I did not, because of residual outrage over my mother's childhood invasion of my privacy, look at or through any of the following: medicine chests, cupboards under the sink, drawers in any furniture, printouts on his desk, or even the piece of pink writing paper used to bookmark *How Women Think,* with "Dearest Simon" visible under a deckled edge. Though I have to admit, that one was tough to pass by.

Between each of these activities, I peed. Maybe six times in the space of an hour. All my television appearances so far had been on local stations. Fortune reached umpteen millions of viewers. Anxiety shriveled my bladder to the size of a garbanzo and sent it into spasms.

So when the phone rang as I was doing a final, I hoped, pee, I dashed to the closest phone in Simon's study thinking—I swear this—that it was him calling to wish me good luck. By the time I skidded in, the answering machine had already clicked on. Its volume, turned all the way down, allowed only a shadow of neuter voice to emerge. Innocent as a babe, I turned it up. And heard a throaty woman's voice say, "Simon, it's Claire. Sorry, sorry, I'm calling on this phone, but I tried your cell and it's not turned on. I left a message on your office voicemail, but who knows when you'll pick that up. Anyway, I'm in the Denver Airport about to board, so—I *will* make it back in time for the dinner tonight. I thought to save time, I'd stop by your place around five to help you with your cummerbund and studs. Really looking forward to the night together at your place. Gotta go. Love you, darling."

*Love you, darling? Night together?* I'd met this Claire. The scientist from his lab. Paralyzed, I stared at the phone. When my legs began to wobble, I collapsed in Simon's desk chair, my heart beating a wild tattoo.

Forcing myself to breathe, in-out-in-out, I reached for the phone and checked the caller ID—small prayer here— to see if Claire's message might have been recorded a year ago and by some electronic fluke resurrected. But no, there it was glowing with digital certainty: Claire McKenna, 12/10, 11:54 a.m., along with her cell phone number. That mobilized me. Flooded with adrenaline, I grabbed a pen from Simon's desk and a sheet of paper from the heap in his wastebasket. In a palsied script, I managed to scratch on its flip side Claire's full name and phone number.

Then, because all bets were off now and I was *this* close to a Jerry Springer moment, I reached over to Simon's stack of books and extracted the Dearest Simon note expecting the worst. And finding it.

*Dearest Simon,*

*I just wanted to tell you how much I enjoyed our long, luxurious weekend. Also, I'm returning those sunglasses you left on my porch. Notice I overnighted them. I thought you might need them for your California trip. I really do miss you my darling. The bed seems so awfully empty without you. Can't wait for Christmas together!*

*Love and many kisses,*

*Jordan*

Dated the week before, and along the very bottom, next to a tiny engraved turquoise palm tree, the name Jordan Conrad. No doubt the friend from Key West.

Sonofabitch. The brilliant, accomplished, handsome, charming Simon York, with whom I had fallen thunderstruck in love, was, deep down where his heart should have been, just another womanizer. No, not *just another.* Because Simon wasn't your common garden variety womanizer. As he did everything, he did his philandering at top form. This was spectacular cheating. Nobel quality screwing around. Two, count 'em, *two* other women. While I had my proverbial head up my proverbial butt.

Steadier now, gritting my teeth, I scribbled next to Claire's name and number, Jordan Conrad, Key West. What I was going to do with this information, I hadn't the vaguest idea.

But something, I was sure, would occur to me.

# Chapter 36

I slogged through the next few hours in a chilly, drizzly fog, New York's foul weather matching my mood. I have only patchwork recollections: the Ghanaian cab driver handing me his Kleenex box through the partition pass-through, Fortune in the Green Room clattering bracelets, bending her turbaned head to give me a good luck kiss, the makeup man telling me, "Sugarpie, you must stop sniffling because it's making that pretty nose all red, and if you let those tears go, you'll really fuck up this fabulous eyeliner. And, believe me, he isn't worth it."

The makeup man knew. Fleur and Kat watching from Baltimore didn't. Later, Fleur told me I looked cool as a cucumber and sounded perfectly coherent. Kat assured me I was wonderful though she did see my right eyelid twitching, but thought it was because Dr. Rao had a scene-stealing coughing fit whenever the camera switched to me.

Fortune introduced me as not only her favorite gynecologist, which probably didn't make Sam Goldsmith, her own doc and one of my New York peers, jump for joy, but also as an example of how women at any age can look and act as if they're in their prime. This concluded with her shouting, "Audience, does Dr. Gwyn look fifty-four?" And a resounding, "Nooo," and Fortune shouting, "Yes, yes, this is what fifty-four looks like today." Wild applause.

So if I was so gorgeous, so accomplished, and such a hit on national television, why did Simon need Claire and Jordan and a woman in every port to make him happy?

While the camera rolled, I couldn't think about that. I did what I had to do. On autopilot, I covered my talking points and only kicked back into full consciousness before the last commercial break when I realized Dr. Rao was mentioning the title of his book in every other sentence and decided two could play that game. I plugged my defunct clinic and talked about how the only source of medical care for hundreds of women got shut down for lack of funding. Racking up the emotion quotient, I mentioned cancers grown deadly and small problems magnified to morbid ones by neglect. By the time I finished, Fortune was reaching for the tissues she kept on her side table and Dr. Rao was coughing up a storm.

Afterwards, at the backstage coffee klatch for her guests and crew, Fortune corralled me. "Amazing," she said. "Great job on the holiday health list. And I loved how you championed your clinic. You struck just the right balance of righteous indignation and compassion. And so from the gut."

"Well I'm pretty desperate," I said, backing up so I could look her in the eye. "I sent a grant proposal to your foundation. I haven't heard back yet."

She wrinkled her forehead in what I took for sympathy. "Probably because this is our Third World year. The Fortune Foundation decided to dedicate the bulk of funding to projects in Africa, South America, and the Indian subcontinent. My board doesn't like me meddling because I tend to work almost entirely from here." She slammed a hand against her chest and gave a shrug that said "Outta luck, sorry."

Not my day.

"Now," she grasped my fingers in hers, "we have you scheduled again right after New Year's. You're doing resolutions for health. You know, mark the new calendar for Pap tests, do monthly breast checks, that kind of thing. And I'm going to have my producer call you about appearing regularly on the show, maybe four times a year. I think what you say is vital and I love how you say it, Dr. Gwyn. You have an experienced voice, a confident voice. That's what my viewers need to hear, the voice of a woman they can trust because she trusts herself."

The next laugh—really more of a sardonic snort— would have been mine.

It was still echoing inside my head when I dashed onto the street and flagged down a cab to take me not to Penn Station but uptown. If we didn't hit rush hour traffic, I might just make it in time to land a front row seat for the Simon and Claire show.

Why did I make this humiliating journey?

Sure, any all-female jury in the land would convict that man on felony lying and at least two counts of cheating based upon Claire's phone message and Jordan's note. And I am not a masochist. But I am a scientist.

I was the kid who took third place in the science fair with a diorama of Marie Curie's Paris laboratory, and grown up I spend a good part of my life checking and rechecking data. Ergo, I am not constitutionally capable of coming to ironclad conclusions based on hearsay. To pronounce him guilty, I actually had to see Simon York with another woman on East 79th Street in Manhattan at precisely the moment he was supposed to be cruising thirty-four thousand feet over Indianapolis. And guilty beyond a reasonable doubt so that years from now, on a winter night with snow falling and "Lara's Theme" playing on the radio, I wouldn't feel I'd made a ghastly mistake and get a nasty case of regret, which is much worse in your golden years than even osteoporosis.

I planted myself in the deli two doors down and across the street from Simon's apartment building. Only a month or so before, the glow from Friedman's Deli had lit our snow-speckled, boundary-leaping kiss. Now it bathed the street as dusk settled. From my table near the window I had a clear view of his building's entrance, but he couldn't see me unless he peered directly into the window.

Hunger wasn't even a memory, but I ordered the price of admission. "Corned beef on rye. Mayo." The waiter gave me the once-over with basset hound eyes.

"Iowa darling, you don't want mayo. Mustard with corned beef. And, if you don't mind my saying, maybe not corned beef for you. Nothing against our corned beef. I'd stack it up against anything in the city, but it's a half a pound of meat and it would lay on your chest like a dead weight. You don't look so hot. For you, matzo ball soup. Like mama used to make. Mine not yours. Listen to Uncle Nate."

Good idea, Nate. I could take my time spooning it up. And when that ran out, a prune danish. If I hadn't miscalculated, Simon and Claire would be hitting the street in less than a half hour. No wonder he wanted to check and recheck my return train ticket that morning. He needed to make sure I was on my way out of town when he stepped out with his other girlfriend.

Thirty-two minutes later, Simon emerged from the building alone. I'd never seen him in a dinner jacket and my idiot heart gave a lurch. Other men look like Dagwood in a bow tie; this man was born to it. I shoved the prune danish to one side, queasy. It was now established that the defendant was not airborne, not on his way to California, and that he had, at the very least, your honor, lied through his teeth to me.

Then, behind him, Claire sauntered into the frame, hung with enough jewelry to sink a ship. I couldn't see details, just sparkles of many bracelets, big earrings, and a killer necklace above the drape of her black velvet cape. No PETA-prohibited fur for her, although the temperature hovered in the twenties and a light sugary snow had begun to fall. Simon reached back and drew her to his side, then raised her ungloved hand and pressed it to his lips. Guilty, guilty, guilty! If I keeled over right now, would they haul Uncle Nate in for questioning?

Two steps forward for Simon. He scanned for a cab. Nothing. He returned to Claire for what must have been a strategy conference. Just after I ducked out of sight, and as I peeped through a spy slit between the food flecked curtain and the window, he left her and bounded across the street to the deli side.

Now he paced the end of the deli's front window, his back to me. Now he strode past, so close I saw he'd nicked himself during his evening touch-up shave. Finally, he flagged a cab and waved to Claire, who clipped across the street on what had to be four-inch heels. He trotted by me a second time as the cab slowed and this time, as he passed, he turned his head, maybe to inhale the aroma of pastrami. Or maybe, as Claire slipped her arm around his waist, he just glanced at the hooker sashaying by.

Whatever, his full face in blissful ignorance that he'd been caught mid-cheat was the last image I saw before I sunk back into green Naugahyde and closed my eyes.

Enough. I'd had enough. I didn't want to know what came next. Whether Simon helping Claire into the cab gave her arm a fond, familiar stroke. Whether he gathered her to him for a cuddle as the cab pulled away. When I opened my eyes and looked out again, all I saw was my own wretched reflection in the window.

Fleur had absolutely no scruples about saying, when I called her on my cell phone, "I knew something was fishy about that guy. Why do you think you hardly ever saw him? He was jamming that magic johnson of his into any woman within fucking distance."

I gave out a wounded groan.

"Okay, I'm sorry it ended like this," Fleur continued, "but I'm glad you're out of it. You don't need him. You looked like Catherine Deneuve on TV. Screw the bastard."

I sobbed quietly and dribbled into the last of my tea. Nate, his basset eyes tender with compassion, dropped a wad of extra napkins with my change just as Fleur said, "He doesn't deserve your tears. He deserves a swift, hard kick in the ass. Not just for you. He's screwing around on Claire whatsis and the Key West woman, too. You really need to tell them."

"I was planning on it," I said, blowing my nose, pulling myself together. I felt in my handbag for the folded paper with Claire's and Jordan's information. "I may need some help from you and Kat."

"Count on us, Gwynnie." Fleur sounded positively gleeful. "Our pleasure, believe me."

*Chapter 37*

Back home, I crashed for nine hours of exhausted dreamless sleep. I might have made it to twelve, but on Saturday morning, Fleur pounded on my door, stuffed me into jeans, and dragged me off to Kat's house in the suburbs because "you need to be surrounded by friends who'll restore your self-esteem by thoroughly trashing the man you were stupid enough to fall in love with. By the way, you look like shit. All that negativity screws around with your collagen. Turn it off."

I wished I could, but the pain was so deep I couldn't get to the switch. It had something to do with loss and something to do with *being* lost after those months in the illusionary Land of Simon. Which a part of me knew was really an emotional desert the size of the Sahara. But Lord, I was going to miss the oases.

The other pain, maybe worse, was that I felt like the damnedest fool. "Smart, smart, smart," my mother used to mock my A+ report card, "but she doesn't have the sense to come in out of the rain." Sometimes even a crazy mama knows best.

Kat disputed my self-diagnosis. When I called myself a chump for love, she wagged a finger. "Better naive than cynical. Never regret an open heart. *He's* the fool and a bastard to boot," she added with an uncharacteristic lack of charity.

Actually, going to Kat's was a good move. In spite of her being well into her radiation, she'd found the energy to decorate the house for Christmas. For the holidays, Kat always departed from her standard post-hippie modernist style and reversed full throttle into the kitsch of her childhood. This year, especially, the traditional stuff had to bring her comfort. I know it reassured *me* that the world hadn't spun off its axis.

"It's like a Macy's window in here," Fleur grouched. "I didn't know there was this much Hummel in the universe. And the whole house smells like the lady's room in Penn Station. The pine is giving me a headache." She gingerly lifted a snowman soap dispenser. "I can't believe in the shape Kat's in she hauled out all this stuff to decorate."

But it was said with fondness. Fleur loved Kat. She added a sprinkle of chives to the eggs she scrambled for her friend. She cut the crusts off the whole wheat toast just like grandmère used to do for Fleurie when she was a little girl. She even clipped a blossom from the coffee table's poinsettia to brighten the tray she brought up to Kat resting in her bedroom.

Back downstairs, she swung by the kitchen to hook her arm in mine. I was next on her list. "Forget the dishes," she said. "Come on. We have work to do."

———

"Let's see. Jordan C-o-n-r-a-d," Fleur typed into Kat's computer, pulling up the Key West white pages. "How many Jordan Conrads can there be in Key West?"

As it turned out, two. Jordan H. Conrad and a Dr. Jordan R. Conrad. The one with the R. was a plastic surgeon.

"Jordan could be either gender. You don't think Simon is a second Stan, do you?" Fleur asked.

"That would be the icing on the cake. No, the stationery was pink. It's got to be the MD," I said. "Simon would want to boff the doctor." I wrote down the phone number.

"Wait, wait. Plastic surgeons always put their photos on their websites to reassure prospective patients they're not getting the aesthetic standards of Quasimodo," Fleur said. "Let's see if Jordan R. Conrad, MD, is a Jewish guy with hair transplants or...bingo!...a strikingly attractive redhead of the XX persuasion educated at the University of Dublin."

"Figures." I bit my lip over the well-defined cleavage in the V of Dr. Jordan Conrad's suit and no glint of gold on the fingers that steepled under her perfectly sculpted chin. Unmarried and—pulled up her CV in a PDF file and calculated—thirty-one.

"Thirty-one! She's a baby. Well, that tears it. Did I even have a chance in this crapshoot called love?" I asked wistfully.

"You mean because she's young and beautiful? Listen, Simon's hitting on everything with a snatch is as much about love as rape is about sex. This is a power thing. An ego thing. Want more proof?" She did a bit of fancy finger work. "Dr. Date is a match-up website for single medical professionals. I decided to play a hunch after you called yesterday. And...voilà."

I read: "'Distinguished British physician of international renown searching for exuberant, understanding, loving lady who wants only the best life has to offer—kindness, consideration, and a caring heart.' Oh, my God." I stared at Simon who stared back with limpid eyes as he invited me and five thousand other women to email him. "Jesus, Fleur, can you tell when he joined this site?"

"Doesn't say. But he's still on. Three months after meeting you."

"What's that flashy thing?"

"That flashy thing is an icon that means at," she peered at the screen, "eight minutes past noon, New York time, or 9 a.m. California time, wherever he may be, your erstwhile boyfriend is at this very moment prowling for pussy. Now," she swiveled her chair to face me. "Do you believe this betrayal had nothing to do with you and everything to do with the pigginess of Simon Swine? Right. I like that look on your face. Like an Amazon warrior. Tears all dry? Good. Time to call Jordan Conrad."

"I will," I said. "But first, Claire McKenna. Don't you have coffee brewing? Go pour yourself a cup. I don't want you breathing over my shoulder while I break this poor woman's heart."

———

It took only a couple of minutes to convince Claire McKenna she wasn't Simon's one and only. She choked up a bit, but she wasn't all that surprised. "I was wondering when the other shoe was going to drop. I thought I'd caught him playing around last year. But he swore there was no one else and I wanted to believe him. Damn. I had a feeling when I ran into you," she said. "Women just know that kind of thing in their bones. So I asked him straight out. He said I had trust issues."

"Me, too. All of Simon's women have trust issues. I wonder why."

"Of course, he denied everything. He said you were a colleague from Baltimore working under him on a very important project."

"Yeah, well, working under him anyway. He told *me* you were on his lab staff, nothing more. He made me feel I was paranoid for even suggesting an unprofessional involvement. 'I never mix business with pleasure, my darling.'" I mimicked Simon's upper-class British accent.

"Liar," Claire said. "Lying, conniving, cheating liar." The little clicks at her end of the phone may have been her biting her nails. "Did you ever hear of someone named Beata Karnikova?"

"Bitti," I said. "Her too?"

"They had a hot affair years ago. I think maybe while he was married and that's why Cynara finally dumped him. He swore it was over. But when he was in Prague last summer, he didn't pick up his cell phone for nearly a week."

Sounded familiar.

"Does the name Jordan Conrad ring a bell?" I said.

"The cousin in Florida? Oh, jeez, not a cousin, right? What's wrong with us?"

I was still working on that. "Not a damn thing," I said, to buck us both up. I gave it my best shot: "Except we fell in love with the fantasy, not the man. It happens all the time. And give Simon his due; he's very good at creating the fantasy."

"Wait till I get my hands on his fantasy next week. I'll wring body parts he doesn't know he owns. I just wish he were coming back sooner. I don't want to lose this head of steam."

"He'll be at my place on Friday night." I had an interesting, diabolical thought. Why not? Why not indeed? "You're more than welcome to come down to Baltimore, Claire. We can make it a threesome. Now won't *that* surprise him?"

Without hesitation, Claire said, "I love it. Ha! Wonderful! Next Friday. I'll be there."

"Not next Friday, this one. He's planning on flying from California to D.C. for the GRIA meeting on Friday. He's going to stay the night at my place."

"No way. He was supposed to be in California for a week, through Sunday," she said. "He never told me he was going to GRIA."

"He's giving a paper," I said.

"That's impossible. He would have told me. I would have known."

"I can tell you what the paper's about." I flipped the sheet with her and Jordan's names and numbers. "I have the first page here. I read it on the train coming home. Actually, it sounds interesting. Original. An innovative approach to detecting ovarian cancer." I rattled off the title. When the silence at the other end went on a beat too long, I became alarmed. "Claire? Are you all right?"

"Can you read the whole page, please?" she whispered finally.

I read it.

"Where did you get that?" she asked after I finished.

"The paper? From Simon's wastebasket. In his office at the apartment. He had a load of stuff he'd printed out and trashed. I needed something to write on. I grabbed it."

"That's my work," she said. "I'm the one who should be up there. Simon York is standing before hundreds of the best scientists in the field giving a paper on *my* research."

Well, that wasn't uncommon. "He's the senior. The lab director," I said, making my voice soothing. "You know science. It happens all the time. I agree not telling you is really crummy. Still."

"You don't understand. Simon pulled me off this project because he said the line of inquiry lacked promise. I managed to get the experiments done in spite of him. Under the radar for nearly a year. I showed him the data a month ago. He was thrilled. Said my work was a major breakthrough." She sounded about to spiral out of control. "We were drafting the paper together. Slowly. Carefully. You know the rules, Gwyneth. He was going to get a piece of the action. But now he's written it all by himself and he's copping the credit."

A mewling, like the whimper of an animal caught in a trap, came through the phone. I imagined her face white with shock.

"I'm so sorry for you," I said. "It's a really lousy thing to do."

"The lousiest. God. Oh, God." I actually heard her swallow. "Is my name in the author's list? Did he credit me at least?"

I scanned the paragraph. "There are five authors listed. Your name is third."

"Buried," she said. "You know, he's done this before. I've heard gossip. I never believed it. I couldn't and still love him, but you hear things. And if they're true, this wouldn't be the first time he's grabbed the glory whatever it took. But he's always gotten away with it."

"Well, you know the protocol. Go to Simon's boss or his board and lay out your case."

"Please," Claire snorted, "I'll never get an impartial hearing. Simon is a superpower at Brubaker. His cronies would never undercut him. Plus, he's their clinical golden boy with all those private-pay surgeries he does on the foreign jet-setters. He brings in multimillions to the hospital every year. I'm just a PhD. He's a PhD *and* an MD. It's not a fair fight."

I sighed agreement.

"What a prick! He fucked me over in bed. He fucked me over in the lab." Her voice broke. "I'm sorry, Gwyneth. I can't talk anymore right now. This is too much to take. I'll get back to you, okay? And thanks. I know it wasn't easy to make this call."

She hung up.

After Claire's call, I tossed on a jacket and went outside to pace in Kat's garden. I was seething. The man had betrayed my personal trust—nothing new for me. See Stan, op cit. And not to minimize it, Simon's bed-hopping was cruel, wounding, and incredibly vulgar for such a superficially elegant man. But far, far worse was his forking around with the medical profession I loved. Now *that* made me ready to throw down the gauntlet and go for his throat.

I circled the flower garden, the memory of Claire's broken voice replaying, fueling my anger. Pulling my jacket close against the chill of the December afternoon, I stared at a row of shriveled stalks and spent flower heads, the layer of shredded bark over sleeping earth. We were well past the growing season. And yet, as I walked, I thought and, after a while, I felt something germinating. Something wicked and wonderful. It would hit Simon York where he'd hurt most: in his reputation. It would restore to Claire what was rightfully hers and satisfy a bloodlust for revenge I hadn't known was in me. It was dangerous as hell.

It was perfect.

# Chapter 38

O ne down," Fleur said two hours later from her perch on the corner of Kat's bed, "Jordan Conrad to go." She waved Kat's bedside phone at me.

"What's your hurry?" Kat asked, rearranging the prop of pillows against her headboard. "It's not as if you're bringing the Conrad woman good news. Give yourself a few days to recover, to process all this craziness."

"And become really depressed," Fleur chirped.

"I don't think so," I said. "Depression is anger turned inward. My anger is right out there." In fact, it had ebbed since coming in from the cold. In the spicy warmth of the house, sanity bloomed. I decided my idea was a ridiculous stunt. Much too risky. I'd just confront Simon with his cruddy behavior towards me, then try to let it go.

I thought out loud as I helped Kat adjust the tray in her lap. "Okay, I can put off phoning Jordan Conrad. But Simon is another story. He's going to call before Friday and I want him to think everything's just the way he left it when he kissed me good-bye. I don't want to tip my hand. He needs to be blissfully oblivious and standing right in front of me when I let go with both barrels."

"Normally, I'd suggest something nonviolent," Kat said.

"But I'm with you on this one. Give him hell."

"It's the radiation destroying her cells," Fleur said. "That's the only explanation for that last sentence coming from the mouth of Katherine 'The Pacifist' Greenfield." She picked a cookie off Kat's plate. Studied it. Put it down. "I've got a problem. So you tell Simon he's a bad boy, wag your finger, and send him on his way. Seems to me he's getting off much too easy. Don't you have anything bigger than a double barrel? Like a heat-seeking missile. I mean, after what he did to Claire McKenna, he deserves a really big bang. And I don't mean the kind he usually gets from you."

"You know," I said, feeling the insanity rise, "there are moments I think my mother was right and I was born with an evil mind. Because out in your garden, Kat, I came up with something that's either devilishly brilliant or totally maniacal. Something that could blow Simon out of the water and at the same time give Claire a really huge win. The problem is that the big payoff carries a big risk. It could put Claire's entire professional future in jeopardy."

"But of course. The poor soul hasn't had enough pain and suffering. I'm sure she'd sign up for that." Fleur gave in and gobbled the cookie.

"She's a grown woman. And she sounds like a smart one," Kat said. "Let it be her decision."

"And ours," Fleur said. "Tell us."

I did.

"You gotta do this," Fleur said when I finished. "Claire's going to love it."

Kat looked skeptical. "Or hate it. Very risky business. Bottom line, it all depends on her," she said.

"Call her." Fleur reached for the phone.

Kat's hand whipped from under the quilt to catch Fleur's wrist. "Not so fast," she said, playing Ethel to Fleur's

Lucy. "You need to do this in person, Gwyn. What you described is a pretty reckless maneuver. All the more reason to be cautious and deliberate as you plan it. So you need Claire right there in front of you. You have to gauge her response, make sure she won't fall apart if things get dicey. It's going to take a strong personality to bring this off. And you've got to see her face so you can make sure she knows what she's getting into. That's the only responsible way."

I peered at Kat, wavy hair pulled up with tendrils spiraling against her too-gaunt cheekbones. Her face, its Mediterranean color drained by a bombardment of isotopes, made a cameo above the drape of her nightgown. She looked like a Greek goddess—Athena, goddess of wisdom. As always, she was on the mark.

"See her in person." I considered that. "I'm loaded up in the OR for the next few days and we've got to get started stat."

"Why not today?" Kat checked her watch. "It's still early. She could hop the Metroliner and be down here in a few hours. Then all of us could get in on the action." Her wan face lit with the prospect of a juicy coconspiracy.

"You sure, Kat?" I said. "I don't want to overtax you."

"It will be good for her." Fleur gave me a radiant smile. "Consider it entertainment. Like a soap opera. 'As the Stomach Turns.'"

I called Claire who sounded stuffy, as if she'd been crying. I gave her just enough information to clear her sinuses. "Holy shit," she said, and I heard a spark of hope in her voice. "I'm on my way."

Claire arrived at Kat's door looking très chic, very New York. There was the meticulously—to achieve the illusion of carelessly—highlighted hair, the designer handbag, the two-hundred-dollar jeans, and the multiple bracelets on each wrist. Fleur gave her the once-over and twisted her mouth in disapproval. I could hear her thinking "phony." But Claire wasn't and Fleur told me later she'd quickly picked up on what I'd sensed on the phone: Claire was genuine. She was also bright, furious, and determined. And the New York thing was more than the outer layer. She wore attitude with a capital N and Y.

She hugged me and shook hands with Fleur and Kat, who'd dressed and descended for the occasion. Within minutes, Claire was leaning back in the club chair in front of a blazing fire in the family room hearth sipping the scotch she chose over wine.

"Before you show me yours, let me show you mine," she said with a wry smile. Gathered around like kids at summer camp, we listened to her spooky story.

It went back more than a year.

First of all, she told us, we needed to understand that Simon ran one of the major-league labs in his field. Staffed with top people. She'd been lucky—especially as a woman, even these days—to have him take her on. Fifteen months ago, she believed she was on the fast track to discovering the elusive test that would detect ovarian cancer in its earliest stages. Hundreds of researchers around the world were hunting for the same prize. At first, Simon encouraged her experiments. They were in a race with at least two other labs and he thought she might be riding a winner. But when her first experiments didn't produce good data, he pulled her off the project.

"Do either of you do science?" she asked Kat and Fleur.

"Kat is a brilliant artist," I filled in. "Fleur is a very successful businessperson."

"I run a dress shop for fat ladies," Fleur said.

"Well, Fleur, you could have done the meaningless shit he shifted me to. And what pissed me off was I knew—the way you know, Kat, when something works in your art—I was sure I was on to something. I begged him to let me continue. He gave me the song and dance about limited resources. That he couldn't play favorites. Even though he loved me." We looked at each other with mutual sympathy. "Finally, he just ordered me to stop. But I couldn't. I knew I was hot. I just needed a few more months. So I did it anyway."

Fleur had been stoking the fire. She turned now, her jaw in exaggerated drop.

Claire said, "Simon works on his hospital cases in the mornings. He gets his patients out of the way first. Then between ten and noon, he comes into the lab and, I'll give him this, he goes sometimes into the night. But I had a window of opportunity in the very early morning when he wasn't there and neither were any of the other staff. I hit that lab every day at 5 a.m. so I could put in three hours before even the early birds got in." She grinned at the memory of her own cunning. "And I pulled it off. No one knew. A couple of months ago, I got the data that clinched it."

She pulled a book from her handbag. "My lab notebook. All the details are in here. Of course, it's going to take trials and human studies. But the basic material is sound. My conclusions will hold up."

"And Simon's response when he found out you'd done it behind his back?" I asked, imagining how enraged he must have been.

"Deliriously happy. Overjoyed. He forgave me every-thing. Simon is the most ambitious human being I ever met. And I was part of his lab, after all. If I get a Lasker, odds are the chief gets a Lasker."

The Lasker Award, I explained to Fleur and Kat, is like an American Nobel Prize. "In fact, many Lasker recipients go on to win the Nobel."

Claire nodded. "It's *that* big. So Simon told me not to tell a soul. Not even our own lab staff, who might leak it. We couldn't chance other labs getting a whiff that we were onto this."

"And then he stole your work out from under you," Kat said, shocked. She'd always given Simon the benefit of the doubt in our relationship. But something so unethical, so immoral that affected millions of women? I doubted she could forgive that.

"I understand he wanted to beat the other labs to the finish line." She poked at the ice in her scotch. "But to preempt me, to shaft me in public. And it's deliberate. He's giving it as a post-deadline paper." She explained to Fleur and Kat, "Those are the ones that come in just under the wire, too late to appear on the conference website. I checked. It's not up there. Don't you think that's—"

"Unconscionable," Kat finished for her. "And I assume there's also money involved. Patents. Royalties."

"With something this significant, for the primary scientist it could be like winning the lottery," Claire said.

"So he's a romantic terrorist. And a credit thief. And if you figure in the money, a common pickpocket," Fleur fumed. "He's got to be stopped. You've got to expose him. Pull his trousers down around his knees and let the world see his shriveled dick."

"Wow," Claire laughed. "I like your style. Is that what you had in mind, Gwyneth?"

"Hypothetically," I said. I paused before pounding out the punch line. "I want to take him down at the GRIA meeting. In front of everyone! Well, not exactly me. Us."

"You've got to be kidding." Claire leaned forward in her chair, scotch sloshing. "In front of the whole GRIA gang, the cream of gynecologic research?"

"Gwyn has a seriously demented brain. We're very proud of our girl." Fleur reached over and patted my arm.

I ignored her. "We're going to play stump the scientist," I said to Claire. "I assume since this project is your baby, you've got questions he can't answer?"

"Absolutely," she said, nostrils flaring. "Simon knows the basics, but I know the nuances. And," she let go a final volley in rapid New York rhythm, "I have evidence he hasn't even seen. Analyses I've been working on the last few weeks that I can put it up there in PowerPoint. Unequivocal proof I'm the one who should be giving that paper. Plus," she licked her lips like a starving woman at a buffet, "I've got a smoking gun. A really big gun. With a tremendous amount of smoke. We do this right, Simon York is toast!"

She popped to her feet and hauled me to mine. While I stood there, smiling indulgently, she danced a celebratory salsa around me. At the end, she pirouetted and planted a kiss on my cheek. "He'll never see it coming. Not in a million years. Gwyneth, you're a genius. I'm so indebted."

Across the coffee table, I could see Kat fluttering her fingers in a high sign, my cue to say the right thing.

I let Claire collapse in the club chair, still grinning. I leaned against the mantle and assumed my best mentor frown. "Well, I think we've got a shot to get you what's yours, but I hope you appreciate the risk involved. Not to me. This meeting is all researchers, not my crowd. They won't even recognize me up there. Besides, I'm in private practice, so I'm safe if they do. You, on the other hand, are risking your career by going up against Simon and the heavy hitters in public. That's just not done. There's a good probability this crowd will turn on you and you'll be persona non grata among your peers."

Claire waved a napkin to cool her flushed face. Maybe it was the dance in front of the fire that made her cherry-red, neck up. Or at forty-four she could have been perimenopausal. Late to take such a big chance with her career.

"I don't think so," she said. "Especially if Simon's done this before. There's some untapped resentment out there from other researchers he's screwed. Worst-case scenario," she gulped the last of her scotch, "I've got a job lined up in Finland. This pharmaceutical company has been after me for years. Mucho euros. If I can get credit for this discovery, I can write my own ticket. Besides, we owe this to all the women Simon York's trashed over the years. Like Jordan Conrad." She let that sink in before she said, "On my way to the airport, I called her."

"Ah, the Key West cutie," Fleur muttered.

"Actually," Claire said quietly, "she seems like a nice kid. Yeah, I know she's a board certified plastic surgeon, but she sounds so young. She sobbed when I laid out Simon's screwing around for her. At our age, Gwyneth"—oh hell, I knew she was buttering me up with the "our"—"with our bank of experience, we only got dazzled. Jordan got bamboozled. He told her he was trying to get her a staff position in the plastic surgery clinic at Brubaker so she could move to New York to be near him. He'd been stringing her along with that for more than a year." Claire rolled her eyes.

I was too embarrassed to confess I'd fallen for Simon's line about relocating to Baltimore. He was so slick. And some women are so gullible.

"Jordan thought Simon was going to marry her. Like that crappy jade ring was a four-carat diamond from

Tiffany's." Claire reached in her pocket. "I assume you got one."

Fleur was turning lavender to purple holding her breath.

I fished around in my handbag. "Just last week."

We lay the rings side by side. I said, "He must buy them by the gross in Hong Kong. Every size."

Claire had a musical laugh. Then she sobered. "As long as we're comparing, I have kind of a personal question?"

When I hesitated, Fleur whined, "Come on, Gwyneth. We're all good buds here. And think of it as being on the other end of one of your own nosy scientific surveys."

I nodded to Claire.

"With you, did he come with his eyes open?" she asked, pink flooding her face.

"Oh, sweet mamma-jamma," Fleur rocked in her chair, "is that anatomically possible?"

I nodded again. "A trick to create an instant, powerful connection," I speculated.

"Bullshit," Fleur roared, "with all those women, he was checking to see who he was fucking at the moment."

When the laughter died down, Claire said, "What I don't understand is why. Why did he do this? Have all these women?"

"Because he can," Fleur fired off. "He's high-and-mighty Simon York. At the top of the food chain. Women are just perks to him, like flying first class."

"It's got to be more than that," Kat said thoughtfully. "Because not all who can, *do*. Maybe he was weaned too early." To Fleur's disparaging hoots she insisted, "Well, it's possible. He had a lousy childhood, right? So maybe he's looking for the warmth and love he missed as an infant. And now that he's grown up he can never get enough."

"Kat's close, I think." I'd been giving the topic some thought. "My sense is Simon has all these women to keep from getting close to any one of them. Really close, I mean. He talks a good game, but playing it scares the crap out of him. So he moves from one to another…"

"…avoiding intimacy. I think you have it," Kat said.

Claire had been quiet while we batted this around, listening, fussing with her bracelets. Now she said, "The thing is, I really was in love with him." She looked up at me. "You?"

"I was in something," I said.

Fleur broke the moment of mournful silence that followed with a brisk handclap. "Okay ladies, funeral's over. We have work to do."

"Right," Claire said. "I'm going to call Beata Karnikova. I've heard she takes no prisoners. I know the three of us, plus you guys of course," she swept Fleur and Kat into her field of vision, "can bring this off." She grabbed my hand, squeezed hard, and looked deep into my eyes with her emerald green ones. "This is more than revenge," she said, pupils firing. "This is justice."

"Close enough to revenge for me," Fleur said. "Death to the infidel! Hang the bastard!"

Kat simply nodded encouragement.

"Let's do it," Claire said.

*Chapter 39*

The next four days blurred by. Everyone had an assignment. Fleur finessed Claire's PowerPoint presentation and chatted with the conference manager at the Clay-Madison Hotel, who had a final list of the post-deadline papers—which included, yes, one by Dr. Simon York about early detection of ovarian cancer. And the Colonial Room, venue for the post-deadline session, did indeed have two screens and a sophisticated audio visual system.

Over the phone, Kat, who'd been on the debate team in college and I, the public speaking champion of Ferdinand C. Latrobe Junior High School, rehearsed Claire in confronting Simon and coached her in parrying every possible outraged response.

I got hold of Beata Karnikova just before she departed for America.

"*Zkurvysyne!*" she cursed him out after I let her know she'd been another victim of Simon's worldwide love-scam. The lying *zasranec* had even booked a suite for them Thursday night at the Clay-Madison. "Of course, the idea of sleeping with him makes me physically sick." Which turned out to be the perfect excuse for changing her plans and arriving just in time to get in on our act.

"Weren't we all a bunch of dunces to fall for his duplicity? But his day is coming," she said. "Tell the others I'm foursquare behind this. Just email what you want me to do."

Claire phoned Jordan Conrad and asked her to keep the lid on it for another week—if Simon phoned, she was to play it cool. She sniffled a lot, Claire reported, but she agreed. On another front, Claire put in a call to an attorney girlfriend in Kerns-Brubaker's legal department, who poked around and confirmed that Simon had, in fact, engaged in preliminary discussions about applying for a patent on a novel ovarian CA test. Claire's name hadn't been mentioned.

And, regarding phone calls, I got one from Casanova himself on Tuesday night. All lovey-dovey. My performance was Oscar worthy. Butter could have melted. Ten minutes after we cooed good-bye, Claire called to inform me she'd just hung up on *her* call from Simon.

He really was a low-down dirty *zkurvysyne.*

———

Friday, December 18, 1:45 p.m. Bitti Karnikova and I arrived almost simultaneously for our planned reconnoiter in the mezzanine ladies' room of the Clay-Madison Hotel. She shook my hand in a single chopping motion, then surprisingly drew me to her for a kiss on each cheek. She was a woman I'd characterize as handsome rather than pretty. Mid-forties, shoulders broad as an ox yoke, with generous Slavic features arranged symmetrically under a practical cap of glossy auburn hair. Interesting choice for Simon. I could see her slinging him over her shoulder like a sack of potatoes and carrying him off to have her way with him. Somehow I didn't figure her as his type—then again, who wasn't Simon's type?

"Sorry we're meeting under such circumstances," she said, backing off. "A moment," she held up a halting hand, squatted to peek under the stall behind me, then made her way down the row to check the other five. Finally, she briskly opened, then closed, the door to the handicapped toilet. I was amused by all this Cold War spooky stuff. Then I remembered Bitti had been raised in Soviet-occupied Czechoslovakia. "All clear," she pronounced. "It is important to be careful. You never know who might be listening."

As if to prove the point, a woman dressed in head-to-toe black sailed through the door and swept in front of us to adjust her head scarf in the mirror. She wore no makeup, no jewelry. She peered at my reflection as it observed her. "You do not recognize me?" The accent was Middle Eastern with trilled r's and a phlegmy overlay. "My friends call me Fatima." She turned towards me and winked.

The wink, a flash of emerald iris, cut through the disguise. "For godssakes, Claire, is that you?"

"None other. But I had you there for a moment, didn't I?"

"Honestly, I had no idea it was you until I caught your eye color."

"I figured it would play from a distance. Claire McKenna," she grinned and extended a hand to Bitti, who gave her the hatchet shake. "I decided in case I accidentally ran into Simon in the hall, I'd better not set off his alarms."

"Excellent costume. You see more and more head scarves these days. Alia Rashid is a brilliant scientist and she's draped head to foot in the chador." Bitti resumed leaning against the wall-mounted tampon dispenser, eye on the door.

"Well, this is just an old Valentino suit and a scarf I dug out of a drawer. And I pushed back the bangs," Claire said, facing the mirror, examining her teeth. "Simon's already in the room, by the way. I was behind him in the hall and saw him go in." She applied a slash of lipstick. "I gave him a few minutes and snuck a look at the meeting room. Nearly every seat is filled. The more the merrier is the way I see it. Let the world know the creep for who he really is." She grimaced at her reflection. "God, I haven't slept for days. My face is collapsing from anxiety."

A teenaged girl entered. Bitti waited until she'd chosen a stall, then stepped into one of the empty ones and flushed the toilet. Noise camouflage.

"Okay. Time is flying. We need to move ourselves," Bitti said. "Two good things. First, Angela Barola is chairing the session. Which is helpful to us. Because Angela is a past officer of Centro Italiano Femminile. Very involved in the Italian women's movement. If it comes down to it, she will err on our side."

"Hurray for our team." Claire swung around to grab a paper towel, blot her lips. Her gestures, I realized, were too jaggedy. She was pretty revved up. Eyes shining, color high. I wondered if she'd had a shot or three of her favorite Dewars in the Metroliner parlor car to boost her courage. Or something in capsule form. "That's what I like, a totally subjective scientist."

Bitti flushed another unoccupied toilet. "Second, I set up everything with the young man in charge of the audio visual components. Multiple inputs are managed by a touch panel control system. For the next session, Simon is at the podium and his PowerPoint gets the screen on the left. The screen right side of the stage—remember *right,* as in we are in the right—has been programmed with your PowerPoint slides, Claire. Simple, yes? So, here is your remote. And a name tag for you." She slapped the first into Claire's outstretched palm and pinned the second to her lapel. "And one for you, Gwyneth." She pinned the name tag to my pocket. Underneath, my heart was running a nervous arpeggio. My mouth was dry with stage fright.

"All set, yes? Let us be off then."

We trailed after her like ducklings towards the door. Just before exiting she stopped short and spun around. "Do you pray?" she asked, and before we could answer, she crossed herself. "I don't myself, but it wouldn't hurt."

"Dear Jesus," Claire muttered behind me. And it wasn't a prayer.

## Chapter 40

Ve fanned out. Claire slipped into the last row far right and hunkered down in her chair. I found a man with a head as big and round as Charlie Brown's and planted myself behind him. Bitti landed a seat halfway back on the center aisle. She didn't need to hide.

Within minutes, the room was packed and you could feel the anticipation. Word had got round that Simon York was about to unveil a groundbreaking advance in the early detection of ovarian cancer. This was a major event. Bitti had said they'd let out the expandable walls to handle the overflow.

It took a few minutes for Angela Barola, the moderator, to calm the buzz. Dressed in a drab suit and a prim white blouse, Angela glared at the crowd under eyebrows that had never seen tweezers. She really did look the part of a science nun, one of that breed of women who channel all their passion into science, which they worship like a religion. I took heart from the fact that her introduction of Simon was not as reverent as he might have wished. Angela didn't seem the type to fall for Simon's charm. Unlike a certain three women of Simon's acquaintance who were, however, currently uncharmed and ready to rumble.

As I slouched in my chair trying to duck behind the big-headed man, a wave of menopausal heat rolled over me, leaving me drenched and breathless. A hot-flash ambush, not unusual under stress. I peeled my cashmere sweater away from my chest, mopped my face and the back of my neck, then stared at the wet tissue balled in my hands. And kept staring. I hadn't laid eyes on Simon since the deli debacle in New York and I'd been stalling since sitting down.

Now I counted to ten before forcing myself to look at him.

Deep breath and there he was, crossing the stage, wearing his favorite navy suit and a new tan he'd probably picked up on who knows what California beach with who knows what California girl. Simon York. My Simon. Every woman's Simon. Which I realized, as I palpated all my emotions, didn't hurt anymore. I was pain free. My jaw was tight and there was some tension in my shoulders. But no real pain.

I watched Simon fussing with his laser pointer. With the silver hair and the cleft in his chin, he was still, on a handsome scale of 1 to 10, a solid 15. "Ladies and gentlemen," he began. The rich baritone, the Knightsbridge accent was, as always, velvet.

Simon clicked to the title of his presentation. I searched for Claire behind me and found her. She curled her lip, mouthed "mine" at the slide, and pantomimed slitting her throat. He nodded towards the back of the room. The lights dimmed. Simon began to recite.

Claire let him get through the introduction: five slides laying out the objectives and the preliminary data. For a moment, when he referred to the work as "our" work and the problem as the challenge "we" saw, I thought, *Oh, my*

*God, we'd pegged him wrong,* he was going to cite Claire McKenna, the real hero of this breakthrough. But Claire's name never surfaced and as soon as he began describing the methodology of the experiments, he slipped into the omnipotent I. *I* calculated this, *I* extrapolated that. I, I, I. Ay, ay, ay…. Claire was out of her seat, heading down the right aisle towards one of three microphones set up for questions and answers. Bitti, I saw, had already positioned herself at the floor microphone far left. I felt a new heat wave simmering around my cleavage. *Come on girl,* I roused myself, *no faltering now.* I trotted to the third mike.

The hijacking happened too quickly for the audience to react. Not that practitioners of science generally move faster than the speed of osmosis. But they did shift in their seats. And you could almost hear a collective crick of two hundred necks craning to see who was speaking as Claire said and the microphone amplified, "Dr. York, I'm going to need to interrupt you here."

Claire whipped off her head scarf. I cleared my throat. Bitti tapped her microphone to make sure it was working.

On stage, the speaker was in a dither. Frankly, it was a joy to watch the always unflappable Simon York lose it in public. It was obvious he couldn't quite take in the implications of the panorama before him. His eyes darted from woman to woman to woman. Claire. Bitti. Gwyneth. Together. What the hell could that mean? From the dazed smile and the hunted look, I could see he knew he was in deep trouble.

Swaying slightly, he gripped the podium for balance. And then, like a marionette chinking parts into place, he visibly pulled himself into a reasonable facsimile of together. But not in time to override Claire's announcement that she was Claire McKenna of the Kerns-Brubaker

Medical Institution, a senior scientist in the laboratory directed by Simon York. And she felt she must protest this presentation.

At first, the audience response was a shocked silence. Then a flurry of whispers spun through the hall.

Clutching the microphone, Claire swung to face the crowd. "I'm aware that what I'm doing here breaks precedent. But I also know you're men and women of science to whom the truth is sacred. And for the sake of truth, it's imperative that you see what I'm about to show you." I fidgeted, worried that Bitti's arrangement with the AV guy got botched somehow and Claire's PowerPoint wasn't ready to roll. I clenched my teeth as I saw her thumb press the remote. Relaxed when on the screen behind her, under the letterhead of the Kerns-Brubaker lab, the smoking gun appeared huge and impressive. She turned to read aloud:

> *Claire,*
>
> *I'm sorry I raised my voice to you yesterday. But I cannot seem to impress upon you strongly enough that your insistence on pursuing experiments regarding the CA-gene test is misguided to say the least. There is no promise of success here. Therefore, I see no value in continuing this line of inquiry.*
>
> *Consider this an official notice that this project is cancelled as of today. Let's get together Monday to discuss in person the best use of your considerable talents.*
>
> *Simon*

Claire gave that a moment to sink in, then addressed Simon. "Do you deny writing that memo, Dr. York?"

The room quieted to the absolute stillness of suspended breath.

Unaccountably, Simon's eyes rested on me. Pleading. As if I could save him. I gave him a thin smile and a shrug. He shook his head in lamentation.

"That is my memo," he acknowledged softly. Then louder, "Yes, yes, of course. I wrote the memo." He was vamping, buying time. "But," he held up a finger whose tremor was obvious even from where I stood, "it was written in the early stage of the project and we had further discussions that reversed my earlier opinion."

Claire was bouncing on her toes as if she could barely restrain herself from vaulting to the stage to throttle the speaker. *Nice and easy, Claire,* I soothed. *You've got him by the short hairs. Don't blow your cool.*

I mentally willed her to remember Fleur and Kat's instructions about staying on message. They'd relentlessly coached her almost up to the moment we left them downstairs in the hotel bar where they were waiting for us, nursing a merlot and an orange juice, to celebrate or pick up the pieces when this was over.

Claire did them proud. "That's not true, Dr. York. The truth is you reversed your opinion only after I came to you with the data that proved my theory. Only after," she came down hard on *after,* "I worked on the project for months without your knowledge or approval. Only after," she jabbed her own finger at him, "I brought to you incontrovertible proof that the experiments had been successful beyond even my expectation. That's when you said I'd done it. Proved you wrong. You told me you were happy to have been proven wrong. That I'd grabbed the brass ring. 'Job splendidly done,' were your exact words." Claire's voice fell to a whisper. "I cherished those words."

It seemed to me the entire room squirmed.

"Do you recall that conversation, Dr. York?"

"Claire," he began, as if he'd forgotten where he was, that he wasn't next to her in bed. At the far end of the stage, Angela Barola's head snapped up. "Dr. McKenna," he amended. "This is absurd. Ridiculous. You had my support, my cooperation, my input every step of the way."

"That's a damned lie and I have my lab notebook to back me up." Cheeky lass, our Dr. McKenna. She flashed the next slide displaying pages from her notebook dated weeks after his memo. Then another slide with more pages from months later. I knew everyone in the audience was scanning for Simon's signatures against the dated entries, looking for any scribble indicating he, as supervisor, had been aware of, involved in her work. Nothing.

"As removed from this as you were, you know I didn't have a problem sharing the credit with you." Claire was playing to the crowd. "I observe the rules. But you were my mentor. I trusted you. You never even told me you were giving this paper today. Your betrayal is a breach of…"

For a moment, I thought she'd choked. But, no, someone had pulled the plug on her microphone. This set off a skirmish near the outlet that sent me sprinting toward the fray. Then I saw the tug-of-war had been won by Carolyn Dean, a pal of mine from the Hopkins lab, a woman built like Fleur but with more muscle, who held up the electrical cord in triumph before jamming the plug into the socket. Back at the mike, I managed to catch her eye and send her a thank-you smile. She gave me a knowing look along with a thumbs up, then assumed a belligerent spread-legged, hands-on-hips position at the outlet to let potential miscreants know she was standing guard against further sabotage.

"Shame!" From the center of the audience, a white-haired man rose to shout, and I thought for a moment we'd won over the old bowties. But he was railing against Claire.

He was shaky on his feet and his voice quivered with outrage. "We must not allow this session to descend into anarchy. I insist that the moderator put a halt to this disgraceful display and Dr. York be allowed to continue."

No one told Angela Barola what to do. She noted the outburst with a frown, then flapped one hand to calm the rustle that followed. "Quiet, quiet," she said. "Come to order, please. Everybody settle down." In the back of the room, a Good Samaritan had commandeered the light switch and flicked the house lights on and off for quiet.

So this was the crossroads. Now everything depended on Angela, whose activism for justice was equaled only by her veneration for science. In our case, the cause was just, but the methods were extreme. She could go either way. I stroked the Latrobe public speaking medal I'd worn for luck. My neck under the chain was moist with flop sweat. I said a prayer to St. Anthony of Padua, who protected against shipwrecks. The Good Samaritan flicked light, darkness, light, darkness.

When the room hushed, Angela said, "I agree with my esteemed colleague that Dr. McKenna's challenge to Dr. York in an open session is highly unorthodox, but my feeling is that airing of differences is healthy for the scientific community. I say we proceed and hear both sides of the issue."

Against a chorus of protests, she turned to an old ally. Bitti was known for calm under fire. "Professor Karnikova, you have the floor."

"Thank you, Dr. Barola," Bitti's husky, accented voice cut through the melee. "I ask us all not to lose sight of the big picture. If what my colleagues," she nodded toward Simon, then Claire, "have indicated is true, this work is of overwhelming importance. So let us return to it."

Someone called out, "Hear, hear." There was a scattering of applause.

"One question, Dr. York," Bitti threw her fast ball. "I'm not sure I understand the data on your third slide." And, well-rehearsed by Claire, she rattled off a question that involved specific genetic germline mutations. Greek to me. Evidentially Swahili to Simon.

He stared at her. I'd never seen that brilliant face look dim before, its light reduced to a flicker. "If you give me a minute to find that reference," he muttered as he desperately wheeled through his PowerPoint.

"Of course," she said. She waited politely, fingering her jade ring while Simon fumbled fruitlessly through the notes on his slides and the murmur of the crowd rose. Finally, he looked up wide-eyed.

*Now, Bitti, before we lose control,* I begged her silently.

Maybe she heard me because, God love her, she pronounced with just the right note of solemnity, "In the interest of time, we must move on. Dr. McKenna, perhaps you can enlighten us?" The audience hushed. Claire clicked her PowerPoint and pulled a slide to the screen.

"Here you can see that I used a denaturing gradient gel electrophoresis for the *BRCA1*," she began and then hit them with slide after slide—data recited from memory, details of her methodology, analyses of her findings. Not everything, but enough to show them she knew this project as only its creator could. *Yay, Claire,* I cheered as she finished to a respectable round of applause.

"Another question." That was my voice, strong, unwavering, from the middle aisle. Leaning into the mike, I announced, "Gwyneth Swanson Berke. Johns Hopkins Hospital." An affiliation that went back thirty years to my residency, but who was counting. Hopkins scored major points with this crowd.

A sea of curious faces turned to me. I could feel my

carotid pulse throb. The beat was irregular but not life threatening.

"This woman isn't even a GRIA member," Simon grumbled from the stage.

I nailed him with my eyes. *Ah, my love, that it had to come to this,* I thought. *But you forced my hand, all our hands, with your arrogance, your hubris. Welcome to payback time.* Which felt damned good. And at that moment, I realized that underneath it all—the education, the MD, the beach house, and the cashmere—I was an East Baltimore girl after all. Street smart, street tough, and, for the first time in my life, proud of it.

"I'm registered," I countered with exquisite calm. I'd paid my conference fee online that morning. "I have every right to be here. This is an open session."

"An open circus," Simon croaked.

"Dr. Berke is a respected gynecologic oncologist with a specialty in ovarian malignancies," Bitti said.

Angela Barola rolled her eyes. "Continue, Dr. Berke," she commanded over Simon's breath hyperventilating into his microphone.

"Dr. York…" I launched into a question based on new data Claire hadn't shared with him, material so complex, so esoteric that I knew if I stopped mid sentence, I would never find my way back. So I barreled through. And for my reward was treated to what we had come here for—Bitti, Claire, and I—the utter and complete demolition of Simon York, research scientist and first-rate scumbullion, before a jury of his peers. From *coup de foudre* to *coup de gras* in three months. That had to have set a new record.

Simon didn't wait for me to finish. He was already making tracks as I wound down. Face apoplectically crimson, hands flying, he snatched his notes from the podium, grabbed his briefcase from the side of the stage, and took off. Claire was blocking his path up the right aisle. Bitti owned the left. I suppose he thought I was the least menacing of his tormentors. He headed dead center, directly toward me.

As he approached, ignoring the astonished, muttering crowd on both sides, he drilled me with a look of such profound loathing that I knew it was meant to stagger me. *Not this time, darling.* I stood my ground. Didn't flinch. Glowered back, and before he could circle around me, pulled off my jade ring and held it out to him.

"I believe this is yours," I said sweetly.

"Bitch," he spat, loud enough for the entire neighborhood to hear. Someone booed.

"Better a bitch than a lying dog," I responded, and watched his right hand jerk reflexively and draw back, palm flattened. I could feel the heat of his desire to make contact. But in the end, he clenched a fist, swallowed hard, and pushed past me.

An ancient doc seated on the aisle blared, "Nasty business. Well, York can say good-bye to his Nobel. He's a tainted man."

I was sure Simon heard it. Hell, it was loud enough to be heard in Stockholm. But he continued his furious march to the exit as two hundred people strained to follow him with their eyes. After the door slammed, they tugged their gaze back to the living the way mourners do at a funeral when the coffin lid has been lowered.

"Now," Angela Barola said in a tone that would brook no dissent, "would you like to proceed with *your* presentation, Dr. McKenna?"

Claire razzle-dazzled them.

# Chapter 41

She was still presiding over a rousing Q and A when I decided I'd had enough of arcane biochemistry for one day and slipped from the Colonial Room to report the news of Simon's rout to Fleur and Kat. Claire and I—Bitti was chairing a panel at the next session—were supposed to join them in the Clay-Madison bar, but as I crossed the lobby I spotted them at the far end, Kat stretched out on a plush sofa, Fleur seated in the club chair across from her.

Fleur raised a hand in weary greeting. "Kat wasn't feeling so hot. So I figured maybe we ought to find someplace she could put her feet up."

Oh, shit. I'd warned Kat. I'd practically begged her not to come with us that morning. At 9:30 she was under a linear accelerator getting bombarded with x-ray beams and only an hour later we picked her up at the hospital for the drive to D.C. Then two hours sitting in a bar drinking orange juice and picking at a veggie burger. What were we thinking? As a doctor, as a friend, I should have vetoed her insistence on coming with us. If anything happened to her, I'd kill Simon York. Such was my reasoning.

Kat opened her eyes. "I'm fine," she said. "Fleur's such a wuss. All that talk about her ancestors braving stormy seas in sixteen-o-whatever. She would have been tossed overboard around the Cape of Good Hope for pussyness under fire."

"You had chest pain," Fleur snapped.

Kat sat up. "Breast pain. I had breast pain. Which the radiologist said to maybe expect. Some shooting pains that a few Advil took care of. That and I was tired. Fatigue is a common side effect of daily radiation; tell her, Gwynnie. She wanted to call 911. Jellyfish. All I needed was a little power nap. Shortwave sleep is very refreshing. I'm totally rejuvenated." She swung an arm and snagged my sleeve. "Now tell us what happened in there."

"All I want to know is Claire got hers and Simon got his, right?" Fleur asked.

"Is the Archbishop of Canterbury Anglican?" I said.

"Let me pee first," Kat rustled to her feet, "and then I want to hear it down to the most minute detail. Boxers or briefs?"

"Boxers, the last time I looked," I said with a half smile, aware I'd never be privy to such info firsthand again. "Simon wears Ralph Lauren fitted boxers, black."

"The fact that you know the brand says it was a sick relationship," Fleur muttered. "I am *so* glad you're out of it."

Twenty minutes later, the story in all its glorious gory detail had been told and we were helping Kat into her coat when Claire emerged from the elevator speaking earnestly to a young man with a press tag pinned to his pocket. She spotted us at the same moment we saw her and her eyes lit up. She whispered something to the man and raised a signal for us to wait.

Then she strode over, very self-contained and professional until the last few feet when she broke into a samba and, fingers snapping, sang *sotto voice*, "Wediditwediditwedidit!"

There were hugs all around and she said, "I'm sorry I didn't make it to the bar, but I kept getting waylaid by attagirls and horrible Simon stories and job offers. What an afternoon. Thanks to you all. Did you tell them about it, Gwyn? You look a little washed out, Kat. Sit. Let's all sit. You okay?"

"She's fine. We're dandy," Fleur said briskly. "Enough of the polite chitchat. Gwyn's already told us about how fabulous the three of you were back there. Congratulations. That's out of the way. Now we want to hear the horrible Simon stories. Unless you have to get back to your new boyfriend."

"He'll wait. His name is Steve Something from the conference newspaper. Can you imagine, the project and I," she tried to look modest and failed miserably, "are going to be the lead article in tomorrow's issue. Which is delivered to the hotel room of every attendee."

"Simon's going to pass out when he gets his copy." I savored the image of him reading about Claire's triumph, our triumph, over his room service coffee.

"Don't I wish. But apparently he's not waiting around to read it. I understand he's checked out. One of my well-wishers saw him getting into a cab with his weekender bag and his computer case."

"Now that's kind of sad," sensitive Kat said. Then in the same sweet tone she added, "But fuck him. He deserves it."

We all broke up.

"Come on, tell us the stories about the bad, bad man," Fleur prompted.

"Well," Claire leaned into our circle and said in her most intimate voice, which, it occurred to me with an ouch, was probably also her pillow-talk voice with Simon, "this one woman told me that York ruined the career of her friend, a microbiologist from Atlanta. Bumped her from a paper they were writing together. His board hushed it up, but the poor girl tried to kill herself."

"He's pond scum," Fleur said.

"In another case, he attempted to horn in on a patent where he didn't belong. Which reminds me," she dug around in her handbag and produced a business card, "a biologist from Sloan-Kettering gave me that. His brother-in-law's a patent attorney. Oh God, I almost forgot the best news. One of the docs on the editorial board of *Ovary Today* stopped to tell me they're definitely rejecting Simon's paper and they invited me to submit mine."

"So this means he slinks back to London with his tail between his legs?" Kat asked. "I have visions of him working in a fish and chips shop, getting all greasy."

"Not quite," I said. "He'll still have his clinical work. He's a cash cow for Kerns-Brubaker and he'll keep raking in the bucks for his high-end surgeries. And I doubt they'll pull the lab from under him, though they'll be watching him more closely, right, Claire? In a couple of years, if he comes up with something big, he could be back on top. But I don't think he'll ever get his Lasker Award, not with this smear on his reputation. And no Lasker, no Nobel. Or highly unlikely. So we did some damage."

"And don't forget, you put a major crimp in his willy," Fleur said. "You know that he's going to think twice before lining up his next harem."

Claire glanced across the room at Steve. "I guess I'd better get back to the interview. And there's a session after that I'm going to try to make. Did I tell you I decided to stay for the rest of the meeting? It's the best place to network and I've got to lock in a job, quick. I've got three weeks of paid leave, so I don't have to go back to the lab and face the Evil One, but after that, baby needs work. I told you about Finland, but I'm having second thoughts. Herb Korets of MicroPharmaceutics in Pittsburgh let me know they have an opening in research and development. And there's this Israeli doctor who wants to meet for drinks tonight. From some super lab outside of Tel Aviv that's looking for a new director."

I thought I actually saw Fleur's ears twitch as they perked up. "An Israeli doctor? Gwyn knows a darling Israeli doctor. Could it be one and the same?"

"Dvora Garon?" Claire asked.

"Dvora is a female name," I reminded Fleur with a smug smile. "No, I don't know her. But it sounds like you're not going to be on the unemployment line, Claire. Big decision. Choose carefully," I advised. "You've got a great career ahead. I see a Lasker on the horizon."

"A Lasker? Why not the Nobel? We're talking cancer here. Countless lives saved," Fleur said. "Does it come with money, the Nobel?"

"Ten million Swedish kronor, which is over a million dollars," I said.

"Well, don't forget your old friends."

"Fleur!" Kat exclaimed.

"Jesus, I was only kidding. Kat's losing her sense of humor. Time to go."

We all rose. Claire, her eyes cloudy, said, "Have I told you I love you all? Because I do. You are wonderful women. You're like sisters to me. Better than my sister, who lives in Oregon and doesn't speak to me. Everyone has everyone's email address, right? Bitti's, too? You'll keep in touch, promise? Not just Christmas cards."

We promised, we exchanged kisses, and she scurried back to her interview leaving a plume of Escada behind her.

In the garage, Fleur said, her voice tinselly, all innocence, "Maybe Claire will take the job in Israel. The climate's good. And you could go visit her, Gwyn. Spend a little time. See old friends."

Served me right for confiding in Fleur.

"Why not?" she asked. "With Simon out of the way, the coast is clear. You said this Ben-Gurion guy was a sweetheart, that he thought your shoulders were like two smooth mountains in the moonlight or some equally fatuous bullshit. And he was fantastic in bed. Plus he's eight thousand miles away so you don't have to pick up his socks. What more could a woman want? Hanukkah's next week. Give him a call. Wish him many crispy latkes."

"You're *meshuga,* Fleur," I said, stealing one of her favorite words. "Why don't you just hand me a loaded gun, trigger cocked? Men and I are a lethal combination. They make for pain and suffering."

"I'm with Gwynnie on this one," Kat said. "She needs to take a break. Figure out why she keeps choosing such toxic partners. Take some time to explore her gestalt."

"Like forever. No more men. I learned my lesson with Simon."

"Ari Ben-whatever is not Simon. He's a white hat. All right, a white yarmulke," Fleur pressed. "Look, all I'm saying is think about it. Is it not worth a few of your superior brain cells to consider the possibility of contacting him?"

"Yeah, yeah," I said. But just to get her off my back, because the idea was so preposterous.

## Chapter 42

Giving up Simon, I decided, was going to be like giving up smoking, which I had managed to do twenty-seven years before. What I remembered from that struggle was that the physical wasn't nearly as bad as the psychological withdrawal. The physical cleaned your clock for the first week or two but the psychological took much longer and niggled away at your resolve like water torture.

To help with the psychological part, Kat went out and bought me another book by Fortune's guru Dr. Prasad Rao, the author of *Men Are Coconuts, Women Are Pomegranates.* This one, titled *When the Fruit Rots: A Guide to Organically Ending a Relationship,* had me drinking pots of green tea, practicing meditation—I absolutely drew the line at the high colonics he recommended—and wearing a rubber band around my wrist to snap whenever thoughts of Simon intruded. All I had to do when the gorgeous Simon surfaced was snap! and substitute an image of him on his long march, eyes bulging, spittle bubbling at the corner of his mouth.

But there were deeper issues. Why I chose such toxic men. First Stan, then Simon. How I turned seriously flawed men into my ideal of perfection, down to the cultivated accents and the designer underwear. Even if I never dated again—which seemed like a brilliant idea—according to Kat my self-knowledge could map and maybe redirect my inner emotional river. And she had a life coach who could be my Lewis and Clark. I took another route.

Tracy the manicurist mused while buttering my right hand with Burt's Bees Milk and Honey lotion, "In my humble opinion, you had this cold and distant mother. Tough as nails, but inside really scared and unsure of herself. And also really unpredictable, right? So, all through your childhood, you tried to do whatever it took to make her love you. But she was a nutcase, so she couldn't love anyone. Soak the other hand. Still, what does a little kid know? You just keep banging your head against, like, this wall of ice. So now you're grown up and you find yourself attracted to crazy, unpredictable men. They seem really polished on the outside but are totally insecure down deep so they jerk you around and lie to you. And you can't trust them the way you couldn't trust your mother. You're going to have to keep your hand still or I'll mess up the base coat. But you think if you only hang in there and do everything right, you'll make them love you and be faithful to you and stop lying and hurting you. Except they'll never be able to give you what you need, right. So it's like you're doomed from the beginning unless and until you decide you're worth better. Think about it. Sheer Enchantment or French Cream?"

———

A few days before Christmas I had lunch with Kat to celebrate the completion of her radiation treatments.

She twirled a strand of whole-wheat pasta around her fork. "You doing okay with the Simon thing? I mean, you're not having second thoughts or doing the standard post-affair obsessing, right?"

"To what end? What's over is over." Which was almost true. Occasionally, when I heard the silvery tones of the anchor on BBC News, I had to snap myself.

"See, that's how I feel about my own cancer," Kat said, making a sly comparison. "It's gone. I don't think about it. What's the point? I've done everything I can. Now I need to concentrate on strengthening my resistance. I've found this extract of papaya capsule they say is loaded with antioxidants and ginseng for energy."

Which she needed because her gallery exhibit was scheduled to open in two weeks.

"I'm weaving like a crazy woman. Joel and Dirk—the guys who own the gallery—are leaving space till the last minute to put up this tapestry. And yesterday, I put in three solid hours on the loom and then Summer and I went to the mall to pick out her layette. Her first sonogram isn't until mid-January, so we don't know the gender yet. We bought white and yellow. And purple. They're making infant clothes in purple now. I love that."

"You and Summer are getting along?"

"*Comme ci, comme ça.* I'm not sure she's entirely over my losing my temper with her. I said some pretty nasty things. But bottom line, we're mother and daughter. And she needs me. Will even more after the baby is born."

"So no regrets about Lee the Sculptor?"

Kat sipped her orange juice. "Now there's another 'what's the point?' Lee the Sculptor is probably discoing the night away with a twenty-year-old art student from the Maryland Institute. I was just an interesting interlude. An experiment. Like a trip in the Time Machine."

"Discoing went out around 1982. And there's no way

that man thought of you as an experiment. Lee isn't the type to play with someone's feelings. It was obvious he was falling in love with you. You know he's got to be hurting."

Kat peered at me over the half glasses we all use to read menus. "By now I'm sure he knows he's better off without me. Look, it was it fun while it lasted. But maybe some romances aren't meant to last forever, right? Lee's and mine. Your's and Simon's. I mean, not every love affair has to go the distance. The ones that flame fast fizzle fast. That's my theory anyway. So I would have liked more with Lee," she shrugged. "But I'll still have something wonderful to think about when I'm older and grayer."

She fingered her amber necklace. "Can we not talk any more about men? Between my lost love and your loser love, the whole subject is much too depressing. On the other hand, isn't it exhilarating to know that your recent experience has enriched your self-knowledge and now all you have to do is apply it? The new year is coming. Clean slate. Celebrate. That's what your pal Fortune Simms says. Which reminds me. Fleur and I are planning on going to Annapolis for First Night. We'll wander around and get back in time to watch the Inner Harbor fireworks from her balcony. You Waterviewians have the best seat in the house. And now you can join us."

First Night in our state capital is a big, mostly outdoor New Year's Eve festival with food, music, and street theater. It attracts families primarily, babies in backpacks, kids running around, snot dribbling in the cold. I sighed.

"First Night will be fun," Kat insisted, looking pained for me. "Come on, it will be. I can't deal with your disappointment on top of Fleur's. She was hoping to have a date for New Year's. Did she tell you she went out with a new man the other night?"

"No. Not a word." I was stung that Fleur hadn't shared. We three were best friends. I felt a surge of junior high angst. Left out again.

Kat must have sensed my hurt and hastened to explain, "She's not sure it's going anywhere, so she's not talking about him. It slipped out with me on her third glass of merlot. Anyway, from the little she said, this one is a winner, someone she really likes. And of course, Fleur being Fleur, she thought he was going to ask her out for New Year's after a few dates, but he didn't. So now she's stuck with us. Poor Fleurie. If he doesn't call her again, she swears she's going to give up on The Plan. For good this time. All that effort she put into it, and it's not exactly working out." Kat's violet eyes crinkled above a wry smile. "Then again, what plans ever do?"

—

The week between Christmas and New Year's is the best time for a surgeon to take off. Given the option, most people postpone surgery until January, so ORs across the country are underbooked and a lot of docs check out for the holidays.

Some vacation. Everything I'd been shoving aside during the time I was preoccupied with Simon jumped out and bit me in the behind. Among the holiday cards, regrets from the final funding source considering my grant application, the proposal Dan had helped me revise. So that put an end to my dreams of the Clinic. And God knows there was a need for it. In spite of a protest demonstration—my own patient, Freesia Odum, carrying a Cure Covenant sign, got interviewed on WJZ—the decision was final. The hospital doors would be locked April first. And then there was my father. Christmas was over. No more excuses. I couldn't close my eyes to it any longer. He *had* to be in a nursing home.

Which meant that every day I got up at seven to haul ass around Baltimore with Dan's social worker, the very competent Michelle Isaacs. We drove from Seven Oaks to Birchwood to Maple Grove, the tree houses I called them, outrageously expensive nursing homes with brightly colored Alzheimer's units where my father could play out his second childhood. The best of them were monumentally depressing and Michelle's grip on my arm got progressively tighter as she felt my fight-or-flight response kick in.

"I can't do this," I said, halfway through the first day.

Michelle swiveled her gaze to me. I must have looked the way I felt.

"I'm turning around at the next exit," she said. "You're right. Maybe it's too much all at once. It's kind of hard to take in, you know, in big doses."

"I mean I can't send my dad to one of those places."

"You don't want to send your father to any of the facilities we've seen today," she fed my line back to me, with a twist. "I get it, but honestly, it's just a matter of finding a perfect match for him. Let's take tomorrow off and try again Wednesday."

She didn't get it at all. But I nodded wearily. What was the use? And by Thursday, we'd seen a few decent places. Michelle was in high spirits.

"Okay, we're on the waiting lists. Now there's nothing to do until a bed opens up."

She said that at three o'clock New Year's Eve afternoon. At six, Fleur and Kat pulled the blanket off me.

"Oh, no, Gwyneth," Fleur growled. "There's no way you're spending New Year's Eve by yourself. We leave you here, you'll sob in your pillow all night. It's not an option. You're coming with us." She actually dug her nails into my arm and tugged.

So under duress at first, I shuffled along through the festive, freezing streets of Annapolis, where musicians performed, costumed actors teased, bagpipers played, and crowds jostled. Light from the eighteenth-century electrified lanterns broke like confetti over the crowd, but I must have looked glum because a mime in whiteface scampered up to me, hooked her fingers to the ends of her scarlet mouth, and pulled as if to say "Smile." I smiled and after a while I felt, well, maybe I was part of the human race again.

Then a surprise. We were walking down Main Street sipping cups of hot chocolate when Fleur stopped so short she splashed some of hers down the front of her coat. "Quick. Across the street. With the plaid muffler. Kat, you've never seen him. That's Dan Rosetti, Gwyn's and my favorite gerontologist and my mother's heartthrob."

It was indubitably Dan, elbow locked to a blonde in a down jacket and boots.

"He's cute. Great hair. Is that Connie deCrespi?" Kat asked.

"Who can fuck herself," Fleur said. "Except she has better options. Thanks to me, the idiot."

"Whoa," I said, nearly choking on my hot chocolate. "The last I heard you guys were joined at the hip. Didn't you have dinner together Monday night?"

"We did. Then Wednesday, I get this bill in the mail for her recent legal services. The woman should have given me a discount for fixing her up with Dan. Instead, she's padded it with hours we went shoe shopping. So last night, I called her. I was calm, I swear."

I could imagine.

"But she has a nasty temper. Who knew? Anyway, we get into it and it winds up she tells me if I have a problem with her charges to file a grievance with the Bar Association and hangs up on me. This is my supposed friend. And a countess twice removed. Just goes to show that background doesn't necessarily translate to class," Fleur said, giving me a pointed look. "Of course, I'll never speak to her again. Unfortunately, now I won't know how she and Dan are getting along in the romance department. I could kick myself for squandering such a good man on the likes of her."

"Well, they look pretty cozy," Kat said. "Arm in arm. Who's the brunette with them?"

"That's Connie's sister, Tessa. She inherited the nice genes." Fleur peered. "Hmm. Tessa's had work done since the last time I saw her. Definitely a nose job. "

"She's across the street," I said. "In this mob, I can barely see two feet ahead of me. You can tell a nose job from across a crowded city street?"

"From across the Grand Canyon," Fleur said. "Look, I'm not budging, but if you want to go say hello to them, be my guest. I won't mind."

"You know what? I don't want to," I said. "I can't think of a more depressing way to kick off the New Year than being pleasant to Connie deCrespi. Not only was she a bitch to you, she scooped up one of the last good men on the planet."

"You're right. Most of the good ones are taken, and at our age, the pool of even the lousy ones is shrinking. Makes you not want to put on your bathing suit." Fleur leaned against me under the streetlight as we watched the trio disappear into a pastry shop.

"Now that's a happy New Year sentiment," Kat said. I was close enough to feel a shiver play through her.

"I want to go home," I said. "I *really* want to go home."

So we did. We were back in my condo drinking champagne when the phone rang. We all jumped. I grabbed the receiver, thinking *Oh God, my father*. But it was Harry Galligan, of all people. So we invited him over.

Inviting him wasn't my idea. It was Kat's.

He called from the FRESH party in Annapolis which, as the head of the recreation committee, he'd organized. But lots of rejected spouses do not make for merry revelry and he'd had enough and was about to duck out for home. Unless.

Quick whispered conference off phone. I was definitely not in the mood for men. Fleur uncharacteristically abstained. But Kat had never met Harry, which she wanted to do, and she felt sorry for him.

In the end, she got her way and he joined us on the balcony, where he wound a consoling arm around me. I'd mentioned on the phone that Simon and I had split and I really didn't want to talk about it, but now Kat, for lack of festive conversation, filled him in on the details. Fleur hovered but didn't talk much. She took her good time warming up to Harry. Poor man. He had no idea he represented an entire disgraced gender on the most romantically sensitive night of the year.

Right after the fireworks, I checked out, leaving Harry and Fleur to play Scrabble. Looking beat, Kat said, "I'm right behind you," and headed for my guest room.

At five past twelve, my bedside phone woke me. The lighted ID spelled out only an area code and a location, New York City. Simon, I figured, sozzled on too much Glenfiddich at some black-tie party, calling to tell me off. Or—you never knew with Simon—to declare undying love. I am proud to report that not even for a moment did I consider lifting that phone from its caddy, although I did spend the next three hours churning the bedclothes and cursing his cheating soul.

The next morning I listened to the midnight message on my answering machine. It had been Claire calling from her apartment. She was wine giddy, dateless, fine with that, and just wanted to wish us all better times. The first joke of the New Year was on me.

# Chapter 43

The following Thursday at ten past six, I broke from the freezing, nose-numbing cold into the warm, wine-scented air of the Bentley-Zindell Gallery to join the chattering crowd gathered for the opening of Kat's show. I planned to be at the reception no more than forty minutes so I could train to New York, hit the hotel around eleven, and be fresh for my New Year's appearance on *Good Fortune!* the next day.

I grabbed a drink, scanned the gallery for a familiar face, and found Kat circulating among her guests, taking compliments with her signature skeptical smile. She'd tweezed her eyebrows for the occasion and they curved like the tops of question marks when she said, "Really?" in response to everyone telling her variations on, "Wonderful. Seminal. So vital. We just love your work."

"So glad you could come," she repeated again and again, extending her hand from under the heathery cashmere cape she'd woven for her fiftieth birthday and wore on special occasions. Fleur and I had treated her to the wool as a birthday gift.

"She looks gorgeous. It was worth every penny," Fleur said, sidling up, drink in hand.

When she spotted us, Kat pulled us into her caped embrace like Wonder Woman. "I love you both. I'm so glad you're here. Can you believe the size of this crowd? We pulled it off." She floated off, a cumulus cloud of silvery purple, to greet the art columnist for the *Washington Post*.

Kat and the gallery guys had conspired to schedule her opening reception to coincide with First Thursday in Baltimore, a monthly tradition for the galleries along Charles Street, the main downtown drag. They stay open late, offer wine and cheese, and the cognoscenti drift from exhibit to exhibit. I'd been there when Joel, Gallery Guy A, told her, "We'll invite them for five thirty, get everyone in first while they're still hungry and sober, wow them with your magnificent fiber art, and rake in the moolah. We're not underpricing this time, Kat. Your work is to drool over."

In fact, Fleur stopped to salivate in front of a huge tapestry titled The Healing Earth, which she renamed, "German chocolate cake. No really. See the nibbles at the edge and the coconut flakes on the top? You can almost taste it."

"You've been on that diet too long," I said.

"Not long enough. I've got six months and fifty pounds to go and then maintenance."

"But you can see the difference now. It's really noticeable."

"I still want to get rid of my second chin. Please note that the third one has vanished." She lifted the elegant Talbot profile to show me, squinted, and said, "Oh my stars and whiskers, look who just rolled in. Do you see what I see? Well, *somebody* swallowed a watermelon."

Summer, in a navy maternity jumper and plaid headband, waved at us from across the room, but made no move in our direction. "Let her come to us," Fleur sniffed, shooing the air with the most insincere flutter in the history of hellos. "Let her pay her respects. She can kiss my ahh...ring. Anyway, I want to see her walk with that Graf Zeppelin attached to her front. She's only what, four months in and she's huge. Is she giving birth to Koko the gorilla?"

"She's carrying all belly, which isn't unusual for a first baby."

"Ladies," a familiar voice crept over my right shoulder and I turned into the cologne-drenched microenvironment of my ex-husband.

Now this is tough to confess because it reveals my bitter almond of a soul in the post-Treachery months, but I used to dream of Stan looking the way he looked at Kat's opening.

He was the picture of Dorian Gray out of the closet, every wrinkle revealed, with an insomniac's gray pallor and pouches under the eyes, sagging chin, scrawny neck, leftover gobbler skin draped in folds above his cable sweater. He'd lost so much weight that his scalp slumped forward and you could see—I knew Fleur was staring at— an artificially straight stretch of coastline plugged with tufts of wiry transplanted hair. Which he dyed. Which I knew because they were black at the tips, white at the roots, and fading in between.

"You look spectacular," he gushed to Fleur.

"You too," she managed. "Absolutely amazing."

"You've lost weight."

"You too."

"Yup. Diet?"

"Atkins. You?"

"Not diet," he said.

Fleur shifted her uneasy glance into long distance. "Well, what do you know? Isn't that Summer at the buffet?

And no Tim. The little mother is all by herself and I'm sure she doesn't have a clue how to talk to these artsy fartsy types. I think I'll just mosey on over and find out whether she's still throwing up these days. Better yet, I'll ask about her hemorrhoids. Pregnant women are fixated on their hemorrhoids, aren't they, Gwyn? There's a conversation to keep me from hitting the smorgasbord." She ambled off, abandoning me to the company of Stan, who was swigging his chardonnay.

I took my ex-husband's free hand. "What's going on with you?" I gave him not a wife's but a physician's once-over. Checked the whites of his eyes. Raised his hand and examined his fingernails. You can learn volumes from a person's fingernails. Stan's glowed reassuringly pink, no cracks, no ridges. But his skeletal fingers felt cold and he was going to lose his Columbia class ring if he wasn't careful. "You're too thin, Stan. Have you seen Blumenstein?" Our shared internist.

"I've seen Blumenstein and he gave me a clean bill of health. It's not what you're thinking if that's what you're thinking. I'm negative. I know I look like I'm dying and there are days, God knows, I'd like to die, but I'm not."

Odd, now that we were detached and distanced, I could read him. On a recent visit, my ophthalmologist told me my farsightedness had improved with age. "Brad?"

Bad Brad. A week away from a romantic Christmas vacation in Aruba, Brad told Stan he'd fallen in love with a nineteen-year-old junior college dropout who'd whirled his Tropical Fruit Fantasy at the Arundel Mall.

"Nineteen years old with the brain of a newt. Youth and beauty, how do you fight it?" Headshake with wry smile. "Did you wish this on me, sweetheart? Not that I don't deserve it."

I guess that was as close as Stan would ever come to an apology.

"No one deserves it," I said, which was my sharply pointed shorthand for not quite accepted.

"True. It's torture. There's no other word for it." He plucked a shrimp from a passing platter. "I thought Brad and I had a life together. I honestly thought we'd beat the odds, which aren't great among, well, people like us, for till death do us part. And what really pisses me off is that I didn't see it coming." He said this to me, to *me,* without a hint of irony. "Where the hell was I when he and Pineapple Boy were…"

As he railed on and on, I realized I was hearing more of Stan's innermost longings and pain than I had in twenty-six years of marriage. More now than I really wanted to know.

"It's so damn lonely," Stan said. "He even took the dog with him. So what do I do now? I'm not looking for just…" he changed directions, perhaps thinking better of discussing one-night stands and bar pickups with his ex-wife. "I want something meaningful. How the hell do you begin again at fifty-six?"

Was that a rhetorical question? Maybe he was actually asking for advice, and if I were a better person I would have said, "I'm really sorry Brad left you. I'm really sorry you're hurting and alone and starting over in your mid-fifties. Is there anything I can do? Refer you to a good manicurist for some reality therapy? Lend you Fleur's list of the ten best places to meet men? Call Faith Shapiro and see if she has a tall, gay ballplayer to fix you up with?"

However, I was still smarting from my trip up the basement steps at Crosswinds a couple of years before. And not totally recovered from two decades of a sham marriage. My stock of sympathy wasn't high. Oh, God, had I wished this on him? For more than a year, I'd wished him drawn and quartered, tarred and feathered, battered and bruised. Now I wanted him to live and be well for the sake of my sons. As for his happiness, let him earn it like the rest of us.

———

Ten minutes before I had to leave for my train, Lee Bagdasarian showed up. Fleur poked me so hard in the ribs I reeled, nearly upending Kat's radiation-inspired Triumph of the Scavengers: A Study in Scarlet and Blue.

Then we stood frozen watching him cross the room to an unsuspecting Kat. "How do you suppose he found out about tonight, I wonder?" Fleur said finally.

"It's not a big secret. It's got to be all over the art community. And it was announced in *Baltimore* magazine."

"Uhm."

I didn't like the sound of that uhm. Too musical. Like the warble of a canary who'd mastered Handel's *Messiah*. Self-satisfied, as if she'd brought off something big.

"You didn't," I accused.

"*Moi*? Didn't what?"

"Oh, Fleur, you had no right."

"Right, shmight, sometimes the world turns on its axis, sometimes you have to give it a little push. She'll thank me."

"She'll kill you," I said. But what was the use. And maybe Fleur had the right idea. Nudge fate if fate didn't nudge you toward happiness. And it was comforting to think that, in spite of her frustration with The Plan, Fleur still believed you could manipulate the universe.

"Actually, once she gets over the initial shock, which will not take long, I assure you, she'll kiss my toes in gratitude. I mean for godssakes, look at him. Is that not yummy? I'd forgotten how yummy he is. All those leftovers on Lovingmatch have dulled my palate."

Lee was indisputably attractive. Tall and lean, but with brawny sculptor's arms that flexed muscle beneath the same black turtleneck he'd worn the August day he met Kat at his own show. Maybe he'd pulled it out for luck. Maybe he had twenty black turtlenecks lined up in his closet because he knew they turned him into delectable.

"You keep an eye on Summer and I'll do the Kat play-by-play," Fleur said.

Summer was engaged in who could even imagine what kind of conversation with a woman sporting a pierced nose and pink hair. Then she spotted Lee. You could tell from the jerk of her head.

"Six feet...five feet...closer...closer...forget Summer, look, look, Kat is about to turn around." Fleur fanned herself with her program. My legs melted with sympathetic weakness for Kat. "Touchdown. Oh, nice. Very nice," Fleur commented as Kat looked up, registered astonishment, pleasure, swayed gently, and finally placed one hand on her neck in an unconscious gesture of delight. Lee bent down to kiss her cheek, then nudged her hand away as he slid his lips down into the hollow of her neck and buried them there. Kat, face flushed, eyes glistening, stroked his dark hair.

"Did you see that?" Fleur fanned a hurricane force wind.

"Beautiful. But I can't wait for the credits. I'll miss my train."

"No, not yet." She craned her neck. "What happened to Summer? Did you see her face when Lee kissed Kat? All pinched up as if she was about to have a tantrum." Fleur searched the room. "Where the hell did she disappear to?"

"Well, she's either tearing up the ladies' room or she decided to take the high road and get out of here before she ruined her mother's big night by making a scene." I found a spot for my empty wine glass. "I've really got to get going."

Fleur swiveled to stare at the reunited couple, who were holding hands and gazing goofily into each other's eyes. "You can't leave now."

"I've got to go. Take notes. It will make a nice entry in the scrapbook for the grandchildren."

In fact, Summer did take the high road. Charles Street at an ungodly speed. She'd parked her Beamer three cars in front of my Lexus. I arrived just in time to see the plaid headband duck and disappear into the interior and hear the door make a rather crude lower-class slam for a $60,000 door. I wasted a minute watching Summer maneuver out and, just as I turned my ignition key, she floored that Big Bavarian and took off up Charles Street, jumping the red light at the Washington Monument, zooming pedal to the metal probably all the way to Roland Park.

*Poor Kat*, I thought, *she'll have hell to pay.*

## Chapter 44

Oh, Doctor, you look scads better than the last time you sat in this chair." Marco, Fortune's makeup artist, sketched a coral line to amplify my less than naturally luscious lips. He backed up to appraise his handiwork. "Some hinky *l'affaire de la* heart, as I recall. But you're positively glowing. I take it you two are back together?"

"Well, *I'm* back together," I said.

He tossed his shaved head and hooted. "No wonder Fortune loves you."

Actually, I wasn't sure how much Fortune loved me. I noticed she stopped at the makeup chair across the room to hug the other guest, a former porno star who was pushing her new diet book. "Ate herself out of a job," Marco snickered. "Debby Does Dairy Queen. Gained seventy pounds. Can you imagine? With all that fucking horizontal exercise? Then she claimed to have invented this diet. Some diet. She's been to the loo three times in fifteen minutes." He made a retching sound behind his hand. "What goes down must come up. Oh, here comes Fortune."

But she never did approach, just walked past me with a cool smile and the slightest wave, like her fingers were tickling the air.

In front of the camera, though, she was her buoyant self. Standing center stage in her six feet four caftanned glory, she whipped the audience into a frenzy with the announcement that she was here and now *personally* restamping the ticket that empowered them to take charge of their lives. Then, seamlessly, she led the porno queen through her diet, which sounded like an awful lot of root vegetables to me.

I had the second half all to myself. When she introduced me exuberantly as her very own Dr. Diva, I must have winced because she said, "Look how appalled she is, audience. Listen, ladies, a diva is any woman on top of her game, that's all. And isn't Dr. Gwyn one of those?" Loud applause. "Now tell us what we have to do to keep ourselves fit and healthy for the next twelve months and forever."

After I ran through my list of medical New Year's resolutions, she said, "Now, catch us up on the Clinic. The last time you were here, you described how all these women were going to be without health care when their local hospital shut down. Tell us what's going on in the moment."

So I spoke of the Clinic, of the desperate need for it, how a colleague and I had come up with an expanded version for everyone in the area, but how, in spite of our best efforts, lack of funding ended that plan. By the time I'd finished, voice breaking, she'd taken my hand.

"No money for such a worthy project? Do you think that's fair, audience?"

Unanimous "Nooo."

"Well," leaning forward for that intimate *pas de deux* with the lens that has made her the most popular woman on television, "neither do these people. Here's what some of Dr. Gwyn's supporters have to say. First, one of her patients."

As the screen behind us filled with a huge image, Fortune whispered to me, "Don't try to talk to her. She's prerecorded."

Dear Lord, it was Freesia Odum, decked out in a very stylish sweater set, granddaughter squirming in her lap. "Dr. Berke," Ms. Odum said into her close-up, "hello from Baltimore. You've been there for me when I had no medical insurance and no way of paying for a doctor and I just want to say we know how hard you've been working on the Clinic and we're praying for you. God bless you and God bless you, Fortune."

Before I had time to process that, Fortune said to me, "And now a colleague, Daniel Rosetti, MD, a respected geriatrician, has something to say directly to you."

Dan materialized on the screen, smiling a quirky, semi-amused, semi-embarrassed smile. He'd been filmed in his office. Behind him, I could see the photo of little Chrissy on her mother's lap.

"Hi Gwyn, hi Fortune," he said with his easy grace. "This Clinic is a life-giving project. It worked once and it should be given the chance to work again. We're all proud of what Gwyneth Berke has given to the community throughout her medical career and we're hoping she'll get that Clinic up and running soon." He waved a salute to the camera. "We're here for you, Gwyn."

"There's a lot of love out there," Fortune said when the screen went to black. "You doing okay?"

"Just in shock," I said, tethered to reality only by Fortune's warm hand clasping my chill one and the scent of her sandalwood perfume. I was still not quite getting it, not quite putting the pieces together.

She pulled me to my feet and towed me with her as she strode to the edge of the stage like some elegant, exotic giraffe to the watering hole. "So what do you think, audience? Don't those people in that neglected community deserve a break?"

"Yesssssss."

"Doesn't Dr. Gwyn deserve to realize her dream?"

The audience was on its feet and cheering. She hollered over them, "I couldn't agree more. So let's do something about it. Let's take charge of this. And to kick things off, I'd like to present to you, Dr. Gwyn, my personal check for….one!….million!….dollars!"

She handed me a huge facsimile of a check for one-plus-six-sweet-zeros signed by Fortune Simms.

Although I tried with every Scandinavian gene in my chromosome set to choke them back, the tears spilled. As Fortune whipped out tissues from her always-present box, I blubbered and dribbled and honked. In front of millions of viewers. But what the hell. I was a diva, I could get away with histrionics.

Afterwards, backstage, she swept me into the cocoon of her caftan, saying, "You had no idea? Really? That sweetheart Dan Rosetti didn't spill the beans?" She released me to arm's length. "I'll tell you, woman, I almost gave it away when I saw you in the makeup chair. I had to really keep my distance because I thought you'd read it in my face."

"Honestly, I was dumfounded. Overwhelmed. How do I thank you?" I asked. I was smiling so hard my cheeks hurt.

"By doing the work. Listen, I'm just glad I have the resources to help out. That's what we're here for, right, you and I? Isn't that why we do what we do?"

Gut instinct told me she meant it. I think Fleur was wrong about Fortune. She may be a marketing genius, but she's not a marketing machine. Too much heart.

Speaking of that noted critic, Fleur phoned me on my

cell phone as I was cabbing across Manhattan to Penn Station, so excited for me I thought she was going to spring through the phone to give me a hug. After she flooded me with congratulations, she said, "Listen, we've got a bitch of an ice storm back here. There's no way you're going to be able to get yourself home in that pantywaist car of yours. I've got access to a four-wheel drive and I'll pick you up at the station. Don't argue with me, Gwyneth. I saw the state you're in, falling apart in living color. You'd be in no shape to drive even if your car was a Hummer."

We chugged into an icy Baltimore four hours later. The conductor called, "Watch your step, watch your step, it's slippery out there," and there was Fleur making her cautious way across the platform in her Republican ranch mink coat, open wide to fold me in.

As we climbed the station steps, she spouted questions like a bubble machine, ending with, "Can you relax now that you've got money for the Clinic? Can you take a break before you charge headlong into putting this thing together?" She tightened her grip on my arm as I began to slide. "Fucking ice. Come on, let's get you home. We'll pour you a nice glass of wine or maybe five. Believe me, the weather will look a lot better through rosé colored glasses."

I thought the "we" in "we'll pour" was just Fleur being her royal self. But no, leaning against his SUV, which was parked, motor running, under the overhang in the ten-minute loading zone, Harry Galligan raised a welcoming hand. Then he fished in the front seat and pulled out a bouquet of flowers. Not supermarket flowers, either.

"Harry," I said, "you heard about the Clinic?" Good old Harry. Harry cared. Harry was there for me. Which didn't add up. Confused, I looked from him to an owl-eyed Fleur, then back. "What are you doing here, Harry?"

"I'm the four-wheel drive." He handed over the bouquet.

"Tulips in January. Thank you." I tried to smile but my lips wouldn't stretch.

"Rare flowers for a rare woman."

"Ahh, how sweet."

"Well, I can't take credit for the line. It's Fleur's." And he reached over and squeezed her hand.

He also tossed my suitcase into the back and held the rear door open for me so I knew where I stood. Sat. Fleur slid into the front passenger seat with a proprietary casualness. And it got better as we drove home. I was mostly out of it, but I still had sufficient brain activity to notice we had something going on here. An arm pat from him, some shoulder-to-shoulder contact that strained the seat belts, and, uh-huh, her hand glided over to rest on his knee.

"You okay back there?" Harry asked. "I can turn up the heat. Don't want those tulips to freeze."

"No, I'm fine. They're fine. They'll survive."

He said to Fleur, "How about you? Are you okay, hon?" Not the Baltimore hon-to-everyone, either; hon as in honey—as in voice as syrupy as.

And Fleur, who had never been cold a day in her life, who had an internal generator that could heat a small city, answered, "Actually, you know my neck is cold. Stupid of me, I forgot to bring a scarf," as if she weren't wearing a mink coat with a collar.

I figured she wanted his arm around her which, on those slippery roads, would probably kill us all. But Harry, bless him, gave her one better. First, he turned the heat up and then in a neat single-handed maneuver, stripped off his muffler and draped it around her neck.

A muffler is not a jacket, but close enough. Kat would be so pleased.

# Chapter 45

Fleur Talbot is a woman to whom nothing is secret, nothing is sacred—someone who thinks privacy is one more pinko-wacko item on the liberal agenda or, on odd days, a quirky reactionary notion stashed next to the right to bear arms. This is a person with no qualms about asking the color of your true love's pubic hair. That Fleur kept her budding romance with Harry under wraps for a month is as close to a miracle as I'm going to get outside of Lourdes.

"I just didn't want to put the kibosh on it," she explained. "It started when we went hunting together for your dad. And we went out a few times. It was great and I thought, well, my luck has finally turned. But then I was pissed when he didn't ask me out for New Year's. He was running that party for your gay divorcé group and he didn't invite me. But when he showed up at your place, things between us kind of exploded and we wound up in my apartment." She noted my pursed lips. "Give me a break. See, that's why I didn't tell you. Also you'd gone out with Harry. So I felt I needed to clear it with you, but I never quite got my balls in a row."

"Well, now that your balls are all lined up, congratulations. No really, I'm happy for you." I hugged her for a blessing.

Kat, on the other hand, put her relationship with Lee out in the open from the moment they'd reconnected at her show. Her critically acclaimed show. So she had two good reasons to glow. But occasionally I'd see pain flicker in her eyes and I knew she was eating herself up over her estrangement from Summer. The morning after she'd stalked out of the gallery, Summer sent her mother a raving email, then absolute silence. She refused to take Kat's calls and when Kat went to the house, Tim blocked the door. Which tore Kat up, although she bravely repeated the mantra she and Lee arrived at together: just as Kat must make the decisions for her life, Summer must take responsibility for hers. And, anyway, they had five months before the baby was born to figure something out.

On the fourth of February, Michelle, my father's social worker, called with the news that a male resident at The Elms had died, creating an opening. We had to work quickly before another old man slipped into the empty bed.

"I can't do this," I told her. "I need time to think this through." Eternity wouldn't have been enough time.

Michelle put the screws to me. "If you don't say yes now, and I mean this very minute, we're going to lose it." With more warning, I would have agonized over the decision, but there wasn't time for my heart to be mangled before it was torn apart.

An hour before the move, I sat my father down to explain what was happening. I stroked his hand while I talked about The Elms, trying to sound upbeat. For a year and a half, he'd been disconnected. Now, when we could use some disconnection, he was plugged in and turned on.

"I'd rather go to Ocean City," he insisted when I urged him to think of the change as a vacation. And he cut me off in the middle of my fairy tale about a beautiful house with people to bring him food and make his bed, waving at the latest temp nervously biting her nails across the room, "Hon does that right here. She's my gal. I don't want this other place. Listen, Doc, this is a secret, but I'll tell you. I walk in there, I come out in a box."

Michelle had to take over so I could rush to the bathroom and heave.

It took us all of fifteen minutes to pack his stuff into the car, and isn't that sad? Fifteen minutes to load what was left of eighty years. Some photograph albums, his Bible, the newspaper, an old *TV Guide* in a plastic cover. Although he hadn't been able to read for two years, these things gave him comfort.

Sadder still, while we loaded the trunk, he slumped in the passenger seat, his stare fixed on the steering wheel. He refused to look back at the house he'd lived in for the last six decades. "Bad, bad, bad," he muttered as I slid in next to him. What science decided this man's brain was a Nerf ball of amyloid plaques and neurofibrillary tangles? Bad, bad, bad was right. The situation and your traitorous child, both.

"It's going to be okay, Daddy. I love you," I choked out. He allowed me a watery glance. Then he shut his eyes and turned his head. Just as well. I didn't want him to see my tears as much as he didn't want me to see his. Maybe shame is the last emotion to go. Or guilt. If I'd been the daughter he deserved, I'd have brought him to live with me. Quit my job to watch over him. Michelle said this guilt was a common reaction among loved ones, "but, honestly, Mr. Swanson will be better off surrounded by trained caregivers who can maximize the cognitive power he has left and take all the necessary precautions for his physical safety."

Sounded like social worker gobbledygook to me. All I knew was that he had enough cognitive power to blame me for his eviction from the Streeper Street house. In his room at The Elms, he shook his head no when the nurse patted the La-Z-Boy they'd already moved in to comfort him with familiar surroundings. Instead, he climbed into bed, fully clothed, and lay there, repetitively smacking his fist into the cup of his hand, staring straight up, refusing to look at the droning TV, refusing to make eye contact with me.

"Dad," I pleaded, leaning over, blocking his view of the ceiling.

He swung at me. Missed. But not by much.

"Time to go," the nurse said. She steered me toward the door. "They make a better adjustment on their own, first day. Besides, you look like you could use a break."

So I left him. At home, I collapsed into vacant sleep. Or maybe I dreamed but mercifully blanked it out because when I awoke at nine, my pillow was damp with sweat or tears and my teeth were chattering. My first conscious thought was that I had to see my father. Make sure he was all right. Not wandering. That someone was checking on him. I drove the seven miles to The Elms breathing through a panic attack.

I found him sleeping soundly in his bed, the TV emitting tinny waves of laughter from an ancient *Newlyweds Game*. A dinner tray with a slab of meatloaf half-consumed sat on the side table. So he'd eaten.

Someone had cared for him. Helped him into his pajamas, combed his hair, removed his dentures for a soak. I wouldn't have been surprised if the perp was Dan Rosetti—my doc in shining armor—who was dozing in the La-Z-Boy next to the bed, Roman coin profile etched against the brown corduroy, one arm stretched protectively over my dad's blanket. His other hand rested on a photograph album open in his lap.

I craned over Dan's shoulder to see. Dear God. How long had it been since I'd set eyes on that picture? Me at seventeen, in hip huggers and an angel-sleeved blouse, hair flipped à la Farrah, posed on the Enoch Pratt library steps waving the letter announcing I'd been awarded a scholarship to Barnard. My passport to college in New York, beyond the reach of my mother's long arm. Hence the blazing smile and the eyes clear for once of their underlying sadness.

Maybe it was that I looked achingly hopeful and as beautiful as I'd ever be. Maybe it was that this particular photo lay under Dan's gentle hand. For one or none of those reasons, I found myself biting back tears as I tiptoed from the room.

At the nursing station, I asked, "When did Dr. Rosetti get here?"

"He still sleeping?" The charge nurse chuckled. "He came in a couple of hours ago to check on Mr. Swanson. Calm him down. They talked Redskins, Ravens, some kind of football. Didn't make much sense to me from either of them. I'm a basketball fan myself. Then they both fell asleep. I figured we'd wake Dr. Rosetti at shift change around eleven. Unless you think we ought to wake him now, Dr. Berke." Old-school RN, automatically deferring to the physician. They didn't make 'em like that anymore. Thank God.

As it turned out, I didn't have to decide. When I reentered my father's room I found Dan on his feet, pacing. He raised a hand to me in greeting, but continued to talk into his cell phone.

"Yes, I am sorry. No, I don't know how long it takes for Salmon Annabelle to dry out. That fast, huh?" He winked at

me while talking to her. I was sure it *was* a her even before
he said, "I'll make it up to you. You pick the restaurant
tomorrow night, how's that? Sky's the limit. Listen, I've got
to go. I've got a colleague here with some questions. I'll call
you in the morning."

Colleague, huh? Fine by me.

"Who knew salmon was such a temperamental fish?"
he said after he clicked off.

"Poor Connie," I guessed.

He gave me a sheepish grin. "She was making dinner
for us at her place. Apparently, I ruined it. I've been told I
don't have my priorities straight. She's probably right."

"Well, I for one am grateful you don't." I glanced at my
father, jaw unhinged, snoring heavily. "He was really
agitated when I left. And look at him now."

"He just needed some man-to-man football talk," Dan
said with a laugh. "The shot of aquavit didn't hurt either."
He grinned as he picked up the bottle twisted into a brown
paper bag and draped his coat over it. "Okay, Harald's out
for the night. And if he wakes up, the nurses can handle
him. You don't need to be here, Gwyn. Go home. Get some
sleep. Come on, I'll walk you to your car."

Remembering how Harry Galligan and I launched our
minor romance in the FRESH parking lot, I searched Dan's
face for a hidden agenda. But no, it radiated innocence.
Unlike some people of the philandering persuasion, Dan
was a one-woman man.

"Thanks," I said, "but I'm going to hang out here for a
while. Not for him as much as for me. And I caught a nap
earlier."

"Me too," he said with a laugh. "That old chair sucked
me in." He wound his scarf around his neck. "You do know
he'll be fine, right? Your dad's a pretty adaptable guy. The

good thing is that soon this will be home to him. The lousy thing is that he might forget he ever lived anyplace else."

It turned out Dan was half right. My father remembered Streeper Street deep into the thickening fog. In spite of my mother, his life there shone a light that dementia had to fight to extinguish. On the other hand, once settled into The Elms, he seemed happy. Within a few weeks, he put on weight and his eczema cleared up. Somebody on the staff—not my ex-husband—shaved him regularly. And when I visited, he was usually stretched out in that funky brown recliner snoring through the pandemonium on the Game Show Network, as if he'd never left East Baltimore. Even better, sometimes I found him sitting in a circle with the other Alzheimer's patients, shaking a tambourine as the music therapist knocked out "Margie" and "Blue Skies" on the piano. And he liked the rice pudding.

But still, I couldn't forget he said he'd leave there in a box.

———

Another memorable exit. This from Bethany, who arrived in my office the following week looking more chipper than she had in ages. Roses back in the cheeks, hair recently brightened. Mascara?

"I just came in to thank you," she began. "I really appreciate the reference you gave to Davis Standish."

"Ah, did it work out for you?"

"I begin March fifteenth."

"Congratulations. We're going to miss you." I played with my pencil. "You sure you want to do this?"

"Oh, yes. I have to get out of here. The thing with Seymour and that bitch Mindy. I'm not going to hang around to watch."

"You're positive there's something going on?" I'd sniffed the mild aroma of hanky-panky, but nothing more.

"Oh, please. It's so obvious. I can't believe you, of all people, haven't spotted it."

Of all people. Because I'd caught the action between her and Seymour? Or because, after having had my head up my butt for the duration of my marriage, I should have been the most observant of creatures?

"All the signs are there, trust me. I mean, how much do you have to know to really know, right?" I nodded to show her I got it. Got it? After Stan, after Simon, I could have written the book on it. "So," she sighed, "it's time for me to move on. And California has a malpractice insurance rate cap. Paradise for obstetricians. So anyway, thanks. You know, for everything. I mean it." She extended her hand and we shook. Very professional. Maybe I hadn't exactly been the best mentor, or Bethany the best mentee, but we'd come a long way, the ferret and I. "Oh, I almost forgot," she said at the door, kind of a farewell gift, "we just did Summer Ellicott's latest sonogram. It looks like she's further along than we originally calculated. I estimate her delivery date for June tenth. *If* she goes the distance. Which, of course, I doubt."

"Meaning what? Twins?"

Bethany's eyes took on an uncustomary playful twinkle. "I assumed you knew from your friend. Two boys."

"Really? Isn't that nice," I said, making the comment professionally bland when what I really wanted to do was dance around the room and work my arm into that train-whistle pull my kids used to make while hissing "Yesssss!" Because this was very good news for Kat. There was no way bratty, spoiled, self-centered Summer would be able to handle two baby boys without help. Tim's parents lived in New York, which left Kat the only on-site grandparent. Doesn't God have a wicked sense of humor? Two XYs and at least one of them was bound to inherit Summer's personality. Oh, yes, little Miss Tantrum would really need her mother now.

And maybe Lee the Sculptor could make a mobile for the nursery.

# Chapter 46

On Valentine's Day, Fleur and Harry announced their engagement accompanied by all the bells and whistles. Fleur posted a notice in the *Baltimore Sun* (mostly for Jack and Bambi's benefit—the plump paragraph listing Harry's degrees and accomplishments was revenge Talbot style) and selected a restrained 1.5 carat round diamond set in Grandmère Broussard's Victorian setting. When push comes to shove, we are what we are. In Fleur's case a flower on the venerable Caldwaller-Talbot-Broussard family tree. She wouldn't have been caught dead wearing a fourth-finger flashlight.

"You're not going to believe this. After fifty-five years, my mother wants to know what's my hurry." She made the rotating "cuckoo" sign near her ear.

"She's probably just surprised. It happened so quickly."

"I suppose. But what's the point of waiting? At our age, it's not going to get any better, right? And it gives me a good four months to plan the wedding. That 'me' really is an 'us,' by the way. Kat, you, and me."

"I have a clinic going up, Fleur. I'm not sure I'll have time to be traipsing around the city sampling hors d'oeuvres for the reception."

"What does that mean, a clinic going up? You're laying the brick? You're wearing a hard hat? You check numbers on the computer and order supplies. A couple of times a week you drive over to see whether they've started the build-out yet. This takes maybe three hours, tops. And what do you do with the rest of your free time? Okay, your father. But you're not dating. You work, you exercise, you sleep. Besides, Kat won't go without you and she needs to get out. In spite of getting laid regularly, she's moping around. This Summer thing is really getting her down."

Contrary to my expectations and my mental dance the day Bethany gave me the sonogram results, Summer hadn't sent an SOS to her mother. Kat didn't know she was going to be the grandma of twins and I, under HIPAA regulations that protect the privacy of patients, couldn't disclose this information to her.

All I let myself say was, "Summer will come around when she's up half the night nursing. It's hard to stand on principle when you can't even stand."

———

April brought showers. One of them for Fleur. Quincy as Queenella LaBella hosted it at the Rhinoceros nightclub downtown and billed it on the invitation as a luncheon bridal fashion show. Guests were requested to bring gifts of lingerie.

Fleur provided a guest list comprised mostly of her chums from twelve years of private school, the weight-loss camp in Maine she'd sulked through for two adolescent summers, and the Junior League for which she still did charity work. "Let's shake up the white-glove set. Queenella and company in all their flaming glory should really unlock those jaws and I want to see 'em drop."

Connie deCrespi wasn't invited, of course. But Fleur did invite Claire McKenna, our cohort in crime. Claire emailed her regrets and her new address in Israel. She'd taken the job running the lab near Tel Aviv. By return email, I sent her Ari Ben-Jacob's number and told her to call him. Fleur thought I was, in her words, nutsoid for handing off Ari. But I'd had my fill of long-distance romance and adoration substituting for love.

The elegant Antonia Guest, proprietor of the Gee! Spot, introduced herself at the door. "I'm so happy for Fleur," she drawled. "I love when women get what they want." She reached into a Gee! Spot shopping bag and pulled out a package wrapped in lipstick-red paper. "My latest—a dual action vibrator that glows in the dark. In case Harry gets lost on the way back from the bathroom. And the lingerie," she tapped another box, "is a nightgown with the nipples cut out. But very tasteful. In white lace for the bride."

The Pikesville matchmaker, Hannah Pechter, folded me into her hug. "Was I right? I knew she would get snapped up. This woman is a prize, a genuine prize. I'm just sad she's marrying out of the faith."

Tracy, our manicurist, said, "I'm so proud of her. Strong nails, strong ego."

For the fashion show, Quincy had selected a bevy of broad-shouldered, big-bootied drag queens to parade across the stage in fabulous large-sized outfits provided by Madame Max. The finale turned out a wedding party marching to the strains of Handel's "Arrival of the Queen of Sheba" with Quincy as the groom and a huge triple-lashed Mae West look-alike named Fandango as the bride, attended by six jumbo bridesmaids in tiaras and pastel hoop-skirted tulle. Way up front, Fleur's mother, who'd insisted on coming when she heard that the hostess was Queenella, whom she adored, wiped tears of laughter with a lace-edged linen handkerchief that Fleur said had to be at least a hundred years old.

"That was the most fun I've had in decades," I heard Mrs. Talbot drawl as the party broke up.

"Look at her kissing Quincy," Fleur said, beaming. "The old girl has some life in her yet. See, Gwynnie, we have something to look forward to as we slide down the slippery slope into blue hair and Metamucil."

"Uhmm." From a distance, I gave Mrs. Talbot a professional once-over. "Why is she dragging her leg?"

The Johns Hopkins Emergency Room answered that question two hours later. The MRI showed Fleur's mother had suffered a stroke, probably between the salad and the tossing of rose petals into the audience by the transvestite wedding party. Not life threatening, but she'd probably be left with a weakness on her right side. In spite of which, she vowed to march down the aisle at the wedding of her only daughter.

———

In the wee hours of the first of May, Tim Ellicott roused his mother-in-law with a phone call. Summer was in labor and she needed her mama.

"She needs me," Kat gleefully repeated when she woke me. "She's having twins, Gwyneth. Two boys. Isn't that spectacular? Except she's only thirty-three weeks in. That's really early, isn't it?" After I reassured her, she asked, "Would you meet me there, please? I know Summer would want you there. As a doctor," honest Kat felt compelled to add.

In fact, Summer's OB was top of the line. My partner, Seymour Bernstein. As Kat rushed in, Summer called out,

"Mama, I'm so glad you're here. Did Tim tell you the babies are early? I got through the first few hours fine, but then the pain got unbearable and I threw a major hissy fit. So they gave me an epidural, and now Dr. Bernstein wants me to have a C-section."

Both babies had turned breech since her last exam, so there was no choice.

"Can you accommodate one more in the delivery room?" I asked and watched Seymour shift uncomfortably from foot to foot. Then I realized he thought I didn't trust him with my friend's daughter and that I wanted to stand by in case of emergency, in case I needed to salvage another bleeder. "If it's okay with Summer, the grandmother wants to be there," I said, nodding at Kat.

While I thumbed through a three-year-old *Redbook* in the waiting room, Kat was in a better place, across from Tim on Summer's right side, when at 2:22 a.m., Timothy Arlen Ellicott, III, four pounds two ounces, five-minute Apgar score of eight, took his first breath, quickly joined by Ethan Greenfield Ellicott at three pounds ten ounces, with a respectable Apgar of seven. Mother and babies fine. Father relieved. Grandma absolutely elated.

## Chapter 47

Dearly beloved, we gathered together at the Stony Run Country Club at the twilight end of a warm June day to celebrate the marriage of Fleur Caldwaller Talbot, fifty-five, to Harry James Galligan, fifty-eight, but who was counting, he's a man. Time to raise our glasses to the happy couple.

But first, a little pre-nup chaos.

The two bridesmaids skidded in just in time for the formal photo session, delayed because Kat got a call from Summer, whose preemie twins were finally home from the hospital. The new mother was frantic about the quality of baby Ethan's poopy, as Summer, who always looked like she was smelling it, referred to it. Dressed to kill, we detoured for a diaper inspection. Kat and I pronounced Ethan's production well within normal range for color and consistency. But then we had to spritz each other with much too much L'Air du Temps to mask the residual poopy odor, which seemed to have an affinity for our Vera Wang silk dresses.

By four thirty, the rabbi was officially late, caught on I-95 in an Oriole's traffic jam. He phoned every five minutes to let Fleur know he'd inched along another mile, which made her crazy.

Not having eaten all day didn't do her mental state any favors either. "This dress has a waistline. Ask me why I bought a dress with a waistline. Because I'm a masochist, that's why. Goddamn low-carb diet. I'd swap my engagement ring for a box of Oreos."

In fact, when she wasn't cursing it, she was radiant in her crystal-beaded, tea-length dress, sweetheart-necked to give her *belle poitrine* exposure to the cooling air, and pure white because she said every bride becomes a virgin anew at her wedding and screw anyone who had a problem with that. Her personal problem was that, in spite of the air conditioning, she perspired large round underarm discs, and I had to run to the nearest drugstore to buy talcum powder, which Kat artfully applied to hide the sweat stains. Nice to have a fiber artist around when you really need one.

Another bit of flotsam in the chaos, Fleur's cousin Clayborne, in from Scottsdale to give the bride away, nearly passed out because, despite Fleur's warnings, he'd played eighteen holes in the grilling sun on Stony Run's course that morning while tippling from his ever-present flask of Wild Turkey. Dan Rosetti instructed him to drop his head between his legs, prescribed plenty of cool water and a salt tablet, and predicted Clayborne would be revived in time for the ceremony. Yes, Dan was on board as a member of the wedding party, suited up in black tie and looking dapper. He was Fleur's mother's date. His job was to escort her down the aisle, providing a steady arm as she limped along.

Mrs. Talbot had presented these unorthodox marching orders to Fleur a week before the wedding. When Fleur protested that her mother walking down the aisle with Dan was a departure from both Christian and Jewish tradition, Mrs. Talbot lectured her, and this Fleur repeated in her mother's Bryn Mawr accent: "My dear girl, keep in mind how I stood by when all my friends' children got married. I gritted my teeth and complimented a hundred homely brides and bought a hundred sterling berry spoons and made my way down endless receiving lines and waited for my turn to come. Well, now it has. And yes, precious, it's my turn as well as yours. Weddings are not just for the bride and groom, you know. They're primarily for family. They're like funerals in that regard. The point I am making is that this is my wedding too, at long last may I add, and I intend to have my way on this matter with Dr. Rosetti."

"She's serious about it being her wedding too," Fleur had told me. "You know she has a crush on Dan, and I think this walking down the aisle with him is part of her own romantic fantasy. Well, fine. As long as they don't say 'I do' and fly off to Hawaii for the honeymoon."

Back from tending to Clayborne, Dan sent Kat and me a wink over Mrs. Talbot's head, genial even when trapped. I hadn't seen him in a while. After thanking him for his part in bringing Fortune Simms's million-dollar check to the Clinic, we'd been connecting by phone for updates on my dad's health. Dan checked on my father when he visited his other patients at The Elms. And I knew he was working on getting some of his physician friends to donate time to the Clinic, but we were still three months away from opening. Maybe, if I could pry Fleur's mother from his side, we could find a moment to catch up.

And then the tardy rabbi rushed in to let us know he'd finally made it by detouring around Camden Yards, and the rector at Trinity, a handsome Englishwoman whom Fleur called Father Jane, popped up to announce we were ready to begin.

"Oh, listen," Fleur hushed us to hear the ancient Hebrew love song "Dodi Li" waft from the Chesapeake

Room where the guests gathered. "I am my beloved's and my beloved is mine," Fleur gave words to the ethereal harp music and for one brief moment sweet calm prevailed.

Then the harpist struck up the processional and we bustled into place for the march.

Mrs. Talbot led the procession, in a halting lockstep with Dan. Kat and I, bouquets of calla lilies in hand, were waiting for our cue when we heard Fleur behind us breathe, "Jesus, save me." Which is no way for a nice Jewish girl to talk, so we both turned around to see her half holding up, half holding onto Clayborne and swaying. It was obvious she was in the grip of some kind of meltdown.

"What was I thinking? What am I doing? Getting married for the first time at my age. I've been alone all my life. I can't even share the remote. There's no way I can go through with this." Her eyeballs swiveled wildly.

"Last-minute jitters," I soothed. "Every bride has them."

"No, I mean it. Oh Lord, I have no idea what I'm doing here. I was perfectly happy with my life. I loved being single."

"You did not."

"Did so. And who is this man I'm linking myself to until death? Death. For once I'm glad I'm fifty-five. Maybe I'll only live another ten years with someone who could be a Libyan spy. Well, he's a physicist, he *could* be. What if he has three wives and twelve kids in another state? What if he farts in his sleep? I'm serious. I can't go through with this."

And Kat, who had a nerve transplant with her breast surgery, exclaimed, "The hell you can't. Come on, Gwyn, let's get this show on the road." We circled around behind Clayborne and Fleur and gave them a firm shove through the wide-open double doors onto the strip of white carpet.

Which is how, most certainly for the first time in the history of the Stony Run Country Club and very possibly for the first time in the history of the wedding ritual, the bridesmaids trailed the bride down the aisle.

———

The center held. Fleur in her grandmother's Alençon lace fingertip veil and Harry in the traditional skullcap stood under the wedding canopy and pledged to love, honor, and care for each other until you know what. They lit a unity candle for the Protestants, and Harry stomped a napkin-wrapped glass to cries of *mazel tov* from the two Jews present. They posed for the photographer and accepted congratulations and kisses. In the receiving line, Harry pulled me into a bear hug and whispered, "If it hadn't been for you, I'd never have met Fleur. Thanks, darlin'." And before I moved on, he mopped his own tears from my cheek. And Fleur…Fleur looked as if she'd never had a doubt in the world.

After we adjourned to the ballroom decorated in Palm Beach Pink and Putting Green, a color scheme Fleur called country club camouflage, Harry led her to the floor for their first dance as husband and wife. Then Dan gingerly steered Mrs. Talbot out for a waltz, and Kat—looking healthy and sublimely happy—whirled around with Lee who, out of his turtleneck and into a dinner jacket, could have been a cover boy for *GQ*. As for me, I managed a few steps with Clayborne before his wife cut in and I found myself back at the empty table facing my *salade endive avec d'amandes et des croutons*.

I sipped champagne, nibbled a breadstick, and allowed myself to grow maudlin about Simon. Say what you will about the man—that he was a cheat and a liar and a fraud—short-term, he'd given me one wonderful *coup de foudre*, one hell of a lightning strike, and I wouldn't have missed the flash-bang for the world. Or the payback.

Fleur lowered herself into the empty chair next to me and snatched two breadsticks and the croutons off my salad. "Wedding's over, diet's over. Aw, look at you. You mooning over Simon?"

I dabbed at my eyes with my napkin. "Kind of. I feel sentimental, but not sad. Weddings make you believe that fantasies can become real. And for a while there, I believed mine would."

"I want you to know I specifically instructed the band-leader not to play 'Lara's Theme.'" She leaned in to accept my grateful finger squeeze and showered me with crumbs. "You're not going to believe this, Gwynnie, but I'm glad you found Simon. No, really, and not only because it freed Harry up for me. That craziness with Simon set you up for the real thing. And don't tell me you don't want the real thing. You will when the right person along. Someone you'll appreciate for being what we Episcopalian Jews call a mensch. A truly good human being. You'll see."

"That's sweet, Fleur. But the truth is I'm fine the way I am. Content."

Fleur said, "Content? Ick. Bor-ing."

"Hey, don't knock content. It's a good place to be, a lot better than some of the places I've been lately. What I'm telling you is my life isn't only full, it's fulfilling and, as you would say, that ain't chopped liver, right?" I smiled with the realization that what I was saying was finally what I was feeling. "Besides, even the thought of starting over is exhausting. Lest you forget, I'm fifty-four years old."

"Lest *you* forget, you were also fifty-four six months ago. If you're happy the way you are, great. Enough said. But don't give me the age crap. Look at me. Look at Kat out there, dancing her ass off in three-inch heels. Madly in love with Lee, who adores her. The age thing, the breast thing— none of it matters to him."

True. Kat had been planning on having reconstructive surgery, but now she wasn't so sure. She'd always gone *au natural* anyway, the flower child, and Lee loved her, dents and all.

"He told her he loved her not *in spite of* but *because of* everything that made her who she is. Pretty poetic shit to hear at any age," Fleur said as she shifted her gaze. "Hell, look at my mother dancing with Dan. Eighty-three and she thinks she's fifteen and swooning over Frank Sinatra. I guess she's always had a thing for Italian men. She's really gone over the line with this crush, though. Do you know what the old vixen did? She persuaded me to let her bridge club handle the invitations and write out the place cards, and somehow Dan wound up at table six, next to her, surrounded by his geriatric patients. Lucky man. He'll be talking osteoporosis all evening."

I laughed as I watched him gallantly steering Mrs. Talbot back to the table. "He's such a great guy, he's probably taking it all in stride. That was sweet of him, agreeing to be here without Connie."

"There is no Connie," Fleur said.

"What?"

"Well of course, there *is* a Connie. That kind dies only with a stake through its heart. What I meant is our Dan isn't dating her anymore. He put it more kindly, but bottom line is Connie gave him a raft of excrement about coming to the wedding when she wasn't invited. I smelled the pungent odor of an ultimatum. Her or my mother. Being Dan, he chose not to disappoint my mother."

"Is he all broken up?" I asked.

"Nah, it never would have worked anyway. Beauty and Constanza the beast. So he's currently at liberty. But you do know he's not going to be sitting at home twiddling his various appendages for long. The man is a major catch."

Fleur sucked a deep breath. "On the off chance you might be interested, he thinks you're pretty. No, really, he said that when you walked in this afternoon. And bright. I distinctly remember he said bright." She leaned across to the breadbasket and snagged a roll.

"Come on, Fleur, you're making this up. Dan Rosetti? You don't honestly believe..."

"Yeah, actually I do. Why not? You're free, he's snap-up-able. You're a doctor, he's a doctor. You can examine each other."

"Boy, are you reaching. I told you I don't need a man to make me complete."

"Who said anything about complete? We're talking about having some fun. If something more is meant to be, it'll be. Then again, maybe Dan's not right for you. On the other hand, you never can tell." She swept a storm of crumbs off her bosom. "While you're thinking that through, heads up, baby. He's coming our way."

So he was, smiling his wise smile and looking directly at me. "Gwyneth, I've been meaning to say hello all evening but I kind of got sidetracked. My cheering section." He gestured towards the old folks' table. "I heard that your clinic is really coming along. Congratulations. Which reminds me. I got a tentative yes from Eli Hunt, the cardiologist, for giving you four hours a week."

Fleur drew an audible sigh of impatience, drummed her fingers on the pink tablecloth, and gave him the googly eye.

"Uhm, well, what I really wanted to tell you is that you're looking exceptionally nice this evening."

Fleur allowed him the thinnest placated smile.

"You too," I said. "The dinner jacket. Very Cary Grant."

"Mrs. Talbot says Rudolph Valentino."

"What*ever*. Can't you people continue this small talk on the dance floor?" Fleur grumbled, poking me to stand. I didn't budge.

Dan grinned at me. "Good idea," he said. "Do you cha-cha?"

"Of course she cha-chas," Fleur answered for me. "She mambos, she rumbas, she boogaloos, she…" I sent her a numbing look and she grabbed a breadstick. Dan reached down and took my hand.

The band swung into a slow tune. "I guess this is going to be a fox-trot. You game?"

I nodded.

"I have to warn you I'm not a very good dancer," he said. "I'm notorious for my two left feet. Actually, none of the Rosettis can dance. It must be congenital."

Notorious. Congenital. The man was polysyllabic. Plus he had two left feet. Just my type.

So I did what I'd done all my life. I picked myself up, dusted myself off, and moved on. Right into his arms. And he stepped on my toes once or twice, but we danced.

Ah, did we dance.

# About the Author

Toby Devens graduated from The American University in Washington, D.C., with a B.A. in English literature. She returned to Manhattan where she earned a M.A., also in English, from New York University. She was a writer and senior editor at Harcourt Brace publications when she met her future husband interviewing him at a medical conference. The couple moved to Maryland, where Toby worked in corporate and health-related communications until the birth of her daughter, Amanda. Her poetry, short fiction, and articles have appeared in such publications as *Reader's Digest, Family Circle, McCall's* and *Parents* magazine, among many others. Most recently, she served as senior vice president for an international network of transplant banks, supervising public relations and media outreach. Traveling extensively, involved hands-on, she had a front row seat to cutting-edge biotechnology and medical advances around the globe. Her writing related to medical issues has appeared in numerous professional publications and scientific journals. She continues to write and consult in the medical field.

The inspiration for *My Favorite Midlife Crisis (Yet)* emerged from her most recent sojourn into singlehood. She currently lives in a Maryland suburb halfway between Baltimore and Washington, D.C. Find out more at www.tobydevens.com.